DIRTY LYING WOLVES

The Enchanted Fates Series

DIRTY LYING FAERIES

DIRTY LYING DRAGONS

DIRTY LYING WOLVES

THE ENCHANTED FATES SERIES — BOOK 3

Dirty Lying Wolves

SABRINA BLACKBURRY

 by wattpad books

An imprint of Wattpad WEBTOON Book Group

Copyright © 2024 Sabrina Blackburry

All rights reserved.

Content warning: sex, language, violence, substance abuse, kidnapping, past injury trauma, past parental loss, and manipulation.

No portion of this publication may be reproduced or transmitted, in any form or by any means, without the express written permission of the copyright holders.

Published in Canada by Wattpad WEBTOON Book Group, a division of Wattpad WEBTOON Studios, Inc.

36 Wellington Street E., Suite 200, Toronto, ON M5E 1C7 Canada

www.wattpad.com

First W by Wattpad Books edition: September 2024

ISBN 978-1-99077-832-2 (Hardcover original)
ISBN 978-1-99077-833-9 (eBook edition)

Names, characters, places, and incidents featured in this publication are either the product of the author's imagination or are used fictitiously. Any resemblance to actual persons (living or dead), events, institutions, or locales, without satiric intent, is coincidental.

Wattpad Books, W by Wattpad Books, Wattpad WEBTOON Book Group, and associated logos are trademarks and/or registered trademarks of Wattpad WEBTOON Studios, Inc. and/or its affiliates. Wattpad and associated logos are trademarks and/or registered trademarks of Wattpad Corp.

Library and Archives Canada Cataloguing in Publication information is available upon request.

Printed and bound in Canada

1 3 5 7 9 10 8 6 4 2

Cover design by Lesley Worrell
Images © Curtis Watson, © S-BELOV, © ANON MUENPROM via Shutterstock
Typesetting by Delaney Anderson
Full jacket design by Patrick McCormick

To my husband, Josh. Fine, here's your wolf one.

CHAPTER ONE

JUNIPER

The temptation to run in these new tennis shoes was both thrilling and frightening. But I kept the pace even and smooth as my feet hit the trail, the sound an echo of my lost running days. The crisp morning air filled my lungs, and I kept my hands shoved in the pockets of my jacket. With summer nearly upon the Pacific Northwest, I couldn't expect too many more days like this one. There was no better way to spend a late-spring morning than at the arboretum, the beautiful foliage surrounding me bringing peace and good memories.

The trees around me rustled, unsettling dew from last night's rain and showering the ground below with rainbow specks of water as sunlight filtered through. In my earbuds drummed a familiar beat that lifted me up and pushed me forward. The only thing more perfect than this would be getting back to my apartment with a hot latte in my hands and a long list of movies to binge on a day when I had no plans.

Sabrina Blackburry

A planned couch-potato day was not a usual part of my weekends, but I was tired to the bone—the kind of tired that a draining job and the stress of no money puts on a person. The kind of tired that a nap wasn't going to fix. Tired. Stagnant. The kind of tired that made you want to ignore the buzzing phone in your pocket as your roommate called you. Again.

I debated letting it go to voicemail. Kat had already called me twice, so something must really be up if she was awake before noon and calling instead of texting.

"What's up, Kat?"

"My job blew up!" she squealed, and I yanked one of my earbuds out on reflex, clicking the volume down.

"Do you want to try that again without the dramatics?" I asked. "What really happened?"

"No, for real, June," Kat snapped. "You know all those sirens we heard last night? It was some kind of gas leak in the plaza. Several of the buildings were badly damaged from an explosion or something. The deli was blown to pieces."

I stopped walking. "Are you serious?"

An older couple stared as they walked past me, the lady giving me a snooty look for blocking the trail. Not that it wasn't plenty wide for all of us, but I moved aside all the same.

"So serious," Kat groaned. "I'm helping Mrs. Pataki with whatever survived the blast today but after that I'm probably out of a job."

"She's not going to relocate or reopen? What about insurance? You can't tell me the deli doesn't have enough insurance to fix the damage."

"Even if she does, I won't have any shifts for months until it's fixed. I don't know what I'm going to do."

"First, take a deep breath." I listened to her breathe. "Good. Now, don't worry about your share of the rent this month. I've got savings and I've been in a pinch before when you gave me the help I needed. I pay back when it's my turn."

"But—"

"Then we find a new part-time job for you until we know for sure what Mrs. Pataki is doing."

"Juniper—" Kat sounded as though she had begun crying. "Girl, I don't know what I would do without you."

"You'd be fine, because you're tough once you've got your head on straight." I smiled. "Keep taking deep breaths as you need them, and let me think more about a plan for when I get back. I'm going to finish my walk. I'll pick us up some cheap groceries on the way home, okay?"

"Can you get that spicy miso ramen?" Kat asked, sniffing.

"Sure, I'll buy plenty of them. See you later."

"Okay, bye, June Bug."

Another stone of stress dropped into the pit of my stomach. Using my savings would set me back from quitting work at the sports clinic for something better. Kat had been there for me, though, and I'd be there for her.

I ran a hand through my short black hair. The undercut was cute but it was high-maintenance enough that I was close to letting it grow out again. And hell, if Kat had really lost her job, things were going to be too tight to go to the salon for a while anyway. I shoved the earbud back in place and changed my playlist to something a little more aggressive to pick up my pace. I was walking fast, but not quite jogging. *Shoes to pavement. Clear your mind. Breathe and let your thoughts go.*

With what I had scraped together, we'd manage for a couple of months. Seattle was a big place, and there was always someone hiring somewhere. The work might not be great, but it would pay until we figured out something better.

I let my feet take me where they wanted to go. My head was clouded with money calculations, not really paying attention to where I was going. That is, until the splat of scarlet on the pavement in front of me caused me to stop. Someone had lost a good amount of blood. Recently.

There was no one on the path in front of me. No one on either side of me. No one behind me. But in the grass to my right there was another spot of red.

I headed toward a thick patch of trees. If someone was injured, I might be able to help. Cursing the fact that I had left my first-aid bag in my car on the other side of the park, I ran procedures through my head. I hadn't taken those first-aid courses for nothing.

The morning dew drenched my ankles as I went deeper into the trees. The sounds of struggle made my heart race, and I reached for the pepper spray clipped to the lanyard in my pocket. I shifted my fingers around the keys and my ID badge until I had a firm grasp on the small canister.

"Is someone in trouble? Hello?" I raised my voice enough that others could overhear if this was an emergency.

Rustling ahead confirmed that more than one thing moved. I squared my shoulders and pushed forward, and came upon the strangest conversation of my life.

"Curse you, warlock, for all eternity!" A snarling, pissed-off woman spat out the words.

"Calm down, Amelia," a man with a stern voice said. "We need to secure a safe location before the Lunaria's Dream wears off."

"What the hell did you do, warlock?" another male voice hissed.

Thrashing came after that. Grunts of pain, frustration, and discomfort.

"I . . . told you," an exasperated man said. His tone was clipped, strained. "We have . . . nine hours . . . of this."

Then, growling. Multiple dogs were present, which added an unknown and possibly dangerous element to this, and I hesitated calling for emergency services because there might not be enough time to wait before something worse happened. But the moment I heard the woman's pained whimpering, I was spurred into action, my pepper spray in front of me as I rounded the tree.

"Okay, that's enough!" I snapped. "What are you doing to her?"

Hunched in the pine needles that littered the ground were four huge men, all with varying degrees of injury visible, from scrapes and cuts to what looked like burn marks. Somehow, the dogs were gone. Another man was on the ground, covered in soot and in obvious pain. His once nice button-up shirt was in tatters, and he clutched his abdomen. The woman alongside him was naked. Like, fully naked, with scratches all over her. Her long black hair was a rat's nest, and when her eyes locked onto mine, I shivered. They looked inhuman. Yellow, like an animal's.

As I stood there before the four stunned men, one of them growled at me. These people were clearly in need of medical and psychological attention, but more importantly, this woman and probably the man on the ground needed rescuing.

"Turn back around, human," the man with the stern tone said. "This is not your business."

"The hell it isn't," I snapped, my voice shaking. "What did you do to them? Is this a kidnapping?"

The woman at my feet convulsed, arching her back off the ground with a strained groan. Thrusting my pepper spray in front of me, I trained it on the biggest man. With my free hand, I reached down to try to take a vital from the woman's wrist.

"Don't move or you're getting a face full of pepper spray!" I shouted, hoping someone on the trail would hear me. "I already called the cops, so you had better behave while I help her."

I prayed my bluff would work long enough for me to examine the woman on the ground, because she could be under the influence of any number of drugs. She could be having a panic attack or a seizure. I just needed a moment to see what I could do for her.

Unfortunately, I didn't get a moment. What happened next came fast. Too fast. I-couldn't-see-it fast. My hand was near her wrist, going for a pulse, when the woman on the ground changed somehow.

"Amelia, don't shift!" someone shouted.

"Alpha!"

"Dammit!"

The woman, Amelia, flipped from her back to all fours in less than a heartbeat. Her limbs flailed, and she clawed at her temples in pain before turning to me. In a flash, what was once a human woman had grown a weird, long mouth. Her teeth sharpened into something grotesque and reminiscent of a horror movie. And as I tried to yank my outstretched arm back, she lunged and bit me.

The pain shot up my forearm and right into my shoulder. An echo of pain in my skull rang hard as I instinctively screamed and pulled back my arm. The four men jumped into immediate action. One of them disarmed my pepper spray and flipped me onto my knees, pinning me down. The other three all jumped onto the woman, the *thing*, who'd bitten me.

With my head pressed to the grass and tears blurring my eyes, I witnessed the most bizarre morphing of a human shape I had ever seen. The stuff of nightmares. The woman's face shifted back and forth between human and the odd long-mouthed face that had attacked me. Hair faded in and out. Bones shifted under her skin, making sickening popping sounds. She convulsed under the three men trying to pin her down, and at the same time, in her own way, she was holding them back.

I had one solemn moment of clarity when the biggest of the three holding that creature down turned and locked eyes with me. A semblance of sympathy and regret settled within his expression.

They were having trouble holding Amelia back, and as one errant leg went flying, I failed to move from its path. Pain smashed my temple like a brick as her foot connected, and my vision grayed as my head snapped backwards and I fell flat to the ground.

Chapter Two

DOM

A growl crept up my throat as I stared down at the mess. An alpha wolf and a prick of a warlock were writhing in pain on the ground. Amelia I was loyal to; the warlock was an unfortunate factor I now had to deal with. Three confused packmates by my side were trying to hold themselves together while we faced the unknown next steps of the drugs leaving our system without Amelia to guide us. And now an interloping human had stumbled upon the scene, and Amelia fucking bit her.

What an utter fucking headache. The second we betrayed that merciless vampire Apollo to fight a battle that wasn't entirely ours, Amelia had truly backed us into a messed-up corner. Now our leader was incapacitated by warlock magic and I was left to clean up the aftermath. We had switched sides during the battle and helped the local magical creatures defeat the vampires. Or that was what we were doing until Amelia was thrown into the warlock and his active magic circle. The battle was done, but I wasn't about to stick around for what came next, not when we'd made our share of enemies and our reputation as Apollo's lapdogs would do us no favors. No, we needed to leave and find someplace safe for what came next.

Another annoyance to add to the list: When was the last time we weren't on the run? Fighting? When was the last time any of us saw a bed? And now this shit to deal with. I snarled in frustration as I stood, rounding on the mess of wolves and the pile of warlock on the ground next to me. I had vowed to follow Amelia to the pits of hell and back, as long as we grew stronger, and I meant it. I was her second, and I'd take care of it.

"Pin Amelia down. Our position is compromised, we need to keep moving and now we need to drag an unconscious human with us."

The rest of the pack looked at me, surprised.

"Why the human?" Jack said.

"Because, Jack, she was bitten. Look at her arm, she's going to turn in the next couple of full moons." We probably didn't even have that long. She'd either be back up in a minute or we were looking at serious brain damage from a hit like that. "Move. Quickly."

The wolves held a suffering Amelia on the ground but took turns eyeing the human's bleeding forearm. The warlock and the source of Amelia's problem, Jerod, was stifling pained laughter while he writhed on the ground. The thought of kicking his ass while he was down was tempting, but from what I had seen, he and Amelia couldn't be separated for now, so the warlock would have to stay whole.

At least the human was breathing. With her curly black hair shaved close at one side and a stubborn chin, I'd bet she was going to be a handful when she woke up. Scratch that—she had already been a problem in the two minutes I had known her.

"Dom," Aaron said, catching my attention.

His buzz cut and stern brow were coated in sweat and grime, reminding me of the hellish night we had just endured. I reached down to take the human's phone and pepper spray. Not that it was going to do much to any of us.

He continued, "I can scout ahead for more trees, but we're still pretty deep in the city. What about a hotel for the night?"

"You think we can hide these two moaning in pain as we haul their asses into a hotel room?" I jerked my head to the ground where Amelia was pressing herself against the cool ground and snarling, and Jerod was dry heaving.

"And who knows what this new one will shriek when she wakes up. We're better to find neutral wolf lands or at least some deep woods. There's plenty of national parkland northeast of here, we just have to get there."

Aaron nodded sharply, accepting my answer and holding down Amelia's legs.

"We should have stayed with the fae," Jack grumbled.

"We're getting as far away from this mess as possible before the Lunaria's Dream wears off and we're vulnerable," I said. "You want that dragon, Ryker, to get any ideas when he remembers we were the ones who chased down his mate?"

"I thought we were cured, though," Carson said nervously. "That fae lady, she did something to us before we left, right?"

"She said she would do what she could about how bound our bodies were to the drug," I explained, shaking my head. "We won't go through what we've been through before with the withdrawals, but they'll still happen. And I don't want to be here when we do."

"What do we do?" Jack asked.

This was an alpha's job, and I wasn't equipped to handle the mess we were in without Amelia. But I was second in command, and Amelia was all but useless.

A whimper from the human made me look down to see her curled up, holding her head. She made a gagging sound and I wondered if she was about to throw up. Leaning down, I turned her on her side.

"Phone."

I looked down at my feet where Jerod was hunched over, trying to dig something out of his pocket.

"Your phone? Why?"

"Call a . . . ride," he answered. "Favor."

Reaching down, I pulled a black rectangle from his pocket. But the black rectangle wasn't a sleek smartphone, it was a melted wad of plastic and glass.

I dangled it in front of him so he could see. "Sorry, bud. It's fried from your little explosive exploits."

Jerod groaned and rolled face down. Standing straight again, I crossed my arms over my chest. What would Amelia do? The better question would be what would the old Amelia do? The one before getting us all hooked on Lunaria's Dream for a power trip. Amelia had always been aggressive, but the last decade had been a whole new level in a desperate attempt to gain some kind of advantage over the alpha that had conquered our home. There was a reason we didn't have a proper pack anymore, and the last few years had been spent growing strong enough to do something about it. If it *was* up to me, we'd go back right now.

Amelia was out of commission for a while. Nine hours, according to the warlock. It was up to me. It would take longer than that to get back, but I could convince her when she regained herself. Apollo was gone, we were about to be free of the drug, whether we wanted to be or not, and there was nothing stopping us from going back and fulfilling an old promise.

"We're going home," I announced.

"The castle is rubble now, remember?" Jack said. "We can't go home."

"Not there. Home," I said.

The wolves perked up.

"Home?" Carson asked, excitement creeping into his voice. "Home-home?"

"Home-home," I confirmed.

"Amelia isn't going to like this," Aaron said hesitantly.

"You heard her before, she was considering at least seeing how the pack was doing," I said.

"She probably meant she was willing to call Naomi," Aaron argued. "She's not going to like showing up at Moonpeak in this state. Especially if we can't find her sister."

"It's going to take a lot longer to get to the village than nine hours. We'll head that way and see what she says when she snaps out of—" I looked down at her.

"No," Amelia snarled. "Don't you dare, Dom."

I crouched over Amelia, looking into her eyes as much as I could while she flailed about. "Relax, we aren't getting far with you like this. I'll get us safely to the woods. You can take over when you're yourself again."

Amelia growled and snapped at me, but I stood and stepped back. "Jack, Aaron, grab her. Carson, the warlock."

I scooped the human into my arms and carried her along. "You were in the wrong place at the wrong time. I'm sorry," I said, not that she could hear me.

"Where to?" Jack grunted, trying to keep a hold of Amelia.

We couldn't very well take Amelia around naked in the daylight. At least the rest of us had found a pair of shorts or something. If we had stuck around, I was sure the fae would have tried to help, but they had more dire situations on their hands than we did, what with the aftermath of battle and removing the destruction from human eyes.

"Put the warlock's shirt on Amelia," I said to Carson. "Then, we'll find a more discreet passage through the city."

Carson took the shirt off Jerod and tossed it to Aaron, who was barely able to get a fighting Amelia's arms through the sleeves without ripping them.

"What method of transportation?" Carson asked. "We can't exactly take the bus like this."

"We're close enough to a road from this part of the park," I said. "We need to secure a vehicle. First, we move to the set of trees over that way, where we can watch the road for an opportunity."

We moved quicky. There weren't many people in the arboretum yet today, and we were able to move without incident. The rain and the disaster at the plaza from last night's battle helped. It kept the humans indoors until the scare wore off.

I scanned what I could see through the trees, but I was going to have to get closer if I wanted a clear picture. I could hear motors and cars, but I couldn't see them yet. "Stay here, and watch the human." I set the woman down. "Don't let her choke if she vomits. I'll find us a ride."

The first twinge of Lunaria's Dream sank its unforgiving teeth into me for letting it run out of my system, and my stomach turned.

Great. Another damn problem.

Chapter Three

JUNE

My head buzzed. I felt sick, and I couldn't remember where I was. Around me there was some shuffling. A whimper, a snarl. My head had throbbed even as I'd been fading in and out, but the volume was too much to ignore now.

"She bit me!" A man's voice startled me. "Deal with it."

That voice. I had heard it right before . . .

I gasped, opening my eyes.

Now I remembered.

It was dark, and there were never-ending trees in the open air around me. Wild plants and unruly bushes told me this wasn't the trimmed and landscaped arboretum. I felt around for my phone and pepper spray, but everything was gone.

They were going to kill me. This was where I would die. Me and that naked girl and that guy on the ground.

Pain shot up my arm from a tender part of my forearm as I adjusted my position. The sleeve of my hoodie had been rolled up to give the wound some air. My eyes widened as I realized: that was no woman, it was some kind of wild thing with teeth.

"She's up," someone said.

The blanket I was lying on smelled like my grandad's attic, and it was itchy, but at least it was keeping the sticks from poking me. The men who had taken me had managed to find shirts to wear and the woman-thing was now in a long, knit dress that was a couple of sizes too big for her, but at least she was covered. My head throbbed again. These assholes had let me fall asleep after head trauma.

Everyone, save the two who were on the ground grunting and moaning, was staring at me. From left to right was the big guy I'd locked eyes with right before getting kicked in the skull. Huge, tan, with a short haircut and sharp jawline. Then there was a short one who looked like he had been through boot camp or something, as the way he held himself was militant. Then there was the gangly young one with messy cornsilk hair, and one on the end who was prodding the campfire with a branch and frowning at it before looking up at me.

I had nothing at my disposal. No phone, not even my lanyard and keys. My heart sank. The first guy stood slowly, then took a couple of steps toward me.

As I sat up straight, the pain in my arm stung, bringing surprised tears to my eyes. I scrambled backwards and gripped the bite on my arm.

"Stay back," I hissed, pushing my legs in front of me and managing to do nothing but stir up last year's fallen leaves and twigs, entangling them in the blanket.

The man stopped, raising his hands palms out. "I'm not going to hurt you, but you'd benefit from listening to me for a minute."

"I'm not listening to my kidnapper," I snapped, and kicked back some more until my back was to a tree.

"She's got you there, Dom," the young blond one said. The one poking the fire laughed, then tried to cover it up as a cough.

Dom. He made me nervous; he was a big guy to begin with, and if that muscle definition meant anything, he was an athlete or at least a gym rat.

"Okay, then, does anyone look less scary to you? They can explain it instead."

It wasn't much of a choice. I wasn't going with buzz cut, the young blond one reminded me of a gangly puppy with too much energy, and he'd probably botch the job. The one poking the fire seemed moody.

"I don't want to hear what any of you have to say," I said, my voice shaking. "I want to go back home." *And I want to call the cops.*

"You're in a position you don't know you're in yet, but you're going to need our help," Dom said. "You barged in on us, and while I know what it probably looked like, that wasn't it. We're taking these two somewhere safe to heal."

I glanced quickly at the grunting, pained figures on the ground and then back up at Dom. I couldn't possibly have read the situation wrong, could I?

"How do I know you're telling the truth?"

"You don't." He shrugged. "But you will when the shift starts. Or you can try to ask one of these two, if you can get them to talk at all."

The man on the ground made a choking sound then spit out a wad of clotted blood. I gasped and snapped my eyes back to Dom in concern. "Yeah, that's about how they've been all day. The warlock said it was only supposed to last nine hours," he muttered.

I was breathing hard, trying to stop myself from hyperventilating. I clutched at my chest and pulled my arms and legs in tight to my body.

"Hey, now, relax," Dom said, putting his hands up in front of him, keeping soothing tones. "In through the nose, out through the mouth."

I took in a deep, shaky breath and managed to let it out slowly. Then another. Then I was ready to talk. "Okay, okay." I breathed.

"You've been bitten."

"Obviously."

"No, you've been bitten by a werewolf," he said.

If I had been in any mood for humor, I would have laughed. "A werewolf?"

"And on the next full moon—which is what, three weeks away?—your body will try to shift. If it can't shift completely, it will try the next full moon and you'll get a little closer. If it doesn't happen then, you'll go through the shift the next moon, and the next, until you either shift or . . ."

This sounded crazy, but he looked dead serious. If he had a psychosis, or a mental illness or something, it might be dangerous to argue with him. But then I realized the other three watching this whole exchange didn't seem phased.

Seriously? *A werewolf?* This was all a bad dream and I wasn't just abducted by a bunch of guys who legitimately thought werewolves were real. They had to be on drugs, maybe something recreational gone terribly wrong. Or a cult, what if they were from a bizarre cult? This was it, I was going to end up on a true crime podcast.

And yet, that woman's face wasn't human. "What happens if I don't turn into a wolf?" I asked. "You said I either shift, or . . ."

"You shift or you die trying."

My breath caught in my throat. I was telling myself in my head that what I was hearing wasn't possible. It wasn't, but the serious faces around me and the things I'd seen so far were seriously creeping me out.

I glanced down at the woman on the ground, snarling and curling her legs up to her abdomen. She was in pain, and she was furious. And in the back of my mind, I replayed the bite. Her face certainly wasn't human, but would I call it wolfish? Whatever it was, she was back to normal now. And the men around us, they had the eeriest look in their eyes. The light kept playing tricks on me, giving them yellow, animalistic stares.

"So." I took a cautious breath, wrapping my arms around myself and trying to ignore the throbbing in my head and my arm. "I was bitten by a werewolf. Let's say that's true, can't I go home and deal with it on my own?"

"There is no going back." Dom's eyes held something like sympathy. "And there are beings out there who want you dead because of what you will become."

That was a terrifying thought. I pushed it away. I needed to deal with one problem at a time. "My roommate will be freaking out right now because I didn't come home. I always come home, and I was supposed to bring back food."

Dom turned, studying the expressions of the others. He ran his hand over his short hair again, something he must do when he's frustrated.

"I'm not out here trying to be the bad guy. I've done a lot of shit in my time, but right now I'm taking you to a safe community where you can live through this painful process. You can decide what to do after you're okay. Leave, go back home, I don't care. But I'll be damned if I let a human go and expose us like this. We have a bad enough rap with the other creatures out there, I'm not about to add to it with you."

"You'll let me go home if I go to your community first?" I asked.

"Yes, after that I won't stop you."

Good. This was good, provided his "community" wasn't a bunch of cultists who were going to eat me or something.

"She's still not convinced, Dom," Buzzcut said.

"Who wants to shift?" Dom asked.

"I'll do it."

Young, blond, and full of energy stood from the ground and began to strip.

"Whoa, whoa." I covered my eyes with my arms, ignoring the stinging arm with the bite in it.

Fingertips brushed the skin on my wrist. It was Dom. He had rough calluses on his hands, but he was soft when he touched my arm and directed it away from my face.

"No, you need to see this."

Even with my arms no longer covering my face, I still had my eyes closed. He couldn't make me look at Magic Mike over there. Or at least, I didn't think he could until I started hearing the strange sounds.

Pop and *snap*. I shivered and cringed hard. It sounded just like my leg had at my very last track meet when I'd messed it up. I subconsciously gripped my thigh with my good hand. I watched in horror as a human body shifted into something else.

Bones moved under the skin, reshaping and fusing where they didn't belong. I instantly regretted my medical classes as the names of muscles and bones ran through my brain as I saw them move around. His skin grew fur. The face elongated. A giant gray wolf stood before me, his yellow eyes peering into mine.

I didn't register that I was screaming until Dom's hand flew over my mouth. "Calm down, it's only Carson."

I took a sharp, quick breath. I took *many* sharp, quick, panicked breaths. The nails in my hand dug into the skin on my thigh. I tried to calm myself down using the breathing exercises from my therapist. I tried to keep my eyes closed as I did it, but the moment my breathing was even a little bit under control, I opened them again.

The wolf sat there, watching me. He cocked his head to one side. At one point he tried to inch forward on his belly, but Dom held out a hand and the wolf stopped.

I was grateful, even though I was in no state to show it yet. It bought me time to calm down. Finally, Dom called Carson off.

"That's enough," he said calmly. The wolf stood to shake out his fur, then reversed the process. I went numb at the sounds of the body shifting unnaturally, and I kept my eyes shut tight this time.

"It's okay, he's dressed," Dom told me.

Carson was back in human skin with a pair of shorts on. I sighed and my shoulders dropped some of the stress I had been holding. I shook out my head and tried to relax the rest of my body. Then I looked down at my arm.

The wound had been cleaned of blood at some point, but I could see the larger indents where fangs had torn at my skin. Carson was a wolf. She was a wolf. Were they all wolves? And if so, why were two of them sick?

"Where are we?"

"The woods. Western Montana," Dom answered.

My heart nearly shot into my throat. "Montana? How long was I out? Where is this community of yours?"

"You can call it the village for now. That's what we sometimes call it. And it's in Newfoundland."

"Canada." I felt weak, like I was going to pass out. A feeling that was quickly accompanied by my growling stomach.

"Aaron, rations," Dom ordered.

Buzzcut, I mean Aaron, reached behind him, rustled in some

bags, and tossed over an entire bag of potato chips and a stick of beef jerky. Dom caught them with ease, and handed them to me.

"Here, eat," he said. I kind of shifted where I sat.

"I need to pee first," I muttered.

He jerked his head in another direction, deeper into the woods. "Feel free."

I was surprised at that one. "You don't think I'm going to run away?"

"We would hear you leaving and have no problem catching you," he answered. "Besides, where would you go? We're in the middle of nowhere."

He had a point.

I stood and went as far as I felt comfortable without worrying about getting lost on my way back. The images of Carson turning into a wolf roiled around my head as I allowed myself an internal freak-out. No one would believe me if I told them what had happened.

I returned and ate my bag of chips and jerky, and didn't speak for the rest of the night. The four men were quiet as well. In the end, the only sounds were the crackling of the fire and the sounds of pain from the man and woman on the ground.

"Get some sleep," Dom announced. No one questioned him. He must have been some kind of leader to them. I was tired and stressed, so I was happy to lay back down on my blanket. I didn't know how much sleep I would get, but at least my body could relax.

Wolves.

It was impossible to absorb.

And if what Dom said was right, I was going to be one of them.

Chapter Four

JUNE

When I woke up in the early morning, it was cold. It was still dark out, but I could never get a full night's sleep in a new place. It was a wonder I had slept at all. Two people in pain nearby made noise all night, with varying degrees of frustration and discomfort. I felt bad for them, even the one who bit me. She must have lashed out in pain, and that was something I could understand.

The thought crossed my mind that I could possibly escape. Even if I believed that I would turn into a werewolf like them, I still would rather handle it at home and not in Canada.

Looking around, I admitted internally to having few outdoor skills, and let the idea of finding civilization anywhere nearby go. I got up and went to the bathroom behind a tree and came back highly dissatisfied with the lack of clean clothes to wear.

"Feel better?"

Dom's voice made me jump. I whirled, running into him standing against a tree nearby. I had passed him and hadn't even noticed.

"Easy, tiger. Just checking in that you're okay," he said.

"You scared the crap out of me." I wrapped my arms around myself as I took a step back, my heart beating fast.

Dom let out a curt laugh. "Didn't mean to."

Amelia was making whimpering sounds and the guy on the ground looked to be having some sort of small seizure. Whatever was happening to them, was it going to happen to me too?

"The plan now is to drive straight through to North Dakota before dumping the car and crossing the border," Dom said.

I turned back to look at him, or as much of him as I could see in the dark. "'Dumping the car'?" I narrowed my eyes at him. "Is your car stolen?"

"Stolen from thieves maybe. We traded our last ride for this one that was about to be taken apart by a chop shop. What are they going to do, report us?"

"Do all . . . *werewolves* . . . make a habit of keeping stolen cars?"

"No. We do what we have to, but you'll see the village is a much more normal place. You'll be comfortable there," Dom said.

"Why are you telling me this?" I asked.

He shrugged. "I thought you'd want to know. I would. And you're sort of one of us now. The plan is no big secret."

One of us. It wasn't the most appealing place to be in, but it was better than being a hostage or a kidnappee.

"Fair enough," I mumbled. "How are we crossing the border? Is there a border patrol? I don't want to get caught with a bunch of highly suspicious people."

He raised an eyebrow. "Highly suspicious?"

"I said what I said." I put my hands in my jacket pockets, shrugging.

"We'll walk through the woods. I can smell a human a mile

away, we don't have to get anywhere near them, and you'd be surprised how much of the border is unwatched farmland. There are some cameras and sensors around, but we've got a prepared spot to cross. Witchcraft lets our kind go through unnoticed by other more concerning things that could be watching. Paid a pretty penny for it, too, or at least Apollo did."

"Witchcraft? And who's Apollo?" I bit the inside of my cheek, mulling over the concept of witchcraft when mentioned by a living breathing werewolf.

Dom's face darkened. "It doesn't matter, he's dead."

"I'm sorry for your loss," I said.

He grunted and moved. His body language was now cold as he turned away from me.

I followed Dom back to camp, if you could call it that. Aaron and Carson were already somewhat awake and yawning. Carson took one look at Dom and turned to the last one of them whose name I still hadn't learned yet.

"Get up," he mumbled, prodding the sleeping man's arm. "Time to go."

The sleeping shape groaned, but he did sit up.

"Start scraping camp," Dom said. "Who needs a hand?"

The camp sprang to life. Dom and Aaron worked together to clean up Amelia and the other guy, making them take sips of water while they were at it. Jack and Carson loaded up the belongings, and I sat with a bottle of water to watch. Where one needed help, another hand would appear to assist. When something bigger needed doing, they would move in tandem. And Dom was the one orchestrating it all as if he'd done this a thousand times before.

Food was packed away, blankets rolled up, and the prone figures were hauled off to what turned out to be one of those vans that could seat like twelve people. My after-school program growing up used to pick me up in one of those, so I was familiar enough with the layout when they all loaded inside.

For lack of a better term, the patients were in the back rows. I sat in the middle area next to Dom. Apparently, he wanted to keep a close eye on the back seat while we drove. Carson and Jack, the last member of the pack, sat behind Aaron, the driver. The front driver's seat, which I was surprised wasn't taken, was filled with the blankets and food from our campsite.

"Toss me a water and something to eat that isn't potato-based," Dom said.

Jack leaned forward to rummage through the dwindling pile of food in the front passenger seat. "Uh, looks like just jerky left."

Jack handed back three sticks of heavily processed and questionable preserved meat products. "That's the last of it."

Dom sighed next to me. "This is why I didn't want you getting the food."

He snatched the sticks from Jack and silently passed one to me without even looking at me. I was surprised but grateful as I took it.

"Potatoes and all their products are perfect," Jack snapped back. "You just don't like good food."

"What I don't like," Dom drew out, "is a bunch of junk food that isn't going to power us through to Newfoundland. Just because you can burn all this oil and grease off with our metabolism doesn't mean it's okay to eat it constantly."

Jack huffed, sitting back in his seat with his arms crossed, while Carson failed to cover his snickering.

"Aaron, you get something when we stop for gas. Jack and Carson can help me try to feed these two in the back," Dom added.

Jack and Carson both groaned.

"Amelia bit me last time," Carson complained.

"And Jerod threw up," Jack added.

Dom leaned forward, close to Carson's and Jack's faces, and spoke dangerously quietly. "Until Amelia is back at full power, I am in charge. My job is to get us all there alive, and together. Amelia is ours, and we take care of our own no matter how unpleasant the job. The warlock, by extension, is our problem until we figure out why they're like this. If you want to lead, challenge me for it."

That shut them up real fast.

Dom gave each of them a heartbeat's attention. "If you don't want the job, then sit down and don't question me again."

My eyes widened and I shied away from Dom, not that I could get that far away in the van. A few words came to mind. *Intimidating*, for one. Maybe *jealousy*, too, if this was how far he went to watch out for his friends. His tactics could use a little polishing, but the results were unquestionable.

Dom looked down at me with a sideways glance. "Calm down. I'm not coming for you. This is pack business."

"Pack?" I murmured. "As in, a pack of animals?"

Dom nodded curtly and faced forward again, watching the road ahead of us slip under the van and away. "As in a pack of wolves."

We rode in silence for a while, nothing to see out the window but alternating farmland and trees. Jack had dozed off, Dom sat watching the road ahead, and Carson was fidgeting with something while I just laid my head against the window and contemplated everything that had brought me to this moment.

"Aw, what? Your name's fucking awesome," Carson said.

I turned around to see he had a familiar driver's license in his hand. Shooting up straight, I reached for it. "Hey!"

Dom was quicker, and he took the whole wallet from Carson's hands. He looked down at it and a slow smile spread across his lips. "Juniper Gunn."

"Give me back my things," I demanded.

"No can do, Juniper," Dom said, sliding my wallet into his back pocket. "You can have it back at the village, once you've fully grasped the situation."

I sank as the weight of it settled over me. My license was pointless when I was a thousand miles from home with no car. And then there was the whole werewolf thing. If I survived, which I apparently might not, how was I going to get home?

"We'll be there before you know it, Juniper." Carson turned in his seat to face me. "No hard feelings, it's for the good of the wolves."

Carson was such a puppy. A gangly, golden retriever puppy. My mouth flattened into a thin line as I tried to come up with an argument, but when nothing surfaced, I sighed. At least he wanted to cheer me up, unlike a certain growly asshole. "June. Just June."

Leaning my head against the cool glass, I watched the same repetitive scenery fly by. If nothing else, it was something to focus on outside of the bite on my arm and this supposed village of werewolves ahead.

At least I knew all the names now.

And they knew mine.

Lord help me.

CHAPTER FIVE

JUNE

My head bounced as a pothole in the road jarred me awake. I was leaning against Dom. Jolting upright in my seat, I looked around, eyes wide. We had reached some microscopic town in the middle of nowhere, with a gas station and almost nothing else.

Dom's cut jawline ticked with some kind of annoyance. Was he pissed I fell asleep on him? I couldn't tell, and he had his arms crossed over his big chest, staring straight forward as Aaron pulled up to a dilapidated gas pump.

"Aaron, food. Jack, Carson, get back here with me," Dom ordered.

And the rest obeyed.

I was sort of pushed to the side as the ones trying to help Amelia and Jerod eat something moved to the back of the van. I used the moment to get some fresh air, slipping out the door.

"I'm, um, going to the bathroom. A real bathroom," I said.

I was pretty sure no one had heard me, or at least no one was paying attention, until Dom leaned his head out of the van. "I trust you. And we're here to get you the help that you're going to need, okay?"

"Okay."

The inside of the gas station was little better than the outside. The walls were covered with neon beer signs, relics of days past. Chipped paint caked the walls in at least four different layers, peeling around the doorway, and a collection of rather suspicious hot dogs warmed on the rollers behind the counter. An old man sat, blatantly looking at a magazine of women he probably shouldn't be looking at on the clock, and I had to clear my throat to get his attention. He shifted his eyes up, clearly bored and wanting me to speak my piece and leave him alone.

"Excuse me, do you have a bathroom?" I asked.

He reached under the counter and pulled up a block of wood with a key tied to it with yellow twine.

"Around back," he said. "Bring back the key or I'll report your plates."

I took the key off the counter and went back outside. Glancing over at the van, I could see they were struggling. I was glad to not be a part of it. Around the corner and to the back of the gas station, I found a thoroughly unimpressive bathroom door that looked like someone had tried to kick it in at one point. I pulled my hand inside my sleeve and opened it.

With the exception of the sink, the bathroom was filthy. I cleaned myself up. Hands, face, neck. My arm had scabbed over but the punctures from the teeth were red and irritated; at least now they were clean. I looked into the mirror, pulling my fingers through my hair as much as I could. I used the toilet, refusing to actually sit on the seat and thanking past June for all the squats and leg days.

Then I spent a good ten minutes hyperventilating as I came to terms with the fact that I was going to turn into one of those wolves. I had flashbacks of Carson shifting that first time in the woods. It still made me feel sick. More than once I had almost brought myself to tears with the idea of my body shifting like that into something else. At least I could distract myself with other thoughts, like my impending return to a job I didn't like and my unemployed roommate's panic as we tried to figure out how to make it another few months in our apartment. You know, no big deal.

When I took the key back to the counter, an ancient plastic phone caught my eye. I set the block on the counter and looked out the dusty front windows of the gas station. No one was looking my way.

"Hey, mister, can I use your phone?" I asked.

He looked up from his magazine and took the key back. "Make it fast."

He unceremoniously plopped the phone on the counter and went back to his reading material.

I quickly dialed one of only two numbers I had memorized. I prayed Kat would answer.

"Hello?" Kat said, uneasiness in her voice.

"Kat! I wasn't sure you'd pick up an unknown number," I said.

"I could kick your ass! Where are you? Are you hurt?" Kat's alarm rang through the phone. I looked up to see if the guy at the counter could hear. If he could, he was ignoring us.

"Listen, I don't have a lot of time. I'm going to—" Guilt hit my chest hard. I shouldn't feel guilty—they'd abducted me—but I could kind of see their predicament. I mean, if the world found out about wolf people, it would get messy. "A distant relative's house. It's an emergency, I'm sorry. Don't worry about me, but I'll send you plenty of money to take care of rent and groceries until I get back. Maybe a couple of weeks, or at least as soon as I can."

"Wait, family? What happened? I was so worried when you didn't come home, I didn't even sleep last night. The cops didn't take me seriously at all either."

"I'm fine," I assured her. "Promise. I'll send the money as soon as I can. And don't you worry, focus on you and the deli situation, okay?"

"Stay safe out there, and whatever happens, I'm sending good vibes your way. But when I see you next, you're going to sit your butt down and tell me every single detail about why you left town without telling me."

"I will. I have to go. Thanks, Kat. Later." I hung up the phone and slid it back to the man at the register.

"You want anything?" I jumped as Aaron came up beside me and set an armful of gas station food on the counter.

"Oh, you were right there?" I asked sheepishly.

"Yeah, long enough to hear you didn't give us away," he said. "You *want* anything before I pay?"

"That's it? No reprimand? No telling Dom?" I asked.

"Do you want me to? I don't see the need. Do you want anything else while I'm paying?"

I looked down at the counter. Any meatish products Aaron could find were stacked with some frozen breakfast sandwiches. Granola bars, power drinks, and canned food like soup and beans. He even had a stack of T-shirts too.

Turning to the disappointing selection of toiletries, I plucked a bar of soap off the shelf and added it to his pile. If I had to have another gas station bath, I was going to do it with soap. I grabbed bandaging supplies for my arm while I was at it and set them down with everything else. "Do you need a hand carrying it all?"

"Nah, you can go back out," he said, and turned to the cashier. "Hey, I'm ready to check out if you're done with your nude mags. I need all this and pump two."

"I'll just go back then," I muttered, a mix of impressed and embarrassed at how he called out the cashier, and made a quick exit.

I walked slowly. I didn't want to get back inside the van if they were still flailing around, trying to feed Amelia and Jerod.

"This was only supposed to go on for nine hours, warlock." I heard a growl from inside the van and stopped.

Warlock. They had said that when I found them in Washington Park, but now it had a whole new meaning. If werewolves were real, that meant warlocks were real too?

I stepped away, not wanting to hear more. Instead, I waited for Aaron to come out of the gas station, and opened the front door for him to put in the bags.

"Do you want a fresh shirt?" He held up the stack. "You can pick between 'Big Sky Country' or this one with horses on it."

"Big Sky Country, I guess. Thanks," I answered.

The shirt had long sleeves, which was nice since I was going to ditch my jacket. It smelled like campfire smoke and there was still blood on it from my arm.

I took the shirt and went around to the other side of the van to put it on. I was wearing a tank top under my jacket, but I still didn't want to stand where that creepy cashier could see me. With my jacket gone and Big Sky Country pulled over my head, I already felt cleaner. Washing my face had helped, too, and if I could get something to eat, that would be even better.

"All right." Dom's head popped out of the van. "We're done here, let's go."

After the others had resettled into our unspoken seating arrangement, I climbed into the van last. Aaron passed a bag to Jack as he pulled out of the gas station and back onto the road. Jack rifled through the bag and handed out some form of makeshift lunch.

"You didn't get any chips?" Jack complained.

"We've got enough of those left," Aaron said.

"Aw, no gummy worms?" Carson asked.

Dom reached forward to take a handful of granola bars and a drink. "We aren't living off of potatoes and sugar until we get there. Alice will whoop your ass if she hears what you've been eating."

"If she's still there," Carson said sadly.

A cloud fell over the van. Those few words put a damper on whatever peaceful mood the guys had kept until now. Dom's face darkened, Jack and Carson looked like kicked puppies, and Aaron pulled a pair of sunglasses he had just bought from the bags and slid them on to hide his eyes. Someone was throwing up behind me, and the smell in the van immediately hit all of us.

"For fuck's sake, Jerod. Hold it in," Aaron growled.

"Pull over," Dom grunted. "Get way off road. We'll clean this up and start up camp."

I looked at the clock on the van console, surprised. It was only a little after midday, no reason to stop yet.

"You feeling it too?" Jack asked. "It started to hit me right before the gas station."

"Hopefully it isn't as bad as usual," Carson added. "That's what the fae lady said, right?"

"Feel what? What's going on?" I asked, but I was met with reserved silence.

"Pack business," Dom finally answered, and I laid my head against the window with a sigh.

We drove a few more miles down the road and then Aaron turned onto an overgrown gravel road, and into the trees we went.

The stench was bothering me, but I could keep it together until we got out of the car. The others, however, didn't look well. Jack was the worst, hunched over, holding his head. Dom looked uncomfortable, too, but he was stubborn, sitting up through whatever it was that was bothering him. Carson looked fine, but nervous, and so did Aaron, as far as I could tell.

The path through the trees clearly hadn't been used in a long time, and the van jostled and bumped as we eventually ran out of gravel road and onto rocky ground near a stream. Maybe I could manage some form of bath situation while we were here.

We got out and everyone pitched in to make camp. Aaron was busy with the fire and Dom dumped a pile of blankets on a log nearby. He turned to me with a frightening expression, and spoke low.

"Stay here. There's a lighter for the fire and food in the bags."

"Where are we?" I asked.

"If I had to guess, it's some hunter's land that hasn't been used in a while. Cross your fingers that it's offseason for whatever they hunt," he answered.

I froze. "What about bears?"

"There's not going to be anything at this site tonight," Dom said. "Listen, do you hear anything?"

No, I realized. Though there was still daylight, even the birds were silent, as though they knew a predator was here. My lips parted as I met Dom's hard stare. There *were* predators here, and the biggest one was staring right at me.

"Nothing is going to come here, not with the smell of so many wolves. Stay put, don't wander."

I pressed my lips into a thin line. "Are you going somewhere and leaving me alone?"

"We are," he said. "Nothing you need to see right now, you've had enough to take in already. We'll be back in a few hours. Don't follow, and don't wander. For your own safety."

"You're putting an awful lot of trust in me," I murmured.

"Believe me when I say this is a last resort situation for us. Now, stay here. You're only putting yourself in danger if you leave."

The intensity in his eyes and words was scary. But after everything I had already seen, it was sinking in how much I didn't want to go through this wolf thing alone, blind to what was happening.

"Okay."

"Good," he said. "I'll come back when I can, June."

A chill ran down my back. Was that the first time he had used my name? It sounded rough on his throat. I shook my head. There was something seriously wrong with me if I thought this pseudokidnapper was any sort of sexy.

"Get it together, Juniper," I muttered to myself, busying my hands with laying out a blanket.

Dom, Aaron, Jack, and Carson carried Amelia and Jerod deep into the woods. The muscles of Dom's back bunched as he moved through the trees, capturing my attention until he disappeared.

And then I was alone.

CHAPTER SIX

DOM

I couldn't get into the woods fast enough. Carson and Aaron were doing better than me and Jack; the withdrawal wasn't giving them any trouble yet. So, they carried Amelia and Jerod. I had scooped up several power drinks—the electrolytes would help us get through this mess somewhat better than we would without them. I drained one of them, then ditched my clothes.

Lunaria's Dream. A concoction stumbled upon by our people centuries ago, brewed by powerful witches using rare ingredients, but the effects were impossible to ignore: a wolf on steroids; drink one vial of the stuff and you're riding high and feeling light on your feet. Keep drinking it on the regular and you're faster and stronger than you've ever felt before. Stop taking it suddenly, and you crash into the depths of hell, which was where we were all headed since our last hit of the stuff was days ago.

The others followed suit, ditching clothes and stretching their limbs. Aaron set Amelia down by me while Jack and Carson carried

Jerod a few yards away. Twin screams, one at my feet, drew my attention, as Amelia and Jerod reached for each other.

"Bring him back!" I shouted, and the distress in them both eased as Jerod returned to within whatever invisible distance they required. Staring hard, I pieced together why this felt so familiar. It all came back to that last battle, when Amelia was thrown into Jerod's magic circle, making a mess and damning them both. Last time we tried to move them from each other the same thing had happened. I frowned down at Amelia. "You guys really can't be separated more than a few yards, can you?"

She couldn't answer.

"Fuck. Blightfang, shift if you can and ride it out."

"Dom," Aaron said. "Do you want me to take a watch?"

"No, I'll keep my skin on. Let me take care of Amelia," I said. "You three keep an eye on the warlock, but otherwise he'll be the same as he's been the last two days. Go, shift, heal." I jerked my head in the direction of the others. "Try to keep it away from June. She's already scared of this shit, let's not show her our worst side."

"Got it," Aaron said, then he looked down at Amelia. "Take care of her."

Any of us would do everything we could for Amelia, even if she hadn't really been herself these last few years. Whether she would admit it or not, she was still our alpha. We were barely more than kids when so much of our pack had been killed. Not this one, not the Blightfang. Our first pack back home in Newfoundland. We lost our parents, we lost our homes, we lost our alpha. The only reason we didn't lose ourselves was Amelia. Alpha Liam's kid 'til the end, she pulled our asses together and vowed to go back when we were strong enough to face our old pack and challenge the new alpha for her rightful place.

I sat down with a grunt, wiping the hair out of Amelia's eyes. She was groaning, holding her ribs tight. She opened her eyes and looked up at me, sweat on her brow and her eyes dull with distraction. Her breath was heavy, but otherwise she was faring better right now than she had been.

"What?" she snapped.

"We're starting to come down off the Lunaria's Dream," I said softly. "Jack's already begun."

She grunted and closed her eyes again. I brushed a leaf off her bronze arm, paler than usual, and she growled at me.

"You can't shift, can you?" It wasn't really a question since she would have taken a wolf form to take on this painful curse if she could. "I'll stay here with you tonight."

That opened her eyes again. "Don't . . . need to."

"I know." I shifted over a foot or so to lean against a fallen tree. The harsh bark of the evergreen scratched my bare back.

My head was pounding, and the abdominal pain was setting in, but it wasn't nearly as bad as usual. I had forced myself to eat something after the gas station, but the appetite drop had already begun. This was the easiest I'd ever had it and, if I had it my way, I wouldn't take that shit again.

It had seemed like such a good idea at first, taking the drug. It pushed our boundaries, let us train longer and fight harder. I was the first to want to back down from it, but Amelia craved what it dangled in front of her. Power, and the promise that we would get stronger. Maybe it did do that to some extent, but the shit we did for that bastard leech Apollo to keep getting it never sat with me. I don't think it sat well with any of us, but sometimes you do what you have to do with what you have in front of you. Sometimes that means starting down a path in life fueled by bad decisions that you made from the vantage point of your teenage years, and the only option you see in front of you is to keep going.

Leaning my head back, I willed the pounding in it to ease.

Apollo was dead, so that option was long gone, along with the rest of the Lunaria's fucking Dream. I peeled one eye open again and grimaced as I added light sensitivity to my pounding head.

"Guess Lady Thea wasn't full of crap after all," I said. "We help the fae with one battle and the healer of the Winter Court magics away most of the symptoms."

And of course, that was the moment Jack threw up, particularly audibly, several yards away. I laughed low, as much as I could manage through my own discomfort.

Amelia growled, holding her ribs. I leaned my head back against the tree, trying to ignore the afternoon sunlight that was threatening to pierce right through my splitting skull.

I smelled the others shift. Aaron and Carson were first. Jack took a bit longer, probably because he was already going through his own symptoms.

"When this is over, if we're better and you still aren't, I'm going to kick that warlock's ass for messing with whatever magic got you like this," I said.

Amelia sort of smiled then took in a sharp breath and growled as she arched her back. Her face contorted in pain.

"I'm taking us back, you know," I said. "I know you haven't been talking through whatever this is you're going through, but you have been listening.

"You did a real number on that human. Another ass to haul back to the village." There was no real change in Amelia's expression. "She better not run off, I don't want to have to chase her down and delay our trip."

I clenched my jaw, a strong wave of nausea washing over me. I had to wait for it to pass before I kept talking. I wasn't even usually this much of a talker, but the distraction was good for both of us. All of us. The others could hear me too.

"Any idea what we'll find when we get back there?" I asked.

"No." Amelia gave a clipped reply.

We were deep enough in the woods that a hearty layer of decayed leaves and dead sticks littered the ground. I could hear every step the wolves took as they did what they could to find some comfort. Jack was having the hardest time, but Carson was starting to whimper.

"We're not the same kids who left. You could do something about him this time. Have you even contacted Naomi since then?"

"No." Amelia grunted and rolled onto her side, facing away from me.

"Amelia," I said softly. "You're as tired of living rogue as we are. We can carve out that place in the village again. We've done some shit, but the pack will have us back in the end. You'll see."

"No." She growled and inched away from me, but I could have sworn I heard the hint of a whimper in her breathing. She could act tough if she wanted to, but the truth is wolves aren't meant to be lonely.

Another wave of nausea hit me, and I dropped the conversation. Grunting, I held my stomach, lying back as comfortably as I could.

I had a long night ahead of me, but at least these were the only symptoms I was having. It could have been worse.

Jerod threw up again in the distance.

A lot worse.

CHAPTER SEVEN

DOM

The sickness was passing. I had no way of knowing how long it had been, but when I stopped having headaches and nausea completely, I figured the others would be on their way too. Maybe they already were, since they had shifted into their wolf skins and would be healing faster that way.

"How are you holding up, Jack?" I asked. The wolf nearest to me gave an exhausted whimper but nodded. I looked at the others. "If you're not already coming down off of it, you will be soon. Get ready to shift back and we can go get something to eat. I'm starving."

Amelia was still next to me, clearly exhausted but holding stubborn and not making a sound. She also hadn't met my eyes since I last mentioned the old pack. She was either pissed at me, mulling over what I said, or probably both.

Jerod was doing a bit better, his suffering coming in waves of bad and worse, giving him just enough relief that sometimes he and

Amelia could sleep briefly. I wondered what we were supposed to do with the warlock. He had been digging things out of his pocket for a while now. A little red Hello Kitty pouch. A candle. A knife. A bright-green string. I didn't know shit about warlock magic, but I knew casting components when I saw them. I made my way to Jerod and nudged him with my foot.

"Hey, warlock," I said. "It's been more than nine hours. When is this going to end?"

"Finding . . . out," he managed through gritted teeth.

A low growl of frustration crept into my throat. If he had a way to find out, I wish he had done it sooner. If I wasn't going to be a part of the spell, I was at least going to watch, so I backed up to keep an eye on him. I was still pretty pissed that this accident had happened in the first place. As soon as Jerod could form whole sentences again, I was going to beat the truth out of him until I had an explanation of what was going on.

Jerod was slow going, pausing a lot to hold his stomach or gag. He spit up blood at one point, but nothing too worrisome. When he finally had his string, knife, some kind of powder, and a crumpled-up flower, he pricked his thumb and smeared blood down the string.

Then he spoke a bunch of warlock gibberish, and the string emitted vivid purple smoke. When he finished the string of magic words, and at almost the instant he stopped, an ugly as sin green demon stepped through the thick smoke. Its eyes bulged, its teeth protruded, and its skin sagged. The thing took a good look at Jerod and chuckled.

Okay, that made me smile a little.

When it started speaking in that same gibberish Jerod had used to summon it, I was lost. It was pretty obvious they were having a conversation, but about what I had no idea. There was a lot of back and forth, and Jerod's answers were pained and short, which only seemed to amuse the demon further.

"For the last time, my liver . . . is . . . spoken for," Jerod snapped.

"You need me to step in and kill this thing?" I asked.

Jerod's eyes slid to me for a moment before going back to the demon. "No, I've got it."

Then they went back to their demon language, and I was out of the loop again. Hoped that June was okay back at the campsite. The whole wolf community would come after us if we let a rogue-bitten baby wolf walk away.

A crackling and a pop snapped me back. I looked up Jerod, only to find the demon gone in a puff of smoke.

Jerod struggled to his knees, holding his stomach and waiting for something. When the ugly demon popped back into our world, I growled low. I didn't like this kind of being. It wasn't natural for it to be here, and everything I was made of, the wolf in me, didn't like it.

The demon ignored me and said something to Jerod in that demonic tongue. Then it cackled and disappeared again. The string used to summon it lit in a burst of flame and fell to pieces in an instant. The tie to the demon was gone.

"Shit," Jerod hissed. He dropped from his kneeling position and slumped onto the ground.

I walked over to him, crouching down to see his face better. "Well?"

"Nine . . . days," he grunted.

"Shit." I echoed his earlier sentiment and stood, staring at Amelia. "What happened to nine hours?"

"Amelia spilled the offering," Jerod snapped at me. "The summoned party . . . was pissed."

My face darkened. "Amelia was thrown during a battle, don't make it sound like she did any of this on purpose. The middle of a battlefield was no place for your summoning ritual, warlock."

"My ritual was a huge part of why you're all alive, wolf," Jerod gritted back.

Running my hand down my face, I closed my eyes. Looked like I was in charge for a little longer, and that meant I'd have us to the village before Amelia could take over and turn us back around.

"Fuck. Okay, okay, let's just get back on the road. Aaron, Jack, Carson, get your asses out of your wolf skins and come here. We've got new info."

Nine days. The warlock had intended to trade nine hours of pain to that demon he'd summoned on the battlefield. The incident that knocked Amelia into the ritual had altered it to nine fucking days.

The sun was up by the time we rode out the initial wave of withdrawal. The cravings would stay, a bit of nausea, and I was sure we'd be shaky for a while. But this was far better than it had been in times past. Walking through the woods, carrying the two incapacitated members of our group, we made it back to the van with the first rays of daylight poking through the trees. June was on the ground by a now-dead firepit. She'd scraped a circle down to the dirt and kept a very small fire going until what looked like less than an hour ago, and was stirring in her cocoon of blankets, wide-eyed at our approach.

"Morning," she mumbled, climbing to her feet. "You were gone all night?"

"We were," I confirmed, heading to the van where I opened the doors for Jack and Carson to settle in Jerod and Amelia.

"What can I do to help?" June asked.

I moved out of the way, letting Jack take my place as they situated our leader and the warlock. As I faced June, my stomach was still turning and my mouth dry from the long night. "There's nothing for you to do. Pick a seat and settle in, we're going to drive straight through to where we'll cross into Canada."

Her mouth flattened into a thin line as her eyes darted to Jerod, now being helped into the van. "I have some medical training. I can see if I can make them more comfortable, or —"

"There's nothing." I held a hand between us, snapping more than I had intended to. "Not one thing you can do right now. Their pain isn't natural, and it's nothing you can do a damned thing about. The best way for you to help right now is to get your ass in the van and out of our way."

"I'm not useless," she said in a low, even tone. "But I'll get out of your way. Let me know if you change your mind."

She turned before I could say anything else, and I cursed under my breath. The others were already passing around the food and cleaning up camp, which we hadn't even gotten the chance to use last night. Aaron pressed a bottle of water in my hand.

"She's going to be a wolf," he said. "Don't be so hard on her."

"I know." I opened the drink and drained the bottle.

"She called home back at that gas station, you know." Aaron eyed me, opening his own water. "She settled her shit, and kept our secret. She could have made this a mess, but she didn't."

I studied Aaron's face. He wasn't one to lie and he wasn't one to stick his neck out for anyone else. "Seriously?"

"She's going to be a wolf, so stop treating her like a human. If she's useful, she's useful. It's the way of the pack to find your place."

He turned, leaving me alone by the van with one last look at the woods where we'd spent the night. I stared down at the empty space where June had slept, her blankets now packed up and loaded and the fire checked and extinguished, probably by Aaron.

To be a wolf was to find your place to do your part in your pack. Was this June's wolf starting to show, or was it purely Juniper Gunn? Either way, I felt like the asshole I was, even as another roll of nausea passed through me.

"Fucking Lunaria's Dream." I spat, got in the van, and we drove off.

CHAPTER EIGHT

DOM

Finally. We were in Canada and driving our own ride. We had money—well, somewhat legal money—clothes, and the SUV. It was more cramped than the van, but it was better to drive with legal plates.

Driving through the provinces was invigorating, and being on the East Coast felt like home. We were going back. I could almost taste the air. Sink my teeth in the mountain elk. Look out over the water, depending on where I dared to run. A few days off the drugs combined with the prospects of returning to the mountains I loved was doing a lot to shake the worst symptoms off me, and from what I could tell, it was doing the same for the others.

I glanced in the mirror and swept over everyone in the car one more time. Jack and Carson were passed out. Aaron was waking up from his own rest, ready to take a turn at the wheel. Amelia was stubbornly staying awake and suppressing her obvious discomfort. Jerod was passed out, which I suppose meant he was getting some form of rest.

Then my eyes landed on June. She was watching quietly out the window, not speaking. She hadn't said much at all since I'd snapped at her, and that had been pretty much two days ago. I sighed to myself and turned my attention back to the road.

June was hard to read, but I could tell she cared about other people. And she was brave. Or stupid. Maybe both. You could be both; Jack was both. But June definitely had the brave part. She showed it when we first met. Plus, it seemed like she knew something or other about first aid, the way she tried to take care of Amelia back in Seattle. For all I thought I knew of her, I still didn't know enough. She was an unknown variable, something I didn't typically like. The fewer unknowns I had to deal with, the easier it was to do my job and keep us safe and on track. But we were almost to North Sydney, and we had a long-ass ferry ride ahead of us. The road curved, and it woke up anyone who wasn't already awake. It was only midday, so we had time to waste until the overnight ferry to Newfoundland.

"We at the ferry?" Jack asked, stretching.

"Just about," I answered. "We have downtime. Last call if you want anything from a store before we hit the wilderness."

"Exactly how much wilderness are we talking about?" June spoke up, stretching her arms out in front of her as much as the seats allowed.

Jack and Carson laughed. Aaron cleared his throat. "A lot of wilderness. I don't know what the village has access to right now, since we've been out of touch, but plan to get literally anything you'll want to have with you."

"Electricity?" June asked, panicked.

"They have that," Jack said. "But no internet."

"They may have figured that out by now," Carson added. "I hope they have."

"There were never any signal towers out there, and I highly

doubt anyone has bothered adding them where we're going," I said. "Plan on not having it and be pleasantly surprised if they do."

"Dare I ask about running water?" June asked.

"Yes, there's water." Carson snorted. "You're thinking a little too primitive."

"You'll be fine," I said. "But if you need any personal items and spare clothes, let's stop now. There are places in Newfoundland we can get things later, if necessary, but for now we're going straight for Moonpeak."

"Okay," June said hesitantly. "I guess I could spare a little more of my savings."

"I want to find somewhere that sells fries," Jack said.

"Poutine!" Carson added, practically bouncing in his seat.

"All right, all right. I'll run us by a downtown store and we can wander around for a while. You can split up but be back a couple of hours before departure because we're going to have to sit in line a while to get the vehicle onboard," I said.

"I'll stay with the SUV," Aaron said. "I don't have any other business in town."

"All right," I said. "Amelia, Jerod, you two need some fresh air? I'm sure the boat ride is going to make your situation even more fun."

Amelia growled. Jerod groaned.

"I'll get them some fresh air," Aaron said.

"Thanks. Then I'll watch New Bite," I said. "Jack, Carson, you two can go off wherever you want but you get your asses back here on time or we're leaving you in Nova Scotia."

"Roger," Jack said.

"Sure," Carson added.

"Wait, I'm 'New Bite' now?" June asked.

I smirked and met her eyes in the rearview mirror. "Get used to it. You're about to hear it a lot."

Her lips slid into a pout as she frowned and looked out the window again.

The traffic in town slowed our progress a bit, but it gave good views. The first opportunity I saw for a store that would carry clothes and things that June might need to pick up, I pulled in and we all got out. It was the first chance we'd had to stretch our legs in a while.

"Be sensible but get what you want. Come back to the car when you're done," I said.

"Got it," Carson said.

"Amelia, Jerod, you two need anything?" I asked.

"No," Amelia snapped.

"Sleeping pills," Jerod grunted. "Enough to knock me out completely."

"At best, I'll try to find some melatonin," I said, and shut the door.

Jack and Carson took off for the store with all the energy they had pent up during the long car ride. They'd need a run in their fur sooner rather than later, but I could probably say the same for all of us. I fell into step beside June.

"Keeping an eye on me?" she murmured, unamused.

"Yes," I said. "And making sure you get everything you need. There aren't a lot of places to pick up things when we get there."

She stopped, spinning to look at me wide-eyed.

"I'll get you what you need. Amelia bit you, and I'm dragging you across the continent to watch over your first shift, the least we can do is buy you clothes and things," I said.

"I'm not sure if I should thank you or not," she said. "But I appreciate the gesture. Do I have a budget?"

"Don't bother with that, we can afford it. Just worry about what you can carry, because it's going in your own bag and you're hauling it around. Let's start there."

"Got it," she said.

She picked a red backpack with a good amount of space in it, then made a beeline for the clothing. June grabbed exclusively athletic clothing. A pack of underwear and sports bras, and then everything else was fit for moving around in. I saw the tight jogging pants in the cart, imagining them on her figure. I ran my tongue over my teeth, my canines aching dully as I pictured it.

"Where are the toiletries?" she asked, looking around the store.

I snapped myself out of the image running through my head and cleared my throat. "Over this way, come on."

When it came to personal care items, she was as indifferent as she was with her clothes. I plucked a bottle of melatonin off the shelf while I watched her grab a dozen other things. She pulled bandages, ointments, and medicines off the shelves and threw them in.

"What are you doing?"

"Building a new first-aid kit, since mine is about four thousand miles west of here." She threw a roll of medical tape in the cart. "I feel naked without it."

"You carry a first-aid kit everywhere?" I asked.

"I'm a physical therapist assistant. I'm between semesters now, but I'm also going to school part-time to knock that *assistant* off my title someday. I've also had a number of first-aid, CPR, and EMT beginner classes. I like to be prepared," June said matter-of-factly.

Well, that explained the kind of person who jumped in to help Amelia, armed with pepper spray and nothing else.

"How noble of you," I said. "Grab what you want but don't forget you're carrying it."

"I know," she said, giving me a pointed look. "You keep reminding me." She turned, not leaving any room for more conversation, and grabbed herself a toothbrush and toothpaste. This wasn't how I wanted to learn more about my unknown variable.

"I didn't mean anything by it," I said, catching up behind her as we kept walking. "It really is a noble pursuit. I'm sure the pack physician would be glad to have a hand while you're there."

That caught a little more of her attention as she pushed our cart toward the entertainment section of the store. She turned her head slightly, and I could see the curiosity in her eyes. "You have a physician?"

"Of course, you can't be caught in the middle of nowhere without one," I joked. "It might be disconnected from the human world, but it's still a functioning society. Even we need doctors sometimes. Cooks, tailors, butchers, hunters."

She hummed and moved on. A pillow, a handful of books, and a flashlight later, she stopped.

"Food?" she asked.

"Don't worry about food," I said. "Anything else?"

She glanced over the cart, carefully taking a mental inventory. I watched the gears turning behind her eyes as she thought it out, then she looked up at me. "Just a phone charger for when you finally give it back."

"Okay." I laughed. "Those are near the front. Let's go."

Jack and Carson met us at the front and I paid for everything on my card, and we rolled the carts to the parking lot.

"Pile in," I said. "Let's get down to the port."

Once the car was loaded, I slid into the front seat next to Aaron, who volunteered to drive the rest of the way through town.

I sat back in my seat, pleased to have a little more of a picture of who Juniper Gunn was. The more I knew, the more I could account for keeping our group safe. That was the only reason I was taking any interest in her.

Right?

Anything else would be a dangerous distraction. I looked over my shoulder to where June was sitting in her seat, opening her medical supplies and packing them neatly into the front pockets of her backpack.

She looked up, our eyes meeting as though she sensed my gaze on her. I noted the curve of her lips, the way her hair brushed her forehead before she swept it back with her long, elegant fingers.

"How long until departure?" Jack asked.

"Three hours," I said. "You'll have an hour before you need to get back to the car."

"Hell, yeah, I'm going to Tim's," Carson said.

June dropped her head again, not saying anything as she went back to meticulously packing her bag. I shook off the odd feeling I got when watching her and laid back against my seat once more.

Interesting woman indeed.

CHAPTER NINE

JUNE

I moaned, a deeply contented sound as I smiled and stretched my legs on the viewing deck of the ferry. I was sure I got a few odd looks from the other passengers. I didn't care.

For three day—three long days—I had been cooped up in one car or another or walking across abandoned farmland. My butt hurt. My back was knotted all to pieces. I hadn't had a good stretch in far too long.

The moment our car was loaded into the belly of the ferry and we were free to go to our seats, I made a beeline for a free space to just . . . walk. How weird would it look if I started exercising? A few lunges sounded useful right now, even if they would earn me a few stares. I sighed and looked out over the water for a moment before retreating back inside.

I had been worried for nothing about fitting in on the boat. The werewolves were right at home, and Jerod and Amelia both managed to get seated without arousing suspicion from their obvious pain and disgruntled expressions. Jerod pretty much sat down and popped a fistful of melatonin. I questioned the wisdom in that for what amounted to basically a human who was already going through enough symptoms without adding side effects on top of that. But he was still breathing, so I stayed out of it as he fell asleep. Dom kept a close eye on everyone anyway. Amelia toughed it out for a while, but took a very large dose of ibuprofen and seemed to settle down a bit as she stayed put in her seat.

And I finally had a taste of freedom after being cooped up in the most bizarre and upsetting situation I have ever been in.

As I came inside, I spotted my empty seat between Dom and Jack. They both looked occupied enough; they wouldn't notice if I was gone just a few more minutes. When we came in and got to our seats, I'd seen the computer kiosks. If I hurried, I might even have internet access before we got too far from port.

My heart raced as I had to wait a minute for someone else to finish before I could use a kiosk. As soon as my fingers hit the keyboard, I went straight to the site I used to send Kat money.

"Come on . . . come on." I furiously typed in my info, racing to get the transfer completed before we lost signal. "Yes."

In went Kat's email address, and out went most of my savings. At least Kat could keep our apartment afloat for a couple of months; more if she was careful. I hoped she would be careful. I had just logged out and stepped away from the computer console when a voice made me jump out of my skin.

"All done?" Dom said.

"I was making sure my roommate could pay the rent." My heart was pounding.

"Walk with me," Dom said. He didn't wait for me, but turned away from the kiosk and headed toward the door to the outside deck.

The moment the door opened, the nighttime air had me tightening my new fleece jacket around me. Pulling my hands into my sleeves, I followed Dom onto the deck, from which you could see the stars reflected in the rippling water. The wind sent a chill across the area and chased most of the passengers back inside. Dom leaned on the rail, watching the water lap against the boat and not speaking. It was probably the most privacy we were going to get on the ferry, and I was dreading what he had to say. I eyed him sheepishly, feeling as though I had been caught with my hand in the cookie jar.

"This must all be pretty frightening for you," Dom said.

"I'm still kind of touch and go with how unbelievable it all sounds."

"New bites usually feel like that for a while. Until their first attempt at shifting, anyway." Dom turned from the view of the water and looked me in the eyes. "We've done a poor job of getting you ready for what's ahead, and I'm sorry about that. I'm not much of a teacher."

I studied his profile as he looked out at the water, the moonlight highlighting the sharp lines of his nose and jaw. He was head babysitter in all this, that was for sure. "You may not be a teacher, but I can tell you're doing your best to watch over everyone."

"I do what's needed of me for my pack. Always."

"I think I can relate," I said. "Some of us get stuck with all the caregiving, huh?"

Dom huffed a laugh, finally turning to study me. "Care to elaborate? I don't know much about you."

"I could say the same about you," I replied. "But sure. I grew up with my grandparents. Grandad passed when I was eight. Granny three years ago. When you're the healthy young person in the house, you end up doing a lot more than a kid should have to do. Then there's my roommate. She's my best friend, but I'll admit I do baby her. I guess the role is just ingrained in me at this point."

"I can see it," Dom mused. "All you need now is a set of scrubs and a stethoscope around your neck."

Elbowing him lightly, I couldn't keep the smile off my face. "Shut up, at least I know what I want in life for the most part. Not everyone gets to say that."

"You're right, they don't." Dom watched the water for a few quiet heartbeats. Studying his profile, I could see that he was actually attractive when he was relaxed. It made me realize he'd mostly been a ball of stress since we'd met, and from the bits and pieces I'd gathered from the group, they had just been in some kind of traumatic conflict. That couldn't be easy on anyone, but I respected Dom for coming up with a plan and keeping everyone to it.

"Okay, New Bite. Ask all the wolf questions burning a hole inside that head of yours. I can feel you staring."

"All right, did you struggle like this when you were bitten?"

He looked at me strangely, confusion plain on his face, then he laughed. "No. You've seen too many old movies. Most of us are born this way."

"Really?" I asked sheepishly. "You're not pulling my leg?"

"Really. Raised in the village, the pack all take a hand in the kids. Had a dad, mom died when I was younger. Had friends, neighbors, a house, the whole deal. Cases like yours are not that common," he answered. "But back on the subject of what's ahead, you should know about the hierarchy of a pack. Do you know much about wolves?"

"Maybe?" I said. "I haven't really thought about them since probably a report in middle school."

Dom nodded. "All right. Well, have you heard the term *alpha wolf* before?"

"The boss wolf, right? I thought that was a myth."

"In the wolves you know, sure. For us it's very much real. We have roles in the group that keep us strong. Everyone does their part, and speaking of that, I owe you an apology for the other day."

I bit the inside of my cheek. I hadn't expected an apology, especially so many days later. Then again, this was the first time we'd been alone since that morning. "Thank you."

"When we get to the village you'll meet the alpha, his beta, and any warriors on patrol. These are the top of the food chain, so to speak. Their roles are to keep humans, other creatures, or rogues out of the territory and away from the village."

"Got it. Boss, vice-boss, and cops," I said. "I need to know them? Anyone else I need to know about?"

Dom chuckled as he turned back to me again. "That smart mouth is going to get your ass handed to you."

"By you?" I asked, then frowned. I had no business playing around with this guy. He'd been kind of a jerk so far, if I was being honest. And the second I had this shift thing under control, I was going home. I'd probably never see him again.

"By someone at the pack, I'm sure." His mouth twisted up at one side. "Everyone in the pack has a job, we cover all the things needed to keep us going. Trackers to keep an eye on the territory and watch the migration of animals, spot where the wild foraging is growing in and when the season starts. We have warriors to keep the pack safe from anything that would threaten it, animal or otherwise. The alpha is the unquestioned leader of the pack. They will be the strongest wolf with the most dominant presence. You physically won't be able to resist a command unless you turn out to be one hell of a wolf when you turn."

"What are the chances of that?"

Dom laughed. Probably not a good sign. "Astronomical," he answered.

"Figures," I said. "So, how does one get voted alpha?"

"It's less like a vote and more like a fight to the death," Dom answered.

"You're not serious."

"I am," he said. "This isn't a human civilization, June. We have different rules, morals. The wolf code of honor means something. Respect a dominant wolf but never call yourself weak either. A pack helps each other. It's a tight community, no one knows a stranger. No one goes hungry. Everyone has a place."

"You're saying things I love and things I hate about this village."

Dom shrugged. "Save your judgment until you get there. I'm just filling you in so you're prepared when you arrive. You'll be expected to meld in with the pack pretty quickly, so be ready for a lot of 'finding a place for you' going on."

"But I don't need to find a place or whatever. I'm not staying," I reminded him.

Dom sighed and ran his hand down his face. "June, I won't stop you from leaving if you're able to."

I narrowed my eyes at him. "What do you mean?"

"Wolves have a strong sense of community. When you fall into place, your wolf won't want to leave. You'll have a stronger force inside you to guide your instincts, and sometimes what you want and what those instincts want doesn't line up," Dom said. "You're going to have a hard time convincing your wolf, those instincts, to leave if they want to stay."

"That's not possible." The notion of losing that kind of control over myself made me uneasy. "I have a career, ambitions, friends, all back in Seattle. I have school in a couple of months, I was thinking about taking a semester full-time if I could get away from the clinic I'm at now. I can't just drop my life like that for a condition that happens one night a month."

"June," Dom groaned. "It's not a condition. It's an alteration of who you are. You'll be one of us, and you'll seek out our communities whether you like it or not. You don't want to live rogue, trust me."

"What's a rogue?" I asked.

"A wolf or small group of wolves who live outside of a pack dynamic. A rogue wolf is a lonely and powerless wolf. Do not go rogue, June. You'd be chewed up and spit out in a year."

"I still can't picture it."

"Clearly. Promise me you'll give the village a chance. If you really, truly don't feel like you can live there, at least cooperate with them long enough to find a rank in the pack. After that, you can possibly negotiate joining a pack closer to home once you've gotten a feel for your wolf and what you can do. You might have a rank beyond just pack member, and if you do, that will be important information for a new pack to know."

"Rank, like a score? How do you get a good rank?" I asked.

"Dom!" Carson was at the door of the ferry, waving to get our attention. "We're having some trouble with Amelia, and she's going to lash out at the people in the row behind us if we don't stop her soon."

Dom grunted in frustration and turned to me one more time. "We won't know your rank until your first shift, and there's nothing you can do to alter what you are. It would be like changing your eye color or how tall you are. It's just . . . what you are."

"Oh," I said softly.

"Just think about what I've said. I don't want you going down a bad path because you made your decisions as a stubborn human without even knowing what it's like."

Then Dom turned to Carson and followed him inside. "Get her to some fresh air and see if you can get another dose of those pills in her. I'll find her something to eat and see if that helps her disposition."

"Got it," Carson answered as the door closed.

And then I was alone. Alone to think about what Dom had said. About belonging. I shook my head and turned to watch the water again. It was too hard to picture. Melding into a strange society because we shared a common . . . curse? Ailment? Whatever it was supposed to be called.

I was happy in Seattle, right? Sure, rent was high and pay was low, but I had Kat and I was helping people. What would a village of werewolves in Canada have for me?

I went back inside, immediately spotting the guys taking care of Amelia. It was clear they all cared for each other deeply. It was nice, in a way, to have that sense of community. Could I have that too?

It wouldn't be easy to wrap my head around it. But I supposed I could try.

CHAPTER TEN

JUNE

We loaded back into the car, got off the ferry, and were on the road again, but I was too anxious to rest. The sun was finally up, and I had been munching on a box of Smarties, which were very much not what I thought I was getting when I bought them, so I was having chocolate for breakfast as we sped along the Trans-Canada Highway.

All anyone would tell me was that we had to go a few hours on the highway and after a while, we'd turn onto a dirt road. That was it. Then again, it was a village in the mountains that the humans didn't know about. Still, I didn't like it.

I tried to read but ended up reading the same pages over and over. Leaving the book aside, I watched out the out the window. In the end, I gave that up, handed Jack the rest of my box of Smarties, and glued my eyes ahead to watch the highway.

"This it?" Aaron asked out of the blue. He slowed the car down, pulling to the side of the road where a few scant tire tracks indicated anyone ever drove this way.

I sat up straight, paying close attention to Dom in the driver's seat.

"The big *X* tree is gone, but this must be it," Dom answered. He rolled down the passenger-side window and in some kind of silent agreement, Aaron stuck his head out and seemed to . . . smell around.

"That old geezer still comes through this way. This is it." Aaron pulled his head back inside.

"All right." Dom inched the car forward, bumping as each tire left the pavement and we got onto the dirt road, making progress once more.

The car climbed around the trees. Over hills, zigging and zagging to climb to a new height. In fact, as the trees thinned and thickened, I caught glimpses of the mountains around us; it felt like we were in one of the dips between peaks, but I couldn't quite tell.

Something inside me stirred. Exhilaration maybe? Not quite excitement, but it was a kind of enthusiasm to be here. It was subtle but it came on suddenly, like I had crossed a line into something.

"Ahh, feels good," Jack said.

"Patrols will be here any time now," Aaron warned. "Be on your best behavior, we're not pack anymore. Only visitors."

"For now," Dom said.

We left the trees again, and the grassy fields revealed a better glimpse of the distance. There were mountains and a blue ribbon that lay across the green below. A river, or a long lake. A puff of wind rolled over the scene ahead, and I watched as it rustled the plants in its wake.

"Here they come," Dom said.

I frowned. "Who—"

Howling.

My heart smacked inside my rib cage. A thundering of giant paws trampled the ground near the car as wolves, *huge* wolves, emerged from the trees behind us and caught up with the SUV.

"What's happening?" I asked, panic leaking into my voice as I clutched the backpack in my lap with a death grip.

"They're smelling us," Dom said, slowing the car down. "And if we don't stop and talk to them soon, they'll attack."

Dom and the others were calm enough, so I tried to let that fact reassure me. Oh god, I was about to meet wolves. Real wolves, from this village. The place we had been coming to with no stops for days. It was finally time.

The car came to a bumpy stop in the middle of the thin dirt path. Dom was the first one out of the car, barely waiting for the engine to shut off before his opening his door. The others weren't far behind, but since Amelia and Jerod were staying in the car, I did too. Just because I was inside the car didn't mean I wasn't pressed to the glass, straining to catch every detail as it happened.

Dom and the others stood shoulder to shoulder in front of the car as the big gray wolves circled us.

One of the wolves was very white in the face, probably older than the others. He walked calmly up to Dom, got his nose right in his face, and let out a huff of breath that rustled his shirt.

"We're here for a couple of reasons," Dom said, out of nowhere. "First, we want to visit family and friends, upon Alpha's approval. We'll stay on the grounds but not in the village."

The other wolves that had been circling came in and sat down in a semicircle, as though they were a bunch of kindergarteners sitting down to story time. One of them even lay down at Aaron's feet with a soft but excited yip.

The big wolf huffed, then changed as the rest watched. De-forming and re-forming under the skin. His body shifted and popped as he lost his fur and morphed into an old man. His naked skin was leathered, like when you spend all day in the sun for decades. His white hair was long enough that it brushed his shoulders, and he kept a scraggly beard. Despite the obvious years under his belt, he was as well muscled as an athlete.

"That's one reason." The old man spoke. "What else?"

"A personal problem to sort out between Amelia and a warlock we picked up," Dom answered.

The old man's eyes shifted to the car, and I gasped when I saw them shining yellow. Not a color I had ever seen on a person before.

"Why isn't her ass out here telling me all this?" he asked.

"Amelia is indisposed." Dom calmly crossed his hands in front of him as he spoke, standing casually. "You can address me as our party's temporary leadership."

"Is that it?" The old man looked through the car windows straight at me.

"No," Dom said. "Not quite."

Dom walked around the car and I leaned away from the window just in time as he opened my door.

"Come on out," Dom said quietly. "Chin up, shoulders back."

My sneakers hit the grass, and something in the fresh air here gave me the urge to run. Not run away, oddly; it was a different sensation. The desire to take off running for the joy of it.

"Come on," Dom said, and he walked back to the line of wolves. It snapped me out of my sudden odd desires, and I followed him.

The wolves seemed even bigger once I was outside the car. I felt so small, and every one of their yellow eyes was on me. Following every step I took, watching me curiously, sniffing the air. The sniffing was going to take some getting used to.

Dom stopped and gestured for me to stand next to him. Chin

up, shoulders back. He reached over and pulled up my sleeve, revealing the bite mark on my arm. A few growls of disapproval rippled through the wolves. My heart was beating hard, and somehow, I felt like this was a test. It probably was.

"You really fucked up this time, didn't ye, boy?" the old man said, eyes burning into mine. The accent startled me, almost Irish in tone. Not that I was an expert in the Newfoundland dialect, but he sounded nothing like Dom and the others.

"Not even a how are ye gettin' on?" Dom asked, but the old man didn't look amused.

"Mind now. Answer the question," he said.

Dom sighed, scratching the back of his neck. "Will the pack take her or not? Otherwise, she's stuck with a bunch of rogues."

The old man finally took his intense eyes off mine and spit on the grass at his feet. "You know we will."

"Thank you, Smokey," Dom said.

"Two of you, go back and send word," Smokey said to the wolves at Aaron's feet. "Tell Alpha we have visitors camping and a new bite to place."

Two wolves stood and took off, running down the dirt road in the direction we had been heading. Then Smokey turned back to me once more.

"What's your name, New Bite?" he asked.

"June," I said, keeping my voice even.

"Smokey. You want me to kick this one's ass for getting you into this situation?" he asked, while jabbing a thumb in Dom's direction.

"Not right now, thank you. Maybe later, I haven't decided yet."

At that, Smokey let out a wheezy laugh, patting me hard on the shoulder and almost knocking me down. "All right, June. You're clear to go on, and I guess these boys will have to take you there.

Dom, we'll run with you to the pond. As long as Alpha says you can stay, you boys can use the old cabin out there."

"Thank you, Smokey," Dom said. "All right, let's go."

Dom patted the hood of the car as he rounded to the driver's door and got back inside. The rest of us scrambled after him, and by the time I clicked my seat belt, Smokey was a shaggy gray wolf again, ready to run alongside the car.

"It had to be Smokey," Amelia growled.

"Yup," Dom said, and with no further elaboration, we left.

Now that the intense moment was over, I felt more at ease, especially when Smokey had laughed. It was fun to watch the pack run with the car, weaving around the trees as we passed them and racing each other and nipping at heels when we were in open spaces.

It probably took us a good half hour to get to our destination, really showing how big this territory must be considering how far off the highway we had already come. After I took in the novelty of riding alongside a bunch of wolves, I looked around the car. Everyone else held some amount of excitement, save for the two in the back. They were all talking over one another, and I had to lean forward so Dom could hear me.

"Why don't you guys have that accent?" I asked. "If you're from here, I mean."

Dom shrugged. "Fell off while we were in the city, I guess. We've been gone a long time, and blending in did us better than standing out."

Makes sense.

"Who is Smokey, is he the beta?" I asked. Surely he was important, whoever he was.

"I doubt it, but I don't know who Evander has at his side now," Dom answered.

"Who was it when you left?" I asked.

The car fell silent.

Oh. Bad move.

"The old beta is dead," Dom said shortly. "The pond is up ahead. Pay attention to your surroundings so you can learn your way around."

The road curved as the car maneuvered around the trees. The wolves ran ahead, bounding for the pond that was coming into view. It was a beautiful, sunny spot once the trees opened up. A breeze teased little ripples across the water's surface and a wooden cabin sat a little way back from the water.

The wolves that had run ahead were walking around the pond or sitting in the shallows. Smokey was the only one I could identify, and he was standing near the cabin, waiting for us.

Dom parked, and we finally left the vehicle. My legs were like jelly, and I almost fell when I took my first step, all my muscles screaming at me.

"Jack, Carson, help the two in the back," Dom said. "We'll wait to unload when we've gotten permission from the alpha, but some fresh air might help them for now."

"Got it," Jack said.

"There's Hannah," Aaron said. One of the wolves that had run off at Smokey's command was now bounding toward us.

Smokey shifted, and so did Hannah. I looked away. I had seen a lot more nudity in the last hour than I had bargained for.

"Permission granted," Hannah said. "Alpha Evander will be by tonight to talk to you guys too."

"Thank you, Hannah. Go help your mom, I'm sure she's getting a room ready," Smokey said, then turned to me

"Come on, New Bite. I'll take you into the village, bring your bag." Smokey stared, watching me for a reaction, and so did the other wolves lounging around the pond.

I looked back at Dom. I hadn't thought I'd have to do this part alone, but here we were. Dom was no help either; he just tapped his chin, gesturing for me to lift my head.

"Lead on," I said, and turned back to Smokey.

And with that, I followed a naked old man and four wolves down the path. The village ahead and Dom and the others behind.

CHAPTER ELEVEN

JUNE

Smokey and I crested a hill maybe half a mile away, giving me my first glimpse of civilization.

I didn't know what I thought I was going to find, but this wasn't it. The village didn't look that rural at all. In fact, for a small town, the presence of several landmarks made me feel relieved. There was a water tower, and generators poked out from behind buildings. There were even solar panels tucked away on a few rooflines. A general store was one of the larger buildings around, save for a huge structure set at the end of the main path; or at least it was much bigger than anything else within eyesight. The houses themselves were mostly white, but with a few colorful ones mixed in. It was all very cozy. Relaxed. Peaceful.

At the edge of the first real street was a set of numbered wooden boxes. Smokey went up to one of them, lifted the hinged lid, and pulled out a pair of sweatpants and a shirt. Once those were on, he pulled out a pair of sandals.

"These boxes are all around the edge of the village," Smokey explained as he slipped the loafers on his feet. "Undress here, run in your fur, get dressed again for the village."

The boxes were like lockers then, only there weren't locks on them. There didn't seem to be that many people living here, so maybe theft wasn't a problem. But rather than stop our progress to ask Smokey more questions, I had to catch up as he finished putting on pants and shoes and walked off without warning. Heads popped out of windows. Folks who were outside stopped to watch as we strolled down the main street.

"Mornin', Smokey." A woman walked out of her house, wiped her hands on her apron, and said, "Who is this?"

"New bite," Smokey said simply.

The woman's face perked up as she raised her head slightly to sniff the air. "Welcome to Moonpeak! Where ya longs to?"

"Where . . . what?" I asked.

"Where are ye from?" Smokey supplied.

"The States," I said, still wrapping my head around the local phrase. "Washington state."

"We'll have a yarn later, Eva," Smokey said, steering us past her and on our way.

A cautious smile and a wave back seemed to please her. I appreciated the friendliness as we passed, and she wasn't the last one. Lots of folks said hi to us as we walked down the gravel, which started at the edge of town. I didn't see anything paved, but I guess at least gravel wouldn't turn to mud in the rain, so it was better than no street at all.

When we were more than halfway into the village, I looked at Smokey, who didn't seem to be turning off the main path anytime soon. "Smokey? Where are we headed?"

He looked back over his shoulder. "You'll need to meet the

alpha first. Once you're in the Moonpeak pack, you can get settled in."

Smokey led us to the large building I had seen when we first arrived in the village. It was white with deep-blue shutters on all the windows. The door matched, and it had a gorgeous garden to the side with a big fire pit and Adirondack chairs in the middle.

"This is the pack house, Alpha Evander lives here. You won't have to come here much, but this is where Alpha's office is, on the main floor. If you have a request for anything, you'll make it here."

As Smokey and I walked up to the front door, a knot formed in my stomach. The inside was nicely decorated. Every window had deep-green curtains on it. The entry area was two stories high, and I could look up the grand wooden staircase to the second floor, which looked mostly to be bedrooms.

"This way, New Bite," Smokey said, and I followed him down a hall on the bottom floor.

It wasn't far; we passed what looked like a library and another office before coming to the end of the hallway, where a big set of double doors opened into another simple but tastefully decorated room. There was a set of leather chairs in front of a big wooden desk. A bookshelf on the far wall held a number of little ships in bottles, probably a hobby.

"You wait here," Smokey said. "Alpha will be here in a minute. I've got to make a quick report."

"Okay," I said and walked over to a window with a nice view of the village.

Smokey left the room, and I settled in to watch the village move about its business. So many people were active in this small space. Neighbors helping neighbors, people visiting each other, and others who were doing outdoor chores like chopping wood or gardening.

I turned at the sound of footsteps behind me to see a big man with a neat black beard and cleanly combed hair. He looked fresh out of the shower or something. He had sharp blue eyes and wore a polo shirt. He might have been roughly old enough to be my dad, maybe a little younger.

"June?" he asked in a pleasant voice. Friendly. He stuck out his hand for me to shake.

"Yes, that's me."

"Nice to meet you, I'm Alpha Evander. Why don't you take a seat and we can have a chat."

He sat behind the desk and gestured to the leather chairs in front of him. I thought he would be more frightening, but instead he reminded me of a professional. A businessman or something. I slid my backpack off and set it on the floor next to one of the chairs, then sat down.

"Smokey explained that you've been bitten. I'm happy to welcome you to the Moonpeak pack on a probationary period until you are able to shift. We'd be happy to have you and help you get settled into life here for a while."

"Thank you, Alpha Evander," I said.

"While in the pack there are a few rules to abide by." He smiled. "We gather every full moon to run as a community, and on the new moon we have a pack picnic. Community is important to wolves, very important. This probation is a little bit for us to get to know you and you to get to know us. If you fit in, of course, you can ask to join Moonpeak when you have your first full successful shift. Sound good?"

"Great," I said. I wasn't planning on sticking around anyway, so the no-pressure approach was welcome. It would seem Dom had gotten it wrong. Maybe I could go back to Seattle right away after all.

"Excellent." Evander smiled. "Linda can help you get settled in. She runs a small dorm house for visiting unmated females. Smokey will take you over there, and be sure to try one of her sweet rolls if she's made any, they are the best you'll find anywhere."

What the hell is an unmated female?

"I will, thank you." I stood, collecting my backpack.

"Our next picnic is in a couple of days," Evander said. "Full moon is a couple of weeks after that. I'll talk to you again before your first moon." He stood and walked me to the door of his office, where Smokey was standing outside. "Let Linda know if you need anything, all right?"

Alpha Evander handed me over to Smokey. "Take her to Linda's," he said. "I'll talk to you later about our visitors."

"You got it," Smokey said.

"Take care." Alpha Evander waved us off and closed the doors to the pack house behind us.

"He seems nice," I said. "I thought he would be scary."

"Make no mistake, New Bite." Smokey stopped. "Don't cross an alpha, they can bring a world of hell down on you, and Alpha Evander is no exception."

With that ominous bit of advice, I caught up to Smokey, who had started walking again. We turned off the main road, not that there was too much more than the main road in the first place. A two-story house with fresh yellow paint offered a warm welcome. Someone had given it pavers up to the door that were nicer on my feet than the gravel, and potted plants littered the front porch. I couldn't say all of them looked alive, but they were there nonetheless.

"Linda will take good care of you," Smokey said. "I'll leave her to it. You tell her if you have a problem, you hear?"

"Thank you, Smokey," I said.

Linda came out of the house wearing a flannel shirt and dark jeans. Her yellow hair was tied up in a bun that had probably been much neater when she first put it up this morning. She had various things on her, from flour on her sleeves to dried dirt on her knees to something that looked like powdered sugar wiped on her hip.

"Hi there!" She had a big warm smile, and the first thing she did was pull me into a surprise hug. "You must be June, I got ye a room ready. Smokey, 'ow's she cuttin'?"

"Best kind, b'y. Can I leave her with you, Linda?"

"Bye, Smokey, I got her from here," Linda said.

"Yes, b'y, Linda. Take care, New Bite," Smokey said as he walked back down the path.

With Smokey gone, Linda pushed me back at arm's length and studied me up and down. "Aren't you a cutie? You look like you could use some lunch."

"Yes, please." Her energy was infectious.

"And I bet you want a shower." She looked down at herself. "Why don't we both have one, I didn't realize how many of my chores I was still wearing. After that I'll fire up a scoff."

Following her into the house, I could see there were knick-knacks everywhere. Teacups and plates hung on the wall in the big eat-in kitchen to the left of the entrance. A living room full of plush couches and wooden ducks to the right, although the central focus seemed to be a beautiful stone fireplace. A candle was burning with a spiced, earthy scent that wasn't quite to my taste but added to the cozy charm of the house. Straight in front of me was a staircase that creaked as we climbed to the second floor.

"I paint all the doors different colors so it's easy to remember where you are," Linda said. "Sometimes visitors are only here a day or two and that's not always enough time to remember your way around."

I saw what she meant; the upstairs hall seemed easy to get

turned around in, but every door was a different color of glossy, bright paint.

"I hope you like green because you're about to see a lot of it," Linda said as she opened a door near the end of the row. A green plaid bedspread was laid over a double bed in the corner of the cozy room. There wasn't a closet, but there was a wooden wardrobe where I could put my stuff. A small bookshelf sat next to the bed, acting as a nightstand at the same time, with a little lamp on top. The shelf itself held a few things to occupy the time. Crossword puzzles and word search books sat on it along with an old coffee cup of pencils. There was a checkerboard and a few classic books to read if I got truly bored.

"Thank you, it's great."

Sleeping in cars and on ferries hadn't been comfortable. I also appreciated having some privacy, which I hadn't gotten on the road.

"The bathroom's the light-blue door, yeah?" Linda said, taking my backpack off my shoulders and setting it on the bed. "When you're ready to eat, come on down to the kitchen. Did you see the kitchen when we came in?"

"Yes, I did."

She smiled and reached out to lightly squeeze my shoulder. "My daughter will be home soon, too, you'll see her at lunch. I'll leave you to clean up, but I'd love to get to know you. Welcome to the village, June."

"Sounds great," I said. Linda left the room, closing the door behind her.

I hadn't been mothered so much in a five-minute span since I'd left for college, and it was a bit overwhelming, but still a comforting welcome. Picking through my backpack, I grabbed some fresh clothes and soap and things for a shower. Time to clean up and eat.

Maybe this village would be fun while I was here after all.

Chapter Twelve

DOM

The old hunting cabin was even more of a piece of shit than I remembered. It was a good place to carefully tread back into Moonpeak territory, though, and once word spread that we were here, I expected a number of visitors.

I was digging through the cabinets for what food may have been left around, but it didn't look like there was any. Carson was helping stock the kitchen with the things we had bought in North Sydney. At least with Carson helping Jack shop, we had some decent food for building our energy up. Still, there were a fair number of potato products as well.

"We're going to have to go hunting," Carson said. "I don't think this is going to last that long."

I shut the cabinet door I was at and walked over to him. Looking through the last of the food he had put away, I saw mostly canned vegetables, nuts, seasonings, a couple of onions, some apples. Some jerked meat, but nothing that would last five wolves very long. Lots of foods that would be a part of a meal, but no fresh meat.

"It'll have to wait," I said. "No hunting on pack lands without permission. We're outsiders now, remember? We get to sit pretty on our asses until Alpha sees fit to come deal with us."

Carson's shoulders fell, disappointed. "Damn, that's frustrating. I grew up here, I want to run down the hills and stalk the elk. Why do pack politics have to be so hard?"

I exchanged a look with Aaron, the only other one to argue we shouldn't have brought Carson with us back then. He was just a kid when we left. Sixteen. Amelia had let him come, saying he had the same fire in him that we did because of what happened. We were all left in the same boat when Evander became alpha, after all. Every one of our parents died trying to either stop the challenge or to challenge Evander when he took over, desperate to avenge Alpha Liam or at least to stop the ascension of Alpha Evander. They must have seen something in Evander that made the risk worth it, but all I knew was that it left a bunch of kids orphaned and eventually rogue. What kind of place did a bunch of kids have in the new structure of a pack that had killed their parents? None, and so we left.

"If you're done, go get Aaron and watch for visitors," I said, trying to distract him.

"You expecting anyone?" Carson asked.

"Smokey. Maybe Alpha Evander. Just keep an eye out, will you?" I closed the last cabinet and turned to him. "While we have permission to be here, I expect the alpha will want to come by and set some ground rules."

Carson stopped in the doorway on his way out. "She'll be okay, right?"

"Amelia?" I glanced at her bedroom door. "Yes, just give her time."

If she's not, our trip back here was all for nothing.

"Dom," Carson called. "Smokey's coming!"

I left the kitchen and went out the front door, the screen door creaking as it swung shut behind me. Aaron was outside with Carson, and Jack was still in the cabin doing who knew what.

Up the path, Smokey walked as though he had all the time in the world. There was a little blood on his mouth, he'd probably caught his own lunch on the way here. While most other wolves only hunted on the full moon or as their role in the village asked of them, Smokey barely left his fur. In many ways, Smokey was an odd wolf.

Once he was close he paused and shifted. He shook his head and brushed the hair out of his face as he walked over.

"How are ya now?" he asked.

"Good, and you?"

"Not so bad." Smokey tilted his head and crossed his arms.

"Got a little something on your mouth, Smokey." I gestured.

He wiped it with the back of his arm. "The goose didn't come with a napkin, boy."

Carson laughed. I shook my head. Same old Smokey.

"How frequent are the attacks?" I asked, shifting to business. "Are you still getting hit by those strange rogues?"

Smokey ran his tongue over his teeth, taking a moment to stare me down. "They stopped not long after you left. About when the challenges to Alpha's position slowed down."

Clenching my fists, I kept my voice even. "You know what that looks like. Why didn't anyone push it?"

"Folks here seem unbothered by it," Smokey said. "Folks I would have thought wouldn't let it go. Folks who usually cause a fuss to get things evened out."

"You're telling me the attacks started when Evander came, then they stopped once he was the unchallenged alpha of Moonpeak?" I asked.

"That's about the way of it," Smokey said.

"Weird," Aaron said.

"Very," I agreed.

"Don't go poking around unless you're really ready to do something about it, ya hear? Now, what happened with this June kid?" he asked. "Did she walk up and ask for a peck on the arm or did one of you boys screw up?"

"Amelia bit her." I crossed my arms. "She's in a bad state right now. June thought we were hurting Amelia and came to help. Amelia lashed out. Teeth. Skin. We took June with us. That's about it."

Smokey gave me a dark look.

"Amelia did it, did she? What's wrong with her?" Smokey asked.

"You want any clothes?" I asked, encouraging him to follow me into the cabin.

Smokey scoffed. "This isn't the village. No need to get pants involved."

"Mm-hm. I figured."

When I opened the door to Amelia's room, she was on the bed on all fours, one of her hands gripping the headboard. It looked like she had brought her claws out enough to start tearing it to pieces in her pain and frustration. The T-shirt and track pants she was wearing had some notable claw marks in them too.

"What happened?" Smokey asked, frowning as he took in the sight of her.

"Some shit with a warlock." I shrugged. "It's supposed to be over in nine days. After tonight we've got three to go."

Smokey leaned over her, getting close to her face to investigate.

"Amelia," Smokey said, putting as much wolf in his voice as he could in his human skin. "Put your fur on."

Amelia glared at him, grunting, holding her ribs.

"She can't," I answered for her.

Amelia turned and snarled. Then she spun back around to her visitor, locking furious eyes with Smokey. "Leave," she managed.

Smokey looked down at her. "And if I don't, what are you going to do about it? Claw me like your headboard? Say some pissy shit?"

Amelia raised an arm to take a swing at him, but in her weakened state he caught her arm and lifted her off the bed with it entirely. Amelia hung there, snarling and fighting as much as she could.

"You were gone for ten damn years, Amelia," he said sternly. "You drag your ass back here . . . no. You didn't even come here, did you? Dom dragged your ass back here. You'd probably still be running away, eh?"

Amelia growled, lashing out at Smokey, but he was able to fend her off easily.

"Listen here, girl. You ran. Your ass ran, and I know why you did it but you're an alpha's daughter and that shit can't fly. I hope the last decade of pissin' around with leeches and whatever other shit you got caught up in is behind you." Smokey dropped her back down on the bed. "I hope half of what I heard isn't true. If it is, then you're even weaker than I thought you were."

Amelia snarled.

"Pissed? Good." He laughed, which pushed Amelia to the breaking point. "Get mad. Get worked up. Get over this warlock shit and come find me when you're done. I'll beat the alpha back into you down at the training fields. Do you know how long Naomi cried? The whole pack? You were Alpha Liam's pride and joy. I'm glad he died before he could see this shit."

Oof.

"Where's my sister?" she demanded.

"Naomi's been living in the pack house with Alpha. Been there nearly the whole time, and she barely comes out," Smokey said.

My throat tightened. Naomi, the softer side of Amelia. Where one twin filled Alpha Liam's shadow with the promise of a future alpha, the other was the match to their gentle mother. Naomi would never have fought Evander, not physically. The implications churned in my gut. "That can't be right," I said.

Smokey stared me down. "It is. Don't like it? Shape up and do something about it. You lot went off for a damn decade, what did you expect to happen here? The village is in a cloud of passive acceptance, and the last of our strong upcoming wolves left. You. You left."

I was on edge now. "If you're so discontented, why didn't you challenge Evander?"

Smokey offered a dark laugh. "You forget, I was Liam's witness. I bound myself to the code that I would respect whatever outcome was of their challenge. Liam lost, and I'll be damned before I break the last service I was able to offer him. Liam was a damn good wolf." Smokey turned his ire back to Amelia. "And look at the apple that fell so far from the tree."

"Fuck off . . . Smokey," Amelia growled. "I was . . . getting . . . stronger."

"You were getting weaker." Smokey looked down at Amelia, a frown deep on his jaw. "You thought you were tough shit with the vampire, but all you were doing was flexing someone else's muscles. What kind of wolf did you turn into, girl? What self-respecting alpha wolf takes orders from anybody?"

Ouch.

Amelia was livid, but she couldn't do much against Smokey as she was now. She snarled and took a swing that missed. She kicked out a leg, but all she managed to do was break off a bedpost at the foot of the bed. Smokey laughed again.

"When you're ready to get your ass back on track, you come and find me," he said, then turned and left without waiting for her response.

I followed Smokey back outside. The others had stayed out front, but they would have been able to hear all of it. Aaron had his head down in shame. Jack and Carson looked absolutely gutted. Smokey stopped in the dirt and turned to me.

"You, too, boy," he said.

"What about me?" I said.

"When you're ready to stop playing butler to the pampered princess, you find me," Smokey said, jabbing a finger in the middle of my chest.

"It's her right to inherit Liam's pack," I growled. "I've followed her this far and I'll follow her to hell and back if it means putting her in her rightful place."

Smokey spat on the ground between us. "There is no rightful place in this world. You take it with your own two hands or you die trying. There is no help in a fight to the death, and all your coddling is weakening you both. Ask her if she even wants it, because from where I stand, it looks like she wants her revenge and can't see past it to decide on her future."

He shifted into his fur and bounded off, back on whatever run he was taking this afternoon.

I watched him go with mixed feelings. I was angry that he'd insulted Amelia, but I couldn't argue that I thought we'd gone down the wrong path to gain strength. I hated living rogue, and in our isolation we had become hardened. Hard enough to come back for retribution. I'd watched Evander kill my father. During the challenge, he caught Dad's neck with his teeth and broke his spine. The sound of it snapping still echoed in the worst of my dreams, and I wanted nothing more than to do the same to Evander. All five of us had a similar story.

"What's the plan, Dom?" Jack asked.

"We wait for Amelia to recover. She's the alpha wolf, she's included in any plans we make."

They were restless. Without purpose, wolves will turn on themselves. We all needed a distraction. Something to do with our hands. I couldn't forget that we also needed to survive the next three days.

"Aaron, see if the pond has fish or turtle we can catch and eat. Jack, scrub the kitchen pots. I'm sure there's a delicious layer of dust on everything out here. Carson, clean out the vehicle. Sweep, air it out, get it cleaned up as best you can."

"Right," Aaron said.

"Got it," Jack added.

Carson nodded. Then the three of them went about their tasks.

Back inside, I checked on Amelia. She was struggling through pain and fury, and I wished I could take it away for her.

There shouldn't be any regrets from the last ten years. I grew, we all had, but some part of me that was still the beta's kid following around the alpha's kid as though there was no question that we would be the next to watch over Moonpeak. Aaron, Jack, and Carson came from some of the best warrior stock I'd ever known. We should have been the ones to take over, not Evander, and especially not after the bloodbath that gained him what he had now. How could we have stayed here and watched him stand where Alpha Liam stood? Amelia made the best call she could have at the time, and we followed her willingly. We did a lot of shit I was not proud of working for Apollo, but there was no arguing with the results when we were all stronger than before. We didn't have a chance at challenging Evander before, but now . . .

Smokey was wrong; our time away was not wasted. We were all different wolves for the experience. Harder, stronger, faster ones.

So why did it feel like I was in the wrong?

Chapter Thirteen

JUNE

Showers were magical. Beautiful. Wonderful gifts from the heavens above to us mortals. I stood under the hot water as it ran down my face. I'll admit I moaned a couple of times. No shame in that. And after I was done standing under the hot water, I got my soap and shampoo and scrubbed myself from head to toe. Twice.

I turned off the water with a sigh. Stepping onto the light-blue rug, taking one of the matching towels, and wiping clean a space in the fogged-up mirror, I finally felt relaxed. I had time to comb out my hair. I took my sweet time with my toothbrush. And after I toweled off completely, I put on a pair of sweatpants I hadn't gotten to wear yet and a gray sweater.

It didn't take long to put my things away, and then I made my way downstairs to the smell of baking bread. My stomach growled as I stepped into the kitchen, and I wasn't the only one there.

Linda was standing over the stove, and a teenager I recognized from when I first arrived yesterday—who looked like a smaller version of Linda with blond hair and dimples—and another woman with a big smile who was maybe my age were at the table. They all laughed as I stepped into the kitchen.

"What's so funny?" I asked cautiously.

Linda cleared her throat, smiling. "We heard your stomach, dear. This is my daughter, Hannah, and Carmine."

"You heard my . . . oh." I covered my stomach with my hands, as if that could stop what had already happened. "Nice to meet you both."

"Don't worry about it." Linda waved a ladle in my direction, then went back to stirring. "The hunger is just setting in. It's perfectly normal."

"Honestly, I don't see how humans can eat so little and still have the energy to do anything," Hannah said.

"Have a seat. I'm dishing up my famous five-alarm chili. I hope you can handle a little spice," Linda said.

"I sure can, thanks." I took a seat at the table.

The other woman, probably in her mid to late twenties, looked fierce. This was the expression of a woman who had seen some things in her time and conquered them all. Her brown eyes were sharp as she studied me back. Her hair was a shiny auburn, and it fell behind her in a loose braid. She was more freckles than face.

"How are you adjusting?" She had a delightful French-Canadian accent. "I heard a thing or two that you were human."

"Adjusting to werewolves being real?" I asked. "Honestly, not well. Better right now, I guess. The shower helped."

That earned another laugh, just as Linda was setting bowls down on the table. She pulled a container of sour cream from the fridge as well, popped a spoon in it, then grabbed a steaming pan of fluffy brown rolls from the oven and got everything on the table.

"Thank you," I said.

"Thanks, Mom," Hannah echoed, reaching out and carefully grabbing a hot roll with a napkin.

"Yes, thank you," Carmine added, then took a big dollop of sour cream and topped her bowl with it. I followed her lead, then took a bite. Hot damn, it was good.

Linda took a seat in front of her own bowl, sighing with a big grin as she scooted her chair in. "Eat up, girls. I made plenty. Oh, Carmine, are you going for another run tonight?"

"Mm-hm," Carmine hummed around a mouthful of chili, then swallowed. "I can't shake the restlessness. I don't want to get my hopes up, but I've got a good feeling about this moon."

Linda reached over the table and patted Carmine on her arm. "You'll find them, you're still young."

Carmine snorted. "Tell that to my *maman*. She wants grandpups."

"Grand . . . pups?" I asked.

"Oh gosh." Hannah turned red and smiled as though she was in on a secret.

"Ah, we call our young *pups*," Linda explained. "Let me fill you in a little bit about what function I serve here in the Moonpeak.

"First, mates. This one is usually the hardest for new bites to accept," Linda said. "You see, the moon has blessed each of her children with a mate. You'll be familiar with the term soul *mate*. You typically only get one."

"Are you serious?" I laughed nervously. "A soul mate? I'm not big on fate and destiny."

The three women at the table looked at me blankly.

"You're serious?"

"Most packs have a place for wolves who are traveling to find their mates to stay," Linda explained. "Of course, there are other reasons to visit a pack, and I'm happy to accommodate those wolves too. But traveling to find a mate is the most common."

"Carmine is looking for a mate? And she's staying here for a while to see if she finds them in this pack?" I asked.

"That's right," Linda said, stirring her sour cream into her chili. "At some point, you will too."

"Whoa, I don't know about that." I shook my head. "I'm not looking for a man right now. I can barely take care of myself."

"If you don't go looking, they will. And when they find you, you'll know it." Carmine shrugged.

"A pack is like one big working beehive," Linda said. "All the parts work together. Everyone participates. If you can help with something, you do. And if you are unable to do any kind of work, you are taken care of. We regularly take meals and spend time with our elderly or sick wolves in their homes."

"Back in Quebec," Carmine said, pointing her spoon at me, "we take our elder wolves into the pack house where Alpha and Luna make sure they are well cared for. It also opens up their old houses for newly mated wolves to start their lives together."

"Many packs do that, yes," Linda said. "It's a great way to care for the wolves who came before you. Wolves put a lot of emphasis on the community."

"What Mom is trying to ask is if you have any skills to bring to the pack," Hannah added, taking a big bite of her roll.

"I'm working on a physical therapy degree, and right now I work at an orthopedic clinic as a PT assistant. Aside from my job, though, some skills I have are . . . I guess cleaning, but I'm not the world's best cook. I've been a substitute teacher before, too, if there's a school around here."

"Very nice skills, June," Linda said. "Let me just find out if Doc could use a hand." She looked down at her bowl, not moving for a moment. It looked like she was spacing out.

"Are you okay?" I asked.

"She's on the link," Hannah said, taking another spoonful of chili.

My mouth popped open as I stared at Linda. "You're not serious."

Linda looked back up at me and said, "Doc's busy today, but that's fine since you're getting settled in. If you come by in a few days he'll be happy to show you around his workspace, though he won't need help often, so you might want to find more than just helping Doc out to spend your time on."

"Okay, I can do that," I said. "Can we back up and cover the fact that you can read minds?"

Carmine laughed. "*Mon dieu!* The humans really don't know anything about us, do they?"

"Mom, how many fingers am I holding up under the table?" Hannah reached an arm below the table, and I bent to see.

"Two," Linda answered without looking.

Gawking, I earned laughter from around the room. "It's a lot to take in, dear," Linda offered. "You'll get used to it over time."

"What we know about werewolves is from movies and books. It's all made up," I said.

Carmine shook her head. "You have to stop saying that."

"'We,'" Hannah said seeing my confused expression. "You said 'we' as in 'we humans,' which isn't true for you anymore."

"The mind link is like making a phone call, but more efficient," Linda explained. "I can speak to other members of Moonpeak through my inner wolf."

I stood up straight. "Like reading minds?"

"No, no. It's all voluntary," Linda said. "No one can read your mind. It's like a phone call."

I nodded, but I absolutely couldn't accept telepathy as a werewolf thing. I was struggling enough with the turning into a wolf part, no need to add less believable things on top of it. And this mate thing, it was a stretch too. But the mind link . . .

"Wait, Dom and the others didn't do this link thing," I said. "I just spent several days with them, and they never once did that."

Linda made a sad face. "They aren't a pack, dear. They can't link."

"You came here with rogues?" Carmine asked, surprised. "Are they sick? Did they attack you?"

"What? No," I said defensively. "The bite was an accident, and I shouldn't have stuck my nose in their business."

"They aren't typical rogues," Linda said to Carmine. "They have pack history here, and one of them has alpha blood. Amelia's presence is probably what kept their minds in one piece."

Carmine looked between me and Linda. "Okay, so were they chased off? Did they disgrace the pack?"

"It's old business that Alpha doesn't like being discussed," Linda said, strained. "You girls keep eating, I'm done. I'll be out back in the garden if you need me."

Linda got up and cleaned up her bowl. She didn't rush or anything, but it still felt like she was avoiding something. It would seem Dom and the others were a touchy subject around here.

"That was odd," Carmine said, then took another bite of chili.

"Alpha Evander doesn't like us talking about the old alpha and beta," Hannah said.

"Dom and the others have something to do with the old alpha and beta?" I asked. "Wait, I haven't met the current beta yet."

"Oh, we don't have one," Hannah said, frowning. "Listen, I'm going to go help Mom. Don't worry about cleaning up. Set your bowls in the sink and I'll get them later."

"I've been to fifteen different packs in the last two years," Carmine whispered across the table once Hannah was outside, "and this one is definitely not like the others."

"How long have you been here?" I asked.

"Two days," she said. "But I promise you it's been long enough to see the strangeness here. Watch yourself. Lay low until you get through your shift, and if you want to leave this place, I'd be happy to bring you home with me. My pack knows how to raise a wolf, they will take good care of you."

"Thanks," I murmured. "I'll think about it."

"*Oui*, yes. Think on it." Carmine got up, scraped the last of her bowl into her mouth, and set her things in the sink before she retreated upstairs.

My mind oscillated between liking and hating this place. I needed more answers. Real answers, from Dom.

CHAPTER FOURTEEN

JUNE

I decided to take a walk through the village, gaining a sense of direction while locating Dom. It also gave me a chance to keep an eye out for some of the weirdness that Carmine mentioned. I had a scrap of paper from one of the crossword books and a pen in my pocket to take notes in case I ran into anything.

On the surface, Moonpeak looked peaceful enough. But I wasn't about to let that lull me into a false sense of security. I kept my eyes sharp and my ears open. Linda's road led to the main street. I walked to the crossing and looked around. A few people were out and about, and from here I could see several wolves running in the grassy area near the pack house. I shivered, still getting used to the sight of them. Then I turned my head in the other direction. If I passed the general store and kept going, I could make it to the trees and eventually to the pond where I last saw Dom. Was he there now? Could I talk to him? Was it allowed?

Well, no one said I couldn't, so I started walking.

Now that I was here and thoroughly convinced I had to settle in for a vacation ending with me sprouting fur, Dom was going to give me some answers, and give back my phone while he was at it. Not that I could make a call from out here, but at least I'd have my music.

Hands in my pockets and shoes to the gravel, I kept a good pace. I smiled and nodded to anyone I passed, making it as casual as possible. Outside I tried to look calm, but inside my heart was beating fast. I didn't know why it felt like I was doing something I shouldn't, but it did. I was almost to the edge of the trees when a voice behind me made me nearly jump out of my skin.

"Where are you going there, girlie?"

I spun around to find Smokey, naked as the day he was born, scratching his beard and waiting for an answer from me.

"To see if Dom is at the cabin," I answered.

Smokey gestured to the grassy fields away from both the direction I was heading in and from town. "Walk with me."

I looked at the trees where the road turned to dirt, and where I knew the cabin would be if I kept going. But I sighed and followed Smokey instead.

"The boys are busy right now, Alpha needs to see 'em."

"Oh," I said. There went that plan.

"What's on your mind, New Bite?" Smokey asked as we walked down the gentle slope. There was plenty to admire here. Tiny flowers bloomed in the grass. There were even a few butterflies making their lazy way from blossom to blossom. The view was phenomenal, and I could really get used to it.

"I'm not sure," I admitted. "I've got a lot of mixed feelings about this wolf stuff."

Smokey hummed. "But it seems to me like you don't got a choice. It's your reality now, and if you don't embrace it you're not

Dirty Lying Wolves

going to turn in your first couple of moons. Hell, you may not turn at all."

I winced. "And if I don't turn . . ."

"You die," he said simply. "Life moves on, you were never cut out to be a wolf in the first place."

"What can I do to shift faster?" I asked.

"Far as I can tell, and I've only seen a handful of bites in my time, you need to accept it. Embrace that wolf, girlie. It's in you now, and it's going to come out. Don't fight it." Smokey shrugged.

"A wolf in me?" I asked.

Smokey chuckled. "You'll figure it out soon enough. Tell me about yourself, New Bite. You ever been in a fight before?"

"A fight?" I asked. "I'm not much of a fighter."

"No warrior, then." Smokey scratched his chin. "You much of a runner?"

Yes. No. Used to be. "Not really," I admitted.

"You got any other special skills?"

"Physical therapy and first aid," I said. "When I go home, I'm finishing my PT degree."

Smokey stopped in his tracks and laughed. He laughed so hard that he held a hand to his lower back for support and started coughing at the end of the laughter.

"Go home? Girlie, this is now home. You ain't going anywhere until you shift, and who knows when that will be." Smokey chuckled, wiping the corner of his eye. "You aren't gonna be the same person on the other end of that shift, you hear me? So if you want some advice, if you're smart you'll wait to make any plans until you know who you are afterward."

"I have a life to get back to," I said. "An apartment, a roommate, and my job."

"You might want those things now, New Bite," Smokey said.

"But you're not doing yourself any favors by holding on to those so tight. Life out here, she's slowed down. Tell me, do you know how to live in the moment? Enjoy yourself? When was the last time you really felt free to live how you wanted for a day?"

My throat tightened, remembering the wind pressed against me and a track under my feet. I didn't know why Smokey's words painted an image from so many years ago when I'd finally let go of my running days, but it was an unwelcome reminder.

"Look, Smokey, I'm tired and overwhelmed by all this new wolf stuff. All I really wanted to do this afternoon was get my phone back from Dom and ask a few questions."

Smokey crossed his arms. "Dom is occupied, but I'm not. If you have wolf questions, I'm here. Believe it or not, I do care about you. Even if it's only for now, you're Moonpeak, and that means I'm here to help you."

The little houses of the village atop the hill were picturesque. The sky was crystal clear today, the breeze playing with the tall grasses on the slope, as though everything was trying to remind me to relax.

"Okay, Smokey. I need someone to talk to. Linda is nice but—"

"She tiptoes around things like she doesn't want to step in a pile of shit," Smokey finished.

I laughed. "Not my exact words."

"Linda's a peach, but she's too gentle for a wolf. I'll tell you how it is, and you can take it or leave it. So, shoot, New Bite, what's on your mind?"

"Something happened, with Dom and the others. I want to know what's really going on."

Smokey grunted and gave a sharp nod. "At least you're not a dimwit.

"Amelia and the kids left after our last alpha was killed,"

Smokey started. "I'm guessing that's part of what Linda wouldn't talk about."

I nodded.

"Figured as much. There's only one way to become an alpha. You've got to belong to the pack, and you challenge the current alpha to the death. You better have some complaints about him, too, because if you don't have a reason to challenge him then the pack won't back you, even if you win."

"Oh," I said. "What was wrong with the old alpha?"

"Wasn't anything wrong with him for years. Decades. Liam was a good wolf. Strong. Fair. Ran things well, kept us in the budget. No one went hungry." Smokey scratched his chin. "But in those last few months, we had a bunch of weird shit happen. Rogues were coming in, and Liam made some bad calls. Got good wolves killed.

"Which is why Evander challenged him. Now, Evander wasn't from Moonpeak. Wandered in one day and joined the pack after a while. Said he was bitten but didn't get on with the rogues that did it. Pretty strange for a bite to be strong as an alpha, but who knows why the moon does what she does. Anyway, Evander challenged Liam over all this mess, and he won. No matter how much the rest of us didn't like it, we had no grounds to complain. Evander did it all by the code, and that was that."

"Wow," I said. "So Alpha Liam got killed, and Evander moved in?"

"That's how it works, girlie," Smokey said. "Now, by the book as it was, we didn't make it a week before Evander started rubbing people the wrong way. He didn't want people talking about Liam anymore, even though they were still grieving him. That didn't set with the old luna or the beta. So they challenged Evander too. Both lost, both died. Pretty sad shit."

"Oh my god." I put a hand over my heart. "They were still grieving! He didn't let them off easy?"

"Nope. Now all three are dead in the ground, and their kids ran off in a rage," Smokey said.

"Their kids ran off—" My eyes grew wide. "Amelia and Dom? And the others?"

"Amelia was Liam's oldest," Smokey explained. "Dom was Beta John's only one."

Quiet overtook me for a moment while I absorbed everything. "Thanks for telling me."

"Don't mention it. And if you want to talk more, Linda can point you my way. See you at the picnic tomorrow."

"Picnic? Oh, right." I remembered Alpha Evander saying something about it.

"Now, go on before you're late for dinner," Smokey said. Then he walked off to shift into his shaggy gray wolf.

I waited long enough to watch him bound off into the trees. A strange guy, but a friend. I thought. Some of my questions were answered but I was left with a host of new ones. What exactly was this place I was getting mixed up in?

CHAPTER FIFTEEN

DOM

The dull knife at the cabin was doing a poor job of slicing the bread I'd gotten from the general store, but jagged sandwiches would be better than nothing to a group of wolves who needed to eat. It was a long night with Amelia and Jerod; the exhaustion of the last seven days was taking its toll, and now we had just over a day left to go.

"Ugh, sunlight," Carson grumbled as he shuffled out of his room.

"Feeling any better?" Aaron asked from the couch.

"Yeah, actually. Nausea's gone," he said as he came over to grab a sandwich I'd already finished making.

"I think we've seen the last of it, and I'll be glad to never take Lunaria's Dream again," I said, Aaron nodding along with my sentiment.

"Take one to Amelia and the warlock," I added. "We may be feeling better, but they're still going through their sickness, and they need to eat something."

"Got it." Carson stuffed his sandwich in his mouth to carry it as he grabbed two more and disappeared down the hallway.

"You better, too, then?" Aaron asked.

"Yeah." I cut the last sandwich in half and tossed it on the plate, then carried it over to the living room where Aaron and Jack were already sitting. Aaron was working a knot out of his boot laces and Jack was still half asleep, head laid back and eyes closed.

"Eat up," I offered as I set the plate in front of them, taking one for myself. "Today's the picnic, we're getting announced to rejoin the pack."

Aaron pulled the knot loose, untying his booth and relacing it straighter. "I'll eat once I've cleaned up. So, we heard back from Evander?"

"Yeah, he came early with Smokey while you all were still asleep. Here's the deal: we'll be on a bullshit probation."

Jack snorted, sitting up and grabbing a sandwich. "Asshole."

"Don't expect too much out of this, stick to the plan," I said. "We train up, find out what's been going on here for the last decade, get Naomi, and then skin that fucker alive. We have to wait for Amelia, obviously, but I'll help her get back in shape."

"Agreed." Aaron nodded. "I'm glad to be back. My head's clear, my wolf is itching to run. I don't like how Evander made his way into the pack. I'm ready to see him dead."

"Yeah, it was a confusing mess back then." Carson came in and sat by Jack. "The weird rogue attacks, all the warriors that were—" His mouth fell into a flat line and his eyes disappeared into that nothing space where he'd spent a lot of time in the early days after his parents died. Those were clearly the warriors he was thinking of.

"Killed." Jack scowled. "They were killed, and Alpha Liam

never did figure out what they were doing here before Evander challenged him."

"That bit Smokey said about them stopping after Evander took over doesn't sit right with me," Aaron said.

"Convenient for him, wasn't it?" I frowned. "I want to look into that."

"Yeah," Aaron agreed. "And I'd love to know why Naomi's in the pack house with that prick. There's got to be a good reason she hasn't come running to find Amelia yet."

A pause hung over the conversation while we ate, mulling over the insinuations. How would Evander have anything to do with what should have been a string of unconnected rogue wolves? Albeit sick ones, but those things weren't right somehow. It was like their minds weren't in the driver's seat, they were acting on violent instinct. And then there was Naomi, like a little sister to me and yet none of the messages I'd tried to send her over the years had made it. That, or she hadn't responded. There was no way she hadn't heard we were back, so what was going on in that pack house?

"We try to find out more." I broke the silence. "No matter what we find, the plan stays. Get information, find Naomi, and challenge Evander for what he did to this pack ten years ago."

JUNE

"There's a cute one," Carmine said, pointing across the grass at a pair of shirtless guys throwing a ball back and forth. "Too bad, he doesn't smell like the one I'm after."

We were sitting on a thick blanket in the grass as the morning sun rolled overhead, peeking through the clouds that came and went. A large pit had been dug in the grassy fields south of the village and a few wild-caught animals were being roasted in it. Two deer, some ducks, a goose, and an elk. It smelled amazing, which surprised me since I wasn't usually big on meat.

"How will you know he's the one you're looking for?" I asked.

Carmine looked around the field. The picnic was in full swing as clusters of folks gathered and chatted in little knots of friends who set up blankets and games around the smoking meat.

"You just know," she said. "I can't explain it well since I haven't experienced it yet, but I've grown up seeing mates and watching wolves find theirs, and you just know."

"That's not very helpful," I said.

Carmine laughed and tucked a stray lock behind her ear. "You've got to start leaning on your intuition, June. A wolf's intuition is no joke."

"I'm not going to pick a life partner on a gut feeling," I said. "But I'll cheer you on if that's how you find yours."

"You bet it is." She grinned. "I'm going to jump his tail so hard, then I'll drag him into the woods for a week straight."

"And do what?" I asked, my eyebrows knitting together in confusion.

"Oh you sweet thing." Carmine cackled wickedly. "It's not for a tea party, I can tell you that."

"Whoa!" I said. "Too much information. You're going to screw a guy you just met because he smells good?"

"You bet I am. And if you're lucky enough to find your mate, you'll want to do it too."

I didn't know about that; the wolves' intense desire to pair off was a bit strange to me. But if what Smokey said was true, I might understand it better on the other side of the shift. It was both frightening and reassuring at the same time.

"What did you do back in your home pack? What was it like growing up there?"

"Ahh, home." She sighed and stretched out on the blanket. "Papa's the Man at Arms. A strong wolf. Fierce. And maman cooks for the pack house, she makes some of the best food I've ever had, even having traveled so much in the past few years. I'm a pack warrior, through and through. I was hoping to find my mate in my home pack, it's much bigger than this one. I will admit, the wandering life to explore other packs has been exciting."

"You really think your mate is here?" I asked.

"Hmm. *Je ne sais pas.*" She shrugged. "I have a feeling that I should be here. I hope it's because I will find my mate, but I can't be sure."

I fell back onto the blanket, joining Carmine in looking up at the lazy clouds overhead. "Have you always wanted to be a warrior?"

"Always," she said. "I take after my papa completely. I live to protect the pack. I love them with my whole heart."

We stared up at the sky for a while. I closed my eyes, content to lay there and smell the cooking meat and listen to the blurred chatter of the people talking around us. The smell of the grass under me, the distant calls of birds. I could fall asleep like this; my jogging pants and big sweater were cozy, too, and the warmth from the sun added to everything was making me dangerously ready for a nap.

Carmine yawned. "Males incoming."

"Hmm?" I asked, still not opening my eyes.

Two thuds landed on the blanket on either side of us, and my eyelids flew open. The man closest to me was clean shaven with light hair and dimples. The other had a darker, more rugged look to him.

"Afternoon, gorgeous," Dimples said.

Both guys were staring at me. Not us, not Carmine, me. I sat up slowly.

"Um, afternoon?" I inched closer to Carmine.

"We couldn't help but hear about you, New Bite," the other said.

"We thought we'd come to meet you. Scent you out. Who knows, we might be mates this time next month." Dimples wiggled his eyebrows at me.

"Back off, guys," Carmine growled. "You're making her uncomfortable."

"Sorry," Dark and Rugged said. "That's not our intent."

"If you want a mate so bad, go out and smell her like the rest of us," Carmine said.

Dimples shrugged. "But what if it really is the new girl here? I'd hate to miss out on the chance of a cute thing like her by leaving before she shifts."

He leaned in and sniffed my neck. I even felt fingers brush my backside.

"Hey!" I pushed him away.

He was gone in a flash when someone behind us lifted him completely off the blanket and threw him onto the grass away from us.

"Back off." Dom's deep tones rumbled overhead.

Dom was standing behind me and scowling down at Dimples. He looked good, healthy. Better than he had since I'd met him. Dom's eyes were unplagued by dark circles and troubles, his body was moving with no stiffness, and I had to admit the relaxed, healthier appearance looked really good on him. His hard eyes shifted away from Dimples down to where I sat, and his face softened.

"You all right, New Bite?"

I managed to nod, inexplicably flustered. Or maybe it was the asshole who just got thrown onto the grass that made me feel that way.

"Dom?" Dark and rugged said. "When did you get back?"

"A couple of days ago. I'm surprised word hasn't already spread."

Dimples had recovered by now, getting worked up and walking up to Dom. "Hey, man, we were just scoping out the new bite. Who are you to stop us, her mate?"

Dom growled low, his eyes flashing, and I could have sworn they turned yellow for a moment. An intense energy was coming from him, and the hairs on the back of my neck stood up straight. Instinctually my eyes drifted downward, but not before I watched the two guys flinch hard.

"She's a human who doesn't know a damn thing about the customs of our mating, and apparently neither do you. Get your asses away from her, and if you want to know if she's your mate so bad, you wait for her to shift."

"Whatever, let's go back to the game," Dark and Rugged said, and the two offending wolves left.

Carmine licked her lips, and I could have sworn her teeth had grown to fangs as she eyed Dom up and down.

"Fuck, why couldn't *you* be my mate?" Carmine asked.

Dom chuckled, sitting down on the blanket next to me. He looked into my eyes with a soft smile. "How are you holding up, June?"

"Getting used to it. I can even use some of the lingo now," I said. "Thanks for getting rid of those males. See?"

Dom and Carmine both chuckled before he looked at me again. "I have something for you."

He reached into his pocket and pulled out a familiar device with pink earbuds wrapped around it.

"My phone!" I snatched it and tapped the screen. Dead, of course.

"I'm sure by now you understand the importance of secrecy here," Dom said. "Besides, there's no reception."

"At least I have my walking music," I said, clutching it to my chest. "Thank goodness I bought a charger."

As I inspected my phone, Carmine looked at Dom strangely. "You smell great."

"Thanks, but I'm not interested," Dom answered.

"No, something on you smells really, *really* good," she said.

"In that case, the other wolves I've been traveling with are wandering around here somewhere," Dom answered.

"I'll take a walk." Carmine winked and stood up, sniffing the air as she went.

"That wasn't weird at all," I said.

Dom chuckled. "Someone I've been with smells good to her. Real good. She's sniffing out a potential mate."

"Gross," I said.

"You say that now," Dom said. "But when it hits you, you'll know what we mean."

"Mm-hm," I hummed. I'd believe it when I saw it.

Dom frowned, leaning forward.

"You're not smelling me, are you?" I asked, leaning away even as my cheeks flushed and my heartbeat picked up.

"What's that spiced scent?" he asked. "Were you around smoke?"

Frowning, I lifted my shoulder to smell my clothes, and then it clicked. "Oh, no, it's these candles Linda keeps in her house. I've never smelled anything like them before. Kind of spicy and earthy."

Dom was quickly lost in thought, and I took another sniff of my clothes. I'd been getting used to the candles, but was there something wrong with them?

"Attention, Moonpeak!"

The voice boomed across the field, stopping the chatter and

games. Evander was standing near the smoking pits of food, an arm raised to gain attention.

"Welcome to the new moon picnic. I'm glad we could all join together on this fine summer day. I only have a few announcements, then I'll let our cooks begin cutting the meat." Evander grinned wide, and his eyes drifted to me. "First, and I'm sure you've mostly heard by now, we have a bitten wolf joining us for her first shift. June, come on over please."

Several heads turned my way, and I instantly froze. "Well, crap," I whispered.

Laughter scattered around the field.

"They can all hear what you just said," Dom murmured, amusement plain on his face.

Heat swelled to my face as I scrambled to my feet and walked over to Evander.

"Not big on public speaking, eh?" he asked. "Don't worry, you won't have to do this again. Moonpeak, this is June Gunn. She's a bitten human from . . . Where are you from, June?"

"Seattle," I said.

"Wow, pretty far." Evander grinned, then turned back to face the pack again. "June will be with us for a bit while she shifts, and maybe we can convince her that Moonpeak will make a good home. Please welcome her if you see her around town. June, thank you, you can go back to your blanket."

Carmine had returned and was sitting in her original spot. As I sat back down, some applause and calls of welcome followed me.

"And one more announcement before we eat," Evander said, pulling the attention back to himself again. "We have a few new old additions to the pack. They were here under old rulership, but have returned to us on a trial basis. They will be welcomed into the village for the next two weeks, then will run with us on the full moon, when they can become full pack members. I'm sure some of you remember Dominic, Amelia, Aaron, Jack, and Carson."

I looked over to see Dom's blank reaction. Whatever he was thinking, he wasn't letting it show on his face.

"Welcome them with open arms, as you would an omega!" Evander said, spreading his arms wide in gesture. "They need the most help of all of us after living as rogues for the last ten years. Now, come on up and we'll serve the food."

Murmurs rumbled around the grass, and Carmine growled low.

"What?" I asked. "What's wrong?"

"That was a backhanded compliment if I ever heard one, an omega? Really?"

Carmine shook her head, turning to me. "An omega is someone who is weak, doesn't have many uses to the pack, and it's an outdated term anyway. The children and elders who don't work anymore, people like that. It's nothing shameful when used correctly, but for a group of wolves in their prime, that alpha just basically called them useless."

Dom's jaw twitched. "Don't worry about it."

"This is so backwards," Carmine snapped. "What rank were you before you left?"

"The beta's son," Dom said and stood up. "June, I'll see you later."

We watched him go, and my chest tightened at the thought of all he'd already been through, only to be slighted here in front of everyone.

"Another for the list of weird things in Moonpeak," Carmine grumbled. "Omega, my ass."

"Come on," I murmured. "Let's get some food and talk about it later. I want you to teach me about ranks, but not here."

"Right, tonight, under Linda's roof," Carmine said. "Come on, I want to get up there before the elk is all gone."

"Okay," I said, and we went to get in line for the delicious smoking meat.

Another for the list of weird things in Moonpeak indeed.

CHAPTER SIXTEEN

DOM

As soon as Evander announced our temporary acceptance into the pack, the buzz of the mind link roared to life in my head. I shut almost everyone out completely, not ready for the overwhelming sensation I had almost forgotten about. Anyone with a wolf on pack lands could try to talk to me now. Fantastic. There were plenty of people I wasn't ready to talk to yet.

At least we got to eat, though. And it smelled like home in the way that only an open-air roasted picnic in these mountains could. The meat was nearly picked clean when we got there, being last in line and all. But with the food distributed, we stood at the edge of the activities with our plates. Aaron was watching a picnic blanket of kids playing. Jack was ignoring everyone but us, and sat on the grass with his back to the field. Carson was so consumed with his plate that he wasn't paying any attention to anything. And my eyes kept wandering around, scoping out the faces I knew and the faces that were missing. Dead.

"Amelia would have lost it at that omega comment," Aaron said.

I snorted a laugh. "Then it's a good thing she wasn't here."

"What's tonight's plan?" Aaron asked.

"One more day for Amelia to be back on her feet. Evander said someone will find us a house in the village we can stay in, but I'm sure it's not a priority. That doesn't mean we sit on our asses, though. If we're to make any moves in a month, we had all better be in top shape. I'm talking daily training, and keep your eyes out for anything funny."

Aaron took on a serious face as he nodded sharply. "I'm going to join Smokey's morning border runs. Should we keep someone at the cabin while Amelia's still like this?"

"Yeah," I answered. "We leave in shifts. Speaking of which, I'm going back now to watch her. I only came for the announcement."

"And to give June back her phone, right?" Carson asked.

The moment June's name left his lips, my eyes shot over to where she was sitting in the field. Laughing on her blanket and talking to Carmine and Hannah.

"Yeah," I said. "I'm going now. Something out here is really distracting, it's putting me on edge."

Aaron's eyes followed my gaze. "I'll go back to the cabin, you run it off." A slow smile spread across his lips. "Try to keep your instincts coming from the right head."

Giving him a light shove, I walked away. "I'm going for a run."

I waved as I walked up the slope and to the edge of the village, then disappeared. It had been a long time, a very long time, since I'd had this kind of time to myself. I loved them, they were my brothers. My wolves. My pack. More than the rest of Moonpeak, they were my family.

But they had a way of driving me fucking nuts.

Slipping into the trees and around the bend to the cabin, I started taking off my clothes. Inside the cabin, I shifted as I walked back to Amelia's door, then poked my big gray head in.

I'm going for a run. I used the link. She looked up from the bed, exhausted, and nodded. Sweat-soaked clothes, tangled hair, bags under her eyes. I didn't know that I'd ever seen her like this before.

Take more of that melatonin, I told her, then left. I didn't believe for a second that she'd do it, but I had to try.

Fuck off, Dom, she said through the link as I left the cabin. We were so close to done with this bullshit warlock fuckup, and then hopefully we'd have the old Amelia back. Not the Amelia we grew hard with in Toronto, but the old Amelia. Moonpeak Amelia.

Out of the cabin and once my paws hit the dirt, I lifted my head and breathed in the fresh air. The beast inside me hummed, content and excited for what we were about to do. Run, it urged. And I did.

Grass under my feet. The scratch of low-hanging branches sweeping along my back as I raced into the trees. My paws, picking up the morning dew from the grass, were damp by the time the cabin was out of sight. The light smell of deer that had passed by recently, unaware of how lucky they were that I wasn't hungry right now.

I tore through the mountains, letting my muscles bunch then spring as each paw hit the ground. My heart lifted higher than it had in years, no other patch of dirt under the moon's light felt like home the way the Long Range Mountains did.

The wolf in me wanted to push faster. I was more than happy to let him. We chose a slope to run up, pushing hard and weaving through a few trees and boulders. After finally reaching the top of our goal, we turned sharply and went back down.

My nose twitched as I scented another wolf. A strong wolf. An old wolf.

I looked around, my eyes darting upwind as I spotted him. Smokey.

Smokey came up on me like a bat out of hell. Charging and rounding behind me to nip at my heels.

You want to race, do you, old man?

I want to see what living soft in the city did to you, boy.

So be it. I ran hard, shooting away and putting some distance between us. But he was fast. His wolf was about as big as mine, and I was a born beta. Then again, Smokey was impressive all on his own, that was why he was Master of Arms.

I ran, and Smokey caught up. I took a sharp turn, and Smokey mirrored it. I rushed up to a big tree, jumping high on its trunk and leaping off to land behind him, and he barked out a laugh.

Cute tricks. Now show me how you fight.

Okay, I could play this game.

We trotted to an open space and began to circle. Smokey didn't have any tells when he was about to attack. But I used to have a slight movement with my back left paw before springing forward, a habit I had since dropped. Smokey didn't know that *yet*.

I twitched my paw and waited for the split second it took Smokey to come at me before I moved sideways and lunged for his neck. But the old bastard was slippery, and he twisted away at the last second. He gave me no moment to recover before his counterattack.

Smokey lunged and nipped at my front leg, then slipped away as I tried to bite him back. I growled, huffing as we rounded each other again.

When Smokey lunged, I barely dodged him, but it let me rake my claws down his shoulder as I jumped off him to push him away and gain some distance.

Not bad, kid.

Not bad yourself, old man.

Smokey barked out a laugh and lay down on his belly. I lay down, too, though years of doing dirty work for Apollo had taught me not to drop my guard. I was still ready to spring up at a moment's notice.

You've got a few tricks, I'll give you that, Smokey said through the link. *But you're weaker than you should be.*

I'm working on it, I said. My wolf growled. *We all are. Aaron wants to join you on morning patrol. I'll probably urge Jack and Carson to do the same.*

A morning trot through the flowers isn't going to build those wolves back up, Smokey said.

I barked a laugh. Patrol with Smokey was hardly a trot through the flowers.

And while those boys are at least taking a leisurely stroll with me, what the hell will you be doing? Smokey asked.

I yawned, letting myself relax a bit. Smokey was obviously done testing whatever he wanted to see from me. *Helping Amelia. She needs more of a challenge than the others can give her, so I'm putting my all into helping her.*

Smokey nodded his shaggy gray head. *She's an alpha, that's for sure. And with some mountain air and a few beatings, I could probably get the both of you into the shape you should be in.*

We'd appreciate it, I said

What's your big plan then? Smokey asked.

We don't have any plans, I said.

Bullshit you don't, Smokey snapped. *I know it, you know it, and if Alpha Evander is half as smart as a pissing squirrel then he knows it too.*

We don't, at least not a finished one. We'll think it through when Amelia is better. Are you going to try to stop us? I asked.

Not if you do it by the code, Smokey said. *You know that. But I'll be damned if I don't do my job the whole way, so you watch your step, you hear?*

I'd expect nothing less from a formidable old bastard like you.

Smokey barked out laughing, his wolf throwing his head back and his fangs shining in the afternoon sun. *It's good to have you kids back. About time we got some alpha blood running in these mountains again. It will do some of these cocky warriors good to get knocked on their asses by someone other than me.*

Amelia would make a great alpha, I said. *Liam's daughter, through and through.*

She's not the only one with that potential around here, Smokey said.

Are you saying Amelia could have competition here? I growled. *Who?*

Smokey just watched me for a moment. I thought he wouldn't answer, but then he stood up and turned his head toward the pack. *Alpha needs me for something.*

He began walking, then, a short distance away, turned his shaggy gray head back to me. *Funny thing, that alpha blood. It can spring from all sorts of unexpected places. Did you know Liam's father was a beta?*

I shook my head, a chill running down my spine. Liam had been a giant of a wolf, wiser than anyone I'd ever known, and I had no idea he hadn't been anything but alpha-born from a long lineage. *No, I didn't.*

Liam worked his ass off to pull out what he had inside of him. But even if he hadn't, any real wolf could have seen what he was. It doesn't take a genius to smell an alpha.

He looked back at me over his shoulder. I didn't know what to say, or what he was trying to say. Or maybe I just didn't want to hear it.

I'll see you when you're ready for a good beating. Not one of these love taps like earlier. Take care, Dom.

Smokey left, leaving me and my wolf in the mountains with more than a few tasks ahead of us. Amelia was almost out of her nine days of this sickness, and I had to find Naomi. Then maybe we could get some damn answers.

CHAPTER SEVENTEEN

JUNE

Sitting at the kitchen table, the jar labeled BAKED APPLES in scratchy letters in my hand, I was wondering why the old neighbor woman would give me pie filling as a gift. Hannah was making toast and eggs, and Linda was peeling potatoes in the sink as the early morning sunshine filtered through the window, blanketing the room in a warm glow.

"Morning, lovely wolves!" Carmine sang as she came downstairs, wearing a sweatshirt and basketball shorts. Her auburn hair was pulled up into a ponytail, and her grin took up almost as much of her face as her freckles did.

"Morning." I echoed her.

Linda turned around from the sink. "Morning, Carmine dear. You look ready to go."

"There are a few trackers who haven't been in the village for a couple of weeks, and I thought I'd wander the outer parts of the pack territory today. Maybe I'll run into an interesting smell." She wiggled her eyebrows.

"Maybe you will." Linda laughed. "A few of our trackers are pretty handsome, and unmated."

"Can I go with you?" I asked.

"Of course." Carmine smiled. "Why do you think I wore comfortable clothes? I was hoping you would keep me company—I won't cover the ground as fast without my wolf, but that's okay."

I grinned. "All right then, after breakfast?"

"Oui." Carmine took a seat next to me.

"Toast incoming." Hannah turned from the counter and slid two small plates across the table. "Eggs in another minute."

"Thank you, Hannah," Carmine said. "June, may I have some of that?"

She pointed to the jar I'd been holding.

"Oh, sure, but I think it's a dessert or something. Baked apples, maybe?"

Hannah snorted a laugh from the counter. Linda cleared her throat. "It's bakeapple, dear. It's a berry, and that's a jam."

"Really?" I looked at the jar again; it made much more sense than trying to figure out why someone would give me only half of a dessert.

"Welcome to Newfoundland," Hannah mused. "Here's a spoon, try it on your toast."

"Oh, before I forget,"—Linda turned, wiping her hands on a towel—"Doc says he's ready for you to swing by on Thursday. He's out on a supply run for a couple of days."

"Sounds good," I said. "I'll make sure to go then."

"It will be nice to have a pack physician in training," Linda said.

"Oh, no. I—" But Linda had already turned back to peeling her potatoes.

I can't stay here.

Hannah interrupted my thoughts by setting the scrambled eggs on the table. "Eat up, freshly laid this morning."

And that was that. If I had learned anything about wolves, it was that nothing could distract them from food. So breakfast went on, and my protests remained silent. After breakfast I went upstairs to change, digging out something to wear for the walk.

This place was easy. Easy, and slow. No one was in a rush, save for the wolves running around the fields outside the village. Neighbors were friendly, no one was on a schedule. It was becoming more and more apparent that I'd left a rat race behind in Seattle. What I wouldn't give to have time for more walks, to read more books, to get enough sleep before waking up for a new day of caring for my patients. I could almost picture it, but there were still things about home that I couldn't stop missing. The ease of a grocery store and limitless restaurant options, for one. Kat, obviously. I guess there wasn't much to miss about the parks, considering I had all the nature I could handle right in front of me.

Shaking my head, I pulled on a pair of leggings and socks. Why was I even comparing the two places when I'd be going back in a few weeks?

Carmine knocked at my door. "Are you ready to go? *Allons-y.*"

"Coming." I finished tying my sneakers and we left the house. The air was fresh, and the sun was bright when we began walking down the slope and away from the village.

Carmine shot me a sly look. "You and Dom. Is he the one who bit you?"

"What's with that face?" I asked. "No, he didn't bite me. That was an accident with a wolf named Amelia. Dom and the guys brought me here so I'd be safe when I first shift."

"Can I see your bite?" she asked.

"Sure."

It was healing nicely, considering it was over a week old, and had already lost its pain. It was just sort of ugly now.

Carmine inspected my arm and whistled. "This Amelia did a number on you."

"Yeah. I was trying to help her, it was an accident." I shrugged. "I'd like to talk to her about it, actually."

"Wait, she's here?" Carmine asked.

"Mm-hm. But she's sick," I answered. "So we haven't really communicated."

"Ah, I see. Good luck, then, I hope you find some peace between the two of you. Now, back to male talk . . ."

"Carmine." I shoved her playfully. "Is that all you can think about?"

"Listen, June," she said. "I've been craving a mate for the last two years. I'm headed toward forty, after all. Moon knows my maman is running out of patience for grandpups. So, yes, I have males on my mind. I'm starting to wonder if I should give up and settle with someone else who's mateless."

"What?" I stopped in my tracks, shocked. "You're almost forty? You look twenty!"

Carmine threw back her head and laughed. "Silly human, wolves live three or four times as long as you. Well, not you anymore. I'm still thirty-seven, but forty is nothing. It's true that most mates find each other somewhere in their twenties, but by no means am I too old to find mine."

I paled. "Am I going to live that long?"

"Yes." Carmine winked. "You are."

"Oh," I breathed. "Okay."

"Back to males!" She clapped her hands, holding them in front of her. "Not gonna lie, that Dom was a juicy piece. Maybe he's mateless too."

"You're into Dom?" I asked.

Carmine shrugged. "I don't know if I'd settle down with him or anything, but a romp in the woods might be nice, if you know what I mean."

"Ugh, I'm afraid I do." I grinned.

"What's the matter, don't you find his type attractive?" she asked.

My heart skipped a beat. I hadn't asked myself that question before, but I found that I already knew the answer. "Yeah," I agreed sheepishly.

"Great, do you want to tag team him? I've got an itch that could use scratching."

"No!" I shouted, eyes wide. "No, I'm okay."

"Suit yourself. Oh, and I saw some other good males at the picnic yesterday. Did you see that guy helping turn the meat in the pits? The one with the scar on his arm?"

"Yeah, he was cute, I guess," I said.

"Or maybe the one with—" Carmine stopped and stuck out her arm to stop me as well.

"Wh—"

"Shh." Carmine's face was serious as she tilted her head, listening and scenting the air.

"Another wolf is here, and something smells . . . weird," she whispered. "I'm going to shift, stay on your guard. If I tap my paw twice in your direction, run back to the village."

"Okay," I said nervously.

Carmine took off her clothes and handed them to me. Without having anything else to do, I absently folded them neatly in my arms and carried them as she shifted. Her fur was stunning. So far, most of the wolves I had seen were varying shades of gray and white. Maybe one or two brown ones at the picnic. But Carmine was a reddish-brown shade that reminded me of autumn leaves, something a bit like her hair color. It made me wonder what color my fur would be.

I shook my head. Now was not the time to admire something like that. We had to be on guard. From a wolf. A wolf who, if they were an enemy of some kind, could outrun me in a heartbeat and eat me.

Did werewolves eat people?

I didn't have time to ponder an answer to that as Carmine began sniffing the air, walking back and forth. She stopped, perked up, and walked forward. A howl in the distance sent a shiver down my spine. Carmine lifted her head and howled back.

She trotted back over to me when she was done, and shifted back to her normal self. I handed her the clothes I was carrying.

"What was all that?" I asked.

She pulled on her shorts as she answered. "Alpha Evander. He's coming this way now."

"And the howling was what, exactly?" I asked.

"A general sound of 'is someone there?' and my answer of 'yes, over here.' As soon as I could tell it was Evander, there was no reason to hide. This is his pack, after all, and I'm a guest on his lands."

Evander emerged from the trees wearing loose shorts and a T-shirt. He ran his fingers through his hair and waved at us as he got closer.

"Good morning, June. Carmine. What are you girls doing out here so early?" he asked.

"A walk to smell out males," Carmine said. "Same old, same old."

Evander chuckled and turned to me. "And you brought June with you?"

"She's good company," Carmine said. "You've got a good one here, Alpha Evander."

"Do I now?" He took a closer look at me, and I could almost see the gears turning.

"Alpha Evander," Carmine said, "I smelled something really strange at the same time I noticed your wolf. I almost didn't recognize you at first. What was that?"

"Ah, yes. I'm out here looking into something that was reported on pack lands. I turned everyone else away from it, I didn't realize you girls would be here on a walk. For now, I suggest you go back to the village, you can walk again tomorrow."

"Okay. Thank you, Alpha Evander. Come on, June. Let's go."

I thanked Evander too. And then he walked away in the direction he had come from. Carmine watched him go with her eyes narrowed on his back the whole time.

"Something isn't right," she whispered. "Your Dom and his friends are from before Evander was alpha, right?"

"Yes," I said.

"Let's go pay them a visit," Carmine said.

CHAPTER EIGHTEEN

DOM

A squeak and the slam of the screen door woke me up. I flung an arm over my eyes, realizing the sun was assaulting me through a gap in the blinds.

"Breakfast," Jack called.

I grunted, sitting up as Aaron walked through the open door to the room where I'd slept in the bed opposite Amelia's. "When'd you get back last night?" he asked.

"Dunno. Three or four." And then I'd crashed. When I didn't see Naomi at the picnic and couldn't go into Evander's pack house, I'd exhausted myself trying to find a place on pack lands where I'd pick up her link. No luck.

I grabbed one of the doughy fried treats in the kitchen and headed for the jam on the counter. "Amelia's nine days should be up soon, when she—"

My head snapped to the hallway. There was a noticeable absence of struggle and moaning. I dropped my breakfast back into the basket and went to the doorway. There Amelia was, sleeping peacefully for the first time in so long. She looked a mess, but a peaceful, exhausted mess. Nine long days were finally over.

She's out, let her sleep. The warlock? I asked over the link to just the guys.

Aaron went straight for the room where we'd bunked him with Carson. *He's waking up, Carson's still out.*

Let Carson sleep, bring the warlock here.

Aaron helped Jerod from the room while I shut Amelia's door, and we all gathered in the living room. He'd lost weight, having thrown up many of his meals over the past nine days, and he sank onto the couch in a filthy T-shirt and unkept hair. I stood opposite, staring down at the cause of this mess, waiting for an explanation. Aaron was on his left, Jack on his right.

"Anytime now, warlock," I said. "What the fuck happened?"

Jerod gave a weak laugh, sweeping his hair out of his face. "The deal with Zopphandomet was broken the moment that she-wolf knocked apart my ritual. Which is a travesty, because behemoths are almost impossible to summon, and I pulled it off. Is Dani okay?"

Dani, his friend, the witch from the battle. "Yes, her and the dragon are fine."

He sighed, smiling as he laid his head back on the couch. "Good."

"How exactly does Amelia falling into your ritual make this"—Aaron gestured to Jerod—"happen?"

A door in the cabin slammed open, and sleeping beauty was awake. Amelia, claws out, held herself in the doorway to the bedroom as her eyes rolled wildly in search of something until they landed on Jerod.

"You," Amelia snarled. "What did you do?" She didn't wait

for an answer before she pounced on the couch, pinning Jerod in place with one hand at this throat.

"Air . . . darling . . ." he choked out.

"Amelia, we can't get answers if you suffocate him," I said.

She let go, stepping back from the couch and flexing her fingers, stretching everything out. Taking a deep breath, she turned to stare at me. "Everything's different. Haven't been postwithdrawal in . . ."

A long time, I finished over the link, just the two of us. *It's been a long time, Amelia.*

Her eyes shone, almost watering over, as she paused and assessed everything in her body. The feel of it, the way it moved. I had to admit, it felt slower off the Lunaria's Dream for the first couple of weeks, and there would still be that little itch of seduction in the back of our minds, wanting to fall back into the comfort, the power. But this, this had to be our new normal. There was no more Apollo and no more drugs.

"Welcome back, Amelia," Aaron said, barely above a whisper. She turned her attention to him, emotions turbulent on her face.

"Amelia?" Carson's sleep-roughened voice came from the hallway, and it broke the tension. A heartbeat later Jack, Aaron, Carson, and I were wrapped around Amelia, glad to be done with the last few weeks of our lives.

"Touching," came a snide remark from the couch.

I turned to Jerod, eyes narrowed. "All right, warlock. What happened after Amelia fell onto your spell? In the woods you said she spilled an offering and your summoned demon was pissed about it."

"That he was. To know what went wrong, you first need to know what part of my spell you fell into. That cup, or chalice really, held the essence of my soul, which I put on the line as bait for a deal with the behemoth. The offering was a connection to me." He met Amelia's gaze. "So when you fell into it, you bled into it. Into a cup of essence of soul. A cup that acted as the offering plate to a demon."

"That doesn't sound good," Jack said.

"Indeed it's not, my friend, it's good to know you're as sharp as you look," Jerod drawled. Jack's face contorted in confusion as he pieced together what that might have meant.

"So she was under the same contract as you," I clarified.

"Then what was that bullshit?" Amelia asked.

"You adding blood to the chalice is essentially a third party barging into our deal, and the behemoth did not care for that," Jerod said. "Nine hours of agony in exchange for his time, that's what I offered and what he accepted. I knew I'd go through some kind of hell, but it was supposed to be manageably temporary. His species of demon feeds off pain and torment. You'd be surprised to find how many demons feed from emotions or sensations. Much easier to contract away for services than, say, an arm."

"So it's done now?" I asked. "You can go back to wherever you came from and we can move on?"

"Not quite." He sighed. "I believe we felt a certain . . . fusing. Back before the contract began. Do you remember the pain being different before midnight?"

Amelia narrowed her eyes at him. "Yes, I do."

"I think both souls were fused together in the process, and our physical distance is going to be limited until I can untangle this mess," Jerod said.

"You *what?*" Amelia rushed at Jerod again, pinning him to the couch.

A howl of fury booming through the cabin doorway caught us all off guard, and I kicked myself for being so distracted. Every head in the room snapped to the doorway as a great auburn beast burst in. Her wild yellow eyes locked onto the couch, and she full-body tackled Amelia, who shifted and snarled, letting out a howl right in the other wolf's face. The other wolf bowed her head; a demand for submission from a wolf with alpha blood wasn't easy to fight off.

"Wait! Carmine!" A human voice was calling as it came in the cabin's front door. Amelia looked up and snarled, and the auburn wolf took the opportunity to lunge and start the fight again.

"Shit," I snapped, and whirled back around to the front door where June was coming in, panicked. With no time to explain, I lifted her and shoved her into a corner, putting myself between her and the fight.

Pressed together, it would be easy for me to block any stray teeth or claws that came our way. "Rule one, June, don't throw yourself between fighting wolves."

"Carmine! Dom, why is she a wolf? What did she have here?" June said, her heart beating fast as she looked up at me with wide eyes.

"What are you talking about?" I asked, watching the circling wolves carefully.

"She just flipped out and yelled 'Mine' and ran in here!" June cried.

"Fuck," said pretty much every wolf present with a human mouth to say *fuck* from. That meant exactly one thing to the wolves; Carmine had found her mate.

"Back down, both of you!" I snapped, and waded into the wolves to shove them apart. "You, Carmine was it? Shift."

Carmine whined, still watching Amelia.

"Now," I demanded.

Carmine shifted out of her wolf form and into the person I'd seen with June at the new moon. Her eyes were still wild as they darted the room and then settled on Jerod.

"Oh shit," I whispered.

"*Tu es blessé? Je me battrai pour toi. Laissez-moi vous aider!*" She pushed past the rest of us to make her way to Jerod, cupping his face in both hands. "What is wrong with your eyes, *mon amour*?"

"Carmine," I said calmly, "he's not a wolf."

Her expression changed to shock. "*Je suis* . . . I am Carmine. It is nice to meet you."

For the first time, possibly ever, the warlock was speechless.

"What is happening?" June asked.

Carmine grinned, and the rest of the room might as well have been on the other side of the mountains, for all her attention was on Jerod.

"You smell amazing." She ran a tongue over her canines.

Jerod cleared his throat, now somewhat recovered. "Jerod Chang, ninth level warlock extraordinaire."

Carmine beamed, inching closer to him. "Spicy, I like it."

A slow smile spread across Jerod's face. "I believe we need to have a private chat."

She nodded vigorously.

"The incident you were witnessing between myself and Amelia—"

Carmine cut him off with a growl, looking over her shoulder at Amelia, who had also shifted back and was now pulling on a T-shirt.

"No, no, let's not start another fight over it. We have a lot more important things to cover right now. The incident you witnessed was from myself delivering some unfortunate news," Jerod said, looking between Amelia and me. "As I was saying, we need to separate our souls carefully, and we probably don't have much wiggle room away from each other. We can test that now, if you like."

"Yes," Amelia said, frowning. "Please take your impending fuckfest outside so I can speak to my wolves."

"Done," Carmine answered instantly.

"Are you serious right now?" June asked.

"Very." I ran a hand over the back of my head. "I'll give you the birds and the bees and the wolves talk later."

"Jerod, will you come with me outside?" Carmine put all the suggestion she could into her tone.

"This seems like one of those instances where you buy a guy dinner first," he mused.

"All right, out," I said. "Go figure this out in the woods. We need to talk in here."

We watched them go, and as the room settled down, we all found a seat in the living room. June was still absorbing what she'd just seen, and I found myself easily rubbing a hand on her back. "You okay?"

"I think so," she said. "That was intense."

"It's about to get a little worse. Do you think you can calm down on the porch for a bit? Take some breaths and get that heart rate down. I'll come out for you soon, and then we can have a little chat while I walk you back to the village."

June nodded, eyes lingering on Amelia for a moment before she gave me a strained smile. "Sure, I'll go do that."

Once she was gone, I found the room staring at me. Jack was grinning like a dumbass, and I rolled my eyes as I took a seat. "We need to catch you up, Amelia. Did you hear much of what we've talked about around here?"

"Enough," she answered. "Enough to know my sister is in that house with that bastard, and Smokey's the same pain in the ass he's always been."

"We're taking patrols with him in the mornings," Aaron added.

"And working out at the fields. Between all that we've been running paths at night trying to pick up Naomi's link."

"And?" She looked strained. "Have you contacted her yet? Is she okay?"

"We don't know," I said. "We haven't gotten to see or hear from her yet, but Smokey says she's there. We were mostly waiting for you to get past that mess before we made any solid plans."

She looked down at the floor for a moment, and I could see the muscle in her jaw tick, which told me she was thinking hard. When her bright eyes came back up, they found me. "Thank you, Dom. I wanted to kick your ass for dragging me back here, but I agree. It's time to take down Evander."

"And take back Moonpeak!" Carson added.

Amelia gave a halfhearted nod. "The only thing I want right now is Evander's entrails scattered across the mountains. First, we focus on that."

I nodded, glad for not having a fight on my hands, but also reflecting on her choice of words. When we'd left Moonpeak she said nearly every day she wanted her pack back. At what point had that fallen from being her main goal?

"I think we decided that you'd spar with me, right?" Amelia was turned to face me again.

"As much as you want," I agreed. "We're ready to get in top shape. What about the patrols for Naomi?"

"Continue them," Amelia said. "Go in twos, no reason to be caught alone with that snake in the pack house. Don't trust him or anyone overly loyal to him. Go at night, and link the group regularly whether you've found Naomi or not."

The room agreed, and Amelia stood up. "I'm taking a shower, are we stocked on supplies out here?"

"We're being granted housing in the village," Aaron said.

"The plan was to move in when you were better."

"We can pack up today," I agreed. "I'll be back soon, I'm going to walk June back and fill her in on a few things."

"Is that what the kids are calling it these days?" Jack smirked, and I did my best to ignore him as I left the cabin.

CHAPTER NINETEEN

JUNE

Jerod and Carmine, who would have guessed. After all that searching, it was pretty hilarious that she mated with the warlock and not another wolf. I didn't even know that was possible, but it was hard to argue with what I'd seen.

After I got my breathing under control, I didn't have much else to do but sit around waiting for Dom and enjoying the scenery. It was rather peaceful. The nature around me was all a beautiful, tangled mess. For all the parks and trails I could walk back in Seattle, I liked the look of the untamed trees here better. The only thing missing was a place to buy a latte.

The screen door creaked open and Dom emerged.

"Are you feeling any better?" he asked.

"Yeah." I stood up, glad to finally be doing something. "Actually, Carmine and I had a weird interaction with Alpha Evander. And I think she wanted to ask you some questions about the pack before he came, but I don't know what her questions may have been now that she's otherwise occupied."

Dom snorted a laugh. "That's putting it mildly. So, what did Evander do that was weird?"

"He might be messing with something that smells suspicious. We were walking this morning, and Carmine sensed something weird. So odd that she didn't recognize that it was Alpha Evander at first."

Dom's brows knit together as he frowned. "Did she describe the smell?"

"No," I said. "But Alpha Evander said something strange was reported on pack lands and that he sent everyone else away from it so he could investigate."

"And you don't believe him?" Dom asked.

I shook my head. "Something wasn't right."

"I should be a good wolf and tell you to trust your alpha."

"But?" I urged.

"But I'm not going to." Dom looked around, glancing at the cabin behind him. "Let's take a little walk."

It wasn't far past the cabin that the wolf territory opened up into the wide fields where we'd first met Smokey. A light breeze rustled the grass in waves as it rushed across the rocky ground.

My eyes wandered over to Dom. Always so serious. He was staring into the middle space between the two of us. I had so many questions about him. If he was a beta's son, how strong was he? I understood why he and the others left the pack all those years ago, but why come back?

"How old are you?" I asked.

I asked the question before it registered that I probably didn't want to ask it out loud, and I slapped a hand over my mouth. "Sorry, you don't have to tell me."

Dom's serious facade crumbled as his face spread into a wide grin, laughing at me. "Where did that come from?"

Heat rushed to my cheeks as I glanced away from him. "Carmine is almost forty. It was kind of a shock."

"Ah." Dom nodded. "I'm sure it was. Wolves can live maybe four hundred or so years if they aren't killed first. It's hard to have an exact estimate, you don't meet too many old wolves."

"That's really sad," I murmured.

Dom shrugged. "There's a wide world of supernatural things that you have no idea about yet. It's not always a safe place to be."

The thought of a whole world that was unknown made me shiver. It was the same reason I was afraid of the bottom of the ocean or deep space.

"Wait, but there are a few old wolves here in Moonpeak," I said. "What about them?"

"Moonpeak's very isolated. The two packs in Newfoundland keep to ourselves. Other than the occasional traveling young wolf, we don't attract unwanted attention." Dom stopped walking and stared at a mountain peak in the distance. "I'm thirty-four. It's not so much in wolf years."

"You left when you were twenty-four?" I asked.

"Twenty-three. My birthday was the next month," Dom answered.

"I'm so sorry," I said. "That must have been awful."

Dom's jaw twitched. "Who told you?"

"Smokey," I said.

"Look, June, I brought you here because there are good people here who can take care of you. I'm no teacher and I'm no babysitter. The wolves here are better at this stuff."

"But I trust you. And I'm asking you."

Dom sighed and stopped our walk. He scratched his head and

looked down at me with tired eyes. With a grunt, he sat down on the ground then laid on his back, putting his arms under his head for support. "All right, New Bite. I brought you here, I'll answer your questions. But after this, I have things to do, so I can't promise I'll be around. Deal?"

Sitting down next to him, I pulled my legs up to my body and wrapped my arms around my knees. "Deal. First question, where is Evander's beta? Does he not have one? Is that even allowed?"

"He doesn't have one and I don't know why," Dom said. "Next question."

"Am I the only one who's suspicious of Evander?" I asked.

Dom chuckled. "You being nosy is what got you bitten back in Seattle. Keep your head down and worry about yourself. You've got a full moon coming up in a couple of weeks."

I frowned. "That's no way to get help with a problem."

"Look." Dom rolled onto his side, propping his head up with an arm as he faced me. "We don't need help with this, we need focus. Your intuition's spot on, but I promised to bring you to a good pack and I did. Amelia and I have a plan and we need time to get ready. I won't say anything that would be dangerous for you to know, but I won't be leaving you here with an alpha you can't trust, got it? I'd hate to have dragged your ass across a continent just to see you get hurt when you got here."

Dom had been a lot of things since we'd met. A leader, a planner, and sometimes a jerk, but mostly for good reasons. I respected him a lot after the trip we'd just been through together, even if I hated the decision he'd made to bring me with them. I could at least understand it, and it was hard to admit now that I was here, but I had no idea if another solution would have even been possible. And if I was going to be stuck here for a while, I wasn't going to sit here unprepared. "You're going to challenge Evander."

Dom sighed and laid on his back again. "Nosy *and* sharp. Not a safe combination, June."

My name from his mouth was so rare it caught me off guard. I shrugged. "You guys might get hurt, and I wouldn't want to see that happen."

"No one comes out of a challenge unscathed," Dom said softly. "That's why you don't need to be a part of this, it's our fight and we've been working toward it for years. You don't need to be involved."

Leaning back, I let my eyes drift down Dom's profile. He carried himself so tense, alert. The way he got everyone moving in the best direction he could at the time, the way he made sure everyone was fed and warm. Maybe it was a wolf thing, or maybe I recognized the group caretaker when I saw it. "Growing up, I was the responsible one."

He raised an eyebrow at that, but let me continue.

"I split my cupcakes in half when someone dropped theirs, I made sure Granny was taking her heart medication when she had trouble remembering to do it, and I'm the one in the office everyone expects to go on errands and do the coffee runs."

"You're starting to sound like a doormat," Dom teased.

"Maybe, but I think you can relate to what I said." Sitting up, I crossed my legs and plucked a piece of grass, holding it taught. "I think you're the caretaker, just like me, or at least something like it. They respect you, you're a leader. I respect you," I said softer. "But you're going to snap under that pressure if you don't have support." I pulled the blade of grass tighter, and both our eyes stayed on it as it snapped in two. Dom was silent, still watching the grass as I dropped it.

"Maybe I did think you were a jerk for half the trip here," I said. "But that's not what I think anymore. I think you're a guy who lives life making the tough decisions for other people. And I think I'm a nosy enabler who doesn't like to see people get hurt. So, if you'll let me in on your plans, I want to be ready to help where I can."

"Why?" he asked. "Why do you want to risk anything to help us?"

Shrugging, I sighed through my nose. "Honestly, I'm not sure. It's in my nature, I guess. I like the pace of this village, the community here has so much love for each other and no one is left behind. None of these people deserve to be under Evander's thumb. Something isn't right here, and I'm not going to sit by if I can help."

Dom reached out a hand, and I took it. "It's a deal then, New Bite. I'll let you know when we're ready to make a move."

"Deal," I said, heart pounding at the unknown danger I may have just forced my way into. But I wouldn't regret it, I could feel that in my bones.

"Hey, if you see a woman who looks like Amelia, let me know right away. We're looking for her twin, Naomi."

"Naomi? Got it," I said. "I'll look for her on my morning walks through the village."

"You're really taking to this place, aren't you?" he asked, a boyish smile taking years off his face, and I couldn't help but smile back.

Yes. God, yes. It was in every breath of fresh air I took. It was in the walks I went on every morning, it was in the wolves I'd met, and the kids I watched playing in the fields, and the deer and elk and produce I'd gotten to eat. It was in everything about this place.

"Yes," I said. "But I have a life at home. I'm torn."

"Tell me more about it," Dom said. "You've seen where I come from, tell me what you're leaving behind."

"Kat, my best friend," I said.

"The one you sent money to?" Dom asked.

I nodded. "She's ninety percent anxiety, ten percent sweetheart, and I love her to pieces. She keeps me sane when I have bad days at work."

"The therapy clinic," he said.

"Yeah. It's what I want to do, but the environment there isn't ideal."

"You are a caregiver, aren't you?" he mused. "What else are you leaving behind?"

"My morning walks."

"You're right, can't walk out here," he teased.

I shoved him playfully. "Shut up."

"What else are you leaving behind?" he asked.

"My apartment, we finally got it decorated so cute, and it was right down the street from a coffee shop."

"Name a block in Seattle that doesn't have a café," Dom said.

"Fine, fine." I laughed. "I love Kat, and walks, and coffee, but Granny and Grandad are gone. I was going to do a semester at school this fall, but I guess I could do that online. Are you trying to convince me to stay out here?"

Dom shrugged. "I'm trying to convince you to follow your heart. You look like you live your life stressed."

I grimaced. "Maybe."

"All right then, let's talk about your shift instead. Anything about it that has you stressed? We can talk about it and see if I can help alleviate your concerns."

"Shifting," I said. "I've accepted that it's going to happen at this point, but it still scares me. You'll probably laugh, but I don't like pain."

"No one does," he said. "There's nothing funny about that, and it doesn't make you less of a wolf. Maybe think about it like an athlete would, have you played any sports?"

Once upon a time I lived and breathed track, until the accident. "Yes."

"Then you remember pushing limits," Dom said. "Pushing yourself, think of your shift like that. Your body will be strained, yes, but get in that headspace you get into when you're at the top of your game. When you pull through to the other side, you'll feel like you've conquered the world."

I knew exactly what he meant; I could almost taste the sweat and feel the sun on me during some of my best wins on the track. "I think I can do that."

"Good." He nodded. "Any other worries?"

I frowned. "This mate stuff is too bizarre for me. I'm picking my own partner."

Dom chuckled. "All of this stuff you've heard is unavoidable, it can be avoided if you really want to, except the shift. If you really want to go back to Seattle, do it. You might have to fight your inner wolf on that if she's comfortable here, but it can be done, and I'll do what I can to find you the nearest pack where you can be happy and safe. Your first shift is our responsibility because Amelia bit you, but if you really want to go after this, I'll help you. Same goes for this mating stuff, if you can and want to resist it, then do so. Rejections don't happen often, but they do happen, and no one is going to force you into it."

I shrugged. "That does make me feel better. It's just that Carmine and Jerod were both ready to jump right into it, no questions asked."

"Carmine has had this expectation to find a mate since she was born, it's part of our culture to accept the partner the moon made as our match. Not all, but most, are happy with that arrangement. And Jerod, I still can't believe Carmine's match is that warlock, but he's a part of this world, too, and he knows damn well what a mate is.

His friend, a witch named Dani, she was also mated to a shifter. It's rare, but it's possible."

"They accepted it because they've seen it, then," I murmured. "But I haven't lived with this, and I don't handle the unknown very well."

Dom shrugged. "Let's say you meet someone and you've never smelled anything or anyone better in your life. You've found them, and from what they say, you'll know beyond the shadow of a doubt. Let's say you meet your potential mate, nothing has to happen until you've marked each other, and any decent wolf will wait for you to be ready. You can take all the time you need to get to know them."

"Oh, I like that. And I can still say no?"

"Always."

"What's the mark thing?" I asked.

"It's a bite, and before you ask, no, it's not painful. It goes right here." Dom reached out with a gentle hand to brush the skin on a sweet spot on my neck. I gasped, and as though my body betrayed me, I moved my head back and exposed my neck a little more.

Why did I do that?

Dom's breath caught, I heard it. And then he snatched his hand back and stood up.

"Did that answer your questions?" he asked, clearing his throat.

"Yeah," I said. I held a hand over that spot on my neck, my face bright red. "Thanks."

"Don't mention it." Dom wasn't meeting my eyes anymore when he spoke. "Let's get you on the way to Linda's, I don't think Carmine is going back with you right now. I've got training to do, I'll keep you in the loop when we're ready to challenge Evander."

"Right," I mumbled.

Dom started back and I followed. My heart was still thumping in my chest. This whole conversation had sent my head spinning, but at least I got to tell him about the weird thing with Alpha Evander this morning.

I admired Dom's strong back as we walked into the tree line and back to the cabin. I didn't know what gymnastics my heart was trying to do right now, but it had better stop before I shifted. I had enough to think about right now, and I didn't have time for this mate business.

The full moon was in less than two weeks, and I needed to be ready for it.

CHAPTER TWENTY

JUNE

"June," Dom moaned into my neck. I inhaled his scent, my fingers digging into his back. I looked into his yellow eyes as his fangs grew, and he bit down hard on that tender spot where my throat and shoulder met. The pleasure that shot from my neck to my very core made me scream into his chest.

"Ah!" I shot up in bed, a cold sweat on my forehead as I gasped for air.

I looked around the green bedroom. I threw off the covers and put a hand over my panties. Damp. Again.

Groaning, I closed my eyes. This was getting ridiculous. For the second night in a row, I was having dreams about Dom. I guess I could chalk it up to Dom being good-looking and honest with me, but that would be pathetic. Was I really that easy? Was I so touch-starved I'd jump on the first guy who laid a finger on my neck? Was that all it took to get me wet now?

I swung my legs over the edge of the bed and went to my

backpack to pull out my shower things and a new outfit. I was frustrated in more ways than one as I made my way into the bathroom and cranked the shower as hot as it would go. The moment it was remotely warm, I climbed in.

What exactly do you think is going to happen between you and Dom, huh, June? Crushing on some dude who dragged you to Canada.

I furiously scrubbed my body and washed my hair. Teeth brushed, face washed, dried off, I left the bathroom feeling a lot better.

I rolled my shoulders back. Lift the chin, relax the muscles. Let the tension melt off. I took a deep breath, and let it out slowly. There, now maybe I could do something with my morning.

But as I went down the hall to the green-painted door that signaled my room, I heard sounds coming from the yellow one. Carmine's room. I tossed my old clothes onto my bed and hurried to the yellow door.

"Carmine?" I called.

The door swung open and she was the most disheveled I'd ever seen her. Auburn hair was everywhere. Bags under her eyes. A giant smile on her face.

"Morning, June," she said.

"Good morning, sleeping beauty." I grinned. "Is your mating with Jerod going well, then?" I was still uneasy about the whole mating thing, but after the conversation with Dom was finding it easier to be happy for two people who'd at least consented to it.

Her smile dropped a little. "Actually, there's a bit of a problem with that. Let's talk outside."

She ducked back into her room. It was just as yellow on the inside as the green one was green. Carmine had a suitcase on the bed and was putting her things into it.

"Are you leaving?" I asked.

"*Non.* I'm packing to live in the cabin with Jerod while we're here in Moonpeak," she said.

"With Dom and the others?"

"They're moving into the village. The cabin will be for myself, Jerod, and Amelia."

"*Amelia?*" I asked.

She shut her suitcase and zipped it with a sigh. "*C'est tout.* Walk me to the cabin?"

"Sure," I said.

"Morning, girls. Breakfast?" Linda called from the kitchen.

"No, thank you," Carmine said.

"No thanks," I echoed. "I'm helping Carmine move her things and then today's the day I'm visiting Doc."

"Right! I nearly forgot you're going to start helping Doc. Have fun," was our answer from the kitchen. My nose twitched as we neared the front door. That spicy, earthy candle was burning again.

"What is it?" Carmine asked.

I frowned at the candle for a moment, then tipped it to drip wax on the shelf where it burned. I blew on it until it was dry, peeled up the disc of wax, and put it in my pocket. Carmine raised an eyebrow in question, but we left the house and went several yards before she asked about it.

"What was that for?" she asked.

"I've got a weird feeling about these candles. I've seen them around the village but they aren't sitting right with me. I was thinking maybe someone with more experience in this supernatural stuff who wasn't from the village might know if there's something off about it."

"That's not a bad idea, my Jerod is brilliant, perhaps he can take a look," Carmine offered. "But I have a more important question than that."

"You do?" I asked.

"Spill. Why do you smell like a wolf in heat?" Carmine grinned.

"I do?" I asked, panicked. "I . . . had . . . oh my god." My face turned bright red.

"Did our little June have a naughty dream, perhaps?"

I covered my face with my hands and nodded slowly, which only spurred more laughter from Carmine.

"It's okay, June," Carmine said. "Many wolves get revved up before their change. Think of it as a kind of puberty. There is a lot going on in your body, and wolves are openly sexual beings. It's part of nature, there is nothing to be embarrassed about."

I groaned. "Second puberty sounds awful. How do you wolves go through it?"

Carmine shrugged. "We don't. Our puberty happens at one time, around our mid to late teen years. We begin to feel the first signs of a wolf in us, and then one full moon we just . . . shift."

I frowned. "That's not fair."

Carmine laughed. *"C'est la vie."*

"I'm going to have to learn French if I ever come to visit you, aren't I?" I asked.

"I will translate." Carmine winked. "My brothers would love you."

"You have brothers?" I asked.

"Four of them, and I'm smack in the middle," she said.

I made a face, holding back a smirk. "How are they going to receive the news about your warlock mate?"

"With congratulations or with a fist, there will be no mild reactions to him." Carmine beamed, flashing her fangs. "He is wonderfully spicy. I love it."

"He's spicy?" I asked.

"He's got a sharp wit and a quick tongue. And he's clever and passionate."

I shrugged. "I didn't get to know him well on our trip here. He was indisposed, I guess you could say."

"Yes, I know," Carmine said. "He told me everything. Believe it or not, we did some talking when I wasn't riding him like a horse."

I put a hand over my face. "Too much information, Carmine."

She flashed her fangs. "Not for a wolf."

I shook my head and looked forward. I had been letting my feet follow where Carmine was walking, but I realized we were already at the trees. The cabin wasn't much farther ahead.

"Carmine," I said softly. "After you left with Jerod, I talked to Dom."

"Oh?" She glanced over at me.

"I told him about our encounter with Evander." My next words were pickier, as I didn't want to reveal that Dom and the others were planning to challenge him. "Dom found it strange, too, and they want to do something about it. He's on our side in this . . . whatever is going on in Moonpeak."

"Hmm." Carmine nodded. "Well, I was going to leave after we untangle the problem between Amelia and Jerod, but if I can help while we're still here, I would be happy to do so."

"Did you find out what happened to them?"

"Jerod and Amelia are connected by the soul. He has a plan to undo it, but for the moment they cannot be separated, and I cannot claim him."

"That sounds complicated and disappointing. I'm so sorry."

Her only answer was a shrug.

"I was thinking, Evander said that something was reported on pack lands and he went to investigate, right?" I asked.

"Right."

"That means someone else has seen it, too, right?" I asked.

"We could ask some of the ones who patrol, since they would be the most likely ones to have found the strange thing and reported it," Carmine said. "Wonderful!"

"Yeah, I was thinking Smokey," I said.

"And I can talk to some of the warriors," Carmine said. "I've got enough in common with them that I could find their training field and casually bring it up while I'm kicking their butts."

"I'd like to see that." I laughed.

Carmine shrugged. "Who knows, you might be warrior material, too, once you shift."

"I'm not much of a fighter," I said. "I'm more of a put you back together kind of person."

"Mm, that is useful too," she said. "But warriors will always be needed to protect the pack from danger."

"I can respect that," I said.

We stopped talking as we neared the cabin. I could hear a commotion outside, but couldn't see it.

Carmine whistled. "Mon amour, I'm back!"

The front door to the cabin opened and Jerod stood there in what must have been a borrowed pair of sweatpants, which were way too big for him, and a pink apron, with no shirt.

"Welcome back." He waved with the spatula he was holding. "I'm making pancakes and mystery meat patties, if you're hungry."

"Great!" Carmine brought her suitcase up the stairs and set it inside the cabin as I followed her. "It smells like elk."

Jerod shrugged. "Aaron brought it back last night and said I could use it, so I did. There's barely anything in the pantry here to work with."

"We'll go into town to the store later," Carmine said. She turned to me and grinned. "Do you want to come with us?"

"Ah, that might be a problem. Amelia, remember?" Jerod said. "We haven't been able to get more than a quarter mile apart, and even that is incredibly uncomfortable."

"Oh, right," Carmine said.

"I'll go," I offered. "Make me a list and send me with some money and I can try to get whatever you guys want."

That perked her back up. "Are you sure?"

"Oui."

She snorted a laugh. "Please, never try to speak French again. Okay, I would love it if you could get a few things. Thank you, June."

"What's this about getting things?" Outside the cabin and coming up the stairs was a shirtless and sweaty Dom, followed by Aaron and Amelia in a similar state.

My face turned hot, thinking about the dream I had just had, and I shifted my eyes to Jerod, suddenly extremely interested in the frilly hem of his pink apron and definitely not the little trail of hair that led from Dom's navel down into his pants.

"June offered to go get us some supplies," Carmine said, tearing a piece of paper from a notepad on the fridge and beginning to write things down. "Mon amour, come add to the list. Oh, June, hand me that wax, I'll give it to him."

I pulled it from my pocket and handed it over, which provided me a moment to walk away from Dom and collect myself.

"I'm taking a shower," Aaron announced and went past us to the bathroom.

Amelia grabbed a piece of meat right out of the pan Jerod was frying it in and ate it. "I'm going for a run."

"Not too far," Jerod said.

"Don't remind me," she hissed, and left through the front door.

"You can probably get most of what you want in the general store here in the village," Dom said.

"Non. We need clothes for Jerod, though I say he doesn't need to wear any at all."

Jerod clicked his tongue. "Darling, I'm going to need to go out of the cabin sometime, and I can't do that naked."

"I suppose I don't want the other females to see you," Carmine said.

I cleared my throat. "Is that the list? Just clothes?"

"No, hold on." Jerod looked over Carmine's list and wrote a few things at the bottom. "I doubt you will find much of this in Newfoundland, but I have a few items that would be nice to have if you can track them down. I'd like to be able to summon my familiar, among other things."

Dom walked over and looked at the list.

"Soy sauce . . . rice . . . pickled pigs' feet?" He looked up at Jerod. "The comb of a rooster and a pound of dried grasshoppers? You aren't going to find all of this in the village."

"And she may not find it all in whatever town can be found anywhere near here," Jerod said as he handed me the list. "But any of it would be very nice. Thank you, June."

"Sure, no problem." I took the list, glancing at it.

Dom stiffened and scowled.

"Company," Carmine muttered, frowning.

Alpha Evander walked casually up the path to the cabin. He wore a polo again today, making me wonder if that was the only kind of shirt he had. As usual, his appearance was very neat and trim for a werewolf.

"Good morning," he said.

"Morning, Alpha Evander," Dom said.

"Good morning, Alpha," I said, nodding.

"I hope you two will be comfortable here for the remainder of your stay," he said to Carmine and Jerod.

"Yes, thank you, Alpha Evander," Carmine said. "We will get out of your way as soon as Jerod and I are adjusted to this new situation."

"It's no trouble at all, Carmine." Evander smiled, then narrowed his eyes at Jerod. "So, June, what's the list for? Shopping?"

I glanced down at the paper in my hand. "Oh, yes. I was going to try to get a couple of things in town somewhere that we can't get here."

"Excellent!" Evander beamed. "Settling right in then?"

"Oh," I said. "No, I—"

Behind Evander, Carmine furiously shook her head.

"Yes, I love it here," I said.

"Great," the alpha said as he turned to Dom. "You should take her since you have a car. Do you think you could do that, for the pack?"

Don's jaw tensed. "Yes . . . Alpha."

"Good," Evander said, patting Dom hard on the shoulder. "June, make the trip count. It's not often we get to go out for supplies. And stay safe out there, you're not in Moonpeak territory once you reach the highway."

"Yes, Alpha," I said.

Evander glanced around the room one more time before settling on me again. "Actually, June, you should join me for dinner when you get back."

Dom stiffened. "Dinner?"

"Of course," he said. "Naomi would love the added company, and I can get to know one of the new wolves."

Naomi! I stole a glance at Amelia, who had gone pale and still as death. "I'd love to."

"See you tonight," Evander said as he turned away. "I hope your trip is enlightening."

"I'm going to go change," Dom said. "Let's get you into town."

"You don't mind?"

He looked me up and down in that silent way of his. He clenched and unclenched his jaw. "I don't mind. Wait here."

Then he went into one of the rooms and shut the door. How was I going to spend hours in a small metal box with Dom? After the dreams? After what just happened with Evander? And after I'd agreed to dinner?

"Oh, here, June." Jerod pried Carmine off of him long enough to pull out a wallet and hand me a large bill. "For the shopping."

"No, no, no," Carmine said and pushed it back to him. "That's American money. Here, June."

She handed me money from her wallet. "Use this."

"Thanks," I said. "I'll get your change back to you."

My heart thumped in my chest and my eyes widened as Dom came out of his bedroom. He looked good in a tight black T-shirt and dark-blue jeans. Combined with his short hair and the stubble on his chin, he looked like something out of a magazine. A very specific kind of magazine.

"You coming, New Bite?" Dom asked as he passed me, heading to the front door.

I blushed; I could feel it. My whole face heated up as I shared a look with Carmine. She winked at me and pointed to her nose.

Oh shit, did I smell like . . .

I took a deep breath and let it out slowly. "Coming."

Dom clicked his key fob and the car unlocked, allowing me to slide into the passenger seat. It was surprisingly comfortable when it wasn't filled to capacity. My eyes shifted to the driver's seat. The way Dom held the steering wheel put his biceps on display.

Very scenic. And I don't even have to look out the window.

The engine revved to life. Dom pulled the car around the dirt in front of the cabin, and we left the way we had first come into the territory.

As we drove, I had an entirely new view of the mountains. The fields were still a rocky ride but, eventually, we reached that narrow dirt path that carried us smoothly down and through them.

Dom let his eyes flicker to me and back to the road. "Tell me more about yourself."

"Me?" I asked.

"Yeah. I regret not doing more of this on the trip here. You're a good person, June, so what makes you tick? Let's start with what you like to do. Any hobbies?"

"School," I said.

Dom chuckled. "No, *real* hobbies. Things you do for fun. You know what fun is, don't you, New Bite?"

"I like music."

"Still not a hobby," Dom said.

I sighed. "I like walking."

By now he was full-on laughing at me.

"That's not a hobby either," he shot back. "Do you know what a hobby is, New Bite? What about that sport we talked about before, what did you do?"

I frowned. "Track. I ran track, okay?"

"There you go," Dom said. "That wasn't so hard, was it?"

"Kind of," I mumbled. "It's a sore spot for me, okay?"

We rounded a curve and the road turned to take us down a slope. Dom paid more attention to what he was doing for a moment before he turned back to our conversation.

"Wanna talk about it?" Dom asked.

"I guess. Sure, why not. It's old news." I shrugged. "I ran track, and I was good at it. Long distance was my favorite, but I did sprints too. Set a few school records. Got a scholarship to university. There was a big competition and I got hurt. Tore my quad about fifty meters out."

"Ouch," Dom said.

"You could say that. Anyway, it ended my track career, my scholarship, and at the time it felt like my whole life had ended. I spent a long time in physical therapy."

"Ah, some things are starting to make sense," Dom said. "Let me guess, you were going to school for some kind of goody-two-shoes thing anyway."

"Teaching," I said.

"Yup, that's about right." Dom chuckled. "Then the accident, your physical therapist was so great you decided to do it too."

"You make it sound cheesy," I said.

Dom glanced over at me. "No. It sounds like you had a plan, and it had to change. You adapted. It's what a wolf would do."

"Yeah, well." I rubbed the back of my neck. "You wanted to know about my hobbies. That's the only real one that stuck. I loved running."

"You never went back to it?" Dom asked.

I sighed through my nose, gritting my teeth. "Nope. Anything else you want to know? My date of birth? Bank account? Social security?"

"Easy there, New Bite," Dom said. "It's a sore spot, I get it. We'll drop it."

"Good." I sighed.

"I grew up in Moonpeak. My mom died before I could remember her. An incident with rogues," Dom said, and I watched his throat bob as he took a moment before continuing. "Not sure what she'd make of my life decisions, but what can you do? Luna Lily became everything I could ask for in a second mom. I was raised in the pack house alongside Amelia and Naomi. They're like sisters to me. Alpha Liam was like an uncle, and Dad was always there too."

I stayed quiet, not willing to break the story. For whatever reason, it was fascinating to hear what kind of childhood Dom had.

"For a while, we were all three sent to the other pack in Newfoundland, Salt Fur. It's bigger and they have an actual school. The older ones go to school with the humans when they know how to hide what they are. I can't say I had any noble hobbies like track, but I was in a band for a short while."

"You were in a *band*?" I grinned.

Dom smirked. "We were terrible, and I thought I could play the drums. I very much can't play the drums, I assure you."

"It's hard to picture you trying," I said.

He shrugged. "I don't believe anyone stays the same for that long. There are too many stages to life to expect someone to stay the same for all of it. Teenager Dominic was an obnoxious punk who thought he was invincible. Good riddance."

The only thing I could imagine breaking that version of Dom was the loss of his father. It was just too sad. I wanted to reach out and comfort him, but I had no place to be doing that.

"Anyway, after a very short stint in the band with the human kids, I gave up the drums and came back to Moonpeak. I began training more seriously with the warriors and Smokey. My dad did a lot to push me too," Dom said, then he turned to look at me for a moment as we drew near the highway. "I'd barely started getting my shit together when everything happened."

"Thanks for sharing," I said softly. "I lost my mom early too. Car accident when I was a baby, I can't remember her or Dad."

"That's where the grandparents came in," Dom said.

I nodded. "It is what it is."

"Spoken like a little kid who had to explain her family situation to every stranger she met," Dom added.

"It felt like that sometimes." I laughed. "You learn to put it in as few words as possible and they get uncomfortable enough to change the subject."

"So, where did track come in?" Dom asked.

I smiled. "I was the only girl in my gym class who didn't complain about running one year in middle school. Coach Hall pointed me toward track and field, and I did until I couldn't."

Dom nodded as he mulled over my words. We pulled gently onto the paved road and I let out a sigh of relief. The bumpy dirt had been getting to me, and when the ride turned smooth again I was able to relax some.

"Favorite food," Dom prompted.

"Probably pizza. It definitely accounts for a few of the pounds I gained after I stopped running, anyway. Sausage, extra cheese, and peppers. You?"

"Venison, still warm from the kill," he answered.

"Ew, I don't think I'm ready for that kind of answer yet," I said. "What's your favorite human food?"

Dom hummed in thought for a moment. "Poutine."

"Yeah, I heard Jack say something about that before. Or was it Carson? I don't know what that is," I said.

"Then let's find out," Dom said. "There's a little place that serves a great plate of it where we're going."

"Should I be scared?" I asked.

"Of food?" Dom chuckled. "Not particularly."

"What I mean is that I half expect someone who wants me to eat a food, but won't tell me what the food is, to feed me something gross or wickedly spicy or something," I said.

Dom shrugged. "You either trust me or you don't. You'll find out when you get there."

"I don't know if it's a good idea, but I think I do trust you."

Dom glanced over at me, raising an eyebrow.

"Ten more minutes. And while we're there, do you need anything for yourself?"

I shook my head.

Dom nodded. "All right then. Let's get this done."

And we rode into a small town by the water. My heart was light. I was feeling peaceful despite the stress and mysteries that awaited me back in the village. All I knew right then was that when next to Dom I could handle anything that lay ahead.

CHAPTER TWENTY-ONE

JUNE

The town was picturesque, with a group of cute little houses, painted fun colors, by the water. Dom pulled up by a tiny place that looked to be a diner. There were a couple of other cars there, probably a good sign since it was after breakfast but not quite lunch yet, and they still had customers anyway. Dom turned off the engine and slid out of the driver's seat. I followed his lead, but before I had the door on my side of the car fully open, he was already there and offering me a hand to step down out of the SUV.

"Thank you." I took his hand and stepped down. The breeze off the water was cool, and Dom's hand was pleasantly warm.

There weren't many seats, and two of the only tables in the place had been pushed together for a group of old men who were sitting and drinking coffee surrounded by their empty breakfast plates. The waitress was leaning against the counter, talking to them as if this was a daily ritual.

Dom slid into a booth where he had eyes on the door, and I

sat on the other side. The booth was clean, if a bit run-down by the years. The laminated menus had seen better days, and it looked like they were kept behind the napkin dispensers on the tables full time. I reached for one and glanced at it to see what this mystery dish was, but Dom gave me a sly smile as he took the menu out of my hand.

"No cheating," he said, and put the menu back in place as the waitress came up.

"You kids know what you'd like to drink?" she asked. She had a grandmother's smile, and her gray perm was neat in the front and a little wild in the back, where it would be harder to maintain. Her pink apron was ironed within an inch of its life.

"Coffee, please," I said.

"Water, thanks. And is it too early to order lunch?" Dom asked.

"No, honey. Are you ready to order?" she asked.

"Two poutines," Dom said.

"Okay, kids, just a minute." Our waitress went over to the pass-through window and talked to the cook.

"You're really not going to tell me what it is?" I asked Dom.

"No." He grinned. "You'll just have to wait and find out."

"But what about my food allergy?" I asked.

His face fell for a moment. "You have an allergy?"

I stared at him for a moment until I couldn't hold my composure anymore. Then when I started giggling, Dom grunted at me.

"Tease," he said.

"I couldn't help it." I giggled. "I don't get many opportunities to get back at you."

"You don't really have an allergy, do you?" he asked.

"Actually, I'm allergic to kiwis, but I feel pretty safe in assuming that's not an ingredient in your dish from rural Canada." I winked at him.

He sighed with a smile. "It's not just rural Canada that likes poutine, it originated in Quebec and spread from there. But, yes, it's kiwi-free."

"Here you go, kids." The waitress set my coffee in front of me and water in front of Dom. She also set down a saucer of creamer packets and sugars.

Thanking her, I lifted the cup to my nose and took a deep breath before adding cream. I was glad to have a taste of coffee again; I didn't usually go so many days without it.

We watched the window while we waited. There was almost no traffic here, a definite change from Seattle; though a light mist was beginning to fall, and that definitely reminded me of the Pacific Northwest.

The sliding of heavy plates across the table brought my attention back to the present.

"Enjoy."

When I was sure the waitress was gone, I asked Dom. "What are these bits in it?"

Dom chuckled and pointed to the different parts of his own plate. "Here you have French fries. Those 'bits' as you call them are cheese curds. Top it off with brown gravy."

"That does not seem good for the arteries," I said, looking down at my own plate and picking up a fork. "I can do this with a fork, right? Tell me this doesn't have to be finger food."

Dom laughed. "Eat it however you want. Just give it a chance and I'll be happy."

"Okay." I cut a fry in half and got a little bit of everything on my fork. I shrugged, took a bite, and let it sit on my tongue as I chewed very slowly.

I swallowed. "It's interesting. Definitely not bad, just different."

Dom shrugged and downed a huge bite. "Welcome to Canada."

I laughed at him. "You really need to stop welcoming me to Canada or Newfoundland every time I see something local."

Dom smirked and snatched a fry off of my plate.

"Hey!" I snapped.

"Clean your plate or I'll do it for you." He winked. "We've got errands to run."

"All right, hold your horses," I muttered, but I couldn't stop myself from grinning as well.

This was so easy, this time alone with Dom. A part of me ached that it would all have to end, but it wasn't likely we'd be hanging out again when I went back. Watching him as we ate in comfortable silence, I realized I would miss this more than I would have imagined possible. When had it become so easy to be around him?

Breakfast, or maybe it was lunch, was good. The food grew on me as I ate it, and I almost regretted that I wouldn't have it nearby when I went back to Seattle.

I was going back to Seattle, right?

The waitress was kind enough to give me a to-go cup of coffee after seeing how much I was enjoying it. Dom paid, and we left.

Next was the store. The small building looked like it had once been a warehouse or something with its metal siding and industrial beams. Nonetheless, here it sat now as a store run by the lumberjack from the paper towel commercials. He greeted us with a big smile and a wave as I wove through the shelves looking for things from Jerod's list.

There wasn't a large stock of most of the items. It reminded me a bit of trying to buy groceries at a gas station. Nothing was given much shelf space, and the whole room was used as efficiently as possible to get a little bit of a lot of things on display.

At least most of the important basics were covered, so some

of Jerod's items were actually not that hard to find. But part of the list was . . . eccentric.

"I can't find a few of these things," I said, showing Dom the list. "Actually, I never knew a few of these things could be called groceries."

"Some of this just won't be possible," Dom said. "Moss from a south facing tree? How does a tree face south?"

I shrugged. "I have the rice, soy sauce, chocolate chips, lighter, and stuff like that. I don't have the last half of the list, though."

Dom kept scanning and reading out loud. "Pickled pigs' feet, comb of a rooster, dried grasshoppers. Those he can get the good old-fashioned way. I'm sure he could find someone in the village who's going to butcher a rooster at some point, and we can possibly get pigs' feet if he wants to pickle them himself."

I pulled a bottle off a nearby shelf. "I don't know anything about pickling, but I think you use vinegar for it."

"Heh, good call. Let him figure it out on his own. Are we done here?" Dom asked.

I looked over the list. "I think so. Now for clothes."

We paid at the counter, and I asked the man where we could find somewhere that sold clothes nearby. The closest place was not far, but it was only going to have essentials.

"Are there no bigger stores for this kind of stuff around here?" I asked. "I feel like this can't be the only kind of store here."

"There are better options," Dom said, pulling onto the main road again and turning north. "But they're a ways away. I don't want to be off pack lands longer than I need to be. You, too, New Bite. It's not always safe for a lone wolf, especially a lone wolf who can't shift yet."

I tried not to think about what Dom said as we entered the next store. There were a lot of goods that we didn't need, mostly pertaining to blue collar work in the area. Boating things, fishing things, outdoorsy things. It had a definite influence on the kind of clothing I had to pick from. I had a whopping five men's shirts to choose between, two kinds of pants, and one kind of underwear and socks, both in bulk plastic packaging.

"Close enough," Dom said, tossing things in the basket.

"Sorry, Jerod. No dress shirts in sight," I said.

"He's going to have to deal with jeans too." Dom chuckled as we carried our things to the front counter.

I got out my phone by habit to check the time as we walked, then stopped dead in my tracks. My phone. It was working.

"Everything okay, New Bite?" Dom asked.

It was Roaming, but at least I had signal. Not that I'd used any data for days now, surely I had enough left for some calls and texts.

"I . . . yes. Can you pay?" I handed him the bills I had left. "I need to step outside for a minute." Dom's eyes flicked to the phone in my hand. "You can trust me. I understand now. I really do. But I have loved ones who need to know I'm alive."

Dom nodded curtly and took the bills I handed him.

"Thank you." I spun and raced out the door to the parking lot.

I scrolled through my texts. Kat, my boss, some co-workers, a neighbor I would walk with sometimes. I quickly replied with excuses to buy more time. Next, I called Kat.

It rang, and I briefly thought about the time difference and if she would even be awake. I shouldn't have worried because she answered quickly.

"June Bug!" she squealed. "You're alive."

"I sure am," I said. "I don't have long, and I don't have great reception. Fill me in."

"First, are you okay?" she asked. "I had a terrible dream and I keep worrying about you. Take a picture so I know you're alive."

"Kat . . ."

"I'm hanging up now. I'll call you when I get a selfie." The line went dead.

"Seriously?" I turned on the camera, fixed my hair to the best of my abilities, took the selfie, and sent it to her.

She gave me a long stream of emojis, mostly hearts, in reply, and the screen lit up with her face as she called back.

"You are alive!" she said.

"Yes, Kat." I sighed. "I'm alive."

"Okay, so Mrs. Pataki isn't going to open the deli again."

"Oh no," I said.

"It's okay, she's got a cousin-in-law, is that a thing? Anyway, she's got someone who owns a grocery store and is about to open a sandwich area. They're willing to take the whole team. The timing couldn't have been better, the renovations for the sandwich counter will be done in two months."

"That's fantastic!"

"Bills are paid, and it looks like we'll be afloat until my new job starts. How are things on your end?"

"My end?" I asked.

"Your family emergency, duh," Kat said.

"Oh." I looked through the window where Dom was exiting the store. "It's going . . . okay. I'll be here a bit longer. I'll be in touch as soon as I can. Reception is bad out here. Actually, Kat, I gotta go. But you're sure everything is okay back home?"

"Yes, June Bug. You worry about you, okay?"

"Deal."

"Bye, love. Long distance hugs," Kat said.

I laughed. "Bye, Kat."

"Everything all right?" Dom asked as I pocketed my phone.

"Home is still in one piece," I said.

"Ready to go?"

We got into the SUV and Dom left. We had a quick gas station stop, then back onto the highway and back to Moonpeak. I took the last sip out of my to-go coffee and watched the scenery pass by. I missed Kat, that was for sure.

But I was starting to wonder exactly how much I'd miss this place, too, once my shift was complete.

CHAPTER TWENTY-TWO

DOM

The road was smooth, and a little damp from the earlier short rain shower. I had to admit, the fresh air was nice, and the drive was peaceful. But I didn't like being off pack lands and now that I had that mind link back, I wasn't ready to give that up either.

June was grinning like an idiot at her phone, savoring her last precious moments with it before her signal was gone completely. Shit, she had the cutest smile. And her short hair; I'd never considered a female's haircut to this extent before, but the way hers sat when she ran her fingers through it, sweeping it back out of her face, it was enough to drive me crazy.

I gripped the steering wheel tighter as I forced my focus back on the road. The wolf inside of me was frustratingly stir crazy. We were both anxious about something, but I didn't dare consider what that something could be.

I had plenty of shit to be anxious about, and she-wolves shouldn't be one of them.

This was just like when Naomi shifted, and she was just fine. June would be fine too; she was tough. The big difference here was that Naomi I could worry over like a little sister, so what was June to me? I couldn't afford to be this distracted. Crushes among wolves were a waste of time if you had faith about finding a mate, and this thing with June should be no different.

But, fuck, she smelled good.

I shifted in my seat, glad she was glued to her phone and hadn't noticed the hard-on I was rocking. Wolves have too many damn hormones. Fuck and fight, an endless cycle.

Snap out of it.

Being horny was no excuse to bother her. I'd put her through enough. It still killed me that we had to drag her back here, but I knew I wouldn't trust another pack with her shift. Or leave her to sort it out on her own like a lone wolf.

Moonpeak might have its problems right now, but the wolves here were good wolves. Linda, despite tiptoeing around touchy subjects, was a good mother and a gentle teacher for June. And the rest of the village, they would watch over her.

Yeah, she deserved Moonpeak. She already fit in—I could tell. For all my piss-poor decisions and the shady shit I'd done, I knew I'd done this one thing right. She already felt like she fit here.

"What are you thinking so hard about?" June asked.

"I thought you were on your phone."

I adjusted how I sat again, trying to shield the view of my pitched tent.

"Ran out of signal." She shrugged. "Are we close to the village?"

"Not really," I answered. "We're not even on pack lands yet. I didn't turn off the highway very long ago."

"Aw." She sighed and pocketed her phone. "I was hoping I was engrossed in my texts longer than that."

"When we get back to the village we need to . . ." My head snapped to the left and I slammed the breaks.

We were under attack.

Fucking cars. I can't smell anything when I'm inside of one, and I barely caught the beast in my peripheral vision as it barreled toward us. Thanks to the brief rain earlier and the dirt road, the tires squealed on the damp ground, and we slid a bit as a wolf slammed into the hood. If I hadn't stopped when I did, he would have been through the driver's side door and tearing into me and June.

My heart hit my rib cage like a wrecking ball. June was with me, and she couldn't shift yet. The wolf in me snarled, fighting to surface so we could kill the one who dared attack us.

"Stay here!" I yelled, tearing open my door and shifting, ripping my favorite shirt and kicking off the scraps of jeans that clung to my back paw.

The wolf recovered fast, and as he pushed off the hood of the SUV, I got my first good look at him.

He was a rogue, but not like I had been rogue. He was something sick and twisted that had been thrown from a pack. Real sick, he smelled like death warmed over. His eyes were wild as he snarled at me, charging again.

As the thing slammed into me, I tore at its shoulder tooth and nail, freeing a chunk of skin and tossing it aside. The thing didn't seem to notice it was missing any pieces, though, and it backed up to lunge again.

Then I smelled the second one. And the third.

Shit. We weren't on pack lands and I couldn't reach anyone for help.

I circled around the wolf I was fighting, pulling it away from the car and June. I tried to glance around as I went, looking for the other wolves, and cursed as I noticed a fourth one.

There was something giant and terrible about them. They weren't normal rogues, and my mind flashed back to the things that had been killing wolves a decade ago. The things that got Alpha Liam challenged.

Four on one. Most wolves would be dead within minutes.

I dug my claws into the soft earth underfoot. I would not be like most wolves.

Lunging forward, I took another bite at the wolf I'd been fighting, turning at the last second when another rogue attacked from my right.

Slam. I had managed to dodge the first one, but another was there and ready for me when I did.

My wolf and I cried out in pain as sharp teeth bit down on my back. I kicked hard, connecting with the wolf who'd just bitten me and shoving it away, only to be swarmed by the other two that were fighting me.

Under the weight and attack of so many rogues, I struggled and snarled. They ripped at my flesh, and it was all I could do to fend them off my throat. I flailed, and righting myself, took a nasty bite to my leg as I lunged upward and latched my teeth around the throat of one of them.

The others bit and tore at me, but in the heartbeat that I grabbed the first wolf's throat, I tore it out and that was that.

Three on one.

I kicked at the faces of the other two that I had been fighting, buying a little space while I looked at the car.

The fourth rogue was sniffing at June's side of the vehicle, but moved away and ran at me. At least June was safe. Safe-ish.

Turning my attention back to the two in front of me, I lunged again. Tearing and biting and shifting away for when the last wolf joined the fray. I swiped my claws across the face of one of my assailants, causing them to back away for a moment just as the third rogue jumped for me.

Snarling, I scraped my claws over the other wolf that had been attacking me and turned my teeth on the new fighter. I clamped my jaws down over their nose and mouth, puncturing their muzzle and dripping blood across my tongue.

Kill!

The wolf in me fought to bring down the rogues around me. Letting go of the rogue's face, I turned my head and shot forward, clamping down on the throat and finishing the job.

Two left.

But the moment I turned my attention to them, one of them rammed into my side. A few of my ribs definitely cracked, and I spat blood as I rolled across the ground from the impact.

I had to focus on the fight, but I registered the sound of the car moving away. Good, at least June could get back to the pack safely.

Snarling, I tested my weight on my legs as the last two rogues closed in. They were huge. At least warrior class when they'd been in a pack, if they were ever in a pack to begin with.

I got up, ignoring the pain and snapping at the closest wolf. But keeping him occupied meant letting up some of my focus on the other.

Crack.

My back right hip suddenly sprouted teeth as the other rogue lunged at me. I flailed and fought with everything I had, snapping and then tearing off part of an ear. I was sure the other rogue was nearly on me again as well. And that was about when I heard the squeal of tires.

I bit down hard on the wolf at my hip, managing to turn the tides and get on top of the fight. With the weight of my bigger wolf on top of him, even this brute of a rogue wasn't getting out without a fight. It bought me just enough seconds to look up at the other rogue, and watch as the SUV rammed right into it.

My heart could have burst. June was fighting. Fighting for me, and she didn't even have her wolf yet.

I raised the front half of my body up and slammed it back down on the wolf below me. Claws and fangs tore into it until it was nothing but a piece of meat under my paws. My fury at the attack and near panic at June's safety led me rip into the rogue with abandon until it was long dead.

I tried to move forward for the other wolf who was in the process of recovering from getting hit by a vehicle, and found out the hard way that I had taken some serious damage to my hip and leg.

That didn't stop me from pushing forward, though. Just a few more feet to the rogue, who still had a leg stuck under the car. With one last push and the bite of a furious wolf, I took him by the throat and tore flesh from bone.

Blood dripping, I spit the meat from my mouth and slumped over. I had given what I could in that fight, and my adrenaline left me.

A vehicle door opened and human footsteps ran my way. My eyes were closing. I needed rest.

"Dom!" June was shrieking my name. "Dom! Don't go to sleep. No, no, no, no, no. Oh god, what do I do? I don't have my kit on me, and even if I did, I'm not trained to fix wolves. There's so much blood, do you need a tourniquet? What am I saying? Let me find something I can use."

And all I could think was that she was so cute when she panicked.

"How do I get you back to Doc? Can you stand at all? Should you not move, or can you shift?" June ran her fingers over several of my worst wounds. "Shit. Dom, you've probably got some fractures and I wouldn't be surprised if you have a torn ligament. At least, I think that's what that is on a wolf. I know where that would be on a human."

I nudged her hand with my head. Her worried face turned back to me, tears in her eyes and her hands were shaking.

Shifting wasn't the best option, but there was no way June could take me to Doc in my wolf form. I closed my eyes and braced for some pain as I shifted. June backed up, giving me some space, and then came forward to support my chewed up hip and leg, the worst of my injuries.

"I thought you were training for this," I said softly. I reached up to her face and wiped a wet streak on her cheek away.

"If you're well enough to joke, you're well enough to get in the car," she said, her voice shaking. "I wouldn't normally move a patient yet, but I don't know what else to do for you out here. Are you sure you're not going to bleed out on me?"

"Yes, New Bite. I'm sure." She looked skeptical but didn't press the issue. June's arms were surprisingly strong as she helped me sit up slowly, then stand. She didn't let me put any pressure on my worst leg, not that I would have anyway. Once I was in the car, she ran to the driver's side and we took off.

I closed my eyes and laid my head back. It wasn't the introduction I wanted to give June to how werewolves fought, but at least that part was out of the way now.

I grinned.

She'd fought for me.

Chapter Twenty-Three

JUNE

Dom was in serious trouble. I was worried he was going to bleed out despite what he told me, and I sacrificed one of Jerod's new shirts to keep pressure on the worst wound.

As Dom lay back in the seat next to me, all I could think about was if he was going to pass out. I went as fast as I felt comfortable going down the road to the village, Dom having to give the occasional direction. All I had to do was get him to Doc, and everything would be fine, right?

My eyes darted to Dom and back to the road. He had to be fine. I mean, he was a badass back there, right? Those wolves looked more like monsters than the ones I'd come to know in Moonpeak, and he tore into them four to one.

It was so bloody and violent. I shuddered and gripped the wheel harder just remembering it.

"You okay, June?" Dom asked from the passenger seat.

"No!" I shouted, his question breaking me from the racing

thoughts in my head, and all my stress spilled out. "What the actual fuck were those? What was that? How are you so calm? I'm about to go into shock and you're bleeding out and you want to know if I'm okay?"

"Believe it or not, New Bite, I'll be just fine. It would be great if you can get me to Doc to have him set my bones properly before they fuse back together, but otherwise, I'll be fine in a couple of days."

In through the nose, out through the mouth. A few breaths later, I was under control. "Sorry for panicking."

"Don't worry about it, you're new to all this."

The window rolled down, and Dom sniffed the air. "Slow down."

I didn't ask why, I just obeyed. As I kept a much slower speed than I really wanted to, my eyes darted around for whatever he was smelling for. My heart thudded in my chest. Oh god, please no more of those giant wolves. Tell me that wasn't what he was smelling.

A howl in the distance startled me, and I pressed a little harder on the gas pedal.

"Stop," Dom said, reaching a hand toward me. "It's Smokey."

Against the thrill in my heart that told me we should be running for Doc, I nodded and slowed the car to a stop. Six big wolves crested the next peak. Four grays, one brown, and one with the familiar white face of Smokey's wolf. They raced for the car, circling it with what I expected was alert and concern.

Dom started opening the car door as Smokey's big head pushed in.

"I know, old man," Dom said to the wolf. "There were four of them. Follow our trail back to the mess."

"How are you . . ." I started to ask. "Oh, mind link."

Dom and Smokey both looked over at me. Smokey huffed a puff of air out of his nose and snapped his teeth a little.

"I'm not telling her that," Dom said.

Smokey licked at one of Dom's bad scratches. "I'll turn when we get to Doc's. Get going while the smell is still fresh."

Smokey withdrew his head from the car and Dom shut his door again.

"What did he say?" I asked.

Dom sighed, holding an arm over his ribs. "Nothing for polite company. Let's go see the doc."

I glanced in the rearview mirror to see slick paws pounding into the damp earth, muscles bunching and jumping and running. For a fleeting moment, my heart wanted to run with them. But I shook off the sensation and put all my focus back on the road.

Dom stayed quiet while I drove to the village. The path took us right up to the cabin where Dom and the others had been staying. A few heads poked out as we passed. Jack and Carson were carrying a couple of bags out and stared as we passed. Hopefully, Dom was communicating with them, letting them know what happened since I couldn't link yet.

I passed right by the cabin, wound through the short expanse of trees, and then the road opened to the village. I turned right just before the end of the houses and stopped in front of Doc's clinic.

Throwing my seat belt off, I opened the car door and ran out onto the grass without bothering to shut the door behind me.

"Doc!" I called. "Doc, patient!"

A man strode out of the house. His dark hair was cropped short in a terrible mess, as if he'd cut it himself. I ran to open Dom's door. "We have lacerations everywhere, and I suspect at least two broken ribs, and I'm worried about an ilium fracture on his right side."

"June?" Doc rushed forward to help me with Dom. "Welcome to your first day of wolf medicine. Let's get him inside."

We got Dom moved inside; a bed was thankfully close and

ready to go. It looked like any doctor's office, minus the waiting room between the front door and the exam room. A bed replaced the usual exam table and the row of cabinets and countertops on the right wall were a lovely shade of '70s avocado green. Otherwise, it was blessedly clean, and smelled like my office in Seattle. A short hallway of rooms beyond the front area looked to be longer-stay patient rooms, and there was a staircase that probably went up to where Doc lived.

"June, can you grab me the bandages and splints from the left cabinet?"

Doc got Dom on the bed, and I ran to the cabinet. I carried the whole box of splints and three rolls of bandage. If we needed more, I would get it then. As it was now, my arms were already full.

"Hm, some ribs. Just fractures, I believe. Try not to breathe too hard," Doc said to Dom.

Dom laughed but it quickly ended in a grunt. "Okay, Doc."

"This leg is by far the worst. Let's not have you bleed out, shall we? June, the bandages, please."

"Right here." I handed Doc a roll and watched him reach over to a small drawer nearby for an already threaded needle and wire for stitches.

Pulling up a stool from the corner so I could watch, I grimaced as Doc did a quick and dirty line of stitches about a foot long from Dom's thigh and up his hip. Once he was done, he bandaged the wound and moved on to the next badly torn chunk of skin. It was highly unsettling to watch him do it with no prep. No painkillers, no needle holders, he barely stopped to disinfect as he went. Doc talked me through it as he went, and assured me wolves were highly resistant to infection, but it still gave me goose bumps.

Dom took the treatment like a champ. He laid his head back, his brow furrowed, not saying a word.

Dirty Lying Wolves

I let my hand crawl across the edge of the bed to reach for his, not really registering what I was doing until it happened. Just before our fingers touched, Dom's eyes opened and his stare pinned me in place. My breath caught in my throat as I swallowed, his gaze tracing the movement of my neck. Closing his eyes again, he entwined his hand with mine.

"How are you feeling?" I asked.

"Fine. I've been here before, I'll be here again."

As my heart tightened, so did my hand, squeezing his fingers lightly in mine. I didn't want to see him hurt again. He'd already been through enough, from what Smokey had told me. And now he was hurt by those things. I couldn't describe them; they weren't like normal wolves. They were big, and the look in their eyes was so dull. Affected by something else. They weren't right.

"Another roll of bandages, June," Doc said, drawing me from my thoughts. "And hand me that short splint. Dominic, your ankle is trying to turn at a bad angle here. I'm going to have to splint it for a couple of hours while it gets back on track."

The front door opened and Aaron strode in. "Dom, where was the attack? How many?"

"Smokey's on it," Dom said. "Four of 'em. Rogues, but they were like the ones Alpha Liam was dealing with way back when."

Doc faltered a moment trying to splint Dom's ankle. "The ones from before?"

"That's right." Dom nodded. "If those fuckers are poking around again, you're going to need more bandages."

Doc shook his head, finishing what he was doing and quickly taking another bandage from me.

"We have to tell Alpha Evander," Doc said. "If they're back, we're in for another terrible time."

"Alpha Evander already knows."

The door was open, and silently following Aaron inside was Evander himself, looking as neat as a pin. He closed the distance between the door and Doc with a few long steps.

"How is he, Stephen?" Evander asked, confusing me at first until I realized that must be Doc's real name.

"He'll be okay in a couple of days," Doc said. "I'm going to need to prepare if those rogues are back."

"Hold on," Evander said. "I don't want any distress over a one-time incident. I'd like everyone present to not speak of the event until we can investigate further. If they're gone now and there aren't more of them, there is no reason to cause a panic. Understood?"

"Yes, Alpha," Doc said.

Aaron echoed him, and I took the cue and said the same.

"Good," Evander said. He glanced around the room, meeting Doc, Aaron, and me in the eyes. He barely glanced over Dom. "June, I'll see you later."

"Later? Alpha, are you sure—" Aaron nudged me in the ribs, and I yelped.

"Don't argue with the alpha. Ever," Aaron murmured.

"Yes, Alpha. I'll see you later," I said.

Evander didn't pause as he strode out of the house the way he came, the door shutting tight behind him.

Dom grumbled. "Prick."

"Doc," Aaron said, "what do you need if we have more rogue attacks?"

Doc finished up with what he was currently doing to Dom's ankle and looked up at Aaron. "More of everything. More stitching wire, more bandages, more splints. More of this." He gestured to Dom on the bed.

"You done with me, Doc? Can I get a blanket or something?" Dom asked.

"Ah, right. Yes, here you go." Doc reached behind him to a shelf and grabbed a blanket. He laid it over Dom's groin and spread it over his legs.

"Dom!" The door opened with a smack.

"You have an awful lot of visitors for someone who just got back," Doc commented.

Amelia stalked through the room, concern on her face. "What happened? How many? Who do I need to kill?"

Dom chuckled. "I'm fine, they're dead, it wasn't even that bad. Can a guy get some rest now?"

"To be fair, your tensor fasciae latae is separated from . . ." Doc mumbled, catching Dom looking at him with annoyance. "Right, sorry."

"If you really want to help, get down there with Smokey and follow the scent," Dom suggested.

Amelia growled. "I'll have to bring the warlock with me that far out, but we can't let this start up in Moonpeak again."

"Who told you . . ." Dom began to ask when his eyes slid over to Aaron. "Of course. Yes, it's just like the rogues that attacked ten years ago, the start of everything that went down."

Doc threw his hands up. "I'm not a part of this, I'll be upstairs making a supplies list. Call if you need me, Dom."

When it was just me, Dom, Amelia, and Aaron, I spoke up. "Anything I can do to help?"

All the wolves in the room stared at me. Amelia huffed and looked at Dom. Then they seemed to stare at each other for a long moment. Once I realized they were speaking privately through their voodoo werewolf mind thing, I crossed my arms, annoyed.

"Go on," Dom growled out loud. "We talked about this."

"June," Amelia said. "I've not been myself since we met. I want to apologize for biting you. Thank you for attempting to save me back then, and I'm sorry I attacked you."

"You're welcome," I said.

"You're going to meet Evander for dinner in the pack house?" Amelia said.

"That's right."

Her jaw ticked. "You want to help? Find out what he's doing with Naomi. My sister, we can't get to her, and I can't help her if I don't know what's going on."

"I'll try. Something is off, and I want to know what it is."

"That makes several of us," Dom said.

"I'm going to find Smokey and see if I can help," Aaron said.

"Me too," Amelia said, turning to follow Aaron out the door. "We don't leave the village unless in pairs from here on, got it?"

"Got it." Dom and Aaron echoed each other.

Aaron left first. Amelia gave one last soft look to Dom before turning and closing the door behind her. I sighed and took a step away from the bed.

"I'll go, too, and let you rest."

"Wait," Dom said. He reached out and grabbed my hand. "Be careful. I don't want you to get hurt because we dragged you here. If Evander is onto you watching Naomi, stop."

"I will." My voice cracked as I tried to keep my heart under control.

"Good. And don't let him do anything weird to you. He's your alpha, but his authority has its limits."

"Okay." I didn't understand what Dom meant by that, or even what he was worried about happening. But I'd be careful. I wanted to know what was going on, not get myself killed.

"I'll come visit you later," I said.

"Don't worry about me," Dom said. "I'll be fine, and then I'll be training. Worry about yourself, New Bite."

Shit, why did that sound so good to my ears?

"Later, Dom," I said breathlessly.

His eyes settled on mine. "Later."

I steeled myself and turned away before it got any harder to leave. I resisted one last glance as I left, closing the door behind me. I didn't know if it was the wolf taking over in me, or the wind, or just my own imagination. But in the softest breath behind me, I could have sworn I heard one last desperate plea from inside.

Please, be safe. For me.

CHAPTER TWENTY-FOUR

JUNE

As I looked through the few outfits in my wardrobe, I realized I didn't have anything nice to wear. When I'd gone shopping for essentials, I was not expecting to be invited to dinner. I went with the two pieces I had that were plain black—a plain shirt and athletic pants. Hopefully, the black would make it look classy and understated and the shiny swish of the brand logo at my hip could be covered by the top.

What did Evander want with me? Was this really an alpha getting to know a new pack member, or was it something more sinister than that? The image of Evander's expression in Doc's office wasn't fading. Was he disappointed that Dom was okay?

Hopefully, I'd be able to pick out anything too suspicious at dinner. And what about Naomi? Everyone seemed worried about her, so it was hard to say what I would find when I met her.

A knock at my door. I rubbed my tired eyes and walked over, opening the painted green wood and finding Linda.

"Hi, there, June." Linda smiled. "Hannah took those bags to Carmine for you just a moment ago."

"Thanks." I gave a weak smile. "I'm glad to know they'll get there."

Linda leaned in the doorway with a mischievous smile. "So, dinner with Alpha. You must be excited."

"Yeah, I guess."

Linda closed her eyes and hugged her shoulders. "I remember the anticipation before my first shift. I could almost feel something between me and Bruce already. They say sometimes a really strong mated bond can feel it. I wonder if Alpha feels something for you, June."

A chill ran down my spine. The pit of my stomach suddenly dropped, and I was almost nauseated.

No. I couldn't be Evander's mate. Absolutely not.

"Do you . . . do you mean he doesn't always invite a new wolf for dinner?" I asked.

"He hasn't before, no," Linda said. "But we haven't really had anyone join that pack who was bitten since Evander became alpha. Oh, before I forget, I brought you something to wear."

"Um, I don't think I need to dress up too much," I said, raising my hands in front of me.

"Yes, b'y. Don't worry about it, dear. Evander asked me to lend you something." Linda picked up the paper bag at her feet and handed it to me.

My heart sank. "Thank you."

"Anytime. I'll see you tomorrow, have fun!" Linda winked and left.

After closing my door, I pulled the garment from the bag. I frowned at the beautiful blue halter dress in my hands. With a groan, I pulled my outfit off and slipped into the dress that was a bit racy for my tastes. The hem fell above my knee and the front dipped low enough to show plenty of cleavage. There was even a pair of matching sandals in the bag.

"Great," I muttered, looking in the mirror. Whatever Evander's game was, he was winning it. I was all dolled up for him now, and if I didn't get moving, I'd be late.

With a groan of frustration, I went out the door and downstairs. Linda was in the kitchen cooking dinner, and I hurried outside before she could stop me and comment on my appearance. As sweet as she was, she didn't have a clue how I felt about Evander, and had just made an already strenuous night about ten times worse.

My face was pink as I walked down the road, painfully aware that there were wolves that could see me in this outfit. It might have been the beginning of summer, but it wasn't all that different from back home. I'd seen several overcast days and familiar temperatures despite being on the other side of the continent, which meant I should have brought a sweater.

After a painfully long walk, and dragging my feet, I approached the pack house. Doc's house, the last one before I left the village proper, caught my eye. I glanced over at it, wondering if Dom was all right. Then I sucked in a breath as I noticed the big gray wolf in the window. Was it Dom? It had to be. Once I passed Doc's place and drew close to the pack house, I knew I couldn't avoid it any longer and squared my shoulders. At the door, I lifted my hand to reach for the handle when it swung open.

Alpha Evander was there with that smile of his. My question of whether he owned anything other than polo shirts was answered, as he was wearing a nicer button-up and black slacks.

"June, welcome to the pack house. Come on in," he said.

"Thanks," I mumbled, and followed him inside.

He closed the door behind me, and I followed him down a

different hallway than the one I had visited before to get to his office. My nose twitched as I smelled something familiar, and it took a moment to place the scent of those candles that Linda used.

Anything I saw could be important, so I gave myself permission to observe everything carefully. The house was fairly clean but most likely unused. There didn't seem to be much life in it. Were Evander and Naomi the only ones here? The lightest coating of dust was settled on a few doorknobs.

As the hallway turned, we entered a big dining space. It would easily sit two dozen, and was filled with food, but the only one sitting at the lonely table was a woman in a dress that looked eerily similar to mine. She was the spitting image of her sister, with a slightly darker skin tone and longer hair, but it was still basically Amelia at the table.

"Hello," she said warmly. "Welcome to Moonpeak, I'm Naomi."

"June. Thank you for inviting me."

Like a patient on painkillers, she wasn't quite fully alert. Whatever was going on here, I'd bet it wasn't opioids, but something else. . . . The others were right to be concerned, Naomi was going through something here.

On the table, there was salad, a pot roast with potatoes and carrots, and warm, fresh sourdough bread with butter. Naomi sat next to the head of the table, and there were plates at the head and across from her already set up.

"Here, June. Have a seat across from Naomi." Evander pulled out a chair for me, and I took it. This would put us on either side of him. I hated the mirroring effect between Naomi and me, especially with the blue dresses.

"I'm glad you could join us." Evander smiled. "I look forward to getting to know one of the new wolves. How are you adjusting? Linda tells me you're learning fast."

185

Evander reached for a bottle of wine on the table against the wall behind him. He poured a drink for Naomi, then me, then himself. Naomi took his signal and stood, slicing the roast and putting portions on everyone's plates.

I tried to focus on answering Evander while observing Naomi. "It was a big shock at first, but lately I've gotten a little excited about it. I'll catch myself watching the wolves run and . . . well . . ."

Evander nodded, grinning. "You want to join us, don't you?"

"Yeah," I said. "I think I do."

He chuckled and reached over, taking a slice of bread. "I'm not surprised. You have about a week left. You can expect some more intense desires to pop up over the next few days."

"I don't know if I'm looking forward to that or not," I said.

"You'll be fine, June. I can already feel the wolf in you." Naomi gave a long pause, a faraway look, and then adjusted her vision to see me again. "Has anyone told you about your first shift?"

"Some," I answered. "Linda keeps saying I'll find out more the day before."

"She doesn't want to scare you," Evander said. "And she might be right. Your first shift can be intimidating."

I reached over and took a slice of the warm bread. My mouth watered as I slathered fresh butter on it. With food in my hand, I was ready to forget every other problem I was facing for a moment and bite into the sourdough. Oh. My. God. I could eat this every day.

"June," Evander said, pulling me from my warm bread euphoria. "Have you made any friends in the village yet?"

This sounded like one of those important questions with possibly wrong answers. I knew Evander didn't seem to care for Dom, so his probably shouldn't be the first name across my lips.

"I like Carmine," I said honestly. "I'll miss her when she goes back. And Linda and Hannah. I haven't gotten to know anyone else very well yet."

Evander nodded, smiling. Maybe I'd passed whatever test that was.

"You'll meet more when you can run with us," he said. "Take Naomi here. You haven't gotten to know each other, but she's a sweetheart, and I'm sure you'd get along. So caring, such a natural-born luna."

I caught movement on his side of the table. His arm clearly reached over to touch her leg or knee or something. Naomi blushed and looked down at her plate.

I cleared my throat, trying a bite of the roast. "Mmm, delicious. Who is the cook?"

It worked. Evander moved his arm, and his hand reappeared above the table to pick up his fork.

"One of the lovely ladies from the village cooks for the pack house. She comes, cooks, and then goes back to her own home," Evander answered. "You may have met Alice at the picnic? She usually makes several of the side dishes and can be found near the roasting pits."

I nodded. "Well, she does a great job."

"Yes, she does," Evander said, and we all turned to our meals for a few minutes of silence.

I ate, and damn did I enjoy it. But I also observed Evander and Naomi. He didn't move his hand below the table again, but he did shoot her several long glances that could have been that mind link stuff. Whatever he was doing obviously made her pause, uncomfortable. Or maybe comfortable, I couldn't tell. One minute she seemed to want to get away from him, and the next moment she was red in the face and breathing a little heavy. Was this some kind of animal heat thing? What weird thing was happening to her?

"Oh, June." Evander spoke up after a few minutes of eating. "Thank you for working with Doc. Do you have a background in medicine?"

I chewed the bite in my mouth and swallowed before answering. "Yes, actually. I'm studying to be a physical therapist. I'm already a certified assistant."

"How wonderful. Maybe it would be best to have you move near Doc and study full time as his apprentice," Evander said. "It would suit you to fall into company with good wolves in the pack. It would do well for your pack status as well."

"I'll have to think about it," I said carefully. "From what I'm told, I'll need to see what kind of wolf is in me first."

"Of course," Evander said, nodding. "Something to keep in mind, who you spend your time with."

Oh. So that's your game. You don't like me hanging around Dom and the others. Is it because you want them as isolated as possible? Or maybe you just want a naive new wolf in your pocket.

Naomi cleared her throat. "Evander, shall I bring out dessert?"

A quick glance at the table showed that we were all nearly done with our meals.

"Thank you, Naomi. Go ahead," Evander said.

"I can give you a hand," I offered, beginning to stand up.

"No, June. You're our guest," Evander said. "We wouldn't dream of it. Naomi, if you need help, I will assist you."

Naomi's eyes went wide. "No, I can get it. Alice made a pie, I can handle one plate."

So much for getting Naomi alone.

Instead of worrying about it right now, I focused on cleaning my plate and making space for pie. A good thing too. Naomi brought out a still-warm dish. The smell of apples and cinnamon hit my nose and made my mouth water.

"Who's ready for apple pie?" Naomi asked.

Obviously, everyone in their right mind was ready for apple pie. She cut three thick slices and served them. I eyed mine with anticipation, waiting for whatever cue I needed to feel like I could dig in.

Evander took his fork and scooped up his first big bite. Good enough for me. I dug in, and the end of the meal was spent in silent bliss as I had the best apple pie possibly in my life. Sorry, Granny.

Once we were clearly done eating, Evander finally got up from his seat at the table. "June, care to join us for a drink in the garden by the firepit?"

"I would, but I've already had more than I should have," I said, holding up my empty wine glass. "I'm actually already feeling lightheaded. I almost never drink."

Evander chuckled. "The tolerance of a human. That will change when your wolf metabolism kicks in. For now, Naomi can walk you safely home."

Yes!

I smiled. "Thank you, Alpha."

Thank you for falling for my bullshit. As if one glass of wine would do me in when Granny had me join her in her daily glass of red the second I turned twenty-one. No self-respecting Gunn would be drunk from wine this weak.

"Get her to Linda's street, Naomi," Evander said as we all walked to the front door. "I'll see you back in a few minutes."

Damn. What a tight leash.

"Yes, Alpha," Naomi said. Her expression was neutral as we left out the front door. Evander stayed in the doorway, waving us off. I made plenty of show smiling and waving and holding my head as Naomi offered me an arm.

I finally felt like I could relax my shoulders once Evander

went back inside the pack house and closed the door. I turned to watch Naomi as we walked. She looked visibly calmer as well.

"What's going on between you and Alpha?" I asked, hoping to sound casual.

"You're not really drunk, are you?" she asked.

"And you're not comfortable around him, are you?" I said.

She was quiet for another minute before closing her eyes and laughing softly. "You got me."

"What's the deal?" I asked. "You live in the same house, right?"

She looked up at the emerging stars in the darkening sky. "I do, and I can't really say why. I think he helps me somehow." Her brow furrowed. "No, I help him maybe."

"I don't think you're in a good situation," I murmured. "Why haven't you gone to see your sister? Or Dom?"

Naomi frowned. "There's a reason I can't. I don't always remember it, but I keep it in my desk. It's a very important reason."

"They're looking for you," I said. "Amelia and Dom. They're trying to find out if you're okay."

The tension was almost palpable in her.

"What if I swore to keep your secret safe?" I said. "I'm worried about you, Naomi."

And it was the truth. The same gut feeling that rubbed me the wrong way with Evander made me want to look out for Naomi.

"Moon above, maybe I'm the one who's drunk. I actually believe you're sincere about that."

"I am," I insisted. "You can't bottle yourself up forever or no one can help you. You have to let it out somewhere, and I promise I'm a good listener."

"I think Evander is making some kind of connection between us. Maybe a mate connection, I don't know," she said.

"What?" I said, shocked. "Is that even possible?"

She shrugged. "Maybe. Sometimes I'm so sad about my parents and I would give anything to get away from him. But then sometimes he . . ."

"He what?" I asked gently.

She paused her steps. "Evander has this pull over me. And I'm scared. I'm scared that one of these days I'll give in to it, and if I do, maybe I'll end up liking it."

"It's difficult to fight it," I said.

She nodded. "I hate it. I hate it so much, but my whole life is in that house. I've fought it all this time but I'm getting so tired."

"Naomi," I said, "that doesn't sound like a mate to me. Did you feel this way as soon as you met him?"

"No," she murmured. "That's the problem. It's so confusing to be around him, but I also have to stay in the pack house. It's the agreement of me living there and having dinner with him that keeps the pack—"

Her eyes went wide.

"That keeps the pack what?" I asked. "Naomi, what is he holding over you?"

She shook her head. "No, June. Our conversation is done."

She walked to my other side and I saw that we were at the edge of Linda's street. Only two houses stood between me and my destination.

"Thanks for talking to me, June," Naomi said. "And please keep your promise that you'll keep my secret."

"Naomi . . ."

"Tell them I love them, and that I'm fine. Don't come looking for me. Goodnight, June."

Naomi walked quickly back toward the pack house.

Oh. Oh, fuck this guy. I'd seen Linda and Bruce. I'd seen

Carmine and Jerod. These two weren't mates, but I'd bet good money he was trying to play house with her cooped up in that place. My blood could have boiled, I was so angry. Screw Evander. He was doing something shady, I knew it.

Looking down at my dress, I wanted to throw up. What did it mean that he'd dressed us to match? I walked to Linda's door, my shoulders squared and my jaw clenched. Naomi needed out of there, and I was going to make that happen one way or another.

I probably need my wolf first, but I swore I'd get her out of that pack house.

One more week. Bring it on.

CHAPTER TWENTY-FIVE

JUNE

Click. I plucked the toast from the appliance and set it on my plate. I was tired from another night of bad sleep, and it showed on my face.

"Are you all right, June?" Linda asked. She was sitting at the table with a new wolf who had arrived late last night. Someone else looking for a mate, like Carmine.

"Just tired." I offered what I hoped was a genuine smile. "Weird dreams."

The newcomer, Bianca, shared a knowing nod with Linda. She had soft features, and buttercup-colored hair in two long braids. She was pale as the moon, and the simple blue dress she wore complimented her pear-shape beautifully.

"I remember the days before my first shift," she offered. "Strange indeed, but in my pack they say the stranger the dreams, the stronger the wolf."

Strength seemed to mean quite a lot to these people, if even other packs had sayings about it. "We'll see, I suppose."

Bianca slid a jar of jam toward me. "Eat, a full stomach might help you recover from your odd night."

"I'll be sure to make a big dinner for you tonight," Linda added.

My nerves were creeping up on me. Sleep wasn't easy, and I shifted between steamy images of Dom and nightmares of turning into a wolf. The dinner with Evander had been weird, and I hadn't had a chance to find Dom or Amelia after. But I couldn't tell these two that; all they had to know was that I was having dreams.

Yawning, I buttered the toast and slathered that bakeapple jam on it. I bit into it, and was reminded just how nice all the fresh, homemade foods were here. Then, the front door creaked open.

Waving goodbye to Bianca and Linda, I grabbed my toast and headed for the front door in time to find Carmine and Jerod walking into the house.

"June!" Carmine said. "There you are. I haven't seen you in days."

"You've been otherwise occupied, love," Jerod said.

Carmine's grin turned from excited to wicked as she leaned over and whispered something French in Jerod's ear. Then she reached behind him and squeezed his backside.

"Whoa there, Carmine," I said. "What brings you out of your love den? Since you're so obviously not done with this honeymoon phase yet."

She chuckled and turned her attention back to me. "We have to go be within a mile or so of the training grounds so Amelia can keep working today."

"Why so close?" I asked.

"Complications with our entanglement," Jerod explained. "Any farther and it physically hurts."

I winced. "Oof."

"Care to join us?" Carmine asked.

"That would be great," I said.

"Is that your breakfast?" Carmine asked, pointing to the toast. I nodded. "Want some?"

"No, but thank you. Can you eat on the way? We have to get moving."

"Sure, let's go." I took a big bite of toast and walked out the front door, closing it behind me.

"Oh, June," Jerod said, "I have to thank you for the things you got from town. I knew you probably wouldn't be able to get it all, but thanks for what you did find."

"You're welcome." I shrugged. "Some of that list was warlock things. Am I right?"

"Yes, indeed," Jerod said. "But let's just keep that between us, shall we?"

I nodded, looking around to make sure we were far away from prying ears. "Did you look at that wax I gave Carmine?"

Jerod's face turned serious. "I did. I won't speak on any theories I have until I've confirmed a few things, but those candles are definitely suspicious. I'll update you when I have an answer."

"You're so clever, Jerod," Carmine said as she reached out to hold his hand. "I can't wait to take you home."

We walked up the path to the main road and then turned like we were going to the pack house, only after Doc's place we took a sharp right and went over the crest of the hill and down into some trees.

"What were you doing traveling with a group of rogue wolves, and what was happening to you and Amelia?"

"We were barely acquaintances. Allies, I suppose." He set his brown eyes on me. "We happened to be in Seattle not too long ago when a supernatural battle broke out."

My eyes widened. "In Seattle? Nothing like that has been on the news, and that would have spread like wildfire."

Jerod chuckled. "As if the humans would know what was going on. Seattle in particular is a city under a tight leash. Nothing supernatural leaks through the long-reaching grasp of the fae courts there."

"Fae?" I asked.

"You might know them as faeries," Carmine chimed in. "But not tiny little nice ones. Pretty chaotic beings, if you ask me. Never strike a deal with them, never thank one."

"Oh. But still, a battle? Someone must have seen something," I said.

Jerod clicked his tongue. "June, June, June. You're not taking enough magic into account. I believe it was decided they would go with a gas leak. Sound familiar?"

I took in a sharp breath. Yes, the gas leak. The explosion that took out an entire shopping plaza, and not a small one.

"Amelia and I were fighting for the same side. I was performing a remarkably impressive spell when she was quite literally thrown into it," Jerod explained. "Then the usual sob story happened. Her blood mixed with mine, a behemoth demon took out nine days of pain as payment on our souls, and here we are! All caught up now?"

"You're serious?" I asked, as sounds of training wolves echoed from where we entered the woods. Grunting, growling, biting, large things hitting each other.

The trees thinned and the field opened up. A huge space, with odd items scattered about. A giant boulder in the center. Huge logs sat on their sides in one part of the field. Another part held more rocks, though not nearly as big as the boulder in the middle. And there were wolves in various states of shift everywhere. Wolves shoved logs back and forth. Men and women, or males and females,

I guess, lifted huge rocks and tossed them to each other in a line. My head tried to tell me I was seeing the impossible, and for a human, it would have been. But my eyes saw it all nonetheless.

I looked toward the far side of the field, where I recognized Amelia, Aaron, Jack, and Carson stripping next to an already naked Smokey.

"This is our stop," Jerod said. "I'll be close-*ish*. I'm not getting dirty with a bunch of wolves."

"What about this wolf?" Carmine gave him a sly grin.

Jerod's face changed from mild boredom to mischievous. "I suppose I could be persuaded."

Carmine leaned in and kissed him. Jerod immediately went for a handful of ass and Carmine nearly knocked him over with her aggressive affection.

"You guys invited me to come here with you, you know," I mused.

But they were already too far gone, and Jerod's shirt was half off, much to his surprise and Carmine's delight.

I stepped over them, walking into the light of the field and slowly following the perimeter so I didn't get in anyone's way.

It was fascinating to see the pack warriors working on their bodies. A little something inside me stirred. An interest. A curiosity. I suddenly wanted to know more about my fellow wolves, and I wondered if I was going to be a warrior. The possibilities were all wide open for a few more days.

I slowed my walking, almost in a trance as I watched the wolves move. For the most part the wolves in Moonpeak were different tones of gray, but there were a few other colors scattered about. A few different browns. Some with black or white fur mixed in. It fascinated me. More now than it had when I first arrived.

I sighed and snapped out of it. I kept walking toward Smokey and the others. To my surprise, someone else had joined them while I was spacing out—Dom.

I was surprised to see him up and around. My feet knew what to do, though, and I took a step in his direction. The moment I did, Dom's back straightened and some instinct turned him toward me. I met his gaze and took in a sharp breath. His eyes were a vivid yellow. They transfixed me.

Dom walked toward me, and I rubbed my eyes. I looked around to see if anyone else was facing my way. There, a male at the logs. His eyes were brown. No, yellow? I turned another direction. Another male, his eyes were . . . yellow. My lips parted in disbelief.

"June, what's wrong?" Dom asked softly. In my shock, he had managed to walk right up to me.

"Dom. I—" I looked around the field at a few more faces and then back up to him. "Dom, have your eyes always been yellow?"

His face crinkled in amusement, and he let out a soft laugh. "All wolves have yellow eyes. Are you now just seeing them?"

"I could have sworn you all had normal eye colors. I mean, once or twice I'll admit I thought the light was playing tricks on me, but mostly they've been normal colors."

"Oh?" Dom smirked. "And what color were mine?"

A warm hazelnut shade, darker at the edges and inviting enough to stare into for however long my heart could take it.

"Brown."

"Huh. I'll keep that in mind. I think I put gray on my driver's license," he said.

"All wolves have yellow eyes?"

Dom nodded. "You will, too, in a couple of days. Your wolf must be getting close. Have you felt it? Some instincts that maybe you're having a hard time ignoring."

"Yeah, maybe I have." Closing my eyes and taking a deep

breath, trying to ease my distraction. "No, never mind this stuff, I have to talk to you about Naomi."

His expression darkened. "She's in the pack house?"

"I saw her, at dinner. There's something going on with her. Evander might be doing something to her. She believes . . ." The promise she wanted from me, to keep quiet, crossed my mind for about five seconds before I decided her safety was more important than a promise to a stranger. "Something's off. She's fighting it, hard, but she's getting some kind of bond vibes from him. And I'm not sure what's going on with her, but drugs or something else is messing up her focus."

"That bastard," Dom growled. "Is she okay physically? Has he hurt her?"

"No, he's just messing with her head somehow. Do we need to make a move right now?"

"I wish we could, but no." His jaw ticked. "He's suspicious as fuck. Strange rogue attacks, like the ones from before, they were happening back then too. Back before Alpha Liam was challenged by Evander. And now, if he's doing something to Naomi, something must be going on. We're missing something, but I don't know what it is yet."

He continued, "Thanks, New Bite. I owe you for this. I'll talk to Amelia and the others later so we can try to piece this together."

"Yeah, of course." I looked away, scratching an itch on my arm and scanning the field around us. "So, you were working out?"

"Yes. The warriors come here regularly, but anyone is welcome as long as they don't get in the way. Interested in a run around the outer track?" Dom teased.

"Ha-ha, very funny," I said, though my eyes followed the worn dirt ring around the field. "And what are you doing out here, anyway? You should still be resting."

"It's fine, I'm not here to train, just to watch. Come on, let's get a seat and see what Smokey puts Amelia and the others through. It will be fun."

As I followed Dom the rest of the way around the field, I could see Smokey talking to the others. He was pointing to the logs and saying something or other to Jack and Aaron when we got close. When we were near enough to take a seat in some of the remaining grass by the tree line, Smokey turned around.

"Well, hello, there, girlie. You here for some training?" he asked.

I put my hands up in front of me. "No way, I came along with Carmine and Jerod. I'll just watch."

"Hm." Smokey scratched his chin. "I've wanted to see what that Carmine can do. Where is she?"

Amelia looked over, a sour expression on her face. "They're fucking."

I looked at her, surprised. "How did you know?"

She grunted. "This soul-tangling thing is not completely unlike a mating bond, apparently, because I can feel *everything* they're doing through their ownbond. That Carmine has strong and frequent urges. It's been a glorious week."

Jack snorted a laugh.

"Oh my god," I said, my face flushing. "They've been going at it—"

"Nonstop, I *know*," Amelia grumbled. "Smokey, give me my next damn exercise, will you?"

Smokey gave her a wicked grin. "To the rock with you."

Amelia stripped her clothes and shifted. Then Smokey looked me over again, staring at my legs in particular. "You look like a runner. You a runner, New Bite?"

I looked down at my legs too. They weren't as big as they had been when I was in track, but they still had some size to them. Not to mention the thirty or so pounds I'd gained in the last few years since I stopped running.

"I used to but not anymore," I said.

Smokey grunted. "We'll see what your wolf has to say about that."

"Smokey, what do you want me to do?" Carson spoke up.

Smokey turned back to the wolves he was evidently training and pointed around the field again. "Aaron and Jack, you two at the logs for some back and forth. I don't want to see those weak-ass front legs again. Fix it. Carson, you need more laps, you were dragging behind yesterday and you better be ready to go until I say stop."

Carson made a face but nodded. "Yes, Smokey."

"Looks like he's here," Smokey mused. Dom smelled the air and his eyes widened.

"Who's here?" I asked.

Dom grinned. "An old friend from Salt Fur."

A huge wolf emerged from the woods. He had mostly white fur and blazing yellow eyes. Dom and the others weren't the only ones to notice him either; most of the heads in the field turned toward the wolf as he walked down the path and straight to Smokey. He was quite close before I took my eyes off of him and noticed the two smaller wolves that followed. One gray, the other a mix of gray and white. All three of them were carrying something in their mouths.

"Nathan, you made it," Smokey said.

The wolf barked a sort of laugh, definitely looking amused, and dropped the fabric from his mouth. The others did, too, then they shifted. Fur fading to skin, limbs rearranging themselves. And then we had three more naked bodies in the field, before the two men and one woman pulled on some loose athletic clothes.

The big wolf was a total jock type. Blond, tan, dimples, biceps the size of a cantaloupe, the whole nine yards. The girl had cropped black hair, light-brown skin, enviable cheekbones, and a smile that lit up her face. She caught me looking at her and winked. And finally, the last one was a bored-looking teenager. Permanent frown, messy brown hair, and obviously uninterested in whatever they were doing here.

"Smokey, you old bastard," Nathan said, and pulled him into a hug.

"Thanks for coming, Nate," Smokey said.

"My pleasure." Nathan turned to Dom and pulled him into a hug as well. "As soon as you said I'd get to kick this guy's ass, I was in."

Dom laughed and slapped Nathan on the back as they hugged. "Is that what you're doing here? I thought you didn't leave Salt Fur."

Nathan chuckled and let Dom go, looking around. "This place hasn't changed a bit."

"You don't need all that fancy shit you got back home," Smokey said. "As long as what you're lifting is heavy, you'll gain muscle."

Dom shook his head as Nathan chuckled.

"Same old Smokey," he said. "Guys, this is Anna and Matt. My future beta, and my little cousin."

At the mention of a beta, Dom looked at Anna with assessing eyes. She did the same. While they were doing that, Nathan turned his attention to me.

"Oh, um. I'm June," I said. "Nice to meet you."

"You smell interesting," Nathan said, looking at me with confusion on his face. Dom shifted slightly toward me, crossing his arms.

"She's new bite," Smokey said. "Might turn this moon. Who knows."

"Ah." Nathan nodded. "That makes sense. Nice to meet you, June. Good luck this week."

"Thanks," I mumbled.

"Whelp," Smokey said, clapping his hands. "Let's get started. Amelia! Get over here."

We looked at where the wolf was ramming herself against the boulder in the center of the field. She turned our way and visibly sighed as she stopped what she was doing and walked toward us.

Dom chuckled, pulling me aside and sitting down by the trees.

"Let's watch the show," Dom murmured. "I'm sure this will be an enlightening experience for you."

I had barely sat down when Smokey leaned over and told Nathan something. Nathan nodded and charged at Amelia, still in his human form.

I gasped as I watched Amelia pick up speed, seeing what he was doing. They collided, and Nathan's muscles bunched impressively as he rammed into the big gray wolf in front of him and slammed her on her side.

"Nathan's an alpha's son, he'll be in his father's shoes pretty soon," Dom said.

I turned to Dom, alarmed. "He's going to have to kill his dad?"

"What?" Dom's brows furrowed. "Oh, no, nothing like how Evander came here.

"It's not always like that. If it's an alpha just handing off the title to their kid, it's different. Of course, if the pack doesn't think the kid can take over and be a good alpha, you can still have someone else step in and challenge it, but that's not a common occurrence. In Nathan's case, there will be a big celebration and he'll fight his dad, but not to the death, then there's a cake."

I snorted a laugh. "What an anticlimactic way to end that sentence."

Dom shrugged. "Who doesn't like cake?"

The culture of this place was fascinating. On the surface the strength and aggression were frightening at first, but I'd come to view them all as athletes of sorts. They weren't here to hurt each other, not really. Other than that business of overthrowing an alpha, I guess.

A hand brushed mine, and I turned to Dom. "You're going to do great at the shift, I know it."

"How can you be so sure?" My own stomach had turned more than once thinking about it, but all that talk of getting in my runner's headspace went a long way to making me feel like I had some control.

"Instincts? I've been in some bad business for a long time, and you either learn to read people or you get in a lot of bad situations because of it."

"You don't talk much about it," I said softly. "The things you did before. I get that you worked for Apollo, and he was some kind of evil in the world. You were on that drug, and you left Moonpeak to get away from Evander."

"We left to get stronger," he insisted, then eased his tone. "We were always going to come back, but we knew we were just kids. If Alpha Liam could be killed by Evander. If my dad, the warriors, everyone else we looked up to could be killed so easily, we needed time, age, and skills that weren't on our side back then."

"I did a lot of shit I'm not proud of." He turned to meet my gaze. "We killed people. Not humans, but other creatures out there that were in the same business as Apollo. Theft, drugs, territory wars, we did his bidding for all of it."

"And you liked it?" I asked, caution tightening my throat.

He was quiet for a long time before answering. "No, but we saw it as necessary. I'm not sure if it was, not sure if it was the right way to get what we wanted, but here we are."

"You don't want to go back down that path," I observed.

"No," he said. "Never again."

I reached over and wrapped my fingers around his, wanting to comfort him even just a little. "My grandad didn't talk much about his time in the navy, but he did say one thing that I think he'd want you to hear right now."

Dom's brows lowered. "And what's that?"

"It's easy to judge who you were and what you did before, but it's who you are going forward that matters the most." I squeezed his fingers a little tighter. "He'd sum it up by saying everyone loved the guy who climbed uphill, 'cause not everyone can keep that up for long."

"How poetic," Dom said after a while.

"He was a romantic at heart, that's for sure."

"Climb uphill, huh?" Dom murmured.

Smack. I jumped where I sat, then looked over to see Amelia with her teeth sunk deep into Nathan's shoulder. He grunted and lifted her again, smacking her down onto her back.

"Oof." I cringed.

"Welcome to wolfhood." Dom chuckled.

I watched, engrossed in the sights before me. Anna and Matt both took part, taking turns with the exercises and running with Jack, Aaron, and Carson. As for Nathan, his attention was wholly on Amelia, and for the rest of the day, I watched Nathan the man, and then Nathan the wolf, beat Amelia six ways from Sunday.

Enlightening indeed.

CHAPTER TWENTY-SIX

JUNE

"What is that for?" I asked. I was sitting at the table in the kitchen eating a late breakfast of oatmeal and sausage links with Hannah. Linda held up a piece of little black lingerie.

"It's a robe, dear. It's so you won't be uncomfortable in your nudity before the shift." Linda gave me a warm smile and laid the garment over the back of an empty chair.

"I will take this opportunity to go for a walk." Bianca was dressed in a green jumper today that made her braids pop. She had finished her breakfast as I came downstairs, greeted by Linda and the robe, if you could call it that for how short it was.

"Have fun, dear," Linda said as she took Bianca's plate and began to rinse it in the sink.

The newest visitor stopped by me just long enough to pat my back. "Your comfort is priority. Your wolf will have an easier time coming out if you have fewer worries distracting you."

Offering her a weak smile, I nodded. "Thanks."

She gave my back one more pat before leaving through the front door, and I turned back to eye the garment.

"Lots of wolves wear them around," Hannah said, then took another bite of food. "Oo ont ee vee ony one."

"Don't talk with your mouth full," Linda scolded.

Hannah swallowed. "Sorry. I said that you won't be the only one."

My mouth was a grim line as I nodded. "Is it required?"

"Goodness, no, June." Linda waved a hand at me. "If you're comfortable enough, full nudity is acceptable even inside the village after dinner tonight."

I choked on my food. Hannah moved to get me a glass of water. "I didn't mean that! I meant, do I have to use the robe or can I go in my normal clothes?"

Bruce came into the room, finishing the last button by the collar of his shirt. "You'll want the robe. You'll rip your other clothes if you wear them. Especially in your first shift attempt."

I sighed, resigning myself to the robe on the chair.

"Take the robe for now and you can decide later," Linda said, placing a hand on my shoulder. "It's all up to you, of course, but the wolves here really won't be looking at your body. We're all going to be too excited for the moonrise."

"About nine or nine thirty this time," Bruce said. "But you'll start feeling it at dinner."

"You might feel it before that," Linda said. "Just be ready to meet your wolf and don't resist her."

"So, what can I expect?" This was the question everyone had avoided answering all week.

"Let's start with the in-between. What did you picture a werewolf was before you knew we were real?"

"A hairy out-of-control wolf-man in tattered jeans, I guess. The stuff from movies mostly."

Linda nodded. "There's a reason those rumors started, that's the in-between of the first shift. Or at least, one possibility if you start shifting and lose control."

My heart nearly stopped. "Are you kidding me?"

"It's less common." Linda put her hands up in front of her. "But it's not out of the question, so I'm giving you fair warning. But that's what the pack is for, there will be a volunteer crew hanging around to intercept anyone who loses control their first shift."

"What is the shift itself like?"

Linda sighed, exchanging looks with Bruce. "It hurts," he admitted.

"I won't lie to you. Your body will grow a new set of everything. Old skin will peel away, making room for new skin that will shift to fur easier from now on. Bones will rearrange, that sort of thing. It's an important process, but the first time is far from comfortable."

My head was reeling, trying to picture it. Trying to find something else that contorted the body to compare it to. "It sounds harder than giving birth."

Linda shrugged, not denying it. "I know it sounds scary, and difficult, and in many ways it is. But if you get out there and trust your wolf, listen to her, you'll be just fine."

"You will," Hannah chimed in. "I swear it's not as scary after you start, it just hurts. But your wolf! Aren't you excited to feel her?"

"I don't know," I admitted. "What if I panic, or resist?"

"Don't," Bruce offered. "Let it happen. Be kind to your wolf, don't push her away. Remember, she's going through this for the first time too."

Now that was something I hadn't considered. Everyone spoke about these inner wolves as though they were a separate thing, and maybe they were. Maybe I couldn't possibly understand it until it happened to me. At least now I wasn't going in blind, whatever may come. I scraped the last of my oatmeal from the bottom of my bowl and scooped it into my mouth. I scooted my chair out and rinsed my dishes in the sink.

"Feel free to roam the village today as you begin to feel your wolf come out," Linda said as I made my way out of the kitchen. "All the trackers and any wolves that don't keep to the village much will be coming in today, so you might see new faces."

I grabbed the robe and went upstairs to dump it on my bed. Maybe I really would wear it, who knew. From what I gathered, I'd be focused on a lot more than just my modesty tonight.

The village was full of energy today. Children played at full speed, feeling the moon even though they wouldn't shift tonight. The teenagers who weren't shifting would be watching the little ones while their parents took part in the run, which wasn't optional. Some kids would gather at one of the larger houses in town to play games until they fell asleep too. Parents with a newborn walked down the main street, showering her with kisses as they stopped to talk to the other wolves who were outside. It felt more like a true pack today than it had even at the picnic gathering.

I took a deep breath and stretched my legs. I felt like running. Like, for real running. Could I do it or would my leg just fail me again? Knowing what was coming tonight, I didn't have the guts to try. Instead, I fast walked, heading from the village toward the training field. If the wolves in town were this hyped up, I could only imagine what the more aggressive ones were doing down there.

But what started as a casual walk ended abruptly as something small, yet alarming, crossed my path.

I screamed as a hideous . . . British Bulldog? . . . crossed my path. It drooled some orange substance that looked like it was burning the ground it fell on. The thing was red, and had two stubby little tails and spikes all over its body.

It caught a grasshopper in its mouth, but the thing popped and burst into flames.

"Ferdinand!" Jerod ran over, scolding the . . . dog. "I told you not to catch them, just find them."

"What is that thing?" I asked, backing away.

Jerod's innocent smile turned into a wide grin. "You can see him? Don't worry, he's as harmless as a kitten."

Ferdinand burped up a little fire, a molten string of spittle sinking slowly from his mouth to the ground.

"Mostly, anyway. He's a demon dog, and my familiar," Jerod explained.

"You didn't have that thing in the car, I'd remember it," I said.

"I summoned him last night. I was missing some components to do so before. Carmine finds him delightful," Jerod said.

"Delightful, right. Hey, Jerod, can I ask you a question about this mate stuff?" I asked.

"Ask away."

"So, you're completely comfortable with it? I mean, you didn't know Carmine before she ran into the cabin and fought with Amelia," I said.

Jerod nodded slowly, giving Ferdinand one last scratch behind the ears before standing to face me with discernment. "I have seen the mating bond take many forms over the years. Wolves, fae, other shifters, even some demons. I'm not sure if I believe in fate, but after the things I've seen and done I can't disbelieve it either. As for Carmine, I find her passion infectious and her drive to get what she wants matches my own. I'm not ready to jump in yet and accept her bite, but why fight a fated match when we could see where it leads?"

Why fight it, huh?

"Okay, try this. Picture the hottest person you've ever been attracted to. You like their personality, you can tell right away you'd get along and understand each other, and they don't pressure you into anything," Jerod said.

Dom surfaced immediately to the forefront of my mind, and I bit the inside of my cheek.

"If someone like that shows up in front of you, why wouldn't you give that a chance?" he asked. "Carmine comes on strong, but, I assure you, no one makes Jerod Chang do a damn thing he doesn't want to do. If I have any advice for you, it would be to allow yourself to take chances. As long as you don't make any premature permanent decisions, you would probably thoroughly enjoy someone who is meant to be with you."

Meant to be with. It felt good to have another person tell me I didn't have to commit to anything I wasn't ready for, especially another nonwolf. His advice made sense, too, even if letting go and taking chances wasn't one of my strengths. Maybe, if this mate thing did happen to me, I could give it a tiny little chance. Just a little one. "Thanks, Jerod. That makes a lot of sense."

"I usually do," he said.

"Humble too," I teased. "So, what are you doing out here anyway?"

"I've got Ferdinand here wrangling up grasshoppers for me to catch. If I can't buy them, I need to get them the old-fashioned way."

"You wanted a pound of dried grasshoppers," I said. "What was that for again?"

"I promise you, you don't want to know," Jerod said, clapping his hands with a smile. "Do you want to help me catch them?"

"Uh, you're not really selling me on it." I looked down at the dog and took another step back as he began to drool again.

"Suit yourself." Jerod shrugged. "Amelia's been helping me gather ingredients to quicken our bindings. With she and Carmine preoccupied with the upcoming run, I'm on my own."

"You know what? I'll help you catch those grasshoppers. It will help take my mind off of tonight for a while," I said.

"Splendid." Jerod chuckled. "I'm keeping them in this container as we get them. I'll set it here and you can just add yours to what I already have."

I eyed the plastic box he set in the grass. "You don't have many yet."

"No, which is why I very much welcome the assistance. I'll have you know I'm a powerful man, June. I'd owe you a favor for this."

"No worries," I said. "I don't want to tangle with magic. I just want to survive tonight."

"Well, thanks all the same, then," Jerod mused. "All right then, Ferdinand! More grasshoppers please."

Ferdinand barked, and I shivered, as it sounded less like a dog and more like a screaming, tortured soul. Demon dog indeed. But as soon as he was done making that awful sound, Ferdinand jumped around in the grass, sniffing and yipping as little pops of fire went off in a random pattern around him. With each tiny hell portal came a grasshopper, displaced from wherever else around here they had been hopping around in ignorant bliss before being magically transported for capture. The ones that didn't catch fire from their unfortunate method of travel were the ones we went after.

A good distraction for a pending shift.

So for the next several hours I learned a little about warlocks, and a lot about how to catch grasshoppers.

CHAPTER TWENTY-SEVEN

JUNE

"You can do this, girlie." Smokey spoke low enough that the entire clearing couldn't hear him, though I knew many nearby still could.

I had opted for the black robe, tied tight around my middle.

We stood on the training field, where I couldn't go crazy in the middle of the village while I was half shifted. Smokey, naked as the day he was born, was imparting a little wolfish advice. A couple of teenagers were hanging around in case they started their shift too. So here I stood, with a couple of sixteen-year-old boys, ready to get naked and turn into a rabid wolf-woman. Fantastic.

"You feel her, don't you?" Smokey asked. "You feel her in there."

"I feel something," I said, my nerves very clearly making it into my voice. "She's pacing."

"Yes, b'y. She's gearing up to push her way out of you. Let her. Embrace it. It's gonna hurt like a bitch, though," Smokey said.

I rolled my eyes. "Yeah, so I keep hearing, thank you."

"Now, I don't wanna scare you, but we've got you kids down here for a reason," Smokey said a little louder, including the teenagers in his pep talk now. "If you get a little too rowdy, we've got warriors who will be trading off all night so this field will be guarded. Can't let you bust out of here and tear shit up, you hear? We'll let you out of here only if you've got control over yourself."

"Yes, Smokey," we said in tandem.

It was getting dark here at the training field, and the moon was going to rise soon. Yellow eyes peered at us through the trees. I shouldn't have been able to see them as clearly as I did, but the wolf coming out in me was changing my once completely normal human eyes.

It was happening. Finally happening, after weeks of agonizing over it.

"Now, I'll be shifting soon, and I can't do a damn thing about it," Smokey said. "So I can't talk to you unless you get that wolf out of ya and figure out how to mind link me. It ain't that hard, but some wolves just come out stupid. You'll have to figure it out on your own or wait 'til the moon releases us from her grasp in a few hours."

The view of the sky was so vivid here, nothing like back in Seattle. And the moon would be here all too soon.

My palms itched and I was growing increasingly warm under my skin, as though I was basking in a summer sunlight that wasn't there. I looked around to see the other two were uncomfortable as well, but they didn't seem as bothered by it.

A howl in the distance. One started, then another and another. I fidgeted with the tie of my robe. Smokey looked off in that direction and nodded.

"That'll be the run starting. Alpha will lead and the pack will follow through the mountains." He met my gaze head-on. "You can join 'em if you finish your shift this time. If you don't . . ."

The intense howls were either louder than normal or my ears were changing.

"All right, kids, sit by one of the posts here and we'll tether you down." Smokey jerked his head toward a set of logs set vertically in the ground, which more than likely were trees with the limbs hacked off. They were definitely bigger around than I was.

"We're getting tied up?" I asked.

"Not really. The logs will give you something to hold on to and a distraction for the beast if it comes out. Don't want anyone running off without supervision in that state, and this will buy those of us watching you enough time to get in here."

The warriors around the edges of the training field were keeping some distance, giving us some space. But still watching.

"Come on over and let's get you all situated," Smokey said.

We each stood by a post, but he made sure we were nice and spread out from each other. My throat was dry and my skin itchy. While I waited, someone brought over bowls of water and placed them within arm's reach of the potential shifters.

"Moon's blessings to you tonight," the water-carrier offered. "We'll be watching, and singing for your journey."

Smokey took some rope and looped it a couple of times around each of the teenagers. It was nice and loose, but it wouldn't be if they shifted. He came to me last, doing the same for me. When he was done winding it around me and the post, and was tying the ends together, he looked into my eyes and spoke low to me. Behind him, I could hear the low tones of singing from the tree line where the wolves watching us were sitting.

"You've got a big one in ya. I wasn't sure before but tonight I am. Let her do what she wants. Don't you dare fight her, June." Smokey knotted the rope and turned away.

The old wolf walked away, looked up at the sky, and crossed his arms. "Okay, kids, this is it. Get comfortable for the long haul."

Then he walked away to be near the warriors in the trees.

I took in slow breaths and let them back out again. Mind on the goal, push through. Just like Dom told me, I tried to put my focus into it like I used to before a big run. I sat down—something told me to save my energy. I leaned against the post and adjusted the thick rope in my lap.

Time wore on. I was sure it felt longer for me than for the wolves out there running. They had all shifted and were following Evander through the mountains. I could hear them. And the warriors here watching us, they were antsy.

As the sun finally collapsed for the day, one by one they shifted, and their singing dropped away to more wolfish sounds. Some before moonrise, some after. I could smell them in the trees. First they took off any clothes they were wearing. Then they shifted into fur and their bones rearranged themselves. A few grunts accompanied that process. And finally, when they were fully in their wolf bodies, they would pace around the clearing.

Smokey was last. I saw it on his face before he even said anything.

"Sorry, kids, my time is up. Good luck."

He finally shifted. Much faster than the others; from what I gathered shifting was harder the weaker you were. I prayed I was strong enough that this wouldn't hurt much, or maybe not be so uncomfortable every month.

With Smokey gone, or at least I couldn't talk to him anymore, my distress started to rise. My itchy palms grew unbearable, and the tips of my fingers had an uncomfortable prickling feeling in them. I could both feel and hear my heartbeat rising, which was alarming in itself.

In through the nose, out through the mouth. Breathe, focus, reach for the goal.

A mild, burning sensation met my skin down my back. I distracted myself by rubbing my itchy palms on the rough rope around my middle.

As the moon became more clear my discomfort intensified tenfold. I had to stand. I had to strain against something. I turned to face the pole I was tied to and pushed against it, trying to strain the muscles in my limbs because when they weren't being stretched, they were spasming.

My breath was heavy as I watched the moon overhead, and then the first wave of pain began.

I cried out as a bone in my foot snapped. The rope caught me as I fell to the ground. I panted, crying out as the bone shifted. The broken pieces elongated and fused in a new direction, more like a wolf's paw.

Smokey's wolf came out of the trees and sat some distance away. Watching.

A whimper escaped my throat as I looked at him helplessly. But he couldn't help me. No one could.

Don't fight it.

The echoes of all my new friends rang in my head. But how was I supposed to not fight this kind of pain? Tears streaked down my cheek as I gritted my teeth and twisted my body to better look at my leg.

I nearly threw up in my mouth, not ready to see a human's foot take such a shape. All my schooling was working against me as my own skeleton deformed itself.

Crack.

My shoulder tore itself apart as my bones moved on their own. I cried out again. It didn't take long for me to throw off my robe; I didn't want anything touching me if I could help it, and the rough bite of the rope was already enough to handle. I took a deep drink of water from the bowl while I still had hands to hold it.

A thin veil of sweat covered my forehead by the time my leg and shoulder had moved into the positions they were seeking. But as one joint would break or reposition, another was ready to do the same.

I sobbed as my fingers snapped. Knees. Elbows. Neck. Wrists. Everything had its turn. The sharp burn of my muscles as they pulled and bunched on their own was terrifying. To have my body jerked around without my consent was horrifying.

My breath came shallow and sharp, and once my body had contorted for the most part into a canine shape, my face began to turn. My teeth hurt as they reshaped. My jaw creaked as it elongated.

One of the worst moments was when long stretches of my skin would burst open like the seam of an overstuffed pillow. Stretched thin to bursting, and the muscles underneath would grow a new layer of skin and fur as I shed the bloody mess that was the old layer. Bruce had said something about growing new skin that was ready to adapt to fur since my old one wasn't. I hadn't known what he meant at the time, but I sure as hell did now.

The moon was now fully overhead. Every breath burned, and I writhed against the ropes. Just when I thought it wasn't going to hurt any worse, a horrid scream rang through my head as the fur began to prick through my skin.

No, not a scream, but a howl. There was a wolf here, and she was in agony.

She cried out, and I screamed. A disgusting sound as my throat wasn't entirely mine anymore, or even human.

Hurt.

I understood its feelings more than its words. I clawed against the ropes that bound us, growing tighter as I grew larger. I stood, or tried to, against the poll, in a grotesque shape of human and beast. The only part of me that hadn't cracked and broken yet was my actual spine, and it allowed me to sort of stand. Us, to stand. Because I felt everything she felt, and she felt me in return.

We were both panicking, I could tell that much. Somewhere in my reality, I began to struggle. Lash out. Since my hands now had claws, I dug them into the wood. Digging and pulling, hands and feet alike. My eyes roamed my body wildly, or at least what of it I could see. Black fur had sprouted and now pretty much covered everything. The same color and texture of my own human hair.

When the first joint in my spine broke, I lost it.

I howled. My first real howl. It was loud and gruff, and it bounced around the clearing. I thrashed on the post. A part of the ropes snapped as my claws hit it, and I was quickly surrounded by half a dozen wolves. Big gray wolves, a white-faced wolf that was Smokey, and a couple of brown ones. They were the warriors; I had seen them each train on these very fields. But somehow, they weren't nearly as intimidating as they had been even a day ago.

Smokey gave me a sharp barking sound. He wanted my attention. I was panting at this point and still struggling, but the rope was quickly falling away now that it had broken. I tried to look him in the eyes.

Rage!

The wolf and I needed space!

I thrashed, snapping my new jaws at the closest warriors as they growled and backed away slightly.

Smokey lunged forward and bit my hip while I wasn't looking.

I snarled, turning on him.

He growled, snapping his teeth at me.

Back off!

The wolf was pissed, and in a moment of realization, I agreed with her. Something clicked, we merged, I was her and she was me. While we shared this form, we would share our minds.

Back off!

She insisted again. But it wasn't them she was insisting to, it was us. I lowered my body; as painful as this existence was right now, I listened. This was it, this was doing what she wanted. It only took me a few agonizing hours to realize it.

Smokey seemed to pick up on my new, less hostile posture. He backed up and the warriors took their cues from him.

Now it was just me and the wolf, but we were still in ferocious pain. *Snap.* Another joint in our back popped, beginning to shape how it needed to be so we could finally run on all fours.

Pain!

It broke my heart. I was in pain, too, but I felt sorry for the wolf that was emerging. Somehow, she had already captured my heart.

We snarled and snapped, writhing on the ground by our post as we continued to have our back snap painfully.

Finally, I could feel the pain lessening. The merge was almost done. Smokey got in our face as we panted, lying there on the ground. He was looking at me so intently, but I couldn't figure out what he wanted.

Speak, the wolf said.

I don't know how!

She hummed her agreement. We were far too tired just now to try. Smokey wanted to mind link with me, but he would have to let me catch my breath first.

One of the warriors from the side of the field dragged something over. The leg section of a deer. It was raw, but it smelled delicious.

Smokey made room for the warrior to drag it over to me. The wolf and I were so hungry, the moment it landed in the dirt we began to gobble it up. Tendons snapped between my teeth. Bones snapped. Blood coated my mouth by the time we were done.

When we were done eating, I found myself licking the blood around my lips and watching Smokey.

Better? he asked.

I heard him! He was in my head. If I hadn't been warned about this, I wouldn't have believed it. But there he was, talking in my own mind.

Y . . . es, I tried. I spoke!

My wolf was elated. She pushed us up on our paws for the first time. Shaky as we were, I tried to coordinate with her to take our first step.

Good, walk a little more. You're doin' okay, kid, Smokey encouraged me.

I took a step. And another. At first, I was tangling our legs up with my human one leg, two leg mentality of walking, but soon enough she set us straight. I kept looking down at our shiny black coat, our long wolf legs, the sharp claws at the end of our limbs.

All right, boys, announce our new wolf here, Smokey said.

I looked up at the warriors around me. They seemed . . . happy? I didn't know how I could tell, but my wolf surely knew wolf posturing enough that we were certain of it. They threw back their heads, Smokey, too, and howled to the skies.

We were excited. Yes! The pack needed to know about us. The pack! We needed to find our pack. Our whole pack.

I went up to Smokey, licked him once on the cheek, and then my wolf and I clumsily bounded off. Warriors from the field joined me. Smokey stayed to watch the others.

I wasn't going very fast, probably to be expected with these strange and fresh limbs. We were also pretty tired from everything. But surely I could make it to the running wolves, I could almost sense where they were, just a few short miles away.

The warriors on either side of me were full of energy.

Excitement. Yay! A new wolf. Their excitement only raised my excitement even more.

We were just coming out of the trees when a tasty smell hit my nose. Delicious!

Follow? I asked.

Follow! my wolf said.

And we bounded off toward the enticing smell. Me and my wolf.

Finally together, finally shifted.

CHAPTER TWENTY-EIGHT

DOM

Standing in the fresh air, surrounded by Moonpeak wolves ready to join together for the monthly community bonding was the closest I'd felt to home in a long time. The running was a good distraction from June. I told myself she was with Smokey, that she was strong and would push through her first shift just fine, but I couldn't keep still regardless. At training I was a mess, and Amelia was happy to hand me my ass for being distracted. But tonight, tonight was the pack run under the full moon, and that I could put some focus into.

Stretching my arms skyward, I watched the gathering excitement in the open field around me. Wolves I hadn't seen in years were now glancing my way with curiosity. I knew what they must think of me. Of all of us. But I wasn't about to let that get in the way of knowing them again. With each familiar face I approached I got a hug, a handshake, or a smile. Not one of them seemed to hold my absence against me, and a few of them nearly cracked my serious mask, telling me I looked just like my dad when he was younger.

It was almost too much to handle. I was so filled with love from this pack, and it shamed me more that I had left it to Evander. But, no matter my feelings, I had followed Amelia, and nothing I could do now would change that fact. She did get one thing right, though—I knew a hell of a lot more tricks now than I would have if I had stayed in the mountain range.

"What's up with you tonight?" Jack asked, and I turned to see he was talking to Amelia, who was on the edge of the field.

"Everything all right?"

"Yeah," she said absently, curling and uncurling her fingers. She was antsy. "Yeah, but I have an off feeling. I don't see Naomi yet, maybe that's it."

"We'll find her," I said. "We already know she's under that roof with Evander. But tonight is the full moon, she's got to come out to run, and we can see what June was talking about."

"Dom's right," Carson offered, taking one of Amelia's hands long enough to give it a reassuring squeeze. "We'll find her. June said she's healthy, we can work with that."

"You're right." She relented, rolling back her shoulders and looking up at the sky. "But I still feel off tonight."

"Maybe it's the bond with the warlock?" Aaron offered, joining us at the edge of the gathering. The Blightfang now together for the first run back in Moonpeak.

She made a face. "Don't remind me, I'm going to have to do all my running close by. But no, I don't think that's it."

The chatter in the clearing died down as people noticed Evander coming from the pack house, already in his fur, with Naomi's wolf walking beside him.

"She's here!" Carson said, taking several steps forward before I caught his wrist.

"Stop," I said, my heart pounding. Naomi, after all this time.

She was a sister to me, just as much as Amelia was. She seemed steady on her feet; she didn't look as though she'd been skipping meals or anything. It was just as June said, physically she was fine.

"Why?" Carson glared at me. "She's right there!"

"Don't make a scene right at the run," I said. "We'll get close to her while the pack is out in the mountains and try to talk to her then. Is that good with you, Amelia?"

We turned to her for confirmation, but her expression was unreadable.

"Amelia?" Aaron asked.

She shook her head. "I finally find her, and I can't make my mind focus on her at all."

"What do you mean?" I frowned, looking between Naomi in the distance and Amelia right by my side.

"Something's . . ." Amelia curled and uncurled her fingers again, then her eyes shot to mine. "You have to make sure we have contact with Naomi tonight. I don't feel right, something is going on and I can't let it interfere with us getting to her."

"I got it," I said, and Aaron held out an arm.

"No, I've got it." He looked pointedly between me and Amelia. "Evander will be watching you both closely, I can get in close enough to check on her. Dom, stay with Amelia, I'm worried."

She scoffed, snapping out of her daze long enough to be offended. "I don't need a babysitter."

"You're stuck with me anyway." I slung an arm over her shoulders as she rolled her eyes, but I didn't miss those curling and uncurling fingers again. "It's all right, I'll be with you for as long as you need me."

She managed a nod, then Evander's sharp howl caught our attention. A glance up at the night sky told me the moon was rising and the run could begin. I shifted, and so did everyone else with varying stages of speed. Once Moonpeak was wearing fur and fangs, Evander howled again, and we were off.

My heart leaped. Claws to the earth, I was more than happy to run with the pack. Bodies around me, running together under the moonlight as one pack. I was just one piece of a whole, and it was blissful.

At this point, even Amelia was doing better now that she had her fur on, and I was relieved to see it, though her ears and nose kept jerking south, as though something entirely too interesting was distracting her.

When it was time to leave the trees right around the village, I thought Amelia was splitting off so as to not stray from Jerod. When she shot like a bat out of hell straight for a white dot at the far end of the houses, I slowed down.

We got it. Make sure she's okay if you need to, Aaron said.

I jerked my head his way, nodded, then trailed Amelia. The white dot that seemed to be her target was a wolf. Not a wolf I knew, but if they were wandering around Moonpeak, then they had permission to be here, or Smokey would have been all over them. Amelia tore through town, and I was trying to stay on her heels when I saw it all unfold.

Amelia, a big gray wolf in her own right as an alpha's child, towered over this other wolf. I thought it was a kid at first, until I got close enough to sense that it was a full-grown female. Despite her size, she had the aura of power befitting at least a beta wolf, and she was frozen in Amelia's path.

What the hell is happening? I asked, but Amelia immediately shut me out. I was not welcome in her head.

Amelia bounded toward the smaller wolf, stopping right in front of her. They stared at each other before she circled the smaller female. When Amelia lifted her head and howled, my reality shifted.

Amelia made the mating call, and she announced her claim before the whole of Moonpeak as the new wolf joined her.

It explained everything. Amelia's weird feeling, the way she was distracted in this direction. When the wolves began to get more . . . *exploratory*, I knew it was time to bow out.

I ran back to the rest of the pack, my mind reeling. Amelia, mated. Of course it was always possible, but after living among so many other supernatural beings we hadn't put much faith in finding our own mates. It was far too unlikely to be another kind of shifter or a human or anything else out there. But, despite this catching me off guard, I was beyond happy for her. A little envious, but happy. A mate for Amelia meant a luna for Moonpeak once she claimed her place and killed Evander. It would be good news for everyone.

Evander ran the pack down from the village and then up the side of the neighboring mountain, and it wasn't hard to catch up to them. Aaron, Jack, and Carson had questions about the howl, and once I'd confirmed Amelia's mate, I could all but feel the excitement among us. Finally something good had happened to one of us. It had been a long damn time coming.

For a good hour Evander zigzagged us around the gorgeous scenery, light filtering through the leaves overhead as we crossed into forests and the full glow of the moon washed over us when we were in the open. I noted when Aaron began to draw closer to the front to where Naomi was. Good, hopefully he would learn something useful about how to help Naomi tomorrow.

The moon was bright. Smells tickled my nose the game that had dared to stray into Moonpeak lands. Unsuspecting rabbits, deer, and a few other creatures that had crossed this trail earlier in the day. My stomach growled. Nathan and Anna didn't look any better off. We were all ready for the moment Evander would release the pack to the hunt.

In the meantime, I ran with Jack, nudging him off balance and laughing when he almost fell over. I ran with Carson, a bit of a chase through the trees as he tried to keep up with me. I ran with Nathan and Anna as we taunted each other, leaping in each other's way and moving at the last minute. It was glorious.

Evander finally slowed the pace, easing the run for the weak and elderly, the ones that didn't have the same stamina as the alphas, betas, warriors, and trackers among us. It had been hours. Evander brought us to a stop by a crystal clear stream. The pack was happy to take a short break, lapping up water and sniffing around.

I lay on my belly by the stream, drinking my fill, and then enjoying the feel of the cool grass under me. Nathan and Anna did the same.

My ears perked up at a distant sound. The cheerful howling of welcome. A new wolf was born tonight.

Moonpeak! Evander called to all of us. *We welcome a new wolf.*

Suddenly, we were all on our feet. The pack collectively threw back our heads and howled the welcome.

Could it be June? Carson asked me.

I sent him the mental equivalent of a shrug. The answer would come soon enough since Smokey would be sending any new wolves on to meet the pack. But a part of me dreaded it. Did I want it to be June? Did I want something to happen if it was?

I eyed Amelia's large gray wolf, curled around the smaller white one. What was it like? What was Amelia feeling? And how could this affect our plans?

Moonpeak, Evander called, distracting me. *Make your way to the village at your leisure. The moon will release us soon.*

I shook out my fur, turning to Nathan and Anna.

How about that dinner? I asked.

Yes! Anna cried, her wolf excited for the thrill of the hunt.

Go! Nathan said, and we three raced off.

Run, run faster!

The wolf in me was elated. We raced through the stream, splashing our fur as well as Nathan's and Anna's. Over the stream, down the slope, we wove and dodged around trees and rocks alike.

The chase was everything I needed it to be. Nathan had seriously grown as an alpha wolf, that was for sure, because he made me work hard for every inch I gained in front of him. There were times he was in the lead, too, and Anna was at our heels the whole way.

Meat!

My wolf and I raised our nose to the wind. Winding back toward the mountainside the village sat on was the enticing scent of a deer. A buck, specifically, and I shot to the side sharply, taking Nathan by surprise.

Hey! he called, but I ignored him. He turned onto my path but I had already gained several feet on him. That buck was mine!

The scent of it had brushed against low-growing plants. It left prints in the soft earth, and my wolf went wild with the sight of them and the smell of the prey.

Delicious! my wolf cried. *Smell!*

I wanted to chuckle at how excited my wolf was. It was like we were just pups again. But the scent was enticing. Very enticing.

And very much not a buck.

The beast we had been hunting was ahead. The buck saw the running wolves and bolted. I pressed forward, but the new smell was distracting.

I was nearly on the buck's haunches when Nathan shoved me aside, causing me to nearly tip over while running at full speed.

Get your head in the game, Dom! Nathan cried.

I shook my head and ran. We were on top of the buck in an instant, it didn't stand a chance.

But no sooner was our prey good and dead did my wolf practically drag our head into the air again.

Scent! Follow!

And with little other choice in the matter, I did.

I walked forward, trying to figure out what it even was. I could eat it. I could fuck it. Was it a wolf? What *was* that?

Dom? Nathan asked. *You okay, bud?*

I'm gonna eat the liver if you don't get back here, Anna teased.

You will not, you glutton, Nathan snapped.

I ignored them, and my walking quickly turned to running. Weaving through the trees, I pushed into the rocky open ground that would lead me to the village if I kept going. But I didn't even take one step into the clear ground before my world spun.

A stunning wolf. Shiny black coat, blazing yellow eyes. She stood tall with long legs and a narrow frame. Sleek. Elegant. My heart pounded even as I registered there was something familiar about her.

I took a deeper breath, tasting the scent on my tongue, and still making my way across the wide fields to her. And I knew now who it was. The registration of it hit my face a split second before it hit hers.

June.

Our eyes met and widened. She was running across the clearing to me. Her long strides were powerful as she bounded over the grass, but there was something new about her. She wasn't used to running yet. This was a new wolf. A wolf figuring out her body. Her fucking perfect specimen of a wolf body.

And I wanted her. I wanted her more than I'd wanted anything in my entire life. My wolf did, too, and he was happy to explain why.

Mate. He said it. I knew it before he told me, but the word was a trigger. It made the gears in my head spin.

Fuck.

June, she deserved better. She deserved the world. She didn't deserve someone like me.

Mine! the wolf in me insisted.

And he was right. I growled. We were almost on top of each other now. If she deserved the best, then I would just have to become the best. But that was a problem for another night, as our wolves met in a collision of fur under the moon's grace in the open field.

June. She ran her neck and sides along me. Scenting on me. She was probably confused as hell, none of this was natural to her, but her wolf certainly knew what she wanted at least. And so did mine.

June? I prodded. Hopefully she had figured out this much yet.

Dom, she answered. *What is . . . Why do you smell so . . .*

What is your wolf telling you? I asked gently.

She didn't answer, but I could tell she was flustered. In the way she smelled, in the way she moved. If she was human right now, she'd be blushing from head to toe.

That made me grin.

I loosened my control a bit and let my wolf explore June as he wished. It was pretty apparent that June's wolf was in control as well. They rubbed all over each other. Scents entwined, and it was such a fucking tease for me. Hopefully June was handling it all okay. This was going to end in a very serious talk later. But for now I was just happy to have her, to be near her. This was spinning my world around, and the state of the pack was about to be in chaos once we challenged Evander. I had known before that I wanted to watch out for June during the conflict ahead, but now I was terrified that something could happen. Her association with me had just made her a target for Evander.

The moon was making its descent by now, and her hold on me had loosened enough that I knew we could shift soon.

June. I got her attention as our wolves were curling around each other. I'm going to shift into my skin. *Do you think you can do the same?*

I don't know, she answered. *I can try.*

That would have to be enough. I pulled back the reins from my wolf and began shifting. It didn't take long to ease back into my human skin. The moment I had hands I plunged them into the fur at June's neck. It was so soft. Her smell, shit, even in this form her scent was so strong. For a moment I wondered if I'd spend the rest of our lives drunk on the smell of her.

Her shift was much slower than mine. Her wolf licked my cheek once, and then she took half a step back to try shifting. My heart ached. It was a slow process of several minutes as she slowly shrank. Her arms shifted first and she whimpered. Another stab through my heart. Slowly but surely, her limbs began to look more human. Her teeth changed. Her tail disappeared. Her claws changed to fingers and toes.

As she slowly formed back into the June I knew, I held her. The last of her shift left her panting, eyes closed. I pulled her onto my lap, holding her in my arms as her breathing and heart rate finally slowed down.

"Ow," she said softly.

I reached up to brush the hair off her forehead, still slick with sweat. "It gets much easier. This is the hardest day you'll ever have with it."

"Good." She sighed, then looked up at me. "I can't believe we're supposed to be bonded."

"Is it that bad?" I asked.

"No." A sly smile spread across her lips. "I don't think I'd be ready to try this with anyone else, I'm glad it's you."

My heart felt like it would explode. I had hoped, but I had pushed it all down and away. Now, every feeling I had for Juniper Gunn flooded to the surface.

I pulled her up closer to my face. She tilted her head back, eyes wide, and I leaned down to kiss her. Our lips met, hot and hungry. She let out the smallest moan as our mouths entwined. Tasting me firmly but slowly. "That was way better than in my dream," she mused.

"I'm going to have to get the details on this dream," I said.

Aaron padded over, not too close, and set down a bundle of clothing. I nodded my thanks, and he left.

"June." I kissed her forehead, then reached over to grab the clothes. "We need to go somewhere and have a talk. And I want to get inside somewhere before we're disturbed by anyone else."

June groaned and curled into a tighter ball in my arms. "I think it's too late for that."

I glanced up. A long line of wolves were sitting, watching, around the outer edges of the clearing. Aaron, Jack, and Carson looked about as amused as they could possibly be. Amelia wasn't paying much attention since she was hovering over her little female, but she did give me a nod.

"Here," I said, offering June an oversized sweatshirt. She pulled it over her head as I stood and yanked on the pair of shorts Aaron had brought me.

I sighed, looking for the one I needed to speak to. There, near Smokey and some of the warriors. He was already shifted and even wearing clothes. June and I must have been occupied with each other for quite some time.

"Evander," I said. "I request a house for a newly mated pair."

He nodded sharply, arms crossed as he watched us. "South street. Last house. It's already empty and ready for new occupants."

It would do for now.

I led June in the direction of the house and away from the clearing of eyes on us. I didn't like the look some of the males were giving her.

"Are you okay with sharing a bed? Beyond that, we can go as slow as you want."

"Yeah. I just want to get inside."

"Of course." I leaned down to kiss the top of her head and took her away.

My June.

My mate.

CHAPTER TWENTY-NINE

JUNE

It was Dom the whole time. The stupid dreams, the way I wanted to connect to him, this whole time it was always Dom. Every interaction I reflected on from the past weeks fell into place as it all clicked. Silence stretched between us but it wasn't uncomfortable. I was bubbling with questions but I didn't want to ask them yet when they could disrupt whatever chemistry we had going on here.

Between Jerod's advice and the fact that it was Dom, someone I was already indisputably drawn to, I was willing to give this an honest try.

"June." Dom's rough voice scratched at the air above me. I looked up as we approached a little white house with red shutters. "We're here."

"Somehow I didn't picture moving in together before our first date."

Dom let out a soft laugh. "Let's just commit to it for tonight. We have a lot to talk about, don't you think?"

Dom opened the door to the small house with the bare basics in it. There was a bedroom, a bathroom, a living space, and an eat-in kitchen. There was a table with two chairs, but not really anything else in the room. The bedroom had a bed with a mattress, two pillows, and a pack of sheets still in the plastic packaging. Opening the closet, I found a quilt sitting on an upper shelf. The house would need more than a few things in order to make it livable, but for tonight it was plenty.

Dom crossed his arms and leaned against the wall, watching with a smile on his face while I poked around the house.

"What are you thinking?" he asked.

I turned back to him, trying to keep my eyes above the waist. All I could think about were those sexy dreams my hormone addled preshift brain gave me. Dream Dom was nice; in-person Dom was a scalding hot temptation. "I'm wondering what to do now."

Dom laughed. "We definitely need to talk about that. The house is our right to ask for, so I got it while the whole pack was present and Evander couldn't make up an excuse. But you don't have to stay here, tomorrow you can go back to Linda's if you want, or if you want me to go back to bunking with Amelia and you can keep this place we can do that too. Although I don't know how much I want to share a roof with her right now with that wolf she just found."

"I do remember seeing her with someone, I think that was Bianca."

"You know her?" Dom asked.

"Not well, but she seems nice. She just came to Linda's the other day. She's from the north I think." My words trailed off in a yawn.

"You've had one of the longest nights of your life. Let's get you comfortable in case you fall asleep," Dom said.

I nodded and we got to work putting the bed together. The room smelled like it had been aired out recently; nothing was stuffy or stale.

Looking between Dom and the bed, I realized I didn't mind sharing. Like, at all. It surprised me and it didn't. This mate thing was *strong*. But Jerod's advice was still ringing fresh him my mind, and I knew I wanted to at least give this a try.

Once we were done with the bedding, I laid down and my whole body sighed with relief.

"Need anything?" Dom asked, pulling the blankets around me.

I shook my head, "Let's work out our plans, I want to figure out how to make this work while this whole plotting against Evander thing is going on."

He grimaced. "This isn't doing you any favors with Evander. Watch your back, or better yet, stay close to me until this is all over with."

Until this is all over with. After living life here, the draw of Seattle was growing smaller and smaller. Once you helped patch up a bleeding werewolf and uncovered a supernatural mystery, it was hard to go back to the office knowing the most exciting part of your day would be Carol asking if you had any weekend plans. Kat, though . . . maybe I could visit, or maybe she could visit, or maybe I could go down the mountain every day for phone reception. Whatever I figured out, I couldn't disregard Moonpeak anymore.

"I'm in this with you," I said. "I'm nosy, remember?"

"I'm serious," he said.

"So am I. This bond thing was a surprise, and I'm not saying I want this bite thing you guys do yet, but I'm taking some advice I got recently and jumping in." Letting out a breath, I saw the serious crease on Dom's forehead, and I wanted to disrupt it. "Does this mean we're dating now?"

Dom laughed so hard it infected me as well. I was still laughing when he leaned down and paused, waiting for the invitation of a kiss.

All other thoughts faded as I looked into his eyes. I leaned forward and gave him a kiss. Just a brush of my lips on his. My wolf liked it; I could tell that much at least.

Dom's eyes widened, and I turned six shades of red under his gaze.

"Do you want to continue from where we left off back on the field?" he asked, a wicked grin spreading across his lips.

Did I?

I nodded, sitting up to toss away the big sweatshirt. Dom moved as well, taking off his shorts while I was otherwise busy with my top.

"You're the sexiest thing I've ever seen. If you're uncomfortable at any time I can stifle my wolf. I can even sleep outside if you want."

I met his eyes and shook my head. "No. I'm fine with it. I want it."

That changed something in Dom entirely. I took in a sharp breath as he grinned, his fangs elongating, and he positioned himself over me.

"Really?" he asked. "If we start this, it might get a little wild. Are you okay with that?"

"How do you know I'm not the wild one?" I teased.

A wave of something hit me. Happiness? And power. And it seemed to radiate from Dom. It took my breath away, and he leaned down and kissed me. It was warm and fierce, his lips on mine, and my hands quickly found their way as they wrapped around his back, tracing his shoulder blades.

He pulled his mouth away from mine and groaned, putting his face to the side of my neck where he kissed and licked.

"Fuck, June."

I shivered. I moved one of my hands down his side and then toward his lower parts.

"Dom, can I touch you?" I asked.

He smiled into my neck, nipping at me playfully. "Please do."

I trailed my fingers down his abdomen until they bumped into a certain long, hard, *excited* part of him. I caught my lower lip between my teeth as I traced the size of him, eliciting a small moan.

But I wasn't the only one who was exploring. Dom's hands trailed down my neck and shoulders to my ribs. One thumb brushed the side of my breast as he pulled back from my neck to look at me. The question in his eyes was plain. I nodded, and he smiled as he ran a hand over my breasts.

I took in a sharp breath; his hot touch over my bare skin set everything on fire. The empty air in contrast to his touch was cold. My nipples stiffened, and goose bumps trailed across my shoulders.

"Do you like having your nipples played with?" Dom asked, taking one between his fingers and giving it a gentle tug.

"Oh!" That sent a shiver down my skin, but in a good way. The wolf in me was going crazy, wanting more of Dom. As much as we could take of Dom.

"I do if it's you doing it," I breathed.

Dom's hands kept exploring, and mine did the same. I ran my fingertips over his back. His firm stomach. His chest. He touched everything of mine he could. My breasts, my stomach, my thighs.

"June," he moaned. "You smell so fucking good right now."

A finger brushed the high inside of a thigh. I gasped and flinched, closing my legs a bit out of reflex.

"Are you sure you're ready for this?" Dom asked, kissing my neck.

"I do want it. Promise. I'm just nervous."

"June, you're perfect. You have nothing to be nervous about. I want to make you feel good, okay?"

"Okay." I wrapped my arms around his neck and leaned into his chest.

His fingers brushed down my opening slowly. A tease of a motion that left me wanting more.

"Shit, June." Dom brought up his hand and licked his finger slowly as he watched my face. "You're already so wet. Do you want more teasing?"

I shook my head. I was more than fucking ready.

"Hm, I'm not convinced." Dom gave me an impish smile as he put his hand on me again, this time teasing my entrance with his fingertip. "Or maybe I just like the faces you make when I play with you."

Air over my chest was making my nipples hard. My exposed core, my whole body was on display under him. Something in me wanted him to tease me, but something stronger in me wanted him to take me now.

But if Dom wanted to tease, two could play at that game.

I reached a hand low, pulling his erection firmly in my palm. I stroked it slowly, purposefully, up and down.

Dom gave me a low, pleased growling sound. "Fuck, June. I can't even explain how badly I want you right now."

My heart sputtered, a thrill of excitement at his desire. I grasped him a little more firmly and gave him another long stroke.

In turn, Dom moved his finger at my entrance to play with my clit. I gasped, and he moved the wetness from inside me to that sweet spot above my core and rubbed it with the same stroking motions I was giving him.

"Dom," I whimpered. "I don't think I can take much more teasing."

He smirked. "Good, because neither can I."

He removed his finger from me and I pulled my hand back as he shifted his position over me. His hands went to my thighs, his thumbs lightly pressing into them as he nudged my knees apart.

"Beautiful," Dom murmured. "And you're all mine."

I let out a soft laugh. "Does that work both ways?"

"Yes. I'm all yours, June." Dom leaned forward and kissed me. He let go of my thighs, but I wasn't closing them on him either.

"Tell me if you're uncomfortable at any time," Dom said.

"Okay," I whispered.

He kissed me again, and my eyes fluttered shut. It was warm and passionate. His fangs grazed my bottom lip, or at least I thought they had before I realized it was my own teeth that had elongated.

The distraction was enough that it took me by surprise when a firm presence pressed against my slick opening. Dom slid his head into me, and that ache of being stretched open caused me to wince.

"Are you okay?" Dom asked, stopping all movement.

I let out a slow breath. "Yeah, you're just . . . big. And it's been a while."

He gave me the softest kiss. Slow and warm at first, but then picking up in motion. His tongue flicked out, and I opened up for him. My mouth caught fire with his hunger, and I got lost in it. I wove my fingers gently through the short hair on the back of his head. He brushed a lock of mine that had fallen on my forehead out of the way. I had all but forgotten he was inside me when he slid a little more.

I gasped. After the first seconds of stretching for him, any discomfort disappeared and what remained was pure bliss. Once my heart had calmed down, and I was sure he could hear it, he slid in the rest of the way.

"Shit." He filled me all the way. We couldn't have fit together more perfectly, and I laid my head back a moment, just enjoying the feeling of him.

Dom leaned down, planting kisses on my neck. "I move at your command, June."

"I'm ready."

He slid out slowly, then back in. It pulled against all the right places.

"Fuck," Dom groaned.

He picked up the pace a little. I pushed my hips up to meet his, drinking up every inch of him I could.

Dom growled, grabbing the headboard with one hand. I slid my hands down his sides, placing them gently on his hips as I felt the muscles that pushed him into me.

I took in a breath and looked up into his eyes, panicked. "I'm not on birth control."

"I'll explain later, but you're fine tonight. Trust me." Dom kissed my forehead. "But if you've got time to worry, then I'm not doing my job."

Dom shifted on the bed, moving us both toward the wall. He grabbed my butt, two full hands of ass. I was so shocked that I didn't say anything until I found myself pinned upright, and he began thrusting again. All I could do was throw my arms around his neck and hang on tight. It was a whole new sensation. It also gave him better access to kiss my neck, which was heating up big time.

He took the skin between my neck and shoulder gently in his teeth. Fangs grazing, blood pumping. The nerves under his touch there were every bit as sensitive as the parts of me he had teased earlier.

"What?" I breathed. "What is that?"

He nipped my neck lightly, then planted a gentle kiss over the spot he was playing with. He pulled his head back enough to look directly into my eyes. His were blazing with want.

"That is where I'll mark you, June." Dom's voice was low as it crawled over my exposed skin, giving me new goose bumps. "I'll put my teeth in you, and you'll come while we seal our bond for good."

Something low in me tightened. He was damn well close to making me come now, let alone with whatever he was talking about.

"That sounds like something I definitely want," I said.

But Dom shook his head. "I'll mark you when you're good and ready, and I'm not letting you make decisions in this state of mind. For tonight, you'll have to settle for me fucking you silly."

He pushed into me with a particularly strong thrust, taking my breath for a moment.

Okay, fine, I'll settle for this.

"Dom," I murmured, my voice rising. "I don't think I can last much longer."

"Then don't. I can't wait to hear you come undone."

He pinned me tighter to the wall and moved his hands. He held me to his hips with one hand gripping the joint of my leg while his other hand moved my hands around. In one smooth motion, he had my arms over my head and wrists pinned to the wall with his free hand.

My heart went wild.

"Rule one for fucking a wolf, June," Dom growled into my ear, making me shiver. "Dominance is everything."

The urgency tightened inside of me more and more with every stroke. I couldn't move, and it excited me.

Dom's mouth took mine. Biting and pressing hungrily. I was desperate for him. Desperate for his lips, desperate for climax.

"June," Dom warned.

I was too breathless to answer, panting, and nodding with fervor.

Yes. Yes! *Please.*

My wolf agreed passionately. We were an animal in heat. Fucking Dom was the only thing either of us could think of.

Dom thrust upward in one last strong jerk. "Let me see your eyes, June!"

He commanded me. I mean really commanded me. My wolf couldn't say no. I couldn't say no. I looked him in the eye as I lost it all.

"Ah!" A short, breathy yell left me as everything in me rose higher and higher toward that sweet release. The moment I felt his last thrust and the spilling of him inside me, I went to pieces.

My body tensed, riding him hard as we both came. It was both better and worse that I couldn't even move my hands, I was fully on display in my most vulnerable moment.

I was panting hard when it was all done. He slowed down, letting my hands go from where he had pinned them over my head. I immediately wrapped them around his neck for stability as he held my hips, rocking them gently as we both calmed down.

"Fuck, June," Dom murmured. He kissed my neck in that sweet spot where he'd promised to mark me when I was ready. To be honest, I still kind of wanted it, but I was glad he was giving me a chance to learn more first.

He lifted me gently off the wall, helping me lay down on the bed. I stretched, and he laid down next to me.

Dirty Lying Wolves

"That was amazing," I moaned. "When can we do that again?"

Dom brushed his fingers over my hair. "Give me a moment first."

"Seriously?" My eyes widened. "Are you trying to kill me?"

He chuckled and kissed my forehead. "We're wolves, June. You've still got a lot to learn."

As the sun began to peek through the shutters, I welcomed my first morning as a wolf.

Naked, breathless, and consumed by Dom.

CHAPTER THIRTY

JUNE

The warm day stirred me awake. I yawned, prying my eyes open. Slivers of sun fell between the wood slats of the shutters over Dom's chest. Bright, it was probably already midday. I groaned and tried to sit up straight, a sudden shock tearing through my heart as I felt the air on my naked body.

My clothes! Everything was at Linda's.

I put my hands over my face, cursing myself for not thinking to get something, anything, before the whole pack would be up and about. My only option now was the sweatshirt I had discarded somewhere in the bedroom.

"Mmm," Dom mumbled, rolling over and pulling me closer to him with an arm around my middle. "You okay?"

I sighed. "I don't have any clothes."

Dom sat up, sleepily wrapping his arms around me and kissing my neck. "I don't see the problem."

I nudged him off of me, fighting the urge to smile. "Of course you'd say that. But I would still like something to wear other than the shirt from last night."

Dom stretched, grunting. "I'll see if we have anything outside the door. 'S customary to leave us stuff."

I perked up at that. "Really? That would be fantastic."

"Hold on, let me check." Dom stood, walking out of the room and to the front door. I stared at his backside as he walked. I couldn't believe the things we'd done last night. *All night.*

By the time Dom came back inside, I was glowing remembering last night and basking in the feeling of the strange new things about my body. That shift was more difficult than tearing my quad, or at the very least it took a lot longer to deal with in the moment, but now I had this feeling inside me that both was and wasn't a part of me. My wolf. And this connection between me and Dom, it was alive and pulling my attention to the doorway as he came in. He took one look at me and the softest expression crossed his face, but he didn't say anything as he set a few bags on the bed. I was delighted to see my backpack was one of them.

"Better now?" he asked.

"Yes," I said, pulling shampoo from my bag. "Hallelujah!"

Dom poked through the other bags. Paper grocery bags, likely from the general store. "Some soap, towels, canned food. It'll definitely get us started. Make a list of anything else you want and we can figure it out later." I stiffened, remembering the last time we'd gone into town. "Should we bring someone with us? More numbers?"

Dom's expression darkened. "Yeah, we can do that. I'm still pissed about the whole thing, and now even more so. If anything had happened to you . . ."

"But it didn't," I said. "And now we're ready. We move in groups. We keep searching for answers. If Evander won't do anything about it, we will."

247

Mornin', kids, Smokey said, taking me completely by surprise. I shrieked and snatched my red backpack, clutching it in front of me as if Smokey could see me somehow.

"June," Dom mused. "It's just the link. You learned it last night, remember?"

I started pulling clothes out of my bag anyway. "Yeah, yeah, one of those things I'll get used to."

Hello, Smokey. What's up? Dom asked.

Alpha wants me to test June. Find out a little bit more about her wolf. Maybe place her somewhere if she's got any particular skills, Smokey said.

"I thought I was . . ." I cleared my throat, concentrating on the mind link. It was much harder to use that over my own voice when I had a human mouth to use.

I thought I was already a backup for Doc, I said.

And you are, he clarified. *But if you're a natural warrior, or tracker, or beta, or anything else, we need to know that too.*

Dom frowned. *We're a brand-new pair, why the rush?*

I don't question the alpha, so I wouldn't know. But, boy, I'd be on the alert now more than ever. You've got a mate to protect, and the plans you and Amelia got brewin'? Those will affect June.

Dom's eyes slid to me. His jaw tightened. *When do you need her?*

I'm sure it can wait 'til mornin', Smokey said. *Day's already half over anyway.*

I blushed, averting my eyes from Dom with a sheepish grin.

We'll come to the training grounds together, Dom said. *That okay with you, June?*

I nodded. *Yes.*

All right. See you then, Smokey said, and then cut off the link.

"You take the first shower," Dom said. "I'm going to put all this stuff away."

"Great, and after that, you can catch me up on the finer details of your plans with Amelia and the others."

Dom ran a hand down his face. "You and Bianca have definitely affected those plans, I'll have to talk to the others to make sure we're all on the same page."

"You've learned by now I'm an inquisitive person. If you leave anything undetailed, I'm going to find out about it one way or another." I patted his bare chest as I walked by. "Be ready for that, *mate*."

I winked before I shut the bathroom door on him. My heart was pounding. I was used to being a straightforward kind of person, but this felt like a little more than the usual June. Had I somehow gotten bolder? Was it the wolf?

Good! Good job.

I could feel her. My wolf, she thought we'd done the right thing. I smiled to myself and turned on the shower. While I was getting clean, I could somewhat hear Dom moving around the house. My ears were incredible, and even the shower was almost too loud for me now. That was something else I'd have to get used to.

Once I was fresh and clean and out of the bathroom, I found Dom in the kitchen making sandwiches. My stomach growled, and I realized I hadn't eaten anything since the deer leg last night.

"Feel better?" Dom asked.

I nodded, walking up to the counter where he was putting mustard on a slice of what looked like homemade bread. "Lunch?"

"There's venison or chicken. There's also mustard, hot sauce, mayo. Here, why don't you take a look?"

Dom moved aside, taking his plate with three sandwiches on it to the table. I almost asked him about it, but then realized exactly how much I'd been eating before my shift, and wondered if I'd have that kind of appetite forever now. In the end, I made two different kinds of sandwiches and joined him at the table.

"I shot a link to Amelia, she agrees we need to talk. The problem is, some of us can't link. Bianca, Jerod, and Carmine aren't Moonpeak," Dom said.

"Secret meeting then?" I asked. "Away from these wolf ears, of course."

"I'll arrange it for tomorrow night. You go with Smokey, nothing's going to happen to you under his watch, and I'll round everyone up when I can. We'll sort out the details together, we've got to be close to ready."

"All right then," I agreed. "Time to hear the plan."

CHAPTER THIRTY-ONE

DOM

Smokey was already there the next morning, of course. Daylight barely shone over the clearing. He was wearing pants for once, standing on top of the boulder in the center to face the sunrise.

I grunted. "Smokey."

He hopped down and walked over. He eyed June up and down, nodding slowly. "Hmm, yes. Now that I get a good look at you with your wolf in there, you're a strong one."

A growl passed my lips, and I shook my head to pull my wolf back in. Smokey wouldn't do anything to hurt June. Well, anything to hurt her badly. His methods could be a little intense, but nothing she couldn't handle.

"What do I do?" June asked.

"We'll go for a run," Smokey said. "Lift some things. Push some things. Dodge some things. A bit of light exercise so I can observe."

I snorted a laugh. Light exercise, my ass.

"And what will you be doing, big fella?" Smokey asked. "Watching over her like a mother hen?"

"I'll be close by. At least in the near area here. I want to get some training in, but June can handle herself." I looked down at my determined mate and smiled.

That made her happy, which made me happy.

"Yes, b'y. Well, get a-goin' while we trot her around and see what she can do." Smokey made a shooing motion at me. "Go on, get. Nathan wanted to see you."

Nathan?

"All right," I said. "June, I'm close if you need me."

I leaned down and kissed her. She had to be the one to pull us apart, though, and she grinned at me as she patted my chest.

"I'll be fine," June said. "I used to do track, remember? I can handle a little exercise."

"Track, really?" Carson and Aaron came into the training field, Aaron looking tired, but Carson suddenly perked up with excitement. "That's kick-ass, June. Did you have a sports nickname? I bet you did," Carson said.

"That's not a thing." Aaron nudged Carson. "Sounds like a bunch of nonsense you'd see on television."

And I would have agreed with Aaron, but when I turned to look at June to say as much, I noticed she was bright red. Neck to ears red. I grinned, a wolfish smile across my lips as I leaned down to murmur in her ear.

"You did, didn't you?" I asked.

"I knew it! What was it?" Carson asked.

"I . . . uh . . . oh god." June put her hands over her face. "Shotgun."

"Shotgun?" I asked with a frown, then it all snapped into place and I grinned. "Gunn. Juniper Gunn. Shotgun."

"Please don't. High-school kids are dumb and the nickname was dumb and it's embarrassing."

"It's cute," I said.

"Cute?" Carson exclaimed. "It's badass!"

"Hey, you two. If you've got enough time to mess around, you've got enough time to run twenty laps," Smokey said.

Carson's amusement fell from his face. "Now," Smokey added.

Aaron and Carson stripped and put their clothes to the side of the field. I leaned in and gave June one more kiss before walking away.

"Good luck, Shotgun," I said, and she groaned as she walked away.

Nathan and Anna were helping each other stretch, probably getting ready for others to show up.

"Dom." Nathan stood, brushing off his dusty knees as he did so and extending a hand. "Congrats, man. June looks like she can keep you on your toes."

Shaking Nathan's hand, I looked back over my shoulder to where June was currently trying to shift under Smokey's supervision.

"Yeah, that's for sure. Smokey said you were looking for me," I said. "How long are you sticking around? I know you probably need to get back to Salt Fur."

"About that," Nathan said. "I know you wanted us to help get you back in shape, and I'm thrilled you guys are back home, but I have a bad feeling you're up to something. We need to talk."

I frowned, eyes sliding around the field for any ears perked our way.

"Come with us," Nathan said, picking up on what I was looking for.

"Where? I told June I wouldn't go far."

"Just the next clearing over," Anna explained. "Somewhere empty, no equipment."

Through a few trees and into the opening, the first thing I saw was a large gray wolf standing and facing us. I knew exactly who it was too. Her new mate stood to the side stroking Amelia's fur.

"What's going on?" I asked.

"Dom, you're a good wolf and a loyal beta to Amelia," Nathan said.

Anna stepped next to Nathan, hands on her hips. "But you're a level above me too. When it comes down to a muscle-to-muscle fight, I don't win."

"What are you asking?" I asked calmly.

"I think you know." Nathan sighed, patting my shoulder. "Amelia wants to fight you. Now."

Pulling off my shirt, I walked toward Amelia.

"Why would you fight me?" I asked. "We're so close to what we've been after for a decade. Why now?"

Amelia's big wolf huffed, nudging her head toward her mate next to her. With a lick of Bianca's face, the petite woman walked away with a smile to stand near Nathan and Anna.

"Ah. Mates do change things, don't they?" What had I said the night I found out I belonged with June? She deserved the best, so I would become the best?

You've changed, Amelia said. *Or maybe it would be better to say you've grown.*

I could say the same for you, I replied, letting the link keep it between the two of us.

I don't think you're just beta material, Dom. No one does anymore, Amelia said. *Our problem has always been that there are two alphas here. You're my closest friend, Dom. But if we're really both alphas, we have to settle this right now.*

There's nothing to settle, Moonpeak is yours and I'll follow your lead, I said. *What is there to settle?*

Everything. Amelia's head shook toward the village. *Only room for one alpha in Moonpeak. We're making the decision right now.*

All you've wanted for the past ten years is to take your father's seat back.

No, she seethed. *All I've wanted for the past ten years is to tear out the throat of the devil that killed him. And my mother, and my pack.*

And the loser? Where do they go? Moonpeak is home.

Amelia was silent.

Moonpeak is home, I insisted. *Your pack is here, your sister is here. I'm here.*

I'll never make you leave this place, you know that. But I'm not going to go through with you being my beta without testing your limits. Amelia glanced at her mate. *Did you know Bianca is from Winter Wind?*

That delicate, petite wolf was from Winter Wind? An arctic pack, constantly in battles, known for their aggression for survival. And Amelia's way of handling things would gain her nothing but praise there.

She's Alpha Bernard's only child, Dom.

Floored, I stared openly at the petite girl standing by Nathan until Amelia snapped me back to the present.

I have no reason to be proud of how I left this place. I get that now. You want the truth of it? This place hurts. What would I do, take over this peaceful mountain village? Sleep in the bed of my dead parents? Hell, maybe he's changed out the furniture. I'll rest real easy on the bed my enemy slept in.

It doesn't have to be that way, I insisted.

It already is, Dom. Don't think for a second that I'll leave without that bastard's blood on my hands, but this isn't what I crave. I can give Bianca a life she deserves in Winter Wind. This fight isn't about me, it's about you. Now, fucking shift, Dominic.

Reeling from her words, I rolled my shoulders, dropped the rest of my clothes on the ground, and shifted. I was ready to accept what Amelia, Smokey, even Nathan and Anna were saying. I did need to push myself and let go of the barriers in my head that I hid behind, convincing myself that I couldn't be more than a beta. If I was meant to serve my people in another way, I owed it to them to give it my all.

No sooner was I finished than Amelia lunged. It was a good one, too, because she nearly had my throat in her teeth. I turned at the last moment and shoved my shoulder under her chin.

We circled each other. Amelia was sharp today, but I could still sense the otherness around her of Jerod and their connection. It was a distraction to her, a constant tug in the direction of the warlock.

In a flash, Amelia was on me. A gleam of teeth as she pounced. I thrashed upward, slicing her chest with my claws as we tumbled, growling and snarling, into each other.

Amelia snapped down, tearing a part of my ear as I shouldered her weight off of me. We circled again.

You would have been the perfect beta, Amelia prodded. *All the backup I could ever need for anything. You make my job too easy.*

I snarled, lunging at her and scraping across her side before we both jumped away.

Then why push for this fight? I snapped.

If you're really up to the task of alpha of Moonpeak, then I won't get in your way. As my beta you'd just be a crutch for me to lean on!

Amelia barreled into me, too fast for me to dodge. Instead, I leaned into it and we both rolled over each other. Tumbling in the grass, gnashing teeth and swiping claws until we were both sprinkled with thin, bloody ribbons.

I pushed back as she snapped up at my neck, then lunged forward and wrapped my jaws around her own throat while pinning her wolf down with my weight.

What happened to us, Dom? Amelia asked. *When did we stop sparring? When did I not notice what you were becoming? Why I was growing stagnant, and you were holding back.*

I gently moved my teeth away and took a few steps back. Amelia began shifting, Bianca running up to her and gingerly touching the bigger wounds that weren't already closing up.

With Amelia taken care of, I began shifting myself. Anna and Nathan walked over to me, and Anna handed me my shorts.

"I didn't want to believe Amelia when she told me," Nathan said. "But damn, Dom. You might just be alpha material yet."

I had just barely acknowledged myself recently that I could be something more than a beta, but it was entirely different when Nathan said the words out loud.

"Don't celebrate too soon," Anna murmured. "Amelia still has a handicap."

"And Dom still needs polishing," Nathan agreed. "A lot of polishing. Hey, Dom, what are the chances of you coming down to Salt Fur for a week with me and Dad? I think if anyone could whip your ass into top shape my old man could."

"Maybe, everything hinges on June," I said. "I don't want to take her so freshly changed to a whole new territory."

"Yeah, makes sense," Nathan said.

"Dom," Amelia said. She had on loose shorts and a big shirt, her preference for training days, but a stark contrast to Bianca in her white sundress.

"Amelia."

"What a mess," she said softly.

That dropped some of the tension in my shoulders, and I walked over to give her a hug. When was the last time we'd done that? An embrace of two wolves who'd grown up together. Knew everything about each other. There was no fight around the corner unless you counted Evander. No vampires to keep us on edge. No bounties, no enemies. Just us.

"Things change. I still want to floss Evander's teeth with his own entrails, but . . ."

"But after?" I prodded.

She turned back to face me again. "Can't say I've thought too deeply past the revenge, you know that."

"Naomi?" I asked.

"Obviously I'm not going anywhere until we make sure she's safe," Amelia said. "Bianca says we're only a couple of days away if we fly, they have a couple of tiny planes up there for important things."

"I'll take the best care of her, if it comes down to leaving me with Moonpeak." I still wasn't sure how I felt about it, but this place, this was home. I never wanted to be anywhere else, and the fact that Amelia could even entertain the idea of moving to Winter Wind—the moon really does pull us in strange directions.

"We're almost ready," Amelia said. "Jerod said he had a solution to our entanglement problem. But it has to wait for the middle of the night."

"Finally," I groaned.

"Second, we need to tell the others what we decided here today. Blightfang, Bianca, June, and if you'll come, too, Nathan and Anna, you're welcome to be there."

"Absolutely," Anna chimed in. "I want our neighboring pack back to normal."

"Agreed," added Nathan.

Agreed. It was time to take Moonpeak back.

CHAPTER THIRTY-TWO

JUNE

"You're almost there, kid," Smokey said.

I was stumbling over my own paws trying to stand, my vision was fuzzy, and focusing was hard until the final pop that fully melded me and my wolf together. My breathing was a bit uneven, and I was hyperaware of every lungful of air I took in. My wolf shook out our fur, sniffing the air and memorizing Smokey's scent.

"There, that a girl. Second time was easier, wasn't it?" he asked.

I shook my head, a different sensation from a human head nodding. A little disorienting, but I was adapting quickly.

"Okay, Shotgun." Smokey chuckled. "Let's see you run."

I growled. I shouldn't have told them my old nickname. Smokey patted our back. "Don't like it? Make me eat my words. Run."

We trotted down the path, slowly, our paws feeling the forest floor.

"I said run, girl. Not take a Sunday stroll," Smokey barked.

I'm working on it, I snapped back.

I tried to watch how some of the other wolves walked. Which feet they coordinated, and how they alternated their weight.

"Matt, glad you got your ass out of bed today," Smokey said.

I turned to see who it was he was talking to. Nathan's cousin, the moody teen I'd met the day they all showed up. He was walking into the training fields, arms crossed, and already looking bored.

"Hop onto the track with June here and we can test the new pups together," Smokey said.

Matt frowned. "I shifted last year, I'm not a new pup."

"You're all pups to me," Smokey said. "And that wasn't a suggestion. Get to the track. Now."

Matt rolled his eyes but began stripping to shift. I looked elsewhere and focused on watching the other wolves train and run. Watched how they moved certain muscles, shifted their weight.

"Okay, kids, get to runnin' and show me what you can do."

I turned around to see Matt had already shifted. It was disheartening to see how fast he was, and how much younger too.

My wolf whimpered.

Sad?

I sighed. *No, not sad. Frustrated.*

But she didn't deserve me being bummed out. I just had to try harder.

Matt made his way to where I stood on the path. Not nearly as big as his cousin, but the same coloring as Nathan. White with some gray in it. We stood shoulder to shoulder and began trotting along.

I was getting the hang of these feet when Matt suddenly took off.

Hey! I snapped.

He can't hear you, girlie. He's not Moonpeak, Smokey said.

A small growl escaped me as I dug my paws a little harder into the dirt track. We started to actually run.

My heart skipped a beat. The running was exciting but scary. I kept flashing back to a track at school. The crowds cheering us on in the big race. My legs pushing harder, and harder, and harder, and then the snap in my leg, and I screamed—

"June!" Smokey snapped. "Are you running or crawling?"

He was right, I was barely moving now. I shook out my head. I wasn't on the track at school, and I wasn't tearing a quad muscle. I was a wolf, and long since healed from my human injuries. It was just . . .

Okay? my wolf asked.

Yeah, I'm okay.

I picked my pace back up. Trotting, running, chasing after Matt. That was all I needed to do, follow Matt around the field. If I could just focus on that, I could do this. Wolves run, that's what they do. So I had to run too.

The sun was high before Smokey stopped us. I wasn't too tired yet, but learning could be mentally exhausting, and I was ready for a break. Unfortunately, Smokey wasn't.

"All right, come on over," he said. I kept my eyes on Smokey's face, not at all distracted that he was *still* walking around naked even though he hadn't shifted all morning.

I laid down on my stomach in the grass, glad to have the shade. All this fur was warm, but the plus side would probably be the long mountain winters here, where it got cold and snowy.

"June, were you even trying to catch up to Matt?" Smokey asked.

I stayed behind him the whole time, I said.

Smokey snorted a laugh. "You're either the slowest wolf I've seen, or you weren't actually running. Matt wasn't going near his full speed. He was waiting for you to pass him so you two could race properly."

I looked over at Matt, who was sitting in the grass near me. Oops. I laid my head down, embarrassed.

"Never mind, but run next time." Smokey shook his head. "Let's see how your nose is. Come here and smell this bag."

I followed Smokey to a shady spot under a tree, where he held up a sealed bag.

"This shoe belongs to someone in the pack. Find 'em." Smokey dumped the shoe on the ground and crossed his arms, waiting for me.

I looked down at the simple white laced shoe, then back up at Smokey.

"You think I'm joking or something?" he asked. "Go on, get sniffing."

I huffed, but put my head down close enough to get a good scent. I didn't enjoy the process at all, but my wolf seemed to be interested. She quickly took over, having us smell all over it, then the ground around us.

"It was sealed for a reason, kiddo. There's no trail here. Go figure it out," Smokey said. "The shoe stays here if you want to come back for a fresh sniff."

But my wolf shook her head. No, we had this. We turned away from Smokey and happily trotted toward the village.

Dom, I'm going to the village for a test, I thought at the last minute.

Do you want me to follow? he asked.

I'll be okay.

Tell me if you have to stray from the village, he said firmly. *I don't want you alone if those rogues are still out there.*

I will.

With that out of the way, I was free to smell. And smell we did. The brain of a wolf was a fascinating thing. The way things imprinted to our mind like a picture, based on smell alone. I sat back and let her do most of the work since she seemed to know what she was doing.

Up the slope and to the village, we picked up traces of the smell. My wolf was excited, I was excited. We were doing this, we were doing a normal wolf thing that I wasn't afraid to try.

Up and down the main street, the smell was stronger near the end closer to the pack house, but it strayed down a side road just before we reached Doc's. On the road, we found three houses, with one that stood out the most.

Trotting up to the faded blue door, we sat. What next? Did I shift and go in? I hadn't brought any clothes with me. As far as I knew, it was polite to be dressed inside the village limits. What now?

Smokey, maybe I've found the house the smell is coming from? I said. *But the door isn't open, and I don't have clothes.*

I didn't ask you to find a house, I asked you to find the person that shoe belongs to, Smokey said.

Do I have to go in naked? I asked.

I don't know, New Bite. Do you? Smokey asked, amused.

I could go back to my house and get something, or maybe they would let me in as a wolf? Could I figure out how to knock on the door? Or maybe . . .

No.

I turned my attention to my wolf. *No?*

Gone.

I looked back up at the house. She was right, the person we were looking for probably lived here, but that didn't mean they were here right now. And while the scent was the strongest at this house, it wasn't that recent. I didn't know how I could possibly know that. My wolf was probably the one who contributed to that knowledge.

Nose back to the ground, we kept smelling. They had walked in a big circle, then down the road and to the other side of the main street. The person we were searching for had been to a few of these houses, either last night or this morning. They weren't here now, though, and we kept going.

Suddenly, my wolf perked up our head.

Scent!

And we took off. Stopping occasionally to smell the ground or the air, we wandered up the main street to the pack house. This person had walked around the side of the building and into a side entrance. These smelled fresh!

The kitchen door was partially open, and I stuck my head inside.

"There you are! You found me." Alice chuckled. She was stirring a pot on the stove, but when I came in she wiped her hands on her apron and walked over.

"Here, dear. You can shift, I have a dress for you." Alice walked to the coat rack and took down a large, simple dress that would fit most females well enough. At least it would cover me.

"Splendid job, June." Alice patted my arm. "I've already told Smokey."

"I got stuck at your house first, I think." I smiled. "This smelling thing isn't so bad. It seems useful."

"And it is." Alice nodded. "Your nose is the first alert to danger. It can help you find food, or avoid trouble. Take good care of it."

"I'll try," I promised, not quite sure how you took care of a nose.

"I've got lunch for you, that Smokey would keep a pup running around for days before he let them eat," Alice said.

That perked me up.

Alice laughed. "Now, why do you think I had a dress ready? I'm feeding you before you go. I've got to be here cooking, anyway, what's one more mouth?"

"Thank you," I said, and followed her to the kitchen counter.

"Ah, here we are. It's not much, but I hope you like a good ham and cheese biscuit. Still hot." Alice handed me a warm cloth napkin with a delicious scent inside. "Oh, and I made too many *toutons* last night. Take a few with you, that Dominic of yours had a soft spot for them when he was a pup."

My face lit up. "You knew Dom as a pup?"

Alice handed me the basket of toutons. They looked pretty much like a kind of doughnut. Hopefully, that would be how they tasted.

"Oh yes, he's a handful that one." Alice stirred her stew. "But so was his dad, bless him. Not as stubborn as Amelia, but closer than I'd have liked."

Sitting on a bar stool at the island, I ate my lunch. "Did you cook for the last alpha too?"

Alice's face fell, and she spoke in a whisper. "I did, but it's best to not speak of that."

Her eyes flicked to the door that would lead to the rest of the pack house. I nodded in agreement. But it made me mad. My wolf too.

Shotgun! Smokey startled me and I almost dropped my lunch. *What the hell are you doing up there, dolly dress up? Kitchen tea party?*

Lunch, I said. *And she wants me to bring you back a touton?*

Smokey paused for a moment. I waited with bated breath for his response.

Come back with two.

I managed to scarf my lunch down with no further interruptions. Scooting off my stool, I piled a few of the treats into the napkin and gave Alice a hug, leaving the basket behind.

"Thank you again, Alice," I said. "I need to be getting back."

"Take care, dear." She held the napkin for me as I shifted, then helped me settle it so I could carry the ends in my teeth. "Don't let that Smokey bully you too much."

I could have laughed, but then I would have dropped the dessert. Back to training, back to learning what my wolf could do.

At least this time I had toutons.

CHAPTER THIRTY-THREE

JUNE

"June," Dom whispered, gently touching my shoulder. "June, it's time to go."

I groaned, rolling over on our bed. I squinted at the bright moonlight filtering through the slats in the window. "Ugh. I'm still tired."

Moving my things from Linda's hadn't been difficult. And as sweet as she was to help me and others like Carmine and Bianca, I was so glad to have my own place. I was used to an apartment with just me and Kat; Linda's place had too much going on for me all at once. I didn't even remember passing out on the couch, but waking up on the bed, I could tell Dom had moved me here for the night, and the thought made me smile.

"Sorry, love. It's about one in the morning. We have to meet the others."

I pulled Dom's giant T-shirt back up on my shoulder from where it had fallen off. "Okay. Let me put something on."

"Wolves, June. We go as wolves," Dom said.

Right. Wolves.

Dom opened our front door. Easier to do with thumbs, after all. Once we were both ready, I followed Dom outside, and we headed for the meeting place. The village was silent, but we still had to be careful of patrols. Smokey would be up in a few hours, and he would be hard to avoid coming back. Smokey wouldn't lie to Evander if he was asked about us, and we didn't need that complication.

Once the village was out of sight, I calmed down. Even better, we had to pick up Carmine and Jerod along the way. Well, really only Jerod, so he and Amelia could travel near each other.

Carmine was already shifted and outside on the porch of the cabin when we arrived. She nuzzled next to Jerod, who was wearing a tailored shirt and a rather expensive looking pair of pants. His shoes were even polished leather.

Where did he get an outfit like that around here? I asked Dom.

He's in control of his resources again, Dom answered. *His familiar should be able to fetch his clothes with simple instructions.*

I wondered if Jerod ever had a problem with burn holes in his things.

Carmine spotted us first, then Jerod. They walked down the few steps to meet us on the ground level.

"Good evening, wolves. I've finally gathered a few things that should aid in remedying the predicament Amelia and I are in." Jerod responded to Dom's huff. "It's a delicate situation. I'd like to see you untangle such an unprecedented incident while making up a new formula for . . . ugh."

Jerod pinched the bridge of his nose. "When this little meeting is done, I could use a hand. Okay?"

Dom nodded, and the four of us walked away. At Jerod's slower pace, of course.

My wolf loved the night air. The smells and sounds of night creatures were enticing, and it was hard to keep us from distraction as we followed Dom. I even got the chance to play with Carmine a bit since we had to go so slowly. Nipping at each other's tails as we went, racing when we could still keep quiet. Smelling the air and ground for interesting things or to make sure no patrols were close.

Amelia and Bianca joined us after a little bit. Aaron, Carson, and Jack caught up after that. My wolf grew excited with all of us together. We wanted to run around, smelling everyone and playing with them. I reigned her in, though, reminding us both that we were here for something serious.

It was a long hike in human terms, but as wolves we covered the ground at a good pace. We started down a path by the brook that trickled cold mountain water down the slope. Dom had us walk in it a ways to mask our scents, and then finally we stopped in a clear patch of trees.

This is good enough, Dom said. *We're on the edge of the pack lands.*

Amelia shifted.

I panicked for a moment as everyone else did the same. The nakedness still felt uncomfortable.

"You don't have to if you don't want to." Dom stroked the fur on my neck. "But not everyone here is pack, so they can't link with us."

What kind of werewolf was afraid of being naked? None that I'd met so far. I slowly started my own shift, still working out the mechanics of it, while they talked.

"What are we doing here?" Jack asked. "Updates? Change in plans?"

"I have an announcement," Amelia said. "But it waits until the end. First, we fix this problem between me and Jerod."

"Agreed," Carmine said. "Get this mess untangled so we can all move on with our bonds."

Bianca leaned over to me. "Congratulations."

"You too," I said. "I hope you found what you were looking for in Amelia."

She gave me a flushed smile. "I really did. I hope you have as well."

Jerod clapped his hands. "We're going to do a complete soul untangling. I've finally found a demon who could do it and isn't charging me an arm and a leg. Literally."

"We spent all day gathering the price." Carmine wrapped herself around Jerod's arm with a warm smile. "Didn't we, mon amour?"

"How many of us do you need here?" Dom asked.

Jerod looked around, squinting at each wolf. "Actually, just in case, I was hoping all of you would stick around as muscle."

"Just in case of *what*?" Amelia asked.

"These things are a lot like a deal with a drug lord." Jerod shrugged. "Hard to say if you're going to be double crossed."

I held on to Dom's arm a little tighter. "I don't like this."

"It's okay." Dom pulled me in close. "Wolves naturally don't mix well with dark magic. You and Bianca can stay back while the rest of us keep an eye out. Just don't go too far, we travel in groups, remember?"

"Yes, Bianca, you should go with June," Amelia said. "Just in case."

I hadn't really interacted with Bianca much, so it was a little awkward when she walked over to take my arm in hers. Particularly since we were both as naked as the day we were born.

"Come on, June," she said. "Let's watch the show from a safe distance."

I tried to act casual about everything, but I was still on edge, or maybe that was my wolf. Dom was right, I didn't *like* the warlock stuff.

There was a large tree a good distance away and so we leaned against it and watched. Jerod walked around the circle, arranging the wolves as he needed them and marking the ground in specific spots. Carmine followed, dropping what looked suspiciously like teeth over the marks.

"What do you think of this demon stuff?" I asked.

Bianca shrugged. "I'm ashamed to say I'm not as versed in the ways of beings other than wolves. It's a bit unsettling, but it should prove rather educational."

Once Jerod seemed satisfied with everything, the magic proceeded quickly. I could tell he was chanting something, but what he was saying I hadn't a clue. I watched on, wincing as he slashed his own arm open, and then he began to glow red.

The circle lit up; Amelia and Jerod were the only ones in it. All the wolves around it growled. They were shifted and ready for a fight if need be, so their wolfish body language was pretty obviously aggravated.

Bianca next to me let out a shiver.

"Are you okay?" I asked softly.

"Yes, I think so. Just a chill," she said. Then an arm shot out of the ground and we both jumped.

"Ew," I said.

Bianca somehow managed to turn even more pale.

A demon covered in mud, blood, and ashes pulled itself from the ground. It spoke to Jerod in that awful language. They discussed something for a moment, then shook hands.

After that, the demon raised its arms in the air, and Jerod and Amelia hovered a couple of feet off the ground, still glowing. The demon began to do his work. The red glow around the two of them was a massive tangle of illuminated strings.

Pulling and twisting, unknotting and yanking, the demon worked quickly. Until he jerked his head around to look directly at me.

No, it wasn't me, it was Bianca. I looked over at her. She was visibly shaken, and a few red strands were drifting off of her in the same kind of aura as Amelia and Jerod. Bianca's hand flew to her neck, and she winced.

"What's the matter?" I hissed.

She shook her head, gritting her teeth and putting up with whatever it was that was happening. I was concerned, but also afraid to touch her and interfere with the demon's job.

Then a branch snapped.

I whirled around, and a smell hit me. Something nasty. Something only vaguely familiar. Smelling it as a wolf was like having to relearn anything I had ever smelled before. Until I saw the motion, and it hit me all at once.

"Rogues!" I squeaked.

Dom snarled, running toward me. The others came around, too, and I tried to shift while in a panic. It hurt more than when I took my time, but I ignored the pain and pushed through.

June! Dom called. *Get behind us, you can't fight yet.*

I did as I was told, but soon there was more than one rogue to contend with. A whole group of rogues, sick looking and foul smelling. They looked big, dark, wicked—just as the ones that attacked me and Dom before had.

I can't reach anyone, we're too far out. Dom echoed in my head, and I knew he was talking to everyone here that he could.

A snarl, a growl, a fight broke out near me, and I turned, alarmed to see Aaron and Carmine viciously fighting a massive rogue.

Dom, now on my other side, tore into one by himself, and my heart sped up as I watched in concern.

How are there so many? Jack snarled.

Carson whimpered as one slashed a big claw across his chest.

June, Dom brought down his target and turned to face me, blood dripping down his mouth. *You must run within range and get help. Get Smokey, get the warriors.*

But—

Run, June! Dom commanded me, really commanded, with some kind of force that pulled my feet out from under me as I stumbled to stay upright. And I wasn't the only one, every wolf around us flinched, save for Amelia and Bianca, who were entangled with the demon's work.

Run! Dom commanded again, and I bolted.

Dom ripped out the throat of one attacking rogue, only to be pounced on by two more. But it was enough of an opening that I leaped over the space and into the mountainside, where I could get away.

Run!

My wolf was yipping in my head. Overwhelming me. Fueling me. We ran. I ran faster than I had ever run before, my paws barely brushing the ground for a heartbeat before lifting me higher and faster as I ran for my life. And for Dom's life, and everyone else back in the clearing. Because I knew in my heart that there were too many rogues, and it was too suspicious that they were attacking in such numbers when they had never shown themselves like that before.

I growled, running. A bullet through the wind, slicing a path in the mountainside as I came close enough to the village to call for help.

Smokey! I called. *Smokey! Wake up!*

What is it, kid? Smokey grumbled. *I'm about to patrol.*

Rogues! I growled. *A whole bunch of them! Dom and the others are fighting them off, but there are too many.*

Where? Smokey ordered, fully in protection mode.

South, maybe? I'm not sure. Can you follow my smell or something? I asked.

I'll be right there.

I could feel roughly where Smokey was, not far from the training fields. I ran that way, hoping to meet him.

Curving around the village, I swept through the trees easily. When I saw Smokey's old gray wolf, my heart lifted.

Smokey! I called.

I nearly ran right past him, and I had to turn around so we were heading the right direction. I caught up with him easily and kept to his pace.

How many? he barked.

A lot. Dom and the others need help, I answered.

Smokey cursed and tried to run a little faster. I met his speed again. *Listen to me, I'll alert Alpha and some warriors. You get Doc and take him there, okay?*

Yes! I replied and changed course again.

Smokey went his way, and I went mine. I rounded to Doc's house easily. *Doc! Emergency!*

June? Doc sounded sleepy. *What is it?*

Rogues! Near the border. Smokey wants me to bring you.

Hold on, I'm coming!

I continued past Doc's house and to my own. I pushed open the front door, probably breaking the lock, but that was a problem for later. I went straight for my backpack of supplies and bit the straps, carrying the bag back out with me.

Where to? Doc asked.

This way.

I met Doc again, then ran with him toward the rogues. The most frustrating part was having to slow my pace or stop every few minutes for him to catch up. I wanted to run. I wanted to get to Dom. I wanted to make sure everyone was okay.

June, Doc said eventually. *I can smell your trail, just go.*

Without replying, I let my wolf loose, shooting down the mountainside and racing for Dom. Their scent reached my nose before I could see the fight. I could hear it too. Once I broke through the trees and finally saw the mess, I dropped my bag and jumped in.

The glowing mess that was Jerod, Amelia, Bianca, and the demon was the only untouched part of the field. Blood was splattered everywhere, there were bodies down, and I looked from wolf to wolf to make sure none of them were my friends.

Dom was tearing into three at once. Aaron had two, and Carson and Jack were tag-teaming a huge male. Carmine was glorious, her auburn fur matted with blood while she thrashed her way through any who dared come near Jerod or the demon.

Dom! I cried out, just for him.

June. He sounded fueled by anger. *Run back to the village, stay where it's safe.*

Dom was slammed down by one of the wolves he was fighting, and another bit down on his leg hard enough that it snapped.

My heart nearly burst, and I found myself running at full speed toward them then biting into a rogue's neck. It was all on instinct. Messy and not at all thought through. But I couldn't watch Dom get hurt, and I wasn't going to sit by without helping.

Knit the circle, boys! Smokey called, ripping through all our heads, and lifting my heart.

I had no clue what he meant, but he was *here*. At least the others seemed to know what to do. Immediately, they moved around.

Repositioning and forming what I assumed was a more sustainable stand in the battle.

Smokey arrived, a couple of wolves behind him, and joined the fray.

After that, it was all a blur. Gnashing teeth, slashing claws. I was in the fight for a little bit but when Doc arrived he pulled me out of it and we shifted to help the wounded.

As the first rays of light filtered through the trees, giving life to the bloody scene around us, Dom and Smokey fought off the last of the rouges by ripping its belly wide open and letting it fall to the ground.

I tied a splint to Aaron's leg, panting as I wiped the sweat off my forehead. One thing to come out of the fight was that I no longer gave a shit about how naked I was. Once you apply a tourniquet on a werewolf while sitting on his chest with your whole ass on display, nothing else matters.

"Thank you," Aaron grunted, and I laid down on the hard ground next to him, panting.

"Don't mention it."

There was a huge pop in the air above the circle. The demon was gone, and the wolves and warlock seemed just fine.

I laughed. At least as much as I could in the state of exhaustion I was in. At least some of us were fine, and hopefully, their situation was resolved.

"June,"

Dom had shifted. He kneeled next to me.

"Are you okay?" he asked.

"I might need a nap," I said.

He smirked, brushing the hair from my forehead. "That can be arranged."

"Kid," Smokey said. "You did good. See me tomorrow." He

began walking around the dead rogues and dragging them into a pile.

I winced. "Not even one day off?"

Dom chuckled. "Not with Smokey."

I yawned, unable to stop myself. "Alpha never came."

"I know," Dom growled. "I'm going to find out more about that later. But first, you're getting a bath and a nap."

"Is there anyone else injured?" I asked, my eyes closing as Dom lifted me into his arms. His chest was warm. Smelly, but warm.

"I've got the rest," Doc called from nearby. "Take her home, Dom."

"Can do, Doc," Dom said.

I think.

Because it all grew fuzzy as I fell deeply asleep.

CHAPTER THIRTY-FOUR

JUNE

The wind was a bit obnoxious, pulling at my hair and clothes. But I was able to pass through the main village and get into the trees soon enough, where the wind was cut down significantly. I was full of energy and determination, and maybe a bit anxious over what Smokey wanted.

I spotted him easily in the field, so I supposed I'd find out soon.

Smokey wasn't naked today, which was saying something. He had on a pair of sweatpants and some slip-on sandals. He stood next to a smaller male, arms crossed and obviously grumbling at each other.

Great. The perfect time to approach him. I grimaced and stepped forward.

Smokey's head snapped to look at me the moment I entered the field. "Afternoon, sleeping beauty."

I winced. "Hello, Smokey."

"Sorry, June," he said. "I get a bit cranky when I don't sleep well."

"I don't think any of us did, Smokey. It's okay. What did you want to see me for?"

Smokey jerked his head to the male standing next to him. "June, this is Tanner. He's our best tracker."

I gave him a once over. He stood about my height, which was shorter than a lot of the other males I'd seen so far, but he was built like a truck. He wore shorts, and I could see the thigh muscles of a runner. He reminded me of my old coach, actually. He'd seen a lot of sun, and his face and shoulders were absolutely dripping with freckles. He kept his head shaved, but he had a neat black beard trimmed short to his chin.

"Hello," I said.

Tanner nodded sharply. "Hello, June. Nice to meet you."

"I told Tanner here how fast you shot out of those woods last night," Smokey said. "We think you could be a candidate for his team."

"A tracker?"

"The trackers keep things off the pack lands that shouldn't be here," Tanner explained.

"And they're having a hard time of it lately," Smokey jabbed.

Tanner growled.

"Relax, Tanner. I don't blame you. There's something not right about those rogues."

"Agreed," Tanner said.

He turned to me. "The more the merrier, as long as you can keep up."

"She can keep up all right," Smokey said, bringing a hand down on my shoulder. "Run with her right now and see."

"Hmm. But how's her nose?" Tanner asked.

"She passed her first test quick enough," Smokey said. "But I doubt you'll just take my word for it. Run with her, Tanner."

The tracker looked me up and down one more time. "All right. June, you up for a little run?"

I was opening my mouth to answer when Smokey cut me off. "Not that prissy little run you did for me the other day," he growled. "Run like you mean it. Run like last night."

"Yes, I'm up for a run." I glared at him. "A real one."

"Good." Tanner took off his shirt. "Let's get to it, then."

We shifted. It was getting easier for me every time. When it was all said and done, Tanner had a similar build to my own wolf. Long, sleek legs and tail. But his own coat was the more common gray I had seen throughout the pack, albeit a slightly darker shade.

All right, June. Follow me if you can.

Run! My wolf skipped with excitement. Yes, run. We would run, and I'd stop holding back. If this wolf body was going to break like my human one did, it would have done as much last night.

Tanner shot out of the training field like he was jumping a puddle, and I almost lost sight of him.

Taking off, the trees were a blur, much like last night. It was as though now that my feet had the taste of running again, I couldn't stop. My wolf was about to burst with excitement too; our tongue hung out of our mouth for a moment before I pulled it back in and charged harder.

The trees didn't go far before opening up to rocky mountain fields. Tanner was easy enough to spot, and we were drinking in his scent too. My wolf added it to our collection of smells, and we should have no problem recognizing Tanner by scent now.

Faster. Harder. We pushed down slopes and up hills. Tanner was a bolt of lightning, weaving through trees and over rocks in no discernable pattern, making him the most difficult thing I'd chased, probably ever.

Not bad, June. Let's see if you can follow me through the water, Tanner taunted.

We ran along the side of a very steep hill, and Tanner jumped down the sharp slope to a lake at the bottom.

I hesitated, but watching him land with a splash in the water, I saw that it would be fine. I backed up, then leaped off the steep hill, landing with a splash of my own.

Swimming with paws was very different, and I panicked for a moment until my wolf helped us steer upward. We broke the surface of the water and took a deep breath.

Now, where did Tanner go?

We paddled to the nearest shore and shook out our fur. I looked around sharply. There was no sign of Tanner, but there were plenty of trees to hide in. We sniffed the air but didn't catch any hint of Tanner.

Walking into the trees and looking around for tracks, a gray motion caught the corner of our eyes. I whipped our head around, just to see the end of a tail disappear behind some brush.

Yes!

My wolf was excited. We chased after the tail, twisting around a fallen tree and leaping over a puddle. I caught the scent of the wolf in my nose. It was Tanner! Or was it? The smell of Tanner was definitely there, but so was another musk of a wolf I hadn't met.

There, the rustling of a wolf against low branches off to the side. Making the decision that this was some kind of trick, my wolf and I abandoned the not-quite-right Tanner and went after the new one.

I got a much better glimpse of the wolf this time as it ran between trees. It looked a lot like Tanner, but again the smell wasn't quite there.

Deciding to stop, my wolf and I sat in the middle of the trees.

What do we do now?

Smell.

I closed my eyes. My wolf mostly took over when we were smelling things, and I sat back and let her do her thing as we smelled the air around us.

Suddenly, we were on our feet and walking back toward the lake. Nose to the ground, we ran without really looking until my wolf took me to a paw print. One single print in the muddy bank before Tanner had jumped into the thicker grass that wouldn't leave signs as easily.

But now we had him. The smell, the direction of the print, we ran. Tanner had taken a sharp turn, another trick to confuse us, but it wasn't going to work this time. With his scent in our nose and his trail in front of us, there was no way we were going to lose him this time.

More wolves. A distraction. They were intentionally showing small bits of themselves and making noises. I would have smiled if I had my human mouth. Clever, but not clever enough.

The scent was getting stronger, we were getting closer. Through the trees and around large rocks, we chased the trail. As it grew stronger, my heart raced with excitement.

Here!

My wolf insisted we had found where the trail ended. I looked around, confused. There wasn't much around us. A rocky cliff to one side, and a few sparse trees to the other.

Here?

Yes, here.

I looked around again, and the lines in the dirt might barely be claws pushing off the ground as someone jumped. Jumped to . . . a thick but low-hanging branch in a gnarly old evergreen tree. I ran to it, putting our front paws as high on the tree as I could get them, and let out a long howl.

"All right, all right, you found me." Tanner chuckled as he

dropped out of the tree. He had shed his wolf form and hidden as a human. Clever—as a human he was much smaller and it was easier to hide.

I sat down, satisfied with myself as two other wolves came out of the trees to sit around us.

The other wolves threw back their heads and howled. I was so excited that I joined them.

Tanner walked over and patted me on the back. He nodded to the other wolves, then beamed at me with approval.

"Well, boys, we have found ourselves a tracker."

CHAPTER THIRTY-FIVE

DOM

"Again," Smokey ordered.

Paws to the dirt and digging my claws into the ground, I was shoulder to shoulder with a growling Amelia.

Smokey had taken us deep into the mountains. Now that I was making some serious improvements and Amelia was growing even stronger, he didn't want us to be watched too closely. The warriors who had seen us training before didn't need to see and possibly report back to Evander what we were up to anymore. Not now, not when we were only a few weeks from the next full moon. Not when we were about to topple Evander.

The two of us lunged in synch, slamming into a dead tree that was easily as big around as either of us in wolf form. This time I heard a crack as we pushed into it with all our might.

"Okay, ease back," Smokey said.

We took a few steps back, and I eyed the huge tree as it swayed lightly.

"Looks like you're going to fell this one too," Smokey said. "Dom, you do this one."

I sighed through my nose, but obliged. Digging my claws into the earth under me, I sprang from the ground and lunged at the trunk. With my full weight and every ounce of muscle I could spare, I pushed into the tree.

"Your enemy won't always be smaller than you," Smokey said, watching from a safe distance. "And Evander is one big son of a bitch. Dom, you were born a beta but from good stock. Amelia, you were a born alpha, but as a female, you'll always be a bit smaller. Push through the tree, imagine your target a little farther back than the actual center of it, and shove until you're there."

A growl of frustration slipped out as I heaved, one last push. I imagined it just as Smokey had described, and shoved until more cracking told me the tree was about to give.

"Back off it!" Smokey snapped.

I leaped out of the way just in time to watch it tumble over, scattering birds, bugs, and broken branches everywhere. When all the debris was settled, I turned to Smokey.

"Not bad, kid. Not bad," he said. "Do you two want to get something to eat and head back home?"

Do you mean head back home and then get something to eat? Amelia asked.

"You know I don't, girlie." Smokey chuckled. "Come on, no lying around. We hunt like wolves."

Smokey shifted, and I caught my breath after slamming into trees all day. Once he was a grizzled, furry bastard, he led the way down the slope.

The sky was turning gray, a likely sign of rain tonight. I thought of June and her tracking lessons with Tanner. She would probably be thrown for a loop if all the scents washed away, but I suppose if anyone could show her how to get around that, Tanner could.

June was so fucking cute when she came home and told me about the trackers. Whatever our future brought, even if she was my luna, these skills would only benefit the pack, and I had no hesitations about her learning them. And it was always good to see her happy about something.

Dom. Smokey interrupted my thoughts. *Get your head out of your ass and go start a fight with Nathan.*

I swung my head around, looking, and listening. *Nathan? Wait, I see him.*

Sure enough, he was walking with Anna and his little cousin a good distance ahead of where we were heading toward a big grazing field to find dinner. Nathan stood out as the biggest, but Anna's shiny, mostly white coat was eye catching as well.

You want me to start a fight, with Nathan? I asked. *Why?*

Don't question me, boy! Just get in there. Smokey nipped at my tail, and I growled lightly but stayed fairly quiet. The wind was on my side anyway, so I crept toward the future alpha and beta quietly.

Don't fuck it up, Dom, Amelia warned. *You might be able to take Nate, but Anna is no slouch. She's his second for a reason.*

Good point, Smokey said. *Get in there and help him.*

Amelia crouched in the grass and followed my lead toward the Salt Fur wolves.

Grass brushed against my side as I crouched as low as possible. I faintly registered the smell of geese, possibly something we could come back for later if Smokey still wanted to hunt. Nathan, Anna, and Matt walked along, not showing any signs of noticing us.

As I crept into range, Nathan's ear twitched. It could have been a bug or an itch or the wind irritating him, but there was no taking chances with a wolf as strong as Nathan. I jumped, and Amelia was right behind me.

Nathan twisted, snarling, and swinging a set of sharp claws in the air between us, causing me to fall back. Anna was on top of Amelia, and Matt joined them soon after.

The fight was brutal. Nathan was definitely bred from alpha stock. Huge, heavy, and so much muscle to get through. When I wasn't defending myself from him, I managed to get in a few swipes or bites of my own while avoiding the mess behind me that was Anna, Matt, and Amelia.

But Amelia could handle them on her own. The problem was, Nathan knew that too.

In sync, Anna and Nathan jumped way back, putting space between them and their fights, and switched targets. Suddenly, Anna was on me with a whole new strategy and Matt was bouncing between whoever he could reach relatively safely.

What the hell was that? Amelia snarled.

Strategy, I growled. *Do you remember that time in Boston with the wildfire demon?*

Hell, yeah, I do, Amelia answered. *Let's do it.*

Just like Anna and Nathan had done, Amelia and I jumped back. But instead of lunging at different targets, Amelia ran for Nathan and I stayed back for just a heartbeat. Just long enough for Amelia to take up most of Nathan's vision and attention, and then I ran under her.

As Amelia jumped up to attack Nathan's face, I shoved under her and between them. Nathan, preoccupied with Amelia, lashed at her and sent her flying. But he wasn't fast enough to react when I came up to his throat with my teeth.

He was already on unsteady feet, so it was easy for me to shove my weight behind my lunge, and we both fell over, me pinning him down and keeping my fangs hovered over his neck.

Amelia recovered, but not before Anna had rammed her side. But Amelia wouldn't be taken down that easily, and after shoving Matt aside and down the hill a bit, she ran her full form into Anna, pinning her down not unlike I had Nathan. With a glance, the Salt Fur wolves backed down.

"You did all right, you two," Smokey said. He walked through the field behind us, in human form so he could talk to the whole group, not only those of us in Moonpeak.

We took his lead and shifted. I winced as tight, fresh skin where Nathan had gotten his claws in me pretty good pulled in the shift. I glanced at him in satisfaction, seeing a few of my own marks on him as well.

"What the hell?" Nathan growled.

"Keepin' you on your toes." Smokey chuckled. "Getting these two up to snuff."

"Where are you going, anyway?" I asked Nathan.

"Back to the pack. I don't like the sound of those rogues from the other day, and I want to check on everyone."

"To see if they've been spotted there too," Amelia said. "Good idea."

"We didn't see them last time, I don't know if we'll see them this time either," Anna said.

"But we need to stay on top of it anyway," Nathan replied.

"Could you send word if you've had any back home?" I asked. "I'd like to know how similar the rogues are this time compared to before."

"I'll do you one better." Nathan clapped a hand on my shoulder. "I'll be back for the new moon and I'll tell you myself. I'm not done kicking your ass into shape."

"Is that what you called him pinning you?" Anna giggled.

"You nearly caught Alpha Evander by surprise this visit," Smokey said. "He doesn't like that kinda thing too much."

"I know." Nathan rubbed the back of his neck, grinning. "What if I said I like trying to catch him off guard?"

Smokey gave Nathan a serious look. "Kid, my loyalty is still to this pack before anything else, and an alpha doesn't drop in on another alpha unannounced."

"Fine, fine." Nathan sighed. "But I hate sitting around at the borders for approval and an escort. There was a time me and Dad could show up whenever we felt like it."

"That time will come again," I promised.

Anna looked back at me and Amelia. "We'll hold you to that promise. See you guys soon enough."

"Yeah, and we might have to repay the surprise." Nathan punched me in the arm. "Keep an eye out over your shoulder, buddy."

"Keep an eye out under your chin," I said.

"He's got you there," Smokey joked.

"Yeah, yeah," Nathan said. "Laugh it up. That trick isn't going to work on me twice."

"It doesn't have to," Amelia said. "We've been together through a lot of shit. We've got more tricks than that up our coats."

"Take care," I said. "Don't let your guard down with those things out there."

Anna nodded. "We won't."

The three of them shifted, skin growing fur, bodies lowering to the ground and getting bigger. Once they left our pack lands, we too shifted into our own wolf forms, and I was satisfied with how our little fight went down.

We need to remember more of the stuff we've pulled off

together, I said to Amelia. *All five of us. We need to be ready just in case.*

I'm game, Amelia said. *Just in case.*

While I like you're planning and finally acting like real alphas, Smokey interrupted, *you two still have to catch something to eat.*

And while you're at it, catch some extra for the pack stores, Smokey added. *Now, let me see you put some real hustle into it.*

There are some geese nearby, I offered.

Nice try, Dom, Smokey said. *But I'm feeling pretty damn puckish.*

No, Amelia snapped. *No, Smokey.*

You kids need to catch me a big old moose, Smokey said, pleased with himself.

Dammit, Smokey! Amelia snapped.

I wholeheartedly agreed with a growl. We had been at training for hours.

Make that a moose, each, Smokey said. *Now, come on, kids, ol' Smokey's hungry.*

And even under the guise of dinner, our training continued.

Dammit, Smokey.

CHAPTER THIRTY-SIX

JUNE

The shower hit me at my favorite temperature. Scalding.

My skin turned pink under the hot water while I hummed a stupid song that was stuck in my head and scrubbed my face.

Washing away a hard day of tracking with Tanner and the others was a nice treat. They had me running through dirt, ponds, mud. Being a tracker was a lot harder than I'd thought it was going to be. When they weren't training, they were following up on leads of scents reported by other wolves in the pack or by Alpha. Tanner even kept chunks of fur from the recent rogue attacks for us to refresh our memories on and sniff around for. It was kind of gross, actually.

I scrunched up my nose just thinking about it and started to shampoo my hair. I heard the front door open and grinned.

"June?" Dom asked.

"Bathroom!" I called.

Dom walked through the house to the bathroom door. "You're in the shower?"

"Yeah," I said, my answer barely leaving my lips before Dom opened the door and came in.

"Hello, beautiful," Dom said, pulling back the edge of the shower curtain.

"Hey!" I squealed. "I'm kind of busy here!"

"Good, then you won't be distracted when I hop in and shower too."

"Don't you dare!" I flicked some water at him but I was grinning the whole time. "I'll never get to finish with you here."

"Mmm. Depends on what you're trying to finish," Dom said, and stripped off his clothes and climbed in. "Much better. I've been looking forward to a shower since this morning."

"What did Smokey have you doing today?" I asked.

Dom grimaced. "Some training in a pond. Something about using water resistance and weights."

"Eww," I said. "That explains the smell."

Dom growled lightly, putting his hands on my hips. "All the more reason I need under the water right now."

"Whoa!" Dom caught me by surprise as he lifted me up and switched places with me.

I smacked him on the arm. "This shower isn't big enough to be playing around like that!"

"Sorry, June, let me get the worst of it off real quick and I'll happily help you scrub up." Dom leaned back under the showerhead, wiping the water running down his head and torso to brush off some of the dirt and grime.

And I only stared a little bit.

"Are you enjoying the view there, June?" Dom asked, not even looking at me.

Okay, maybe I was staring *more* than a little bit.

"There, enough for now. You finish up first," Dom said.

We traded places again and I finished rinsing out my hair.

"Better?" he asked.

"Better. The shower is yours, but I'm using the sink for now, okay?"

"Whatever you want, as long as I can wash Smokey's bullshit training away." Dom sighed, getting under the water again and grabbing his soap.

I dried off and wrapped my hair in a towel while Dom showered, then took to the mirror for lotion and to brush my teeth.

"Hey, Dom," I said, swirling lotion on my cheeks, "I've been meaning to talk to you about something."

"Yeah?" he asked from the shower.

I bit my lower lip, trying to decide how to bring it up. I rubbed the last of the lotion into my skin and set the bottle back on the sink. "Well, all our friends who've found their mates recently have, um, marked each other. Amelia and Bianca even did it twice."

The water shut off and he pulled open the curtain. "Amelia had to redo theirs because whatever Jerod had done to untangle their souls undid the bond with Bianca."

"Right," I said. "And Carmine and Jerod, they marked as soon as they got back to their cabin that night."

"Mm-hm," Dom agreed. He grabbed his towel and began to dry off.

"I was thinking, tomorrow you're trying to reconnect to the pack at the new moon picnic," I said, "and remind them how strong you are. Show that you could be alpha material."

"I am," Dom said, tossing his towel into the hamper and putting his hands on the sink on either side of me. I looked into the mirror, meeting his eyes as he surrounded me.

Damn, he made my heart beat so fast.

"And I was thinking that if you were doing that, I should do the same as your mate. As a luna," I stuttered.

Dom grinned, leaning his face down next to mine and kissing my cheek. "Juniper Gunn, are you coming on to me?"

"I'm serious, Dom. I'm trying to put on a good show for your cause."

Dom turned me around to face him, not in the mirror but eye to eye. He lifted me and sat me on the sink so we could be at a more even level.

"June, marking you is permanent. Very permanent," Dom said.

"Nothing a demon can't handle, apparently," I mumbled.

"I will say, I've never seen anything like that before." He laughed. "But, June, we're not warlocks, and I have no idea what kind of deal Jerod made, what he had to give up for that kind of service from a demon."

I was also curious, but too afraid to ask Jerod myself.

"When I mark you, it's going to be because you're ready for it, and not because you want to help me show off to the pack."

"Dom." I reached up and put my arms around his neck. "I do want to help you, but I want to be marked by you because I love you, Dom."

He grinned, his eyes lighting up as he leaned in and kissed me. "I love you, too, June. But are you sure? I was going to sort out this mess with Evander before I asked you about marking. You haven't decided what to do about school, or your family, or Seattle."

"As much as I want those things to work out, in my heart, I can't leave this place. It feels right, it feels like I should be here. And for school, maybe I can go to one here in Canada. My job I won't miss. I'll miss Kat like crazy, but I need to be here. I need to stand on Moonpeak soil and run with this pack. Leaving it is no longer a choice my heart can make."

I reached up to cup his face with my hands, planting a light kiss on his lips. "Leaving you is no longer a choice my heart can make."

Dom scooped me up off the counter and into his arms. I squeaked, my towel falling off my head and onto the floor as he whisked me from the bathroom.

"You're sure?" he asked again. "Because I'm ready to do this right now if you are."

My heart pounded in my chest, and something stirred over my neck. That sensitive feeling that took my breath away. All I could do to answer Dom was nod, but he took it with a smirk and dropped me on our bed.

There were no words between us, and Dom pressed his mouth to mine in a deep kiss that distracted me long enough to be surprised when his fingers gripped my backside.

I gasped, wrapping my arms around his neck as I held on tight while he lifted me to him. Our bodies pressed together as tight as he wanted them to be. My breath was hot and fast, and I couldn't get enough of his lips on mine.

"June," he growled into my kiss, pulling his lips away and moving his head down to my neck.

I shivered as he planted a soft kiss on my skin where my shoulder met my neck.

"Fuck," I hissed.

"Not yet," Dom said, grinning into my neck. "Although, I must say I like it when you swear."

A breathy laugh escaped me as he lifted me from the bed. I squealed and held on tight.

"Where are we going?" I asked.

"Bed is too low," Dom grumbled. "I need a counter for this."

A counter? For what?

Mate!

My wolf was going nuts.

Whatever Dom had planned, he had made it to the kitchen and

set me down on a counter. He pushed something or other off the counter behind me as he slid me onto it.

"I've wanted to do this for a while now." Dom flashed me a dangerous grin and dipped his head downward. He kissed my collarbone, then the top of my breasts, then my stomach.

"What are you doing?" I asked.

Dom kissed my stomach again, his hands on my hips as he held me in place. He looked up, his eyes meeting mine, a glint of trouble in them.

"I'm going to taste you, then fuck you, then bite you," he said, simply.

A noise caught in my throat as his fingers slid over the most tender parts of me. My breasts, my neck, and . . . farther south.

"Dom," I breathed as his fingers slipped into me.

"Hold on to the counter if you need to," he said, lowering his head and removing his fingers, quickly replacing them with his tongue.

I sucked in a breath and my arms fell behind me on the counter to hold myself up. Something or other over knocked over, but I didn't care. Dom's hands lightly pressed into my inner thighs, keeping my legs open as he helped himself to the taste of me.

I was hot. My face was hot, my neck was hot, my lower half was definitely hot. My fingers slid through something soft behind me as Dom gripped my thighs tighter.

Dom's tongue was bold in its explorations, and when he put his lips on my clit he set thousands of nerves on fire. I couldn't keep a moan from my throat as he finally lifted his head again.

"Fuck, the taste of you, June," Dom growled, then made his way back up. He kissed my stomach, my breasts, my collarbone, then my lips.

"Are you ready?" he asked.

"Yes," I breathed.

He kissed me softly, reaching up to brush the loose hair off my face, and then pressed his hard self against me.

Kissing me passionately, he moved his mouth harder against me as I opened up for him. His tongue slid inside, then he moved his mouth in rhythm with mine, and I was caught off guard when he slid inside me.

I moved my head back to take in a sharp breath. In my surprise, I moved my hands from behind me to around Dom's neck. When my eyes flicked down to my fingers, a laugh slipped out of me.

"What is it?" Dom asked, pausing his motion and causing me to move my hips, trying to get him deeper in me again.

"Don't worry about it," I said.

He looked down at his chest and around his shoulders where my hands had trailed. White flour dusted the both of us; I had knocked over the jar. Dom smirked, meeting my gaze, and hugged me as he began thrusting again.

It was so good, I didn't realize he was moving his hands behind me until he brought a white thumb up to rub my cheek.

"Hey!" I giggled.

"Payback." He chuckled. "And a distraction."

"A distraction from what?" I asked, looking down at his flour-covered hand.

"It'll be better in a minute," he said. In a flash, he moved his head down to my already flushed and sensitive neck.

I had about a heartbeat's warning as his teeth grazed my skin. I tensed, bracing to be bitten.

My wolf was going insane. Her erratic energy bounced in my head as Dom's fangs grew, and he bit down.

I gritted my teeth, the sensation of pain hitting me for a

moment, but then I sucked in a breath as it was quickly replaced with a hot flood of pleasure.

"Dom!" I cried, holding on to his shoulders for dear life. His thrusting never stopped, and it was almost too much to bear the intense feelings from the sex and from his bite at the same time.

Then my own teeth started aching. I ran my tongue over them, feeling a point where my canines were.

"Dom," I said, a little softer but as much as I could handle at that moment.

Dom moved his own teeth out of my neck gently. "Do it."

I didn't have to ask him what it was I was supposed to be doing, because my wolf was screaming it in my head.

Bite!

Bite. Right. I moved forward and sank my teeth into Dom in roughly the same place he had bit my own neck. It was purely instinctual, biting down and feeling his hard thrust in my core.

Dom grunted, his body stiffening, and he leaned in to bite me again.

It was too much. It was everything.

I unraveled, pulling my teeth from Dom's neck and screaming his name. Dom held me tightly, and even after he spilled himself into me he continued to thrust gently until we were both spent.

I was breathless when he moved back from me, and he had to help me sit upright on the counter.

My eyes came into focus and I found his gaze on me.

"It's over, June," Dom murmured with a grin on his face. "We're marked."

"That was . . . wow," I breathed.

"Are you okay? Do you want to rest on the bed?"

I was dizzy, but it didn't stop me from trying to shake my head.

"Is that biting thing something we can do again?" I asked.

Dom's eyes lit up and his lips curled into a wicked smile.

"It certainly is, my mate," he replied.

And his lips met mine as I realized we were, in fact, not going to leave the house that day.

But it was oh so worth it.

Dom. My mate.

CHAPTER THIRTY-SEVEN

JUNE

"You look gorgeous," Dom said.

I smoothed out my sweater in the mirror, turning to look at myself in as many angles as I could. "I didn't know I'd want to look nice for the pack until now. I thought practical clothes would do the job."

Dom sighed, walking over to me and turning me away from the bathroom mirror. "June, it doesn't matter what you look like, it matters how you act. How you treat the pack. And trust me, you're perfect."

"You shouldn't have let me just buy sports clothes," I grumbled. "And we need to do laundry, this is the best thing I had clean."

Dom leaned in and kissed my neck, right over where he'd bitten me yesterday. I shivered. "And who's fault is it we got flour all over the house?"

I turned red and moved away from the mirror. "Let's just go before we're late."

He chuckled but followed me out of the bathroom as I ran my fingers through my hair.

"Relax, June. The pack already likes you." Dom opened the front door. "You're brave, capable, kind, and you're even integrating into the pack as a tracker. You'll be a perfect luna."

"That's right, I'm really enjoying learning about tracking with Tanner and the others. If you become alpha, and I'm your mate, will I have to stop tracking?"

Dom shook his head. "I don't see why you would, you'd just have to cut back on it some so that you could perform your other duties as well."

I perked up at that. "Really?"

Dom entangled our fingers and lifted my hand for a kiss. "Really."

"All right, then, I'm ready. What exactly do you need me to do today?"

We walked to the usual picnic place. "Today, I'm going to reconnect with old pack members. They'll remember me as a kid who ran away, I want them to know me as a strong wolf who came back. A wolf who cares about the pack. You don't really need to do anything other than mingle and meet new people. If you think you're making a good impression on someone, though, it wouldn't hurt to bring up that we're mates. A good impression from one of us can be a good impression on both of us."

"Got it. Be charming. I can do that, I think. I'll channel my inner Kat, she's the people person."

Dom laced his warm hand in mine. "We aren't here to sew any seeds of displeasure with Evander, though. Today is just positive things, okay? There is enough unrest about his reign already."

"I won't," I said. "I'd rather enjoy myself than think about him anyway."

We crested the top of the hillside next to the village. Looking down on the festivities, I could see there were clusters again. Last month I didn't know any better, this month it felt . . . wrong. Packs shouldn't be this way. Where were the games? The groups talking about a shared interest? The children playing? Because even the children I saw playing were in small groups, and from what I could tell it was the same kind of groups their parents kept. Pack wolves with pack wolves, warriors playing with the children of warriors. It wasn't right.

"I'll start with some of the warriors," Dom said. "They'll be the hardest to win over, and I don't know a lot of them. They've come in while I was away, I need to correct that."

I glanced down at the picnic at a few familiar faces. Amelia and Bianca were talking with Carson, Jack, and Aaron. Carmine and Jerod were talking to Linda. Smokey was nowhere to be found, but if I had to wager a guess, he was on patrol. Then I spotted a mix of people I knew and people I didn't. Perfect.

"Doc's talking with some people by the fire pits. I'll start there, maybe Doc can introduce me," I said.

"Let me know if you need me," Dom said, leaning in to plant a soft kiss on my lips

"I will," I said. Our hands with the entwined fingers fell apart as Dom walked in one direction and I walked another. I made my way to the delicious smell of the cooking food in hopes of getting into some polite conversation with new people.

The hill was a bit slick from overnight rain, the dew on the grass making the trek downward slippery. I watched my footing, keeping my sneakers on the flattest spots I could find.

Once I was at the bottom, I could focus better on where I was going. I was glad to look toward the pits and find Doc in conversation with Naomi. I froze. Was this the first time she'd been outside of the pack house? Her eyes were clear today, and she seemed alert enough.

Naomi's here! I opened a link with Dom and Amelia.

Where is she? Amelia demanded.

I'm near the food being cooked, I said.

Evander? Dom asked.

I don't see him, but there's a couple of big guys by her I haven't talked to before.

See if you can start a conversation, we'll head your way and see if there's an opening for us to get close, Dom said.

Right.

Watching Naomi as I got closer, I made note of Alice joining to talk to Doc. The big guys near them were silent. I built up a pleasant smile and approached. "Hello," I called. "Can I join you? This smell is pretty hard to resist."

They turned to face me. Alice smiled and winked. "You can come over, but no sneaking bites. I've been chasing the pups off of the meat all morning."

I gave a nervous laugh and came to a stop between Naomi and Alice. The two unknown males by them who stood at the pits nodded their welcome.

"I don't think I've gotten to meet everyone yet," I said. "I'm Juniper, are you hunters?"

The pair looked like brothers. Sandy hair, the same gray eyes, and a dimple on the left cheek. But while their resemblance was uncanny, it was easy enough to tell them apart by an obvious height difference. I kept shooting glances at Naomi, who wasn't smiling as she stood by, but this was my best chance to assess who was here and if they were keeping an eye on her for Evander.

"Sure, we know you," the shorter one said. "Dom's mate, right? You made for a bit of a show on the full moon."

The taller one elbowed him. "Don't say it weird like that. He means your wolf is impressive. I promise he's not a creep, just awkward."

"I'm Franklin, this is my brother Danny," the tall one introduced them. "I hear you're with Tanner now?"

My face lit up. "Yes, I love tracking. It's really hard work, but it's challenging and it's important."

Doc nodded. "You're right, it is. I miss having a helping hand around the clinic, though."

"Sorry, Doc," I said.

He laughed and shook his head. "No, no. Smokey was right to show you to Tanner. But if you'd still be willing to help on occasion if I get more on my plate than I can handle . . ."

"Of course," I said. "I do have a passion for health care, and if I can help the pack please let me know."

Alice beamed at me. "I'll be right back, it's time to season those ducks."

"I'll let you know if I need the extra hands," Doc said. "And it might not hurt to keep a few of your supplies in a small case you can carry when you go tracking. You'll be the first on the scene if something happens."

"That's a really good idea, actually," I said. "Thanks, Doc. I'll have to make something."

"You'd be there before me. You're maybe the fastest thing on four legs that I've ever seen."

"Is she really?" Naomi asked, a polite smile on her face. "I'd love to see that some time."

I turned to her. "I don't know if I'm faster than the other trackers, but I'm enjoying it. Maybe we can go together sometime, I do love a good run."

Run!

Shh! Not right now.

"Do you run much, Naomi?" I asked. "I didn't see you on the full moon."

Naomi looked a bit uncomfortable. She coughed. "I was occupied elsewhere. Not feeling well."

Wolf!

Wolf? Yes, there are a lot of wolves around here.

Something was getting my wolf all worked up. Maybe it was the delicious-smelling food next to us. Maybe it was the picnic with our whole pack. I shrugged her off. I needed to focus here.

"I heard you were in a fight with those rogues," Danny half whispered. "I can't believe we're seeing those things again."

"Careful," Doc said with a nervous laugh. "Alpha's been putting a stop to that kind of talk. Says he's looking into it and not to stir up fear."

The group fell into an uncomfortable silence. Naomi's expression flashed with worry before falling back into her neutral mask.

"Still, June," Franklin said, "you must be pretty strong to make it through that fight before your shift. And you got paired with a wolf like Dominic. He was the beta's son, you know."

"He's pretty amazing. But I don't really know how strong I am, you might ask Smokey. He tested me on a few things, but he didn't comment much, so it's hard to know what he thinks."

Franklin elbowed Danny. "Do you think fast and strong make a good hunter? Maybe we should invite her when we go after the picnic game."

"Hold on you two." Alice came back over to the group, finished with the cooking for now. "She's got enough on her plate for this pack as it is, don't you go piling on more."

I chanced a look over my shoulder. Dom and Amelia were a distance away, but their eyes were trained on me and Naomi.

I'm working on it, I told them.

Wolf! I rolled my shoulders, trying to relax at whatever my wolf was trying to tell me.

Wolf? I wondered. *What do you mean wolf?*

Naomi stiffened, her eyes widening.

"Are you okay?" I asked.

"Naomi!" someone called from the other side of the picnic field. Alpha Evander was looking sternly at our group. "Naomi, come here *now*."

Naomi froze and looked into the distance with a strange expression on her face. Evander's shout seemed to snap her out of it, and she turned slowly toward him, keeping her eyes turned off into the woods, where she had been looking a moment ago.

"Naomi!" Evander called.

A small whine came from her throat. Her look of conflict and confusion hurt me. She took another step toward Evander, and I reached out and grabbed her wrist to stop her.

Her eyes finally left the woods, flicking to meet mine with surprise.

"I—" I didn't know what to say. I didn't know what made me stop her from going to Evander, or why it bothered me this time.

"Stay, Naomi," Amelia ordered, walking past the both of us to put herself between us and Evander.

"Amelia." Naomi's voice wavered, and I nearly had to catch her as she swayed.

Amelia looked over her shoulder, glassy eyes brimming with worry pointed at her sister. "I love you, Naomi. I'm sorry I left you."

Naomi's face crumpled as a sob escaped her, and I pulled her into a hug.

"I know I've been gone a while," Amelia said, addressing

Evander. "But in ten years of seeing other packs, I've never met an alpha who would demand a female at their heels like that."

That garnered a lot of attention, and the fields were silent with eavesdropping wolves. Evander's face twisted for a heartbeat before he regained his image. "They say the moon makes every pack different, I don't see why that can't pertain to Moonpeak."

Heat wrapped around my back as Dom joined me in the hug. I moved out of the way as Naomi sobbed into his arms. "Dom, I . . . I . . ."

"Shh." He rubbed her back as she sobbed. "We've got you, Naomi. Whatever's going on, we're getting you out of it. Right now."

"How are those rogues, Evander?" Amelia prodded. "Find out what's going on yet?"

A ripple of whispers followed her comment, and who knew how many private links had just opened.

Shouting. Growling. We all turned our heads to where Naomi had been looking. Some commotion was coming out of the trees.

"What is that?" someone asked.

Mate!

I frowned. We already had a mate.

No! Wolf mate!

Wolf mate? I looked at the trees, then back at Naomi, who had turned in Dom's arms to face the commotion with an expression of disbelief.

"Oh shit," I breathed. "Move! Move out of the way."

I pushed Alice and Doc off to the side, and the hunters took my lead and gave us space. Dom had barely released Naomi from the hug when I put her between us and the charging wolf that was now tearing across the field.

My wolf knew this giant wolf. I knew this giant wolf. His scent was familiar, and his huge size reminded me of Dom or

Evander. This was an alpha wolf, charging at us with desperation in his eyes.

Dom pulled me off Naomi in time for the wolf to shift and scoop her into his arms. A big, naked Nathan held a shocked Naomi. He covered her in kisses, and my cheeks burned from grinning.

The whole pack was silent. I glanced at Evander just long enough to see his face turn beet-red in anger before he dropped it and regained his composure again. The other wolves around us gathered in a large ring around the newly found pair.

"Naomi!" Nathan said. "I can't believe it was you. How have we not seen each other since you shifted?"

Naomi was finally realizing what was happening to her. A smile spread across her face and she wrapped her arms around Nathan's neck. "I don't know! We went to high school in Salt Fur with you."

"But I left to train under my uncle in Labrador your senior year!" Nathan finished.

She gasped. "I was a late bloomer! I didn't shift until—"

Nathan grinned, leaning down and planting a deep kiss on Naomi's lips. She blushed but kissed him back just as hard.

An arm slipped around my waist. "Well, I'll be damned."

I looked up at Dom, who was smiling just as stupidly as Nathan was.

"I'm happy for them," I said. "But how in the last ten years have they not met up?"

Dom's expression grew dark, and he glanced over at Evander, who remained farther back in the field while the rest of the pack was gathering around the happy couple.

"I can think of a few reasons," he answered.

"What the absolute fuck is this?"

The outraged voice startled enough of us into turning to face

Amelia. Bianca was beside her, amusement all over her face as Amelia fumed.

"It was you? You bastard!" Amelia came near them.

"Amelia!" Naomi managed to squeak.

She nudged her way out of Nathan's arms, throwing herself into Amelia's embrace. To her credit, I'd never seen Amelia's expression so gentle as when she wrapped her arms around her sister. After a moment, during which I suspect Naomi and Amelia linked for a few private words, Naomi pulled back. "Don't talk to Nathan that way anymore, Amelia," Naomi said. "He's my mate."

"Leave them alone, Amelia," Dom said. "Personally, I wouldn't trust anyone else with her."

Amelia growled, and Bianca reached over to grab her hand. Sighing, Amelia wiped a hand down her face. "So be it. But if you hurt her at all, I'm skinning you alive, from your dick to your eyeballs."

"If you'll excuse me, I'll be taking Naomi, as we have things to discuss," Nathan said.

He carried her away from the picnic, the whole of Moonpeak cheering them on and yelling lewd suggestions. Tears formed in my eyes, and I wiped them away as we watched them go. And I suddenly felt lighter as I realized one more worry was off our plate. Naomi was more than safe in Nathan's care.

Evander wore a blank expression as he watched the excitement.

"Not much left for him to hold on to," Dom said, low in my ear.

Not much left at all.

Two more weeks and the next full moon that rose over Moonpeak would be a full moon to remember.

CHAPTER THIRTY-EIGHT

JUNE

The smell of metals in the earth beneath me was strong in my nose.

Tanner took me on patrol with him to walk the entire border of the pack. If we just walked, it would take us more than one day to do it, so he let us run some of it since this was my first time. As I got used to the job, I would be able to walk around the very edges of Moonpeak territory and come back into town once a week.

I held my nose to the earth as a light misting of rain coated my shiny black fur. I resisted the near-constant urge to shake the wet off, but all I'd be doing was prolonging the inevitable soaking.

My wolf, more so than Tanner, was teaching me about smells. He told me she would be my best teacher, and he wasn't wrong. She might be the expert, but if I couldn't identify what she was trying to tell me about a scent or a mark she found, then I wouldn't be any use to a tracker team.

June, over here, Tanner said, pulling my attention from the tang of fresh soil in my nose.

I walked over to where he was standing by a tree, nose pointed to a marked-up patch on it. My wolf instantly picked up the smell.

That's damage from antlers. A buck will rub his scent on the trees in breeding season. Turns on the lady deer. Makes 'em horny.

Ew. I chuckled. *That was maybe the worst pun I've ever heard. Why do we need to know about that?*

Hunting, June. Now, these marks are pretty old. Last season, in fact. But this fall when they start appearing fresh, I want you to be able to spot them and tell me or Smokey or Alpha, Tanner said. *We don't hunt the deer in their breeding season, or we'd never have enough deer the next year.*

That makes sense, I said. *Okay, I think I could spot them again.*

Good, Tanner said. *Spotting the first signs in certain animals' changing seasons is vital to our survival. We hunt what is excess, we harvest when it's time, we plant when the season calls for it. Knowing when animals are coming out of hibernation, or mating, or putting on fat for winter is all a part of a tracker's job.*

I thought trackers just watched out for enemies.

No. Tanner moved on from the tree to keep us going around the pack lands. *Wolves may be volatile by nature, but we really don't get attacked that often. Not way out here.*

Not even by rogues? I asked.

Even with Tanner's wolf form to show his expression, I could have sworn his eyes darkened. *No, I suppose those have changed things. I still can't believe we haven't found them.*

I paused a moment before continuing to follow Tanner. Smokey had said the trackers were on the trail of the rogues both times now. He must be disappointed that they haven't found anything.

Hey, Tanner—

Shh, Tanner snapped. *Did you hear that?*

I jerked my head back, my ears flicking around to try to catch what he could have heard. It was hard to sort through the other sounds of nature for something out of place.

Damn. It's Vernon. He's wanting me to see something.

Do you want me to keep going on patrol or . . . ?

You better come with me. I don't want anyone alone with those rogue freaks out there, Tanner said.

He turned northeast and began running around the forested area and through a spacious patch of field. I followed him easily. My wolf loved the progress we made. Since finally letting go of my fears while running, I was enjoying it again. Unfortunately, that meant most other wolves went at a pace a little slower than I ever wanted to go. It's hard to find a good running partner when you're a tracker.

The sun was still high enough in the sky that I wondered if second breakfast was a bad call. I had eaten before leaving the house, when the sun wasn't even up yet, but I had already worked up an appetite, and lunch was still a ways off.

But I didn't want to interrupt Tanner with that kind of thing either. Not until we found out what Vernon wanted. Should I be worried, or was this routine stuff for the head tracker to deal with?

Finally cresting a small hill and heading down a steep slope, I spotted a gray wolf and a brownish one crouching behind a thicket of trees.

Vernon, Tess, what is it? Tanner asked as we approached them. We mirrored their crouching position.

Something weird was here, the gray one said. *Look at these markings.*

Tanner crawled forward on his belly, peering at whatever Vernon had found. I moved, curiously trying to see what it was.

You dug a damn hole outside of pack boundaries, Tanner said. *Why did you even come this far?*

It's my fault, Tanner. The brownish one spoke up. A female with an American accent that surprised me. I had been around the Canadians for too long.

She caught a trace of this on the wind, Vernon said. *I thought she was thinking up things, smelling nothing. Drove her nuts for a good hour until I caught it too.*

Whoever did this walked across pack lands, I just know it, Tess said.

If they did, they didn't touch a damn thing, Vernon said. *We couldn't find a trace of where it was coming from on anything but the wind. That is, until we got here.*

Tanner nodded, and leaned into what I could now see was a hole that Vernon and Tess had dug roughly in the damp ground. A glance at their paws told me they were muddy between the light rain and the digging.

I've never seen anything like this, but it smells like strong magic to me, Tanner said. *June, come over here and get a whiff, but don't touch anything. I don't like the feel of it.*

I crawled over between Tanner and Vernon. The hole was at the base of some kind of bush, so it was pretty full of roots. At the bottom, maybe my human arm's length into the ground, was an open metal box. There were some stones in it with red markings that I didn't recognize and a knife.

My wolf didn't like it at all.

You've got one hell of a nose to sniff this out from back in the pack lands, Tanner said. *But I don't know what to make of it. It's not in Moonpeak, but we're close enough to the humans down here that maybe one of them practices magic. Could be something to look into.*

Are you going to tell Alpha Evander? I asked.

The three of them looked up at me. Tanner sighed through his nose. *Of course, it's his call if we pursue this or not.*

Now I was anxious about being off pack lands, not that I was alone. I wished I could talk to Dom, but our mind link wouldn't work this far away.

Bury it again and try to leave it as you found it, Tanner said. *We'll report it and I'll let you know what's decided about it. Good nose, Tess.*

Thanks, Tanner, Tess said. *It didn't have grass over it anyway, this thing looked like it got buried recently, or dug up and buried again, maybe. They won't notice a thing.*

Good. Finish up and get back on your usual route, Tanner told them, standing up. *Come on, June. Let's head back for today, I've got to see Alpha.*

Okay. I followed him while Tess and Vernon started to put everything back as they had found it. Tanner took us up the slope and into the mountains again, easing my unrest with every step closer to pack lands we got.

Magic. My wolf didn't like it, that was for sure. She didn't like it the first time we smelled it, either, with Jerod and his demon-summoning thing.

I shuddered. But it made me wonder if Jerod had anything to do with it. Maybe he could at least identify it for us.

Hey, Tanner . . .

Maybe it wasn't such a good idea to reveal what Jerod could do, or give anyone reason to suspect him.

Yeah? he asked.

Thanks for teaching me, I said.

Tanner let out a soft, barking laugh. *It's no problem, June. You're fast, and you've got a good nose on you.*

Not as good as Tess, apparently, I added.

No one has a nose as good as Tess, Tanner mused. *But we're glad to have you on the team anyway. We could always use more trackers, I don't want to thin out like we did last time and have to put people on single patrols again.*

Last time. Last time this place was having these rogue attacks. *How bad was it?* I asked.

Tanner took his time answering, and the sadness in his one-word answer was palpable. *Bad.*

We took the final steps back into the range of the pack lands. I sighed with relief, and my wolf even relaxed.

What do you mean thin out like last time? I asked.

Tanner grumbled. *I'm going to be frank with you. The trackers lost a lot of good wolves the last time these strange rogues showed up. People are on edge after these new attacks, and our job is more important than ever. If we can catch the first signs of an attack approaching it might make the difference in how many die.*

My chest tightened. The hurt in his message came through loud and clear. Was Tanner the leader back then, too, or was he filling someone else's shoes?

I'm sorry, I said. *That sounds like it was very hard times. But I thought you said the trackers were some of the safer jobs to have, rather than the warriors and hunters. What happened?*

Tanner went quiet a moment while we navigated a steep, rocky part of our trek back. *Normally, trackers find things. Smell things, scout things. We report. We don't fight unless it's a full-out pack war. It's not our job. Hell, that's why the moon gave us warriors and big-ass brutes like your mate.*

But the rogues were different. They seemed to come out of nowhere, and if they caught you, that was it, Tanner said. *Even if you were a strong wolf and could normally fight off a rogue or two, at least for long enough to slip away, these rogues are different.*

Where are they coming from? I was worried. *How are we supposed to protect the pack from something we can't find?*

That's the big question, isn't it? Tanner sighed. *Come on, I don't want to keep scaring you. Let's just get back to the village, and you can take off this afternoon. I need to report this to a few people.*

Okay.

Tanner left me with more questions than answers, but he wasn't really saying much that I hadn't been told or figured out already. Once we got a little closer, I turned my attention to someone else.

Dom, are you busy? I asked.

For you? Never, Dom replied right away.

Somehow I didn't think it was that simple, but I let it go. *The trackers found something unusual today. Tanner is going to report it to Evander. We need to talk to Jerod. It was magic, hidden a little outside the boundaries.*

Fucking magic, Dom spat. *I'll wrap up with Smokey and meet you at the house. Then we'll go to Jerod.*

We dropped our link, and I focused on following Tanner. One way or another I'd find out about this magic stuff. For the good of Moonpeak.

CHAPTER THIRTY-NINE

DOM

We made our way straight for the warlock's cabin. If anyone could give us answers about magic, it would be him.

We were rounding the curve of the path when the front door slammed open. Out of it rolled a fully naked Carmine with wild eyes and protruding claws. Jerod landed on his back, pinned under her as a cloud of purple smoke emitted from the cabin. The warlock's chest was covered in shallow scratches and he looked more disheveled than I had ever seen him, including during his stint under the behemoth's contracted torture.

June groaned and covered her face with her hands. I chuckled as I watched Carmine and Jerod look up to see us.

"Hello, there," Jerod said mildly, glancing at us from his upside-down state. "Love, we have visitors."

Carmine growled a bit, then sighed as she climbed off of him.

"Bad time?" I asked.

"No worse than any other time of day," Jerod said with a

devilish grin as he righted himself. "One moment, I'm not keen on receiving visitors with no pants on. I'll be right back."

I looked down at June, who was peeking between her fingers as Carmine and Jerod went back inside.

"They're gone," I said. "They'll be back with pants. Probably."

"I'm starting to doubt Jerod is actually some all-powerful warlock," June said as she dropped her hands.

"Did you see him summon a demon in the woods the other night?" I asked.

She grimaced. "Yeah. Okay, I guess he is. He's just . . . eccentric."

I chuckled as Jerod and Carmine came back outside, this time in a dress shirt and slacks and a sundress respectively.

"So, Dom. June. What brings the two of you to our little part of the mountain?" Jerod asked. Carmine stood behind him and wrapped her arms around his neck, giving June a wink from over Jerod's shoulder.

I looked down at June and nodded. She was the one who'd seen the items in person. She gave me a nod back and turned to face Jerod.

"This morning the trackers found something near pack lands that was magical in nature," June said.

"And you want to know if it's mine?" Jerod asked.

"That, or if you could identify it," June answered. "It was buried under a bush."

Jerod frowned, bringing up a hand to hold his chin while he thought. "Buried? What self-respecting warlock, or any magic user for that matter, buries their supplies? No familiar? No pocket dimension?"

"It's not yours, I take it?" I asked.

Jerod shook his head. "Definitely not. Ferdinand fetches my things. Much safer that way."

"Well, if it isn't yours, would you be able to tell who it does belong to?" June asked.

"Possibly." Jerod winked. "Actually, very likely. I'm a bit of a genius in my circle."

"And humble too," I muttered.

"I don't know if I can show you, though," June said, frowning. "Tanner is telling Evander about it as we speak. If we're ordered to leave it alone, I could show you later. If Evander wants to see it for himself or guard it . . ."

"I see," Jerod said. "Well, nothing we can do about it presently, but I'll start investigating the area. That is, as long as Evander will let us stay."

"Jerod is right," Carmine said, kissing him on the cheek. "I'm actually surprised he hasn't kicked us off his land yet."

"What do you mean?" June asked. "Why would he kick you off?"

Carmine shot me a knowing look, then turned to my mate to answer. "I, and any traveling young wolf really, am welcomed here to find my mate. If your mate is not found, or in my case my mate did not turn out to be of this pack, then there is no reason for me to continue to be here."

"Oh," June said. "*Oh*, I get it."

"The only reason Evander let me and the others back in is because we were Moonpeak to begin with. He probably thinks we aren't a threat," I added.

"Or that you're a threat he can deal with," Jerod murmured. His face hardened with concentration as he tapped on his chin.

I narrowed my eyes at him. "What are you planning, warlock?"

"Hm? Oh, nothing yet." He grinned. "I don't plot until I've confirmed my theories first."

I growled a little. "I don't like the sound of that."

Jerod waved a hand at me. "Nothing to be concerned over. I'll even tell you if my suspicions are correct. For now, let's just say I need to push a few boundaries around here. Stick my nose a few places, I think. June, I've taken a look at that wax you brought me and I can tell you a thing or two for certain."

She gasped. "What do you know?"

"It's subtly magicked. The components indicate the intended purpose is some kind of persuasion. I suggest if you encounter it again, you destroy it or avoid it," Jerod answered.

"That's going to be hard to do," June said, then turned to me. "I brought him a piece of that weird smelling candle. Do you remember asking me about it at the picnic?"

My face darkened, recalling the odd smell. My wolf didn't like it then, and now I could see why. "Good to know, but who's bringing them into the village?"

"Whoever is leaving their other magic supplies around, I'd assume," Jerod said. "Just avoid them, I'm working on a solution."

Carmine brushed the hair out of her face and giggled. "You are so smart, Jerod. Maman is going to love you."

"It's less your mother I'm worried about, and more your father and brothers," Jerod said.

"Oh, and the rest of the warriors. And Alpha. And Beta too. Really, you should worry about the whole pack," Carmine added. "But I know they'll approve, even if they tease you for a while."

"Right, teasing by werewolves," Jerod said flatly. "That's something to look forward to."

June cleared her throat. "Let us know if you figure anything out. We can leave you to . . ."

June's head snapped to the left, and she stared wide-eyed toward the village.

"What is it?" I was suddenly alert, listening for anything that could indicate danger.

"It's Tess and Vernon!" June said. "A call for help on the tracker link."

"Go," Jerod said. "I'll see what I can do from here."

June started running, her first instinct still to run in her human form. I tossed off my clothes and shifted, catching up to her easily. She took one look at me and began stripping as she went. Once she stopped and dropped her shorts, she shifted, too, and we took off.

Through the trees, through the village, we ran down the slope, and all I could do was follow June. She was the only one who could hear whatever it was the trackers were saying.

But the bigger problem was that she was starting to leave me behind. I gritted my teeth. I didn't want to tell her to go on without me. Particularly not if it meant she was running into danger.

Update? I asked.

Vernon is down! No, he's getting back up, Tess is trying to defend him from a rogue.

Who all is coming? Who knows about this? I asked.

Trackers know, June said. *Alpha knows.*

I growled. *No warriors? No Smokey?*

I don't know, she answered. *It sounds like it's Evander's decision not to involve them.*

I snapped in anger, snarling as we ran. *The hell it is!*

Smokey! I practically roared in his general direction.

What is it? he asked. *I'm about to catch this goose.*

My anger flared. So Evander was choosing not to tell him.

There's a rogue on some of the trackers, I said. *We're on our way now, heading west and south.*

On my way, Smokey growled. *Is June going on ahead?*

No, she's with me, I said firmly.

She's faster than you, Smokey said. *If a luna can't defend her own wolves, she's no use to the pack.*

She's barely a turned wolf! I argued.

Dominic, Smokey said. *You either trust her, or you don't.*

A shiver crawled down my spine. Smokey had a bad habit of saying shit that needed to be said, right when I didn't want to hear it.

We'll meet you there, I said and closed the link.

Almost immediately, June opened a new one. *Tanner says he's nearly there, and so is another pair of trackers.*

I clenched my jaw as I pushed forward as hard as I could. But even glancing at June, I could tell she could go faster.

June . . . I started, swallowing my resistance. *Go on ahead, I'll follow. Don't do anything foolish, but be there with those healing skills of yours.*

You're sure? she asked, conflict plain in her words.

Go! I shouted.

She took off with impressive speed, so quick even I could hardly believe it. It was like she was getting faster every day.

I shook my head, watching her pull ahead bit by bit. This was no time for admiring June. I opened a new link.

Amelia, Aaron, Jack, Carson, I said. *Get your asses in gear, we need some backup.*

What is it? Amelia asked.

What's goin' on? Carson asked, clearly just waking up from a nap.

Our pack is being attacked, I growled for all of them to hear. *West and south of the village. Get here, now.*

I cut the link and checked on June's progress. Shit, she was already nearly out of sight through the trees.

All I could do now was follow and trust my mate.

My future luna.

And save our trackers.

CHAPTER FORTY

JUNE

Tess. Vernon. I'm coming!

Paws to the ground, I thundered across the distance to where the call for help came from.

What pissed me off the most was Evander's response to the call for help. Apparently, the ass was going to come himself and take care of any threat, no need to involve the warriors.

Fuck Evander. Where was he when we were attacked the other day? When Dom and I were attacked in the car?

I pushed my legs as hard as they would go. I could tell I was getting close; my ears twitched with the hint of a fight.

I see them, Tanner said. *Terry, Ben, June, when you get here circle wide and check for more before you jump in.*

Right, I agreed, and the link dropped.

As I ran hard into the faint sounds of the scuffle, my eyes darted around to look for more as Tanner had asked. The rogues were nearby. The stink of them burned in my nose now, and a small growl escaped me as me and my wolf fumed over their presence in our lands.

I ran a wide circle around where I could hear the fighting. I saw nothing, so I jumped right in. Pushing through some low-hanging branches that scratched along my back, I came out of the evergreens in a burst of speed, scattering pine needles behind me.

There! Tess's smaller wolf was pretty much cornered by a rogue, and Vernon and Tanner were dealing with two others. Vernon had a nasty gash on his side.

I'm coming, Tess! I called.

Something overcame me. I charged, furious. My rage at the rogues, that they dared step their feet on Moonpeak soil and attack our trackers. . . . My eyes were wide and burning with hate as I launched myself at the spine of the rogue that had cornered Tess.

The big brute sensed me at the last second, though, and as I landed on him and sank my teeth into his neck with a light crunch, he turned on me, throwing me down and slashing his claws across my belly. I howled in pain rolled away from him.

Now he was circling me, but I could see Tess in the corner of my vision, ready to attack. She looked much more timid, but brave and willing to try for my sake. It put into perspective that I'd only seen very strong wolves fight these rogues. Their wrongness irked me, put my wolf on edge and made her angry. But what they seemed to do for the trackers was make them scared and overwhelmed.

Which just made me angrier.

The stinging of my belly was nothing compared to other injuries I'd seen from these rogues. I needed to keep my head on my shoulders and get through this fight until help arrived.

June, your left! Tanner snapped at me.

I whirled to see it at the last second as another rogue came in and pounced. I managed to roll away, but it gave the first rogue an opportunity to swipe at me again, catching my shoulder with his claws.

Shit! Where had they come from? I ran the circle around the fight as Tanner had asked. There was no scent at all, no sign of more, yet here more were. On top of the two that Tanner and Vernon were already fighting, they had gained another, and so had Tess and I.

We're here! A voice I hadn't heard yet, but that I recognized as the two sleek trackers Terry and Ben came into the fight. They were still so small compared to the vicious rogues that circled us, though, which strained my heart. I didn't know how to watch them all at once.

The fighting ensued again; this time it was five of them and six of us. Much better odds, but still not enough of us to safely do this.

I shook my head, clearing it and getting back into the fight. I could marvel at the power of Dom and the others later, right now there were sick, twisted rogues on my packmates, and I couldn't let that go.

The fight was vicious and dirty. I ripped into rogue flesh when I could, tried to dodge where I could see. But even then, I caught a lot of claws and teeth sinking in and slashing at me. The other trackers were not doing well either. The stunning contrast of a pack of trackers trying to fight and a pack of warriors . . . we needed backup.

Dom, where are you? I asked.

Just about there, he answered. *How many?*

Five—ah!

Crashing into the fray was another three rogues. *Shit! Eight on six.*

All my attention was then consumed by staying alive. I pushed Tess out of the way of an attack, then bit into the side of another rogue. If we made it through all this, I wanted to train with Smokey like how he trained Dom and the others. What had Dom said about him when we first arrived? Smokey used to be some kind of Master at Arms who kept the whole pack in shape?

I growled at Evander's arrogance. Or perhaps it was stupidity to only keep the warriors trained up. If . . . *when* Dom became alpha, Smokey would be back in business.

A big gray wolf rushed into the clearing. My heart soared! Dom was finally here! I turned to the newcomer in a brief window of opportunity between attacks, only for my heart to sink as I laid eyes on Evander.

It took a lot to keep my wolf from growling at him, we were so mad.

Gather behind me, Evander ordered. *I won't let anything happen to you all.*

Was he serious? This time I did growl at him. *Alpha Evander, we need to work as a team to take them down!*

But the trackers were all listening to him. Ears down, posturing behind Evander as they each submitted to his will. The rogues lined up before Evander, then began circling.

My chest tightened. This was bad. If the rogues all attacked at once, our wolves were all clustered in a neat little bundle for killing.

I growled, snapping at the closest rogue to get it away from the fight.

Juniper! Evander called. *Stand down.*

The command startled me, and a part of me wanted to listen.

Maybe it was my wolf listening to the alpha, maybe it was something else, but it was Dom who erased the urge completely.

June! Dom called.

Dom!

And then he came into the space where we were fighting. Was Dom's wolf always this big? He stood shoulder to shoulder with Evander, but instead of getting behind the alpha wolf, Dom came to stand at my side. With him next to me, all the pressure of Evander's order melted away.

Then the rogues attacked.

We had three, Evander had the other five.

I tried desperately to watch what was happening to the trackers that Evander protected, but I was too busy with the rogues in front of me to really see.

Dom on the other hand was performing brilliantly.

They weren't getting near me, unless I had perfect opportunities to attack while they weren't looking. It was as though Dom was orchestrating the moves to a dance, and my part was much safer than his.

Evander made fighting look as effortless as Dom. We were in control for several minutes before another charging through the forest underbrush brought us three more rogues.

What? I exclaimed. *Dom, more!*

I see them, he growled.

Two of them ganged up on us, and one more for Evander. I watched as the trackers stayed back as they had been told.

And it pissed me off.

Tanner! You guys going to just sit there while we fight for your lives? I snapped. *What kind of wolves are you?*

June, watch your side, Dom growled.

Suddenly, we were back in a fight, albeit an even harder one than before.

We're here! Aaron called. My heart lightened as I saw Amelia, Aaron, Jack, and Carson race into the fray, and then it was chaos once more.

Evander was either too busy or didn't care anymore about his little formation and show of power. We were fighting for our lives and the lives of the wolves of Moonpeak.

Amelia was terrifying. I hadn't gotten to see her fight last time, but it was very in line with her character. She held nothing back as she tore into her enemies.

Smokey came into the field shortly after. He was vicious as well, his attacks precise and destructive. I was so happy to see him joining us at first that I didn't notice the extra couple of rogues who had also come into battle.

Dom was more strategic, positioning and pushing the enemy around as he told the others what they could do or where they could attack from to help our odds.

I was physically exhausted, and turned to help our injured wolves. I helped Tess lay down so I shove her hip joint back in place. I had to shift to do that, but she was more comfortable, so it was well worth it.

Evander roared in pain as he got a nasty gash down his ribs from two rogues attacking at once. It was open and bleeding freely, but he kept up his end of the fight.

Finally, several rogues were down and new ones had stopped entering the battle scene, and we could all relax a little. The pile of bodies at our feet was disgusting meat by the time things calmed down completely.

Panting and exhausted, everyone was in terrible shape, and as

Evander bit down and crushed the throat of the last rogue, the pack laid down and got our first moments of rest.

What the fuck was all that? Amelia snapped, the first to her feet after it was all over. I could only assume she was fueled by her ever-burning anger.

Enough, Amelia, Evander replied. *Now is not the time. We need to see to the injured and get everyone back into the village. We're on lockdown.*

I froze. *Lockdown?*

Evander looked at me, sighing through his nose. *You were very brave today, June. You fought well for a tracker.*

Dom growled slightly but cut himself off. I could tell he was supremely annoyed.

But, Evander continued, *my trackers should not be seeing any battle. Nor should the other wolves of the village. Right now, I'm issuing a command for all to stay within the village until I and a select group of warriors run through these lands and clear out the rogues.*

Alpha . . . Smokey started.

Smokey. Evander cut him off. *You are to run a wide patrol and share my wishes with any who are outside my reach. Trackers, hunters, any who might wander in and out of the edges of the pack lands. Go tell them to come back in for now.*

Yes, Alpha, Smokey said, and he rose to his feet and trotted off. He sounded irked, but he did as his alpha told him to.

Dom, you and Amelia did well today too, Evander said. *Please take your group back to the village and I will call on you later. We need to have a talk.*

Evander rose to his feet before any of us could ask more questions. *I will personally handle a patrol around this area. Tanner, help get the injured back. Can you all walk?*

Dirty Lying Wolves

I think so, Alpha, Tanner answered. *Come on, you heard him. On your feet, let's get to Doc and see to that hip, Tess. Vernon, your side is looking pretty bad too.*

Dom rose to his feet as well. *Come on, June.*

But!

I know, he answered softly. *Come on.*

We stood—Dom, me, Aaron, Amelia, Jack, Carson—and walked the long trek back to the village. Into Moonpeak, and into a lockdown.

CHAPTER FORTY-ONE

JUNE

I woke in the middle of the night, still seething over Evander and the rogues. Dom was asleep, fully satisfied with the way we'd spent our evening. There really wasn't much to do here with no internet or television, so we filled our empty time with more physical pastimes. I was hoping for bonding time and a distraction, and I suppose I got that, but now that it was just me and the quiet hours of the night, I was back to being bothered.

Sitting up and leaning against the headboard, I hugged a pillow to me and looked down at Dom. At my mate. One of the few moments of peace and happiness I'd had since things grew strained over the last couple of days after the attack on the trackers.

Still, I couldn't sleep. A chronic worrier, Gran used to call me.

Maybe so. Maybe there wasn't anything I could do about anything tonight. Maybe I should just wait it out a couple of days as Dom had suggested. After all, trapped wolves grow restless and resentful after too much captivity. He knew the wolves best, and I was sure this would only aid in his claim that Evander was unfit to rule. If anything, in a week at the full moon, Dom's challenge might be backed by the whole pack.

So why couldn't I sleep?

I sighed, sliding down in the bed as quietly as I could. Maybe I could just close my eyes and pretend to sleep until it really happened.

I rolled over once. After a while, I rolled over again. Frustrated, I pushed the covers off of me. Eventually, I pulled them back on again.

Until finally I sighed and got out of bed completely.

I walked through the house and settled at the kitchen table, resting my head in my hands with a yawn.

Sleeplessness, I suppose. Endlessly boring sleeplessness.

Or at least, until I heard the scratching outside.

My eyes popped open. What was that?

Scratch, scratch. It was very light. Even with my wolf hearing, I might not have noticed it if I wasn't already awake. I suppose Tanner had really hammered in my tracker training, because I was noticing every little thing.

I walked to the back window and peered out, only to see something truly unexpected. Jerod's little dog, the one that he said was a familiar, was on fire. Well, it was drooling fire. It had an extra tail and little horns. If I thought it was so ugly it was cute before, it was ugly enough to win some kind of award now.

"What the hell?" I whispered.

Ferdinand was walking around in the field south of my house, scratching at the dirt. He had something in his mouth, other than the lava drool of course, and it seemed he wanted to bury it.

Quickly, I slipped through the front door and around the back of the house to get a better look.

June? You okay? Dom's sleepy voice sounded in my head.

Yeah, I didn't mean to wake you, I said. *Checking on something . . . strange.*

I'll be right there.

While I waited for Dom to come out, I kept an eye on Ferdinand. He would have been lost in the tall grassy field if it wasn't for the glow of his lava. Actually, could that set the grass on fire? More magic, I guessed.

"What the hell?" Dom mumbled, coming up beside me.

"That's what I said." I smiled. "But what is he doing in the middle of the night?"

"I'm going to find out," Dom said.

He walked over to Ferdinand, and I followed. The familiar had found whatever spot he was looking for and dug a hole. Once he finished, he dropped a half-used candle in and buried it.

"What is going on?" I murmured.

Ferdinand patted the dirt down and turned to face us. Tongue out, drooling lava.

"Hello, there, I hope I didn't wake you."

I took a cautious step forward. "Are you . . . talking?"

Ferdinand drooled, his eyes looking in two slightly different directions.

"If you're asking if my hellhound is speaking to you, the answer is obviously no."

"Jerod?" Dom asked. "Explain."

"Yes, it's me. I'm speaking through Ferdie here. Actually, I'm doing a lot of things through Ferdinand, and now that I've happened upon the two of you, maybe you could help me out with something."

"Hmm." Dom eyed the familiar with suspicion. "What exactly do you want us to do and why?"

Ferdinand stopped to scratch his ear with his back leg.

"I'm so glad you asked," Jerod said. "Unfortunately, my demon contact is very secretive and doesn't like being known by more than twenty-six living beings at a time, so I can't share that. But what I'm doing here is fascinating, I assure you. The delicate nuances of what I'm keeping in balance here are well above the heads of anyone below the sixth circle of warlocks, not to mention shifters with no exterior magical abilities to sense the conduit—"

"*Jerod.*" Dom growled a warning. "Get to the point. Now."

Jerod's sigh came through loud and clear as Ferdinand sat there drooling. "Fine, fine. My genius is obviously wasted here. I need help hiding three more things in very precise locations."

"And why is that?" I asked.

"Think of it as me creating a better environment for you all to challenge Evander.

"If my theory is correct, and rarely are they not, I believe there is a great chance of dark magical interference during your challenge. Some of the magical interference you've seen in the area, I think Evander is connected to. Believe me when I say I'm simply preventing what you might consider as . . . cheating."

"Cheating?" I asked, tilting my head. "Isn't it cheating to have your help in the first place?"

"No, no, my dear June," Jerod said. "You could hardly afford my price for cheating. No, I'm only leveling the playing field. Carmine insisted I do something about my hunch."

Dom cleared his throat. "And what has Evander done with you and Carmine?"

"Oh, we're removed from the territory," Jerod said simply.

My heart thudded in my chest. "Removed?"

"Did you think the alpha would let the outsiders loiter around forever? And particularly when he has locked down his village due to a threat? I'm on that miserable ferry boat right now, apparently talking to a pocket mirror while the two of you waste my time with these questions."

"Carmine left? I didn't get to say goodbye," I said.

"No, we haven't left entirely," Jerod answered. "We're going to stay within a day's travel so we can get back in time for the full moon. I have some things to look into, and you think Carmine is going to leave without making sure you're okay here? And a delightful fight to watch on top of it."

"She's very passionate," Dom said. "That's for sure."

"You don't know the half of it." Jerod feigned exhaustion. "Insatiable, this one."

It was harder to hold my tongue this time, but I let it go. Carmine was indeed insatiable when she wanted something. I turned to Dom. "Do you think Amelia and Bianca are gone too?"

"No," he answered. "Not only would Amelia have told me, she would have thrown the biggest fight the warriors here have ever seen in order to stay and see our plan through. Since she is pack, even though Bianca is not, they have all the time in the world to decide which pack to call home."

"Good. I was hoping after this was all over she would stay to help with this rogue situation."

Dom placed a hand on my back, rubbing it gently. "We'll take care of wherever these things are coming from. Right after we take care of Evander."

"And now I wonder if those two things are one and the same," I murmured.

"Back to the point, please," Jerod said. "Will you help me or not? It's going to be a bit challenging to get Ferdinand into the pack house undetected."

"Why do you need in the pack house?" Dom eyed Ferdinand with suspicion again.

"You wolves really aren't that sharp, are you?" Jerod sighed, exasperated. "I need to keep, or hide, five items in a few precise coordinates in order to plant a circle. Two of the locations are outdoors and once buried won't have a traceable scent. The other three... well, I can spell them to not leave a scent as well, but getting them into places might be difficult. Ferdinand will come tomorrow night with the last three items and instructions if you think you can hide them for me."

"I can't honestly believe I'm considering this," Dom muttered, pressing fingers to his temples. "Fine. Send them tomorrow. Do we have a way to contact you?"

"Until you drag your pack out of the dark ages and figure out how to get a cell tower out there, probably not," Jerod said flatly. "You'll have to wait until Ferdinand finds you, I can hear you through him."

"Fine," Dom said. "Send your things, but let it be known that I do not need help taking that bastard down."

"I didn't say you did, big guy," Jerod answered. "Alphas, so touchy. June, I hope you're ready for a life of coddling that big ego."

I started to giggle, and then slapped my hand over my mouth, peeking over at Dom, who wore quite the unimpressed look.

"Anyway, I'll send everything tomorrow. Good luck you two, I'm expecting one hell of a show to entertain me after all this work."

"Count on it," Dom said. "The moment it's within my rights to do so, I'm tearing him to pieces."

"Hmm. Let's hope so. June, if it all goes south, I'm sure Carmine would love to host you at her pack. It might be nice to have another American with me while I acclimate to rural Quebec," Jerod offered.

"No thanks," I said, looking over at Dom. "I have complete faith in my alpha."

Dom gave me a warm smile, reaching over to lace his fingers with mine.

"Suit yourself. I always have contingency plans. Keep an eye out, same time tomorrow."

Ferdinand trotted away from the village as I marveled that not only was he able to go undetected but also didn't set the fields on fire.

"That's magic for you," Dom murmured. "Confusing shit, I'd rather keep it out of here completely once this is all over."

I nodded my agreement. Jerod was an interesting character, but we would have a lot of work to do once Dom became alpha, and the added unpredictability of a warlock wouldn't help.

"I wonder what Jerod thinks is interfering?" I asked when we were back inside. "He thinks there's magical interference, whatever that means."

"We can't write off that box of stuff the trackers found the other day," Dom said. "That's pretty much what started all this. "

Sighing through my nose, I felt a headache coming on. "I guess we wait for Jerod's instructions. If he can really stop some magical interference, we need his help."

"Agreed," Dom said. "We're so close to the moon and the challenge I can almost taste it."

I nodded. "Bring it on."

CHAPTER FORTY-TWO

JUNE

Ferdinand brought three items with him the next night with notes about precisely where to place them attached. Dom didn't look phased, but I was less sure of the items in question when I saw them.

A cracked porcelain chicken needed to be buried in Linda's neighbor's vegetable garden, dangerously close to their front door. A bumper sticker for some radio station in Ohio was to be placed as precisely in the middle of the basement of the pack house as possible, and a knife that had very obviously and recently had blood on it needed to sit on or under the general store's porch

"I'm impressed he really did spell the smell away," Dom said, holding up the knife by the cleanest parts of the handle.

"I don't think I want to know anything about dark magic," I mumbled, looking at the cracked chicken.

"Do you two think you can have this done tonight?" Jerod asked. "As much as I want to say I'm powerful enough to snatch Ferdie out of harm's way if he gets caught scratching at people's doors, I'd rather not risk it."

Dom said, "We can, but the hardest part will be the pack house."

"I'll do that one," I said. "I can do it early in the morning. I'll meet up with Alice and walk in with her before she makes breakfast."

Dom frowned. "I don't like you going in there."

"If we get caught snooping in the pack house, which of us do you think is in for a lot less trouble than the other?" I asked.

Dom grumbled, but he didn't argue. It was painfully obvious that Evander and Dom disliked each other, and that Evander had taken a liking to me. Or at least, he was nice if not suspicious when he'd invited me to dinner.

"I'll send Ferdie back tomorrow night," Jerod said. "Let me know if everything is in place, and I'll activate my spell."

And Ferdinand waddled off.

Dom and I watched him go. Then Dom growled and crossed his arms over his chest. "I'll let you take the bumper sticker if I can take the other two. Go on in and get some sleep, you've got to get up early if you want to meet Alice and make it look natural."

"All right." I leaned up and kissed him on the cheek. "Will you be back before I leave?"

Dom shrugged. "I should be, but if I do this fast enough I might try to sneak out and see if we have a follow-up note from Nathan. I hope we hear back from Salt Fur. I'll see you after you slip that in the pack house," Dom said. "Get some sleep. It's going to take me a bit to watch and make sure the old man running the general store is sleeping. Unless he's found a solution to an old problem, he's a habitual insomniac."

"Okay, I'll see you tomorrow then." I slipped back into the house as Dom shifted forms and prowled off in the other direction.

Warm light woke me up. I opened my eyes enough to confirm that it was barely sunrise, or maybe even just before. Stretching my arms out beside me where I would normally run into a big warm wall of muscles and morning lust, it was . . . actually a bit refreshing for once. I smiled, knowing I'd miss him if this happened more, though.

Dom, you there? I asked, my wolf and I reaching out as far as we could.

Yeah, looking for a note, he said. The signal was very weak, he must be all the way to the borders by now.

Okay, see you later.

Tossing my covers aside, I jumped out of bed and into the shower. A quick wash, combing my hair with my fingers and hoping for the best, I slipped on something easy to wear. Sneakers on, I put the bumper sticker in my back pocket and hurried out the door.

A grin spread across my face as I stretched and began an easy jog. I could loop the village a few times and watch for Alice as well as enjoy my newly regained hobby. The memory of my accident was still vivid, but I'd been forced to acknowledge that my new body wouldn't let me down as easily as it had when I was just a human.

The sound of my shoes crunching on gravel became a welcome beat for me to jog to. It would only last as long as I stayed on the main road, but I could enjoy it as long as it lasted.

The sun came fully up, and a few sleepy wolves began their day. Even though we were now all confined to the village, people still wanted to get outside. Gardens to tend, animals to feed, eggs to collect. The everyday actions that kept the Moonpeak wolves from needing to rely on the outside world.

My running finally took me past the road I knew Alice lived on, and I was excited to see her door swinging open.

"Good morning, Alice." I waved. "Off to cook?"

Alice beamed at me, holding up a basket on her arm that appeared to have bell peppers from her garden in it. "I am! And to do a bit of dusting."

"Mind if I join you? I need a good walk to cool down from my run," I said.

"Of course!" Alice said. "Come on, dear, you can help me peel potatoes."

"Sure." I waited for Alice to get closer to me at her own pace. I stretched, pretending I had come a lot farther than I actually had. As she neared, I fell into step with her.

"So, how has it been just cooking for the alpha and not Naomi?" I asked. "Is it easier?"

"Oh, I can't seem to drop the habit," Alice said. "I've been cooking the same amount anyway and storing the leftovers in the fridge."

"Old habits die hard, I guess."

"Well, they aren't going to waste, anyway," Alice said. "At least there's that."

"What do you mean?"

"I put the leftovers in the fridge, but Evander must be eating them because I find the empty dishes in the sink the next day anyway." Alice shrugged. "Then again, he's a big wolf. He must be hungry with all the extra patrols he runs now to take care of the . . ."

Alice looked around, then cupped her hand to her mouth to whisper. *"Rogue problem.*

"So, anyway, it works out just the same," Alice continued. "Haven't seen much of Alpha lately, usually I'm done and gone before he gets back from the morning patrol, so I leave his breakfast on the table."

"Oh wow," I mused, glad for the trove of information Alice was giving me so freely. "He must be busy."

"Quite right," she agreed. "He is. And here we go, the pack house! Come on in, June. Have you had breakfast yet? I can make you a plate while I'm at it."

In the kitchen, Alice got to work pulling out vegetables and washing them while I peeled the potatoes. Once everything was cleaned, peeled, diced, and in the skillet for a scramble, I saw my opportunity to slip away.

"Alice, I'm going to find a bathroom real quick," I said.

She was busy with the cooking food as she cracked eggs into the pan. "All right, dear. Just down the hall, the door is marked, you can't miss it."

"Thanks." I left the kitchen, grabbing the bumper sticker from my back pocket and looking for a door that could lead to the basement.

I passed the door with a bathroom sign and a few more before I found a hallway with a door at the end. The sign on it read AUTHORIZED PACK BUSINESS ONLY in bold letters. My instincts told me it was the one I was looking for.

Sure enough, the door was locked. But it was one of those old pinhole doors that could be opened without the key if you had a little metal piece to stick in it. Looking around the door frame, I didn't see one, but I did realize that other doors might have what I was looking for.

Back around the corner, I found what I needed on top of the bathroom door frame.

"Bingo." I slipped it inside the tiny hole on the door handle, the faint clicking inside allowing me to turn the doorknob.

The door swung open, and I looked for a light switch by the stairs. Not finding one immediately, I relied on my wolfish eyes to adapt to the darkness.

At the bottom, I could just make out a few hard shapes—tables and shelves—to avoid. I walked to the middle-ish of the room and dropped to the ground level.

I smiled when my fingers brushed the corner of a rug. Easy,

hide the bumper sticker underneath it, and even if Evander came down here, he wouldn't spot it. Jerod was smart to spell its scent away, now I would just have to slip back upstairs, eat my breakfast, and make a casual getaway.

I turned in the dark and carefully made my way back to the stairs I had come from. That was when I heard a sneeze.

My head jerked up and I looked around. Someone else was in the dark basement.

My pause ended up costing me because the lights flickered to life as I was standing in the middle of the room. No cover, nowhere to hide. My eyes darted around, looking for whoever had turned the lights on as there were too many strange scents in the air to pinpoint anything. But instead of finding the source, I stared in horror at the masses of magic paraphernalia spread around me.

Knives, candles, and books written in the strange letters Jerod used. Pictures, markings on the walls and floor, and at the far end of the basement was one giant barred cage. Big enough for a wolf to run just a few paces and then turn around to run back. The floor was well worn, and on the floor in a blanket a figure was lying down. The one who must have sneezed.

"Oh Juniper." The voice from behind me gave me the chills. "When something triggered the alarm at my private door, I had hoped it was simply a mouse."

I spun on my heels, eyes wide as I took in Alpha Evander leaning against the wall next to a light switch.

My heart hammered in my chest.

Dom! I cried.

Nothing.

"Trying to mind link?" Evander asked. "Not in this room."

He walked a few steps to run his fingers over some of the strange markings on the walls. Then he took a lighter from his pocket and picked up a candle from one of the shelves, lighting it as he spoke. "I've already taken that into consideration, I'm afraid."

"What is this room?" I asked, my eyes locked on the candle.

"It's just a basement, June," Evander said. "Where important pack business is conducted."

"What kind of pack business requires magic?" I asked. The smoke from the candle hit my nose, irritating my senses and making my thoughts foggy. I shook my head to snap out of it.

"I use whatever tools I can to keep the pack in order," Evander said. "You can understand that desire, can't you, June?"

His voice was so soothing now. Yeah, I guess an alpha does just want order in the pack.

"Yeah . . . order . . ." I murmured.

"You shouldn't have come down here, should you?" Evander asked softly. "You saw the signs, didn't you?"

"Signs . . ." I remembered them, they clearly stated that I didn't belong here. "I saw them."

Evander looked at me like Grandad when I brought home a bad report card. "What am I going to do with you? Snooping in the pack house of all places. These are dangerous times, you know. All these rogues running about."

"Rogues . . . right," I agreed.

"I can't very well let you go free to spill my secrets, now can I?" Evander asked a question but it was more like he was thinking out loud than actually talking to me.

The smell of the candle was so odd. I could nearly sense something familiar about it, but every time I came close the thought drifted away.

"Why don't you rest here for a while, June?"

"Rest here?" I shook my head. "No, I need to . . . I need to do something."

Something. What was it? Tell someone something? Hmm.

"No, no," Evander said, coming closer and putting my senses on alert. "I must insist."

I froze, hands out, and ready to run on instinct if I had to.

But Evander got to me first. He was definitely an alpha, his speed and strength were every bit of what Dom's were. If only my head wasn't so fuzzy, I could have dodged him but . . .

His hands wrapped around my head, palms on my temples as he whispered something under his breath.

Everything dimmed.

"Have a rest, June," Evander said. "We'll have a talk when you wake up."

And then everything went black.

CHAPTER FORTY-THREE

DOM

Run. Hunt. Find.

My wolf and I prowled the edges of the pack lands that came closest to Salt Fur. The bottom of the mountains where you could finally find stretches of ground that didn't tilt to the mountains' whim. Where you could really dig your claws into the earth and sprint.

The sun was rising, and if I wanted to avoid being found by Evander and his patrols, I might have to dip outside of pack lands while the morning runs went by. Or maybe I could find a message from Nathan and Naomi and slip back still, if I could find one soon.

Or maybe there was no message at all. Maybe the Salt Fur pack trackers hadn't found mine, or maybe it was blown away in the wind never to be seen again. Maybe Nathan never showed Naomi the letter, or maybe she'd forgotten how to decipher the notes we made as kids.

A lot could have happened to it, but I shook off the thoughts and pressed on. They must have gotten it. I had tied it to a damn tree at the edge of their lands, after all. If their patrols and trackers were missing this kind of blatant thing on their lands, then I'd have to tell Nathan to retrain them all. Hell, maybe I could send Tanner over for a few weeks once this all died down.

Once this all died down. I pictured a life with June, protecting Moonpeak. She deserved a place to run free, to go as fast as she could. And with her helping nature, her medical training, her tracking senses, Moonpeak couldn't ask for a better luna.

My chest puffed out, my wolf was beaming with pride over June. Too perfect.

And June wasn't the only one I could see a better life for once this all ended. My best friend would finally have a place where she fit in, and a pack of equally aggressive wolves to lead into battle. Amelia had always sought a fight like a moth to a flame. And Bianca, the petite luna, would be good for her. She seemed to have a good head on her shoulders and could keep Amelia cool when it counted.

And Naomi, she was safe with Nathan. I'll admit, I'd be hesitant to see her go too far away from one of us, either me or Amelia. She was such a quiet wolf before, and it seemed time had only made her more withdrawn. Maybe Nathan could open her back up, he certainly knew how to put a smile on most people's faces. Naomi deserved happiness, she had such a soft heart, we always knew she could be a luna.

I bared my teeth, a wolfish grin as I sped forward. Yes, it was all within reach, as soon as I took care of Evander.

But the sun was good and up, I couldn't delay much longer. A couple more laps back and forth and I would need to sneak back to the village.

My eyes darted to trees, to rocks, wherever they could put a note for me to find.

A branch behind me cracked. It was far away, but it was a branch for sure. Something big passed by behind me, and there were only so many big things in these mountains, most of them being wolves.

I stopped, crouching down, and listened for more clues. The sound of paws hitting the ground told me what I knew could be true: wolves were coming from within Moonpeak.

I saw them, far away so I couldn't tell exactly who they were, and yet the only wolves allowed to be out right now were Evander and his handpicked patrols.

Internally, I groaned. There was no avoiding it at this point, they were too close and my scent was all over the place from running through the grass. On top of that, I was definitely one of the bigger wolves in Moonpeak; there was no use in trying to hide.

I stood up to my full height. My wolf grumbled but conceded that there weren't many more courses of action to take. Not unless we wanted to look more suspicious than we already did.

Sure enough, the wolves caught my scent and headed my way. I recognized three of the warriors as new ones Evander had brought in over the last ten years, and then the bastard alpha himself.

I held in the growl my wolf tried to throw out, and watched with cautious eyes as Evander approached me, his warriors holding back.

The large gray wolf padded toward me, yellow eyes meeting yellow eyes.

Dominic. What are you doing out here? Evander asked.

I didn't answer at first, looking over each of the warriors he had brought with him. Judging the outcome if I had to fight them all. But a fight between alphas would be something else entirely.

I clenched my jaw tight. Thoughts of how equal we truly were tried to slip into my mind as doubts. But I couldn't afford that, not this late in the game. My father may have been a beta, but too many wolves had faith in me to become alpha of Moonpeak.

June had faith in me.

I'm one of the stronger wolves here, I said. *I've already fought the rogues before. I can't sit still without having contributed to the protection of the pack.*

Hopefully, that would be enough.

A noble thought, Dominic, Evander said, the sheen on his fangs visible. *But you still go against your alpha. You are not even a moon cycle with the pack again, and already you disobey.*

The last word had pressure behind it. A command in his voice that told me he expected me to yield to him. My wolf didn't like it, but I lowered my head slightly. Enough to show a bit of submission, but only the bare minimum of a wolf with beta blood.

Evander looked me over again. I thought he was going to say something, but then his head turned and he looked to where he and his warriors had come along the border. A new wolf approached, and Evander backed away from me to meet them.

He transformed back into his human skin. I was curious to see what would make him do that, considering we had so much danger here with the rogues. But my questions were answered when a smaller wolf, a tracker probably, came up to him with a folded white paper held gingerly between its teeth.

My heart dropped. That had to be a note from Nathan and Naomi. If they addressed it to me like I had addressed mine to them, Evander would know why I was out here, and would likely try to make an example of me. I knew that was what I'd do.

"Let's see it," Evander said, taking the note and unfolding it.

My legs tensed, my eyes stayed sharp on Evander's expression. The moment he showed signs of realization, I would have to fight him.

But rather than realization, his puzzled expression just grew to exasperation as he turned the note over to the back, and then the front again.

Thank the moon, the whole thing was well and truly coded.

I was relieved until I watched Evander bring the paper closer to his nose and sniff it.

Naomi. I closed my eyes as my hopes sank. It wouldn't really matter if she was the one to write the note, her scent would be on Nathan enough that it would leave traces on the paper as well.

"Thank you for bringing this to me. Don't speak of it to anyone else, I'll need to have a better look to see if I can figure out what these scratches mean," Evander said, and the tracker bowed their head before trotting off again.

Evander sighed, looking down at the note once more and flipping it over again. Then he turned his eyes on me.

"You wouldn't be out here looking for this, would you?" he asked.

No, Alpha, I answered. *I'm here to protect the pack. Protect June.*

Focusing on my heartbeat, I tried to slow it down. I tried to play on the two basic instincts of a pack wolf. Submission by calling him *Alpha*, and protecting my mate. It would be enough for most wolves to accept, but would it be enough for Evander?

Evander took a few steps toward me, his sharp eyes taking in everything about my shape, my posture, my wolf's agitation, or what of it I couldn't hide.

"You're from beta blood, aren't you?" he asked, more for himself and not really looking for an answer. "I suppose you could make a reasonable protector. Warrior."

I didn't answer as he paced around me. Some unspoken cue made the warriors he'd brought with him walk away. Did he dismiss them? Why would he want me alone?

Unless he was ready for a fight. I nearly grinned, this was what I had been waiting for, and if he instigated it I wouldn't have to wait for the full moon in a few days to claim my title.

Come on, do it. Fight me.

When all of the warriors were well out of sight, Evander smiled. "You're quite close to Amelia, aren't you?"

I paused. Where was he going with this?

"When I let you all back into the pack, I was hoping you had changed. Come to see the light in the last ten years." Evander crossed his arms over his chest, assessing my expression for any change. "It was an unfortunate way to solve the problem, but Liam wasn't doing the job with those nasty rogue attacks, now was he?"

A growl escaped me, no matter how hard I tried to stop it.

Alpha Liam was an outstanding alpha! I snapped.

"Hold on there, Dominic." Evander chuckled, putting his hands up. "I know you would have been close to him, what with your father being his beta and all. I suppose you had grand dreams of following in his footsteps someday, didn't you? Like father, like son. Forever a good line of *betas*."

The way he spit the last word out was like an insult, reminding me of my place. My lips curled back, my fangs shining in the morning sun, which now felt lightly through the trees around us.

"Calm down," Evander said. "Consider what it would mean for you to lose your temper with your alpha here. What was your plan anyway, to back up Amelia in a plea for support against me? It would never have worked—her temper is astonishing, and she isn't fit to lead a peaceful place like Moonpeak anyway. Besides, what claim does she have? I've been a fine alpha for the past decade. The best Moonpeak could ask for."

Bullshit you're handling things here, I snarled. *What about these rogue attacks?*

Evander laughed. Outright laughed at me. In his naked human form, standing face to face with a wolf of my size, and he wasn't even flinching. The bastard was confident in himself, I'd give him that much.

"Oh, I rather like to think you lot are the cause of all the rogue mess," Evander said. "After all, they disappeared not long after you left and reappeared not long after your returned."

We have nothing to do with them!

"Are you sure?" Evander mused. "Do you really believe that? Would the pack really believe that?"

I crouched down, trying not to lose it on him before my rightful full moon. I snarled. If only Smokey was here, or Amelia, or any other witnesses to his behavior.

What's your hold over Moonpeak, Evander? Why did you come here, and what involvement do you have with magic?

"Dominic. It's such a shame you turned out this way"—he looked down at the note in his hand once more, then in a flash, shoved a hand toward me—"because I was willing to tolerate you. Pity."

A stab of pain hit me right in the chest, inches from my heart. If I wasn't in my wolf form, I would have been pierced through the heart by a thin silver blade.

You bastard! I snarled, but then spat up a rush of bile. The silver was very pure, very potent. *Amelia won't let you get away with this! I'll have your heart between my teeth!*

Evander backed off quickly, then shifted into his own wolf form. He lifted the note gently in his teeth and turned to walk away as my vision started to blur. This wasn't normal silver. Whatever it was, I was fading fast.

I wouldn't worry about Amelia, Evander said as he walked away from me. *She'll have her hands full with the alpha of Winter*

Wind. He will be here to collect his daughter and her mate soon. I've already contacted him, and Alpha Bernard doesn't take no for an answer.

Fuck. One of the few wolves with a nastier reputation than Amelia. My weight became too much for my legs, and I struggled to stay upright as Evander faded from sight.

And that was when I heard the growls approach.

The rogues were here.

CHAPTER FORTY-FOUR

JUNE

My head swam. My body ached. The only thing that alerted me to the fact that I was conscious again was the presence of a throbbing headache.

I was on a bed, I think. Or I was on something soft like a bed. My head was certainly on a pillow.

I opened my eyes slowly to a light room. The bedding was soft and floral, painting supplies sat on a table by the window, and the wall was covered in artwork. A scent that I knew I had encountered before but couldn't recall where edged the room with mystery.

Where was I?

And how did I get here? I remembered sneaking into the pack house basement but then it gets fuzzy.

I tried to sit up slowly, but my head swirled and I laid it back down.

"Ugh." I closed my eyes for a moment, and then the door to the room creaked open.

My eyes popped open, and I saw Alice carrying a tray.

"Oh, dear," she set the tray on a table and rushed to the bed. "June, don't get up too soon. Poor girl, you must be so upset."

"Upset?" I asked, trying to sit up slowly. "What happened? Where am I?"

Alice clicked her tongue and shook her head sadly. "You don't remember, do you? It will come back. Poor child. Here, let me get Alpha, he's the best one for this situation. I brought you a bit of soup and toast. Try to get one of them down if you can."

Alice rushed out of the room with purpose, leaving no room for more questions.

I moved the blankets off of me and swung my legs off the side of the bed, looking down in horror to see that I was not wearing any clothes I recognized. Flannel pajama pants and a plain T-shirt. Did someone change me?

Hey . . . I turned to my wolf.

Silence.

That sent a cold chill through my heart.

Hey!

A sense of dread filled me as I reached out and felt nothing. No response.

My nose was fully irritated with that familiar smell now. It was clouding the room, clouding my head. It was like the candle in Linda's house but much more potent.

I frowned, trying to decide where it was coming from, and as I looked around the room again I jumped as I saw Alpha Evander leaning in the doorway. He smelled like he'd been out in the woods. It was jarring to know he could sneak up on me like that.

"I'm sorry, did I startle you?" he said gently.

My muscles tensed, on the defensive.

"What am I doing here? What's going on?" I said.

Evander walked forward. I scooted back onto the bed, trying to keep the space between us as big as possible. I was so disoriented, though. Why was my wolf so quiet? Why was I here?

"Juniper." Evander sat on the edge of the bed. "Don't you remember?"

That smell. That maddening, foggy smell that irritated my head. It was stronger as he walked toward me. I looked over his shoulder and spotted the lit candle on a bookshelf by the door. He must have lit it when he came in. I instantly didn't like it.

"Remember what?" I asked slowly.

"You collapsed after the news," he said. "I brought you up here to rest. Alice helped you get comfortable. It even looks like she left you something to eat, what a sweetheart."

My eyes darted to the tray of food and back to Evander again. "What news?"

"June, I'm afraid there was a bad rogue attack at the borders," Evander said.

My heart stopped. "Oh no . . ."

"There was a wolf who disobeyed the lockdown orders. His safety was . . . compromised."

"No."

Dom? I reached out. *Dom!*

"I'm afraid there were too many of them," Evander said sadly. "Dom was overwhelmed."

"No!" I screamed. "He would never! He's the strongest wolf I know!"

"June." Evander reached out to pat my knee. I jerked back.

"I need to see him!" I snarled. "Let me see him!"

I tossed the covers aside and tried to get off the bed and move toward the door, but Evander was quicker. He pushed me back down, and I was too weak and clouded to fight him.

"June, it's too late. He's gone," Evander said. "You're in no condition to leave right now, you need your rest."

"I don't believe Dom was killed!" I insisted. "Let me see him!"

"June, sit down." Evander commanded me in that way the alpha wolves seemed to be able to do. My body flinched, and in this state, I couldn't fight it. I sank back into the bed, my eyes watering.

Dom? Dom!

Nothing.

"That's better," Evander said. "June, you're clearly distraught. Why don't you stay here for a while? I can't imagine what it would be like to live in that house after . . . well. Why don't you stay here for a while? I'll let the pack know what has happened."

I was numb. My body didn't feel like mine anymore. But Dom couldn't be dead. There was no way it was true.

"Now, why don't you lie back and relax?" Evander said. "You've had a stressful day as it is. In fact, maybe you should take a nap, and maybe if you feel better when you wake up, you can join me for dinner? I can have Alice make your favorite meal if you let me know what it is."

I was taken back by that. On the surface, Evander was acting nice. Then again, didn't he always behave that way? I knew I didn't like him for how he handled his takeover of the pack, but was that my only reason? Was I hating him for something that happened ten years ago? That didn't sound like me, but I just couldn't make my mind remember.

"I can have Alice lay you out a nice dress as well. I'm sure a fresh change of clothes will do you good," Evander offered.

A realization hit me through the fog. My eyes darted around the room again, and I began to piece together what this room reminded me of. Floral sundresses hung in the open closet. The paintings on the wall were all of things that could only be seen from looking out the windows of the pack house. Even the soft scents that lingered here reminded me of her.

"This is Naomi's room," I said.

Evander nodded slowly. "It *was* Naomi's room. Yes."

"Why put me here? Why not a guest room?" I asked, suspicious of his motives.

"Naomi's old room already had clean bedding, clothes, and toiletries in the bathroom. The other rooms are used so rarely, we don't keep them ready for use. I would hate to put you in a dusty room, after all."

Enough heavy suspicion and even the strange candle smoke couldn't cloud my head entirely. Naomi hadn't seemed happy here. Was she a prisoner? Was I a prisoner? And where was Dom really? Because I couldn't accept a reality where he wouldn't survive. Not now, not so close to the full moon and his challenge to Evander.

Flashes crossed my mind. A bumper sticker. A figure lying on the ground behind silver bars. Evander. The basement.

The basement!

I still didn't have all the answers. My memories were still hazy. But I did know one thing, and that was that I couldn't trust Evander.

"Rest, June," Evander said, sliding a bit closer to me on the bed. "And remember that I'm here for you. The pack is here for you. We watch over each other. I know you haven't been with us long, but you belong in Moonpeak, and Moonpeak needs a caring wolf like you.

"It's a shame we lost Naomi at such a strenuous time for the pack," Evander continued. "She was such a nurturer, something I see in you as well, June. Naomi's presence helped the fact that we don't have a luna here. Ah, well. I'm sorry, I'm rambling now."

"Naomi is a luna now," I said. "Or she will be someday. Nathan is clearly an alpha."

"True." Evander sighed. "She's where she belongs now. I hope this pack can go on without the role she filled. At least, until we can find another to soothe the pack in troubled times."

I nearly jerked back from him in that moment. My head swam. If he couldn't find a luna, he couldn't just shove any wolf in that role. Could he?

I shivered. Even if he thought that could be the case, why not look for your own luna in the first place? And, for that matter, all the other important roles in the pack? He had no beta; he'd dismantled the role of the Master of Arms. The trackers weren't even utilized well if they had to tiptoe around what they found with Evander when he wanted to keep things secret.

Liar.

My wolf was starting to wake up. Relief flooded me.

Dom isn't dead.

Both of us were satisfied in the other's confidence in Dom.

But how to navigate this situation?

And who was the person in the basement? Maybe they had answers. Did this mean I would have to play along?

Maybe for now that would be best.

"You know what, Alpha?" I said. "I am tired. This is a lot to take in."

Evander smiled, placing his hand on my knee while I resisted the urge to yank back my leg and kick him in the face.

"Of course, June. Do you want me to bring you the soup Alice made?"

"Yes, please," I said sadly. "I should still eat something."

"Let me get that." Evander left my side long enough to bring the tray from where Alice had left it and bring it back to the bed.

"Thank you," I said. "It smells wonderful."

"I'm glad you still have an appetite," Evander said. "Tell me, what sounds good to eat for dinner? I'll have Alice make it."

"Oh," I said. "Nothing complicated. I don't want to trouble her."

"Nonsense," Evander said, pleased that I was going along with his suggestions if even only a little bit.

"Well, then . . ." Something that would keep her here for a while. Something that could let me maybe talk to her while she had downtime.

"What about a meatloaf?" I asked. "Granny always made that when I didn't win my track events."

"She'd be delighted to." Evander smiled, standing up. "Alice makes a great meatloaf. I'll let her know right now, you get some sleep. And that door over there is a bathroom if you need it."

"Thanks," I said, pretending to yawn and pulling the blankets over me.

"Rest well, Juniper. I'll come to check on you later."

"Okay," I said.

Evander gave me one last pleased look as he left the room, shutting the door softly. A metal sound clicked in the door before I heard his footsteps walking away and down the stairs.

The moment I thought he was far enough away, I tossed off the blankets and tiptoed to the door. Sure enough, it was locked. Not that it would stop a wolf from bursting through it, but he would definitely know if I broke the lock.

With a sigh, I walked back over to grab a piece of toast and start eating while I investigated what I could see and reach from the windows. Not much. Some plants, and really nothing directly below that I'd want to risk landing on if I climbed out the window.

Mate, my wolf whimpered.

I know, I said softly. *We'll find him. And if he can't challenge Evander on the full moon . . .*

I shook my head. *No, Dom will be here. He will. I have to bide my time until he can get back. Whatever Evander did to him, Dom is stronger.*

I eyed the candle, which was nearly out now. The smell was maddening. It muddled my thoughts, I just knew it. But how? Was it magic? Where did Evander get magic?

With a sigh, I sat back down on the bed. Time to come up with some new plans, and play the part of the sad wolf with a missing mate. Maybe I could keep Evander's guard down long enough to get some answers.

Who was in the basement?

Where was this magic stuff coming from?

And where in the world was Dom?

CHAPTER FORTY-FIVE

JUNE

Evander was finally gone. Barely. I had just about gotten the hang of his daily routines, or at least he already had a pattern after the last couple days I'd suffered under his roof.

He woke early, going for a morning patrol. He'd sneak into my room while I slept, or pretended to sleep, and light his damn candle. Whatever fog my mind couldn't shake, I knew that candle had something to do with it.

While he patrolled, Alice would come to make breakfast. She brought me up a plate, then packed the rest for Evander when he returned. She would do some cleaning around the house and then leave.

Evander would return soon after; there was a very little window for me to be alone in the house. He spent time in his office or room until lunch. He would eat whatever Alice had made and left, usually something simple like sandwiches, and bring me up a plate while he checked on me and lit another candle.

The damn candle. I wanted to throw it out the window. I wanted to shove it down his throat. But then he'd know I wasn't playing his games, and all my chances to learn more about what he was up to would be gone.

His afternoon had another run, and Alice was back for a repeat of the morning routine until dinner, which I was expected to join him for.

It was all terribly frustrating, and my wolf would bounce between lashing out in fury and demanding we tear down the pack house, and being almost completely dormant and unresponsive. The whirlwind of anger and emptiness left me disoriented and exhausted.

But never without scheming.

I tried everything. Slipping out a window only to find small spikes in all the places I could possibly put my hands to climb. Getting out through the bedroom door, but it was always locked unless Evander let me out. I tried begging Alice but she was absolutely loyal to Evander's orders. The most infuriating part was that I couldn't remember why she shouldn't be.

But finally, finally, Evander was taking a longer walk than usual, and Alice just left.

Nose pressed to the window, I strained to see the side of the building that would tell me that Alice was walking home. I couldn't see her, but I saw her distinct shadow, carrying its basket now empty of whatever garden vegetables she brought today. Just a few more steps and . . . yes! She was completely off the pack-house lawn and I was alone.

But for how long?

Didn't matter, I had to make the best use of the time I had.

I ran to the door to the bedroom. I had found some of the tape Naomi used when she secured her paper to watercolor on. Even better was that it blended in well with the wood of her door, because when Alice was fumbling to come into my room with breakfast, I slipped several pieces of tape that I had prepared over the inside of the door. And now I got to see if it had stopped it from latching.

I held my breath, turning the doorknob and straining to hear the click of the lock. I did, she hadn't forgotten that part. But pulling the door gently, I heard the most glorious sound. The part inside the door that stuck out and latched it shut was taped down, and all I could hear as I opened the door was the metal from the strike plate brushing against my rushed tape job.

"Yes!" I hissed, whipping the door open and running into the hallway.

But where to start? I could raid Evander's office for suspicious things, but then my smell would be all over the place.

To the basement then. Something bothered me about it, I thought there was a person down there, but I couldn't really be sure. Everything I remembered was so jumbled. But I was determined to find something somewhere that would remind me why I was so against Evander.

I went down the stairs, doing my best to touch as little as possible. The less of my scent I could spread around, the better.

The basement door was locked; I had expected that. But I remembered the trick I did before and went to find the unlocking pin from on top of the bathroom door again.

"Dammit," I hissed. There was nothing over the frame this time. I checked a few other doors around the hall, but none of them had that old fashioned pin thing.

I went back to the basement door and stood still, listening for any sounds in the house. Nothing, and Evander didn't usually sneak back into his own home, so I should be able to make at least a little bit of noise, right?

I cleared my throat, knocking on the door to the basement.

"Hello, is someone down there?" I asked.

Even with my wolf hearing, I couldn't detect anything behind the door.

"Hello?" I called again, a little louder. "I'm not with Evander, if that's what you're worried about. He's not even home right now."

This time there was some stirring. Did I wake someone down there? Muffled sounds that could have been a voice came through the door, but nothing discernible.

"I can't unlock the door, but do you have another way I can get in? A window? A vent?"

They mumbled again, but I still couldn't understand. There was too much basement between me and them; I had to get closer.

"Hold on, I'm going to look for more ways to get to you," I called.

Leaving the basement door alone, I took a step back and looked around. I couldn't get near the far side of the basement from this side of the pack house. Maybe that meant I needed to find my way to the back half.

The kitchen shared the back wall of the house, and while I didn't know what other rooms sat around it, there wouldn't be a particular problem with my scent in the kitchen, so it was a good start.

There were windows, but I knew where those led. There were old pipes that ran up the walls. Not a surprise with the age of the buildings in the village. But nothing like an air vent or laundry chute to be found. The rooms around the kitchen were not useful either. A pantry, a supply closet, and two bedrooms that can't have been occupied at any point in the last several years.

"Take a deep breath, June," I said. "In and out, then think about it."

If this floor wasn't working, the upper floor probably wouldn't either. But I was running out of time, and it would be easier to slip back into my room from upstairs.

I took the stairs two at a time and tried all the doors. Most were either locked or empty. The few guest rooms I had access to were useless, the windows as impassable as Naomi's.

Frustrated, I paced the hallway. I could either try the basement another way or go back to my room before Evander returned, and try to think of another way.

I closed the door to Naomi's room and peeled off the tape so Evander couldn't catch on to my trick. I sank onto the bed.

"Ugh," I groaned into the covers. "Why is this so hard?"

I rolled over onto my back, staring at the ceiling. My throat tightened, and I put a hand over my heart. "Dom, where are you? I need you."

Reaching out for a link, any link, I tried again to contact the village. I couldn't reach anyone outside the pack house. It was like Evander had done something to this place to prevent it.

I rubbed my eyes. I probably looked visibly upset, and while I could use Dom as an excuse to Evander, I really just didn't even want to deal with the discussion it could bring up. I walked into the bathroom to wash my face.

The bathroom was nice, if fairly simple. A shower, a bathtub, a sink. All you really needed, basically. It was wallpapered in a very old-fashioned style and had old pipes to match. As I filled the sink and splashed my face, checking in the mirror that I looked refreshed and normal, the old pipes caught my attention.

Clang, clang, clang.

I turned off the water and froze, listening.

Clang, clang, clang.

One of the pipes that ran down the wall was definitely being hit by something from a lower floor. A much lower floor.

I abandoned the sink and ran to the pipe. I knocked on it three times, just like the sound I'd been hearing.

A pause, then I got my response. *Clang, clang, clang.*

I ran my hands along the pipe, trying to figure out what its purpose could be. Whatever it was once used for, it didn't seem to function anymore, so it was just a piece of old pipe now.

But if I could open it up . . .

From bottom to top, I inspected it carefully. If I stood on the edge of the bathtub, I could reach an old valve of some kind. I put my ear to the pipe, listening for anything that could be running inside. Gas, water, who knew what else. Nothing.

I let out a slow breath and grabbed the valve tight. "Here goes nothing."

I yanked hard, using every ounce of strength my wolf could grant me, and popped the valve right off the pipe. With a yell, I fell backwards into the tub.

"Ouch," I groaned, rubbing my head and shoulders where I'd hit the tub the hardest. But I got back on my feet, looked up into the hole the valve created, and put my mouth near the opening.

"Hello?" I called.

A pause. "June Bug?"

My heart froze. "Katherine? What are you doing here?"

"It is you!" she cried. "I thought they killed you. I thought they killed me! I think they might still kill me. I don't know what's happening."

"Shh, calm down, Kit Kat. Take a deep breath." I paused, waiting for her to do as I asked. "Why are you here?"

"Well, my best friend ran away across North America to a mysterious relative's. Some people I've never heard of. You haven't told me about any Canadian relatives, especially not from the middle of nowhere Newfoundland!"

"How did you know where I was?" I asked.

"Do you remember the selfie you sent me? I asked you to send me something to prove you were okay? You were standing in front of a store, I could see the sign. I looked it up, and there is just the one place with that name. And I looked on Google Street View and sure enough, it was a building in Canada."

"So you found where I was and came all the way out to *Canada*? How did you afford that?" I asked.

"I've been having terrible feelings that something bad was happening to you. I couldn't contact you, and I got a bunch of money and came out here myself."

"And where did you get a bunch of money?" I asked.

"Oh, yeah, that part. So, you know how the plaza I worked in got blown up or whatever? Apparently, it was enough hassle that some new owner bought it out and paid out every single person who had worked in the area a big bonus. I don't know who it was, but they must have been loaded to throw around that much cash."

My jaw dropped. This must be that group of fae Jerod told me about.

"How did you get here? In this house."

"June, I was so scared," Kat cried. "There was this old diner that I was eating at, and I showed the lady your picture. I showed your picture to everyone I could find, starting at the store where you took your selfie!"

"Okay, but focus, Kat. Here, how did you get here."

"Right, right. Well, the diner lady recognized your picture. She remembered you, or rather the guy you were with. You're with a guy by the way? Who is he? Is he dangerous?"

"Focus!" I said. "We don't have a lot of time before Evander gets back."

"Is that the guy's name?" Kat asked. "No, okay, the story.

Anyway, someone saw the car come down an old dirt hunting road. So I kinda . . . followed the road a while."

"You what?" I exclaimed.

"Well, I didn't think it would go so far!" Kat said. "I thought you were holed up in some old hunting cabin or something. But anyway, I was walking and it was growing dark. Then these big animals came out. They chased me down, one of them scratched up my leg real bad, and this guy came out after them and took me."

"A guy?" I asked. "What did he look like?"

"Well, it was kinda dark, but he was naked. Some facial hair, I think. Anyway, he chased off the . . . big dogs? No, I guess wolves or coyotes or something. Anyway, he chased them off and brought me here. He shoved me in some basement and I've been down here for days! June, my leg hurts so bad and I want to go home."

Kat started crying, and my heart collapsed.

Tears flooded my own eyes as I listened to Kat's soft weeping through the pipe. Both of us a prisoner in Evander's house. My throat tightened as I wiped the dampness off my face, then I sucked in a breath.

"Kat," I said, a tremor in my voice. "You said one of the . . . they're werewolves, Kat. You said one of them scratched up your leg?"

She sniffed. "Yeah, it still hurts."

I closed my eyes, my heart sinking. "Did they scratch you or bite you?"

She paused, thinking about it. "I think one of them nipped me, but the scratches are what hurt."

My face fell, and I balled my fists at my side in frustrated determination. "Hold on, Kat. I'll get us out of here somehow. My m— Um, I have friends who will help us."

She sniffed again. "When we get out of here, I want the whole story, June."

"Yes, I promise," I said. "The whole—"

Footsteps. I could barely hear them, but all the training Tanner had hammered into me made picking up sounds like that second nature.

"I've got to go, Kat," I hissed. "Hang in there! I promise."

I hopped off the side of the tub, kicking the broken valve under the sink and slipping back into the bedroom where I could lie on the bed and pretend to nap.

My heart pounded with every movement Evander made. Footsteps outside. The opening of the door, and then some walking around downstairs. Kitchen sounds where he ate the meal Alice had left for him, and then some more walking.

I took deep breaths, in and out. Trying to slow my heart and calm my nerves before Evander noticed anything was amiss.

And it was agony.

After a good long time, and a lot of silent prayers that Kat would keep quiet down there, Evander's steps finally made their way up the stairs.

Slowly, deliberately, he took the steps along the path I'd taken when I was checking the other doors in the hallway.

I caught my lower lip in my teeth. Did he smell me? I'd tried to be careful . . .

The footsteps made their way to my door. A hand on the doorknob tested it quietly, probably making sure the lock was still in place, then he unlocked it and came in.

"June?" Evander called quietly. "Are you awake?"

He was a wolf, he knew damn well I wasn't breathing like I was asleep.

"Resting," I answered, sitting up in the bed now.

"Good, good." He walked over and sat on the edge of the bed, a habit he had formed every time he visited me now. He studied my face, which was hopefully peaceful enough not to arouse suspicion.

"You weren't out of your room today, were you? Helping Alice perhaps?"

Damn, he had smelled me. Think, June, think!

I shook my head. "No. Actually, I'm afraid I gave her a little extra work. I sent something I was wearing with her to sew for me. Naomi and I don't seem to be the same size."

"Ah." He nodded. "That explains the smell."

I tilted my head. "Smell?"

"Never mind. June, I'm here to talk about the full moon," he said.

The full moon. I had today and tomorrow to figure out a plan of what to do on the full moon, then tomorrow night I would get my chance.

"You're not in any state to participate tomorrow," Evander said. "You should stay in the pack house."

"What?" Alarm rang through me as my wolf surfaced, resisting the idea of not running on the full moon with her packmates. "The whole pack will be together! We can't possibly be any safer than as a large group of wolves, running as one."

"June, be reasonable," Evander said. "You're not in a mental or emotional state to handle the strain of it all."

I needed a plan he would go along with. I couldn't challenge him or try to reach out to any of my friends if I wasn't even out of the pack house to try. My eyes slid to the hand on my knee, which I really just wanted to slap away, and I remembered how he was around Naomi . . .

"But, Evander," I said, placing my hand over his. "I'm safest next to my alpha. You've taken care of me so far, what if I need you during the full moon?"

That surprised him, but his expression quickly turned to pleased. He lifted my hand in his, holding it for . . . comfort maybe? Was he trying to comfort me? And he sighed.

"I understand your feelings, June. I'll consider your request," he said warmly.

And then I yawned, trying to excuse pulling my hand away to cover my mouth. "Thank you."

"I'll let you rest. Do you want anything special for dinner tonight?" Evander stood up.

"Whatever you want is just fine with me, Alpha."

"Very well, you get some rest."

He left the room and I laid down like I was going to fall asleep, all the while listening intently as he locked the door and went downstairs to his office.

Shit. Evander had nearly caught me, and now I knew who he was keeping in the basement! If she was bitten, I knew why he'd brought Kat here. He probably expected her to either die or shift into a loyal wolf. Was he using his magic candle on her too? Was she hungry, cold, scared?

Tomorrow night the full moon would be here, and one way or another, this was going to have to end. I just had to hope Dom could find his way back to end it.

CHAPTER FORTY-SIX

DOM

From my room in the pack house, I grumbled as Salt Fur's doctor checked me over once more. I had already been here for days, granted for most of it I was in no shape to leave yet. But now that I could, I was eager to get back to Moonpeak, and to June.

"Relax, Dom," Nathan said. He stood against the door frame, arms crossed and watching the doctor at work.

"I don't think relax is the word for it." Nathan's dad, Alpha Thomas, sat in a chair in the corner and observed my checkup as well. He looked every bit an old fisherman in his flannel and boots. "He is, understandably, irritated at his situation."

"Tonight is the full moon, I have to get back. I have to challenge Evander," I said.

Nathan growled, and Thomas's expression darkened. "We know, Dom. And the Salt Fur wolves will back your claim and ensure the challenge goes unhindered."

"He was trying to manipulate Naomi." Nathan's eyes darkened with a dangerous emotion. "I want to be the one to put that bastard in the ground myself."

We'd already pieced together her information and ours, recognizing that it was those damn candles that had kept her in a fog. Evander was the lowest, most disgusting form of life, and I was eager to put an end to him.

I watched as the doctor got close to my chest, inspecting where the silver dagger would leave a scar. Not something most wolves had to deal with, but silver was a different story.

"Dom has every right to his claim," Thomas said calmly. "Remember John. Remember Liam and Lily."

"Sorry, Dom," Nathan said. "But I'll be there with you. If you don't finish the job, I will."

"Get in line. I think Amelia would be next, then Aaron, then Jack or Carson."

"Those last three have no business challenging an alpha," Thomas said.

"Mm. But it wouldn't stop them," I answered.

"Okay," the doctor said, standing up straight. "The silver came dangerously close to your heart, but I can't see any lasting damage. I don't recommend you going back to Moonpeak to immediately get into another fight—"

I growled, and she held up a hand to stop me.

"But," she continued, "I've been treating alpha wolves for a long time. I know you're going to do it anyway. Please watch out for daggers this time, okay?"

"No promises," I said.

She turned to Alpha Thomas. "I've done what I can for him. I see no reason he can't go now."

"Thank you, Doctor. You may go," Thomas said.

She left the room. I wasted no time throwing the sheets aside and standing up.

"I'm back." A light voice called from the hallway as Naomi rounded the corner and came in, carrying a pile of clothes in her arms. "Done already?"

"Yeah, I'm clear to go. Thanks, Naomi," I said, taking the clothes she was carrying and putting them on. It was like night and day; the way we'd seen her back at Moonpeak was a haunting of who she was. In a matter of days, she was already flourishing here by the sea with Nathan. I'd be forever grateful that she was able to smile again at all.

Nathan gently pulled Naomi into his arms, kissing her softly on the lips. "We'll be leaving soon with my picked warriors."

"I'm still coming," Naomi insisted. "You're not talking me out of it."

Nathan sighed, turning to his dad with a pleading look.

Thomas chuckled. "I can't help you with this one, son. She's your luna, get used to letting her have her way."

Naomi gave Alpha Thomas a warm smile. "Thank you, Alpha."

"I'm sorry we can't send you more backup," Thomas said, turning to me. "But on the full moon, we have our own pack to take care of. I've got a handful that might have a first shift to watch over too."

I shook my head. "No, thank you for any help at all. If those rogues try to stop me from getting back and I can't challenge Evander, our whole plan goes south. So thank you."

"I'm sure Amelia won't let him go completely unchallenged," Thomas reminded me.

"I know, but it sounded like Evander had a plan for her too. I wish I could contact the others, but Salt Fur is way too far from the village."

"I wonder how June is holding up," Nathan said. "She seems like a smart girl, but . . ."

The muscles in my jaw tensed as I pulled up the shorts Naomi had brought me. "She is, but she also has no idea what happened to me. I'm worried about her, she's the type to get herself involved however she can. I'm sure she's either looking for me, or who the hell knows what else."

"Yes, b'y. She does seem determined, I'll give her that." Nathan sighed. "If you're ready, we can head down to lunch and gather the fighters. No need to run to Moonpeak as wolves when we have plenty of time to walk and conserve energy. The moon is still many hours away."

"You don't know how hard it is to not just run straight there," I said.

"Nathan, why don't you go down to the kitchens for a scoff first," Thomas suggested. "Take Naomi with you."

Nathan raised an eyebrow, looking over to his dad and receiving no answers to his silent question. In the end, he shrugged it off and took Naomi by the hand and led her out of the room and down the hall.

Thomas watched them go. I studied the old alpha. A little older than my dad would be if he was still alive, Alpha Thomas looked a lot like his son. Or rather, it was the other way around, I guess. Similar build, tan from the time spent under the sun by the sea where the Salt Fur wolves ran, blond hair, but Alpha Thomas kept a beard. The genes ran strong in this family, that was for sure. And as soon as Nathan was truly out of hearing range, Thomas turned those blue eyes to me.

"Dominic," he said.

Now I was alert. He had only called me Dominic once before, and that was when my dad died.

"You've made some questionable choices in the last few years," he started. My heart sank. I knew, and I was ashamed to agree with him. "But despite the unfortunate circumstances that brought you down this path, you've landed on your feet." Alpha Thomas stood up, looking at me eye to eye and reminding me how big he actually was. We stood shoulder to shoulder, but he still somehow took up a bit more room than I did.

"We did what we had to," I said.

"Hm. You were a big part of what carried Amelia through a time of madness," Thomas said, placing a hand on my shoulder. "I've always regretted not taking you back to Salt Fur with me after John died. But it seems you were where you needed to be after all."

I didn't know what to say to that, so I said nothing. I had no idea he had even considered bringing me under his roof. Not that I gave him much time to ask me; we left pretty damn quick.

"Your father would be proud of you. Liam would be proud of you," Thomas said, taking his hand off my shoulder and sighing. "I'm proud of you, and I know you'll make Moonpeak a fine alpha."

My throat tightened. I had no idea he felt this way, thought this way, about me.

"Promise me one thing," Thomas said seriously.

"What?" I asked.

"When this is all sorted out, you bring that luna of yours here so we can meet properly over dinner." Thomas gave me a warm smile, and in that instant I realized the faith he had in me. How sure he was of my success, to send his son with me to support my cause. To send me back without more help.

Evander had to die, and Thomas had faith that I could be the one to kill him.

"Thank you, Alpha," I said softly.

Thomas chuckled and slapped a hand on my back, guiding

me out of the room and toward the dining hall. "Here's your first tip, an alpha doesn't call another wolf *alpha*. Thomas will do just fine."

"That's going to be strange, since I've known you as Alpha Thomas my whole life."

"You'll have all the time you need to get used to it, *after* you go claim your title."

"I will, Thomas," I answered.

"Good, now, get down there and eat something. Your wolf must be starving, and you need all the energy you can muster to get through tonight. Remember the rules of challenge, and I'm sure Smokey won't let anyone go against the old code."

"No, I'm sure he won't."

Thomas patted my back. "I'll see you after it's all done. Good luck, Dom."

"Thank you."

Alpha Thomas left, heading back in the direction of his office as I went the other way, toward the smell of food.

In the big room there were plenty of wolves seated and eating what appeared to be venison burgers for lunch. It was big enough to sit maybe fifty wolves at four long tables, with a pass-through window to the kitchen, where you could grab the prepared food. Nathan and Naomi were easy to spot, and Anna saw me come in as she was sitting down with her own plate next to a big male I didn't recognize. They waved me over, and I joined them.

"Here, I got you a plate," Naomi said, scooting three burgers my way. "I bet you're hungry."

I took it gladly. "Thanks."

"This is Zach," Anna said, leaning up to kiss the male to her left. Light-brown hair, lots of freckles, and even more muscle.

"Your mate, I take it." I reached across the table to shake his hand. "Nice to meet you. My condolences about being stuck with Anna."

The table laughed at that, and Zach gave a playful warning growl as he shook my hand.

"So, what did my old man want?" Nathan asked.

I shrugged. "A pep talk of sorts."

Nathan nodded, his expression turning into a grin. "I thought as much. He must really see potential in you, he's only ever a hardass to me."

Anna laughed. "No more than you deserve."

Nathan elbowed her playfully. "Watch it, Beta."

"So, who is coming with us?" I asked. "Anna?"

"Hell, yeah, I'm in," Anna said. "I wouldn't miss this for the world. Zach, too, right baby?"

Zach nodded.

"We're also bringing a few new faces, but they're trained up and ready to go," Nathan said.

"I welcome their help," I told Nathan. "If you can get me to the village field before the run starts, I'll do the rest."

"We'll do more than that, Dom," Nathan said, putting an arm around Naomi. "We'll back your claim, and kill any rogues that involve themselves in the fight. He's got some connection to them, and whatever it is, it needs to stop."

"A good set of teeth to the throat ought to do it," Anna added, taking a big bite of her burger.

"If we leave after lunch, we should be able to mostly walk it with some light jogging and get there in time," Nathan said. "Try to reach out and talk to June or Amelia if you can while we walk. I'm sure they'd love to know you're okay."

"Of course. I'm hoping Aaron has made his way into Smokey's morning running group. That is, if Evander is even letting Smokey out of the village at this point. He really locked everything down tight," I said.

"Oof. I can only imagine trying to keep that old man inside the village for so long. I hope he's at least wearing pants," Nathan said.

Naomi smiled warmly up at him and placed her hand over his.

"We'll set everything right," she said. "Dom will win. My sister is firmly behind him and will fight to the death before she lets Dom die or Evander keep his title."

Even after all these years apart, she knew Amelia well.

"All right, then," Nathan announced. "Clean your plates, guys. We've got a walk ahead of us."

And as we finished our plates, my excitement built.

Finally, everything we had been working for. It was finally time.

Time to kill Evander.

CHAPTER FORTY-SEVEN

JUNE

Sleep hadn't come easily last night. I woke up from a mix of nightmares and full-moon energy every hour or so. Forty-eight hours now, and I still didn't know where Dom was or how to free Kat.

My head was clearer this morning. My wolf was awake and alert. My eyes darted to the candle near the door; it wasn't lit yet.

I went straight to the bathroom, turning the hot water on and dropping my clothes in the hamper. After quickly scrubbing down and washing my hair, I stood under the water for a bit.

I stared at the pipe on the wall. My only lifeline to Kat. What I wouldn't give to talk to her a little more, but I hadn't had the chance since that first time. I shut the water off and stepped out of the shower.

Brushing my hair, messing with my undercut and looking in the mirror, I wondered what clothes were acceptable tonight. Lately, even my wardrobe had come under scrutiny, and I felt more and more like I was stealing Naomi's closet.

What does a girl wear to overthrow a corrupt alpha?

I wrapped the towel around myself and walked back into the bedroom, opening the closet door and picking a loose sundress that could be discarded quickly for a shift. Whatever tonight brought, the shift was inevitable for all the wolves.

I barely had the dress pulled over my head and a pair of panties on my ass when the door to my room clicked open.

Startled, I yanked the dress in place and stared wide-eyed as the closet door was pulled open.

"There you are, June," Evander said, a gentle smile on his face. He walked over and lit the candle. *Dammit.*

Of course, I'm right here, asshole! You can sense me wherever in the house I go!

My wolf growled, hard and loud enough that I had to resist it slipping through my own lips as well.

Evander smirked and looked me up and down. "You look lovely, June."

"Thank you," I said, not sure what else to say.

Evander watched me a moment longer, and then stood back so I could leave the closet.

"I have some business to attend to this morning," he said.

I took a step into the room and frowned as I smelled the smoke again.

"Okay," I murmured.

"I was thinking since you will be with me tonight at the full moon, you might like something to take your mind off of things today while you wait."

My eyes widened. "Take my mind off of Dom?"

Evander gave me a sympathetic look. "Poor girl. Yes, June. Alice does quite a bit of cooking for the full moon meal after the run, and I thought you would enjoy helping her downstairs."

My heart raced. I had to play my words very carefully to keep my act up right now. But getting out of this room could mean contacting Kat, or reaching out to Amelia or Aaron or someone in the pack who could tell me what had been going on for the last few days.

"Oh, that would be wonderful," I said. "I've liked helping Alice ever since I arrived in Moonpeak."

Evander smiled, seeming to accept my answer. "Very good. I'll let you finish getting ready and then you can come downstairs, Alice has arrived and is setting up in the kitchen."

"Thank you, Evander. And thank you for letting me out with you tonight. I know you're just worried about me."

"Oh, June." Evander pulled me into an embrace. My wolf threw a fit, and I almost let out the growl building inside of me.

"It's a pleasure to look after all of my wolves," Evander said. "And to make sure you have a safe place here." He smiled and looked me over once more, lingering maybe a little longer than I liked on my legs. "I'll see you later. Don't be afraid to stop and rest if you need it."

"I will."

Alice was in the kitchen peeling carrots over the sink. "There's my June!" She winked. "So glad to see you feeling up to some work."

"What can I do first?"

"Take that basket there and wash all the food in it. It came straight from my garden an hour ago," she said, gesturing with the vegetable peeler to a basket on the counter.

"Got it," I said, and began sorting the veggies. The excuse to work did pass the time, much better than sitting in Naomi's room all day. But under Alice's sharp eyes I had no chance to investigate the house. I could be finding things in Evander's office, or figuring out how to get into the basement.

But at least the morning passed quickly if nothing else. My thoughts kept coming back to Dom, worrying about where he could be and if he was hurt, and worrying about Kat in the basement.

Dom? I tried.

The link didn't really go anywhere. Like there was nothing on the other side to latch on to. Or maybe it was me who was having the problem. My head couldn't shake the cloud, making me second-guess everything I did.

I tried again to reach out to him and failed. I also reached out to Amelia with no results, and in a desperate moment, I tried Smokey too. Nothing.

The only positive now was that I had learned how to make potato salad. I hadn't cared for it much before, but Alice's was fantastic.

Morning turned to midday. Evander came back in, ruining my chances of exploring the pack house. An uncomfortable lunch, and then an afternoon in the kitchen again.

As I pulled the last pan of rolls out of the oven, I looked at Alice, who was mixing some kind of sauce. She seemed to sense as much and looked up at me.

"Oh, June. Don't look so down." She put down the bowl she was mixing in, wiping her hands on her apron as she came to give me a hug. "You look like you're about to cry, dear. I know you've been through a lot these past few weeks, but the Moonpeak pack will take care of you. You're one of us now."

At her touch, the arms of a motherly figure, the tears started falling. I reached out for her, wrapping my arms around her small shoulders and sobbing.

She didn't even know what I cried about, but she didn't have to. She was just there for me when I needed her.

I was crumbling. If Dom didn't return, I didn't know what to do. I didn't know if Amelia was out there. I couldn't reach her, I couldn't reach anybody, and I couldn't let Evander continue on this path. What was I supposed to do, challenge him myself?

My tears finally ran their course. I blinked, wiping off my face as I leaned away from Alice.

"There now, a good cry can make anyone feel better," Alice said. "We're done here, dear. Why don't you go up to your room and rest a bit? We've got a big run ahead of us."

I sniffed, nodding. I wasn't paying very close attention to what she was saying, but I knew she meant well. My mind was filled with other thoughts right now. Thoughts of me, thoughts of my wolf, and thoughts of what I might have to do.

"Yeah, thanks, Alice," I mumbled, and left the kitchen as I tried to dry my face.

Dom. He wasn't dead, he couldn't be. I had to believe in him more than I believed in Evander. So wherever he went, I'd be on his side until he came back. And the one thing I knew he wanted was freedom for Moonpeak.

I took in a shaky breath as I closed the door behind me. Sitting on the bed, I reflected on my options.

"What now?" I asked weakly.

If I could find Amelia, she could and very likely would still challenge Evander.

If Nathan came back, he may be persuaded to challenge Evander, but what would that mean for the future of Moonpeak?

Aaron might do, he was definitely the strongest after Dom and Amelia of the wolves I came here with, but was he strong enough?

Smokey? No. He wouldn't do anything of the sort without a

lot of proof of a bad alpha, and while I felt I had that, my head was so foggy I couldn't remember straight to tell him anyway.

So if all of those plans failed, was it up to me?

What if I have to fight Evander?

No, my wolf insisted.

No? What do you mean no?

Mate. Mate will come.

"I hope so."

I lay there a little longer, trying to reflect on everything Smokey had taught me about fighting. When I was watching Dom and the other wolves train, I never imagined I'd regret not joining them.

Tanner's training was good, true, but maybe not as useful as Smokey's. Still, I wondered if I could drop enough hints to him that something was wrong to make him investigate. He must be annoyed that he just got a tracker, only to have me taken away days later.

Evander's footsteps came down the hallway.

Sitting up on the bed, I watched as the enemy came into my room with a smile. That was what he was, the enemy, and I couldn't let the fog make me forget that.

"Feeling better, June?" Evander asked.

"I'm fine. I just needed a rest. The run will do me a lot of good."

"All right." He nodded. "Meet me downstairs when you're ready, we'll make an appearance together."

"Okay," I agreed. He left, closing the door behind him.

My heart was racing, but I stood with determination.

Get it together, June! Tonight is the night.

I took a deep breath and left. I wished I could stop and tell Kat what was going to happen to her tonight. I really regretted not being able to warn her through the pipe the other day, but I'd run out of time. She was going to be down there, trying to shift, and not having a clue what was happening to her. I had to hope she'd make it through.

But right now, I had the problems in front of me. Evander.

At the front door, Evander smiled and opened it for me to leave first. I did, and he stepped out beside me, and we walked to the field. The sky was darkening and the moon would rise in a few hours.

"I've told them not to bring up Dom," Evander said. "There will be time to mourn later, but this isn't the night to distress you. We will watch the wolves gather and you can talk when you're ready. I'll be right by your side."

"Okay," I answered, internally cringing at his attempts. Where Dom was smooth and rugged, Evander was slimy and fake.

The field was full. Moonpeak wolves in varying states of dress, and a few already shifting for fun. As we arrived, one of the wolves howled out the presence of their alpha.

"Good evening!" Evander waved. "Don't mind me, enjoy yourselves. Socialize, and we will begin the run at moonrise."

A few cheers and waves and the wolves returned to whatever they were doing before we arrived.

I was able to stand next to Evander and not need to speak as he greeted a handful of wolves who came to make polite conversation with him. Meanwhile, my eyes roamed over the field, looking for anyone I could reach out to.

I spotted Tanner, but he was more of a last resort. He didn't know our plans, and I didn't know how far I could push his loyalties without getting caught.

It was a special kind of agony to be looking around a field full of happy people while trying to reach out for a lifeline.

When I spotted Amelia, my heart jumped. Yes!

Amelia! Can you hear me? I tried to link her, but my head was still fuzzy.

She didn't so much as look at me, she was more engrossed in conversation with her mate and the biggest person I had ever seen.

A little more of a search, and I spotted Jack. He actually looked my way, eyes wide in shock.

Jack! I called. *Jack, where is Dom?*

But Jack couldn't hear me either. It looked like he was trying to reach out to me as well, and failing. I sighed, shaking my head. It was no use.

"Alpha." One of the warriors came forward, getting Evander's attention.

"What is it?" Evander asked.

"We sense the warlock returning to pack lands," he said. "Smokey is about to intercept. Orders?"

Evander's expression slipped into annoyance momentarily, then back to the mask of a happy alpha. "Send Smokey. See what he's here for and let Smokey dispose of him as he sees fit if it's not important."

"Yes, Alpha," the warrior answered, and left.

I watched after him, mild interest on my face, but all of my senses were focused in that direction. Jerod? Was Carmine with him? Surely his magic trick would be on our side tonight. He'd figured out the candles, maybe he could help undo whatever hold this potent one still had over me. I put all my focus on that direction of the field, waiting and hoping.

Something stirred in the back of my mind. It was far away, foggy. Distracting.

I shook my head, trying to listen for new arrivals. Hoping that Smokey would bring Carmine and Jerod here.

The thing prodded my mind again, this time it a little more clearly.

I tried to keep my face still, but I could swear I heard the smallest hint of a link. The first to come through since Evander had kept me in that candle-smoke-filled room.

June!

My heart pounded in my ears. That time I heard it for sure.

Dom?

June! he answered. *June, I'm on my way.*

My heart could have burst. My eyes started to mist over but I blinked it away before anyone could see. My head was a swirl with emotion and relief.

Dom—he was fine, and he was coming!

I looked over at Evander, resisting the urge to betray my happiness. I focused on clearing my head before anything else. Breathing in slowly through my nose, exhaling through my mouth, slowing my heartbeat. Breath in, breath out, focus. The minutes dragged on as I practiced focusing on things. A pair of children playing, the leaves of a tree swaying with the breeze, a lone cloud wafting overhead. When a commotion came from the edge of the gathered pack, my heart nearly leaped into my throat.

Smokey's white-faced wolf padded through the crowd, trailed by Jerod and Carmine.

Evander's face was strained as he eyed them. "What's this, Smokey?"

The wolf shifted, allowing the benefit of human speech for Carmine and Jerod since they weren't Moonpeak and couldn't link. I was also relieved that I wouldn't be straining to hear, since my mind wasn't completely clear yet.

"The warlock brings an accusation," Smokey said. Worry rippled through the wolves, shock on many faces.

"An accusation, on the night of the full moon? Surely this can wait. Take them to the cabin to wait for tomorrow."

Smokey shook his head. "I will not, Alpha. The code says we stand to hear an accusation this serious, no matter the moon phase."

Evander's face slipped for a moment. "Still, the moon is nearly here, and we can't speak once we're all shifted."

A good point, unfortunately. Jerod seemed calm, which didn't surprise me, but so did Carmine. She wouldn't let anything happen to him, which meant she knew he had some kind of plan, or at the very least she didn't think this was putting him in danger.

Jerod shook his head, looking up at the sky. "I'll cut to the chase then."

Lifting a hand, he whispered something unintelligible and with a burst of blue smoke a large burst of fireworks lit up the sky above.

"What did you do?" Evander growled. "Warriors! Remove this warlock."

Jerod calmly raised a hand before him in a "hold on" position while he kept his eyes overhead. A screech tore through the sky, and that was when I felt the overwhelming presence. My heart hammered as we all watched the impossible rise above the treetops. Wings, spanning so far I wondered if they could cover the village, flapped as a creature from fairy tales headed our way. My knees weakened as the word formed in my head.

Dragon.

It let out another screech, and descended near the unphased Jerod. Was this another one of his summons? Was this the thing he summoned in Seattle that created that mess between him and Amelia?

The biggest wolves of the pack surrounded the dragon and Jerod, but didn't dare to get too close.

"Dani, thank you for coming," Jerod said, and it was in this moment I noticed the woman in black sitting on the dragon's back. She slid down, the dragon's tail moving to catch her if she fell too fast, and once she was on the ground, she threw her arms around Jerod.

"You should have called sooner! I didn't know where you went," she said.

"Later, I promise. For the moment, I need your assistance," Jerod said.

Howling from the east made my head turn. My heart raced; I could feel him. Dom, he was getting closer. All of them were getting closer.

"What?" Evander snapped, a snarl on his face as he swung his head to the east.

I took off before Evander could realize I'd left his side. Dom was the first of several wolves to emerge, and I ran to him. "Dom!" I cried, throwing my arms around his furry neck.

He stopped, pressing his nose into my neck as I clung to him, nearly sobbing.

So, he brought the dragon and the witch, Dom said.

"You know them?" I asked, stunned.

"The moon rises, Evander!" Our attention turned back to the group as Amelia walked forward from the crowd. A wicked smile played across her lips. Other wolves walked forward behind her. Bianca. A large blond man I'd never seen before stepped behind them as well. Aaron, Jack, and Carson followed, standing in solidarity behind Amelia.

The others in the crowd looked a mix of confused, fearful, and solemn. Many of them looked as though they knew what was coming and wanted to be far away from it when it began. Evander growled, forcing out that pressure of an alpha that sank most of us downward.

"I am the alpha who saved this pack from the rogue attacks ten years ago!" Evander snarled. "Smokey, get this abomination off of my lands!"

Smokey gave a dark look to Evander. "The code, Alpha. Not even you can sway me from seeing it through."

The alpha snarled, turning on Jerod. "And you, what unholy wretch did you summon here, warlock?"

"Me?" Jerod asked casually. "Nothing any worse than what you've brought to these lands. In a sense." He looked up at the dragon, giving him a nod.

"What does that mean, warlock?" Amelia snapped.

Jerod, who had all of the attention until now, pointed our way. "I'm here to help this one level the playing field. You have a claim, don't you?"

Around Dom settled the other wolves who had followed him. Nathan, Anna, and many more that I didn't know. I was so consumed by Dom's return that I hadn't noted who'd come with him.

"You said he was dead, Alpha," one wolf in the crowd remarked.

Several growls of agreement rippled through the field.

"Don't question the alpha," a timid female said, but the glares from those around her silenced any further thoughts.

"He . . . Dominic!" Evander screamed. "How did you survive? I saw you being attacked with my own eyes."

Dom shifted, and I let my arms fall away from him as he stood and glared at Evander with fire in his yellow eyes.

"I survived all right, and I brought back more proof that you are unfit to lead this pack."

If anything, that caused the murmurs in the crowd to grow worse. From the back of the new batch of wolves, Naomi stepped forward.

"She knows," I whispered, looking from Naomi to Evander. Naomi knew what Evander was doing in that house, and now she'd had days of clarity away from that terrible smoke. Naomi's word in this pack meant a lot, but would they be enough to reveal Evander's darker deeds?

"Naomi?" Evander asked in disbelief.

"Evander," she said, her voice shaking. "I don't know how, but you have something to do with the rogue attacks."

Nathan tightened his hold around Naomi as she leaned into him.

"A wild accusation," Evander spat. "Dom, I'm disappointed. Is this all your proof that I am an unfit leader? A bitter plot against me in your father's memory, perhaps? I'm ashamed to have thought you smarter than this."

"Oh, don't you worry about proof." Jerod pulled the spotlight back to himself. "Ryker, would you please take a shape with hands please? I need you to hold something for me in a minute."

The dragon shifted, a human form appearing as his massive body receded into . . . well, still a massive body for a human shape, really. His glowing silver eyes remained, as did a large pair of wings on his back.

"What is this, Jerod?" Dani asked.

"Ah, I need a spot of blood, my dear. And if Ryker could hold something for me, that would be great," he said.

"Enough!" Evander had recovered and was standing like he was about to shift. "Get off of my lands, now!"

Ryker laughed, a dark rumble that was the first sound he'd made echoed across the fields as he stared down Evander. "No."

A chill ran down my back. "He's on our side, right?"

Dom pulled me tight against him with one arm. "I believe so. Or at least, his mate Dani is on Jerod's side."

Dirty Lying Wolves

"Hold on there, Evander," Jerod said. "Smokey, you know a lot about this wolf code nonsense, correct?"

Smokey spat on the ground, then nodded. "You had a piece to speak about Evander hurting this pack. That's to code, you have the right."

"I have a testimony accusing an alpha of dark magic that directly harmed pack members. So I would be allowed to speak here tonight?"

"Yes," Smokey answered. "By the code."

"This is ridiculous!" Evander spat.

Jerod held up a hand, glee plain on his face. "Now, now, let me finish. I promise to be quick. Evander, I accuse you of summoning demonic souls and low-level necromantic sorcery."

The crowd gasped, and I clutched my chest. "The smoke!"

Dom frowned down at me. "Smoke?"

"He, yeah, he was doing something to me. And to Naomi. He has one of those candles, only it's way more potent than the ones in the village. He kept me in a room with smoke from it, my head was in a fog and I couldn't link with anyone."

Dom gritted his teeth. "That's how he kept Naomi under his control and she unable to link with us."

"Preposterous," Evander spat.

"Is it?" Jerod asked. "These so-called rogues of yours, they aren't right. There's something off about them, and it takes a warlock to see it, because it's our magic. Those rogues aren't just stray and sick wolves, they are dead and dying wolves that you've found and stuffed with demonic energies."

Murmurs of agreement. Those rogues were not right, and any wolf who'd fought them knew it. Evander laughed a dark sound. "That is the most ridiculous thing I've ever heard. What proof could you possibly have, warlock?"

"I thought you'd never ask," he said, gesturing toward Evander with one hand and pulling out a small bone from his pocket, snapping it with his thumb. *"Revelare!"*

Evander jerked back, his wide eyes falling to his arm just about where a warlock's mark should be. He hissed, covering the skin with his other hand, smoke billowing from between his fingers. His cry of pain was the only sound in the silent field, but every pair of yellow eyes in the area was trained on him. Panting, Evander fell to a knee as the smoke subsided. Looking down at his own arm, he took in a freshly scarred mark that looked strikingly similar to one Jerod had. Evander's mark revealed his rank in the fifth circle.

"What is the meaning of this?" Smokey asked quietly.

"Can't you tell?" Jerod asked, giddy. "Your beloved yet corrupt alpha is a warlock. Or at least he was, and then he must have been bitten."

Evander roared, charging in fury. Ryker stepped in, just catching him and pushing him back.

"You!" Evander spat. "How dare you? That a measly first circle warlock could even recognize me, let alone reveal my marks! How?"

Dani laughed. "You think Jerod is a warlock of the first circle?"

"Oh, my fault there, Dani." Jerod showed the mark on his own arm. "Do you mean my mark, Evander? I do have an unfortunate tendency to break rules in my coven, and their preferred punishment is to demote me for a while. This is nothing more than a reminder of the last time I disappointed them."

Dani shook her head, amused. "I don't know who you are, wolf. But you stand before a warlock of the ninth order, and the only asshole I know who's ever summoned a behemoth by himself."

Evander's face paled, adding an eerie effect. "That's impossible."

Dani snorted. "Tell that to Seattle."

"Let me ask one question to the wolves of Moonpeak!" Jerod shouted, reveling in the attention of his grand reveal. "Who here has been influenced in a strange way by Evander? Can none of you recall a moment where you could not think straight around him?"

Me, I absolutely could and would speak out against what I now knew was magic used against my will. I stepped forward from Dom's side. "I have! In the pack house, for the last few days. If any of you thought I wasn't acting myself, it's because I wasn't."

Evander snarled.

Naomi stepped forward, her eyes meeting mine before staring down Evander. "I have as well."

Naomi's confession held a lot more weight than mine did—she'd been here for the entire time. But the wolves around us were now turning angry. Some shifting, some stepping closer to Evander. Dom looked close to shifting, fury in his eyes. Amelia was alight with a partial shift.

"Whelp, it's about time to level this playing field, isn't it?" Jerod asked. "Dani, my dear, I need a dash of blood. And, Ryker, could you be a peach and hold something for me? It's a touch heavy."

"Sure thing," Dani said.

"I suppose," Ryker answered. "Is this all you called us here for?"

"Oh, I promise I need you to be the one to hold it," Jerod told him. "Dani, the blood?"

Jerod was looking around on the ground for something as Dani followed him.

"A-ha, right here then." He gestured to a spot on the ground. "If you would, please."

Dani sighed, pulling out a small knife from her pocket and

cutting into her hand. She spilled a few drops of blood onto the ground and Jerod leaned down to press his hand over it.

"Summonitores . . . Befvelzetah!" Jerod commanded.

A pillar of red light erupted from the ground, shooting toward the sky. But it wasn't the only one, as four other identical pillars shot up from the locations we'd hidden the things from Jerod's instructions.

"Those places—"

"I know," Dom murmured. "It looks like our warlock has been plotting this for a while."

"A heads-up would have been nice," I said.

The five points around the village glowed. A shaking in the ground sent alarm through me, and I reached out to hold Dom's arm.

"What is this?" Ryker frowned.

"Whoops, better hold out your hands," Jerod told Ryker. "He's going to dump his burden for you to hold while he works. Just a pesky curse, don't fret too much over it, but don't let it touch the ground or we will all end up in his realm, and I can promise you we don't want that."

"What?" Ryker barely asked when a flash of black vapors blazed across the field to him. Suddenly, Ryker's arms were full of a shadow of some kind, a ball of shapeless energy.

Ryker, on the other hand, hissed out a curse, and it looked as though he was putting everything he had into holding the thing up.

"Argh!" Evander cried. "What are you doing to me?" He had wretched onto the ground in pain, his body sizzling.

"My acquaintance is creating an antimagic field," Jerod told Evander. "I'm afraid whatever you were before you were bitten isn't going to help you anymore. Not here, at any rate. You've done this pack wrong, and now you'll have to face them as nothing more than the wolf you were bitten to be."

Dom stepped forward, his hands growing claws, his fangs sharpening. "Evander of Moonpeak . . ."

"No!" Evander screamed.

Dom continued walking forward and shifting bit by bit, Amelia a few steps behind, a hunger in her eyes. "The moon rises on this pack, and I find your rule lacking."

"NO!" Evander was now writhing on the ground, shaking off his sudden loss of magic and scrambling to shift himself.

"For the reasons of magical influence inflicted on this pack in bad health, I challenge you for your seat," Dom said, and finished his shift into one big and pissed-off wolf.

"So be it!" Evander snarled.

And the fight for Moonpeak began.

CHAPTER FORTY-EIGHT

JUNE

Dom shifted, his wolf fully ready to engage in the fight to the death ahead of them. I could feel it, and it was as if my heart was whole. The sight of Evander, half shifted and eyes crazed in desperation, made me so scared to watch the fight, but I had faith in Dom. I always had faith in Dom.

The revelation that Evander had been using dark magic shocked us all. We'd known something was wrong, but none of us would have guessed it was this. But the moment Jerod showed Evander's true colors, it was like the fog in my head lifted. I saw everything I had experienced in the pack house in a new light.

"You can strip me of my magic," Evander screamed as he shifted, "but you can't undo what has already been done!"

He shifted, howling a high and long note that stretched over the mountains all around us. My heart pounded—something was wrong about his call, but I was too new of a wolf to know what it was that bothered me.

Dirty Lying Wolves

"There is no slipping away from this one, Evander," Amelia cackled as she shifted. Nathan behind me shifted as well. Then Aaron, a big blond male beside Bianca, Jack and Carson stepped forward to shift, and the most pissed-off Smokey I'd ever seen in my life. They easily circled Evander and Dom, clearing the path for their fight and ensuring no one would interfere.

The wolves around the alphas in the field were a mix of rage and upset. I could feel them, my pack. The Moonpeak wolves. They hadn't known what we were planning before tonight, and if they sensed we were going to do something, the revelation of Evander's powers shocked them. I wanted to soothe their worries, calm them down. It was a compulsion, but I fought it to watch my mate fight Evander to the death.

Evander may have used magic to get this far, but he was still a big-ass wolf too. There was no denying that. Even with all the confidence I had in Dom's victory, I still worried.

A few of the pack wolves shifted too. The moon was up, and we had no choice but to succumb to her call. I bit my lower lip. Soon I would have to shift too.

A sudden realization pulled me from the last of the haze in my head and back to someone who really needed me the most right now.

"The basement!" I cried. "There's a bitten human trapped in the basement of the pack house who might shift tonight!"

"Fuck!" Anna cried.

"We will take care of them," Naomi said. "You stay with your mate."

"No, she needs me, but—" Dom and Evander circled each other. Dom struck, slashing across Evander's chest and pulling back as Evander retaliated.

"We will do our best," Naomi promised.

Go! Dom told me. He may have been fighting Evander, but my distress was distracting him. *Go, be a luna, June. But be careful.*

My chest tightened. I was losing the grip on my human body, feeling the demand to shift grow stronger.

"I love you, Dom!" I cried. "Win for Moonpeak."

I ran toward the pack house. Naomi and Anna followed me, still in our human forms, but only just.

"Things are going to get complicated when we shift," I said. "I won't be able to link you two since we're in different packs, but the person in the basement is a friend of mine. She was trapped by Evander and has no idea what a shift is or wolves or any of it."

"Oh, poor dear," Naomi said. "We need to tell her quickly."

"Is she restrained?" Anna asked.

"I don't know," I said. We made it to the front doors and I pulled them open.

Racing to the basement door, I kicked it down. Anna joined me and we made quick work of it, splintering it and tearing down the chunks as we went inside. With the magic nullified, I had a lot less to worry about down here, though the red pillar of light from Jerod's spell was still here, glowing over where I'd hidden the bumper sticker.

Kat was behind the part of the basement with bars. She was on the floor; the smell of fresh vomit filled the room.

"Kat!" I yelled.

Her head pulled up. "June! I'm . . . something's wrong."

"Kat." I rushed to the bars, grabbing them to look in closer at her, and hissing as I pulled myself back from a sudden jolt of pain.

"Silver," Anna growled.

"Ugh," Naomi grunted. "We don't have much time. I'm slipping."

"Why are they naked?" Kat asked. "What is happening?"

I crouched on the ground closest to Kat. She was pale, panting. The scratches and the bite on her leg looked gross. Infected. She would be okay if she could shift tonight, but if she didn't, then she would need medical attention fast.

Her usually vibrant green eyes were dull and exhausted. Her wig was nowhere in sight, leaving her head bald except for the floral tattoo on the side that she'd had done when she was diagnosed with alopecia.

She was shorter than me, and a little bit on the plump side. At least she always had those enviable hips and a really cute butt. The entire, sweet, cuddly Kat was here, and about to go through a full moon.

"Kat," I said. "I don't have much time to explain, but do you know what a werewolf is?"

"This isn't a time for jokes, June," Kat said, her voice shaking.

"I wouldn't joke with you at a time like this," I said. "Kat, I need you to listen closely. Urg—"

Suddenly, it became painful to breathe.

"I'm gone, sorry, June," Anna said. My eyes darted to her briefly. Just enough to see that she was shifting.

"Me... too," Naomi got out, then began her own transformation.

They had both run here naked, so I was the only one with a dress to get off first. I began undressing as I quickly spoke to Kat.

Kat made a panicked sound but was still hunched over on the ground.

"Kat," I pleaded. "When the wolf comes, accept her. She loves you. She loves you as much as I love you. Take— oof!"

I fell to a knee. Claws poking from my fingers. My skin growing fur.

"Kat, take your deep breath. It's going to be okay," I managed before my shift consumed me.

"June!" Kat shrieked, then began sobbing.

My wolf pushed to the surface, my bones shifting and popping. My tail grew and my fangs sprouted.

Friend? my wolf wanted to know.

Yeah, I told her. *Friend.*

But that friend was in pain, and there was little I could do about it.

June! It was Aaron. *We've got trouble, stay in the pack house. I'm sending in more wolves.*

What's going on? I asked, turning to the door.

Evander called the rogues, Aaron said. *There's a whole army out here, they're flooding the field. We're holding them off, but the children of the village need somewhere to go. They can't shift yet.*

Alarm rang through me. I whipped my head back to see Anna and Naomi watching over Kat. It pained me, but there was nothing I could do for her just now, and everything I could do for the kids.

I ran up the stairs, pushing open the front door to the pack house just as Aaron was shoving several running kids up the walk. Three young teenagers, carrying a baby and dragging along two smaller children. So, six right now.

I pulled the door open.

Get inside, hurry! I told them.

They can't link yet, no wolves, Aaron told me.

Ugh, that was right.

Let your wolf take over. Trust her, you're a luna, June, Aaron said, then ran back to the fight.

My eyes widened as I looked over the field. Rogues, dozens of them. They flooded the field, and there weren't enough fighters for all of them.

My eyes darted to Jerod before remembering the antimagic field. He would be no help, nor would his witch friend. Carmine was occupied defending them both, and the dragon that Jerod had somehow convinced to get involved was completely consumed with whatever strange occurrence Jerod had brought on with his magic.

No, the only hope for Moonpeak now was wolves to defeat wolves.

June! Aaron snapped me out of my thoughts. *There are two more kids, I'm sending them your way, keep them safe.*

Any elders? I asked.

A few, I'll look— urgh!

Aaron? I asked.

I'm fine, watch the pack's weak.

I will, and send me the injured! I called back.

I turned into the pack house to come face to face with the frightened young ones. The oldest, a girl of maybe fourteen, held the pack's youngest pup in her arms, trying to soothe his crying. A toddler girl was sobbing as well, and a boy of about eight was doing his best not to look frightened, but it was easy to tell that he was.

Even with the stress and panic washing over me, my wolf did seem to know what to do. I sat back and let her take over.

We walked to the children, brushing our sides against them as we walked around them, and licked the cheek of the toddler. She stopped her tears, or at least slowed them, and grabbed our shiny black fur with her little fingers.

Nudging our nose into the oldest girl's arms, we did what we could for the baby too. He calmed down a bit, but was still upset.

"Where should we go?" the second oldest, a girl, asked.

I trotted over to the basement doorway and jerked my head to the stairs. The children got the hint and made their way down.

Snarling and growling noises were coming up the stairs, and I figured they must be from Kat.

I closed the front door and followed the kids downstairs. The basement was huge, and though it was filled with Evander's weird magic items and shelves of books, it was mostly harmless now that Jerod's antimagic area was in effect. The one thing that would cause any harm now was Kat, and she was safely behind bars that I highly suspected were meant to hold wild wolves.

I trotted over to the bars and looked in. Kat was holding her arm close to her. It obviously hurt her, and I remembered my shift only a month ago. She was in for a lot of discomfort tonight.

Looking over at Anna and Naomi, I could see they were both sitting by the bars and doing their best to make soothing sounds for the incoming wolf. Kat may not benefit from it, but her wolf might.

A crash upstairs drew my attention, and I dashed for the stairs. Stairs that were harder to climb as a wolf than a person, but I scrambled up as quickly as I could anyway.

At the top, I could see where the front door had been rammed into. I went forward cautiously, then a huge crash sounded as a rogue bashed his way into the pack house.

I snarled, lashing out. The rogue who had broken through was big, and I wasn't much of a fighter, but I was also the only thing standing between this vicious beast and the children downstairs.

I snarled, biting into the beast's neck as he swung me around. I was thrown off, hitting my back into the wall and sliding down it.

The rogue stalked forward, sickly yellow eyes hungry for his prey, hungry for me.

Standing and ignoring my spinning vision, I growled. He rushed forward, and I rammed into his chest. I reached upward with my teeth, sinking my fangs into his throat. He made a gurgling, choking sound, and fell backwards, spilling blood all over the floor.

But he wasn't dead, just badly hurt.

The front door, which was only barely hanging on its hinges now, swung open again. Aaron came in, leading the last children and two old wolves. He ushered them downstairs, then turned to the fight I was mixed up in.

June, are you okay?

I will be once this thing is gone!

Aaron lowered his stance, charging.

The rogue was sufficiently distracted by me, so it took Aaron's blow hard. It snarled, spurting more blood as it tried to round on Aaron to retaliate. It kicked Aaron hard, then turned on me and slashed me across the neck.

Ugh.

June! Aaron called.

I shoved forward, ignoring the sting of torn skin and lunging at the rogue. Time to finish what I started at the rogue's throat. He snarled, lashing out at me and catching the fresh scratches across my throat, causing me to yelp as I reached forward and sank my teeth into his neck. One hard bite and it was all over.

The body slumped to the ground. I'd killed it. I looked up at Aaron, panting.

That was amazing, June, Aaron said.

Yeah, well, I think I'm getting the hang of this wolf stuff.

I'll hold the pack house with you, he said. *We need to keep the weak safe.*

Yeah, I agreed. *But what about out there?*

Have faith, Aaron said, walking over to stand by me as we looked out the open doorway into the chaos. *Dom has faith in us to do our part, we have to have faith in him. All of them. Amelia would never let Moonpeak fall, and she's out there with Nathan, Jack, and Carson.*

A pained howl rang from the basement. It had to be Kat.

I squared my shoulders and took up a spot by the open door. *You're right, Aaron. These wolves need us, so here we make a stand.*

Aaron came to stand quietly beside me. *Yes, my luna. I will stand with you to the death.*

We watched solemnly out the doorway, ready for another attack.

Kat howled again, the mad beast surfacing and swallowing the bubbly and gentle Kat whole. All I could do now was pray she lasted the night. That any of us would last the night.

And my first job as a luna began.

Protect everyone downstairs. Let nothing reach Kat while she went through a terrifying and unexplained experience. Protect the pack.

My pack.

My Moonpeak.

CHAPTER FORTY-NINE

DOM

The moon rises on this pack, and I find your rule lacking.

Old words among wolves. Words that Evander once said to Liam, and then my father once said to Evander.

The challenge was issued, and now I had all the wolves of Moonpeak around me to witness the fall of Evander's reign.

But Evander wasn't content to settle things between the two of us. Evander had called the rogues.

Where he could have been hiding them was beyond me. Now that we knew their dark magic origins, a lot of things made more sense. The way they didn't leave enough scent to track. The way they didn't move quite right. The way they didn't seem to act or think beyond an instinct. They were animated somehow, or possessed, or whatever they were. I was sure Jerod could tell us later, but the only thing that mattered now was that they were attacking the pack.

My pack.

I snarled, lashing out at Evander and raking my claws across his nose.

What have you done? I snarled. *You bastard!*

I didn't ask to be a wolf! Evander snapped, catching my leg with his teeth and ripping skin as I dragged it from his mouth. *But I know how to use all the skills at my disposal. Alpha Liam was weak. His idiotic code of honor killed him, just as it killed Lily, just as it killed John.*

The fire of anger that sparked in me was only fueled higher with every loved one he named. I lunged forward, sinking my fangs into the side of his neck, but his thick fur prevented much damage, and I sprang away.

"The basement!" June cried. "There's a bitten human trapped in the basement of the pack house who might shift tonight!"

Fuck.

"Fuck!" Anna cried.

"We will take care of them," Naomi said. "You stay with your mate."

My first instinct was to keep June where I could see her, but that also meant keeping her where Evander was, and the rogues that now came toward the field. My wolf wanted her to go, to be a luna.

"No, she needs me, but—" June's hesitations came through our bond clear as day. She was very torn, but I thought her wolf knew what she needed to do too.

"We will do our best," Naomi promised.

No, that wouldn't be enough for a wolf like June.

Go! I told her. *Go, be a luna, June. But be careful.*

She paused, only briefly, and began running.

"I love you, Dom!" she cried. "Win for Moonpeak."

I squared my shoulders, digging my paws into the earth. I intended to win. She didn't need to worry. I wouldn't be a wolf she needed to worry about.

A furious roar from the side nearly caused me to look, but I kept my eyes trained on Evander. The field around us was still awash in the black haze of whatever unholy thing Jerod had called forth. The glowing red pillars of light still shot up from the ground where Jerod's hellhound and I had buried things, and one from inside the pack house.

Amelia, what's happening? I asked.

Rogues incoming! she snapped. *Bernard and I have the north, you just worry about your own ass.*

Aaron, how bad is it? I asked.

Snarling, howling, ripping noises started to sound around the field. By now, everyone was shifted. The moon was high and the wolves were out. There was panic in some of them as the moon brought the pack to its closest state. I might not have been alpha yet, but I could still tell that some of the wolves were frightened and not able to fight.

There's a lot of them, Dom, Aaron grunted. *I'm worried about the kids.*

Drip. Cool water hit my nose as I spoke with Aaron. The first drops of rain fell, promising a muddy mess of a fight ahead.

Get them in the pack house. Get June. Maybe she can help if the situation with the new bite is handled.

I will, Aaron promised and I could feel him run off.

My attention was placed back on Evander as he slid in quick as lightning. He nipped my front legs and drew back.

Tell me, Evander, I demanded. *Why come all the way to Moonpeak in the first place? Why set up your plot and take a peaceful pack from Alpha Liam at all?*

Liam was a fool, he had a pack of werewolves at his fingertips, and he coddled them! Evander snarled, and we came together in another ferocious scuffle, biting, tearing, and pulling back again.

Alpha Liam was an outstanding wolf! I snapped, rushing Evander and ramming his side as we both toppled over each other. *But look what you did to his mate! His daughters!*

Nothing had to happen to them if they had just bowed down and obeyed their own laws, Evander hissed at me.

That pissed me off. That pissed my wolf off. If I was killed and the new alpha tried to hold on to June the way Evander tried to hold on to Lily, Amelia, and Naomi, then I'd beg the moon to bring me back just long enough to kill the bastard. Thank the moon that Lily had rathered go out with honor, that Amelia had rathered leave to become strong enough to challenge him.

But for whatever hell he had held Naomi under, he would pay.

What did you do to Naomi in that house? I growled. *What did you do to her?*

Nothing, Evander snarled. *Not for lack of trying, the prude bitch. But with her in the house, the wolves would shut up about finding a luna, finding betas and warriors and all the rest of the shit they whined about.*

A wolf for ten years, and yet you know nothing about our ways, I said.

Evander laughed. *The strongest wolf wins, those are your own ways! Allow me to show you which of us is truly strongest, son of a beta.*

The strongest wolf, yes, I snarled. *You went far beyond your wolf, you used magic to cheat.*

I'll show you strength! Evander roared. *I don't need magic to beat a lowly beta wolf like you!*

Evander launched himself at me and I met him head-on. Teeth

ripping flesh, claws raking across skin. I struggled to gain the high ground, sinking my teeth into the meat behind his ear before he threw me off. In turn, he kicked hard as I fell off, scraping claws across my softer stomach and knocking the wind out of me.

A roar of pain and a sharp howl of despair. I finally tore my eyes away from Evander; I couldn't help it this time, because it was where I knew Amelia was.

The sounds of the fight all around us were clear now. Rogues had come from all directions, attacking the village. The strongest of our wolves were trying to hold them off, but they were definitely outnumbered.

Amelia was grappling with a rogue, and a giant white wolf next to her was half down on the ground. His face was caked in a river of red blood, and the tiny white wolf behind them howled in misery. That one was Bianca, I thought. So that would make the big one Alpha Bernard, the bloody winter wolf.

The brute of a white wolf stood back up, but with some trouble. The drips from the sky were turning into a full-fledged rain now, making the earth under us soft and slick. But he roared, fury and rage as he barreled into a fresh line of rogues anyway. His reputation wasn't exaggerated, he was a brutal fighter and a reckless terror when faced with an enemy. It was almost like he was fueled further by being outnumbered, and it reminded me a bit of Amelia.

Fascinating, but stupid. This was not the night for suicide missions.

Amelia, your left! I called to her.

She lunged in, snapping the neck of the rogue she was fighting, and her head snapped left. She ran to join the big white one in his fight, and I almost wished I had enough time to watch them. The pair of alpha wolves, because that giant bastard had to be an alpha, had a vicious grace on the battlefield.

Get back to your own fight! Amelia snapped. *End this!*

Evander rushed at me, and I evaded him at the last moment. The sharp movement brought the extent of the damage he'd done to my stomach to my attention. I likely had blood dripping, mixing with the falling rain, into the mud under me. The rain roared in my ears, wiping out the scents of the field around me until all I could focus on was Evander.

We circled each other again, then I pounced as his eyes flicked away for a moment.

Latching onto him with teeth and claws, I ripped fur and a piece of his ear before kicking away again. He went wild with anger, charging blindly and ramming into my side.

You fool of a wolf! Evander spat at me. *I gave you every opportunity to crawl back here with your tail between your legs, and instead you have the balls to challenge me!*

I didn't bother answering his statements, made entirely to get a rise out of me. But he either thought he could prod something out of me or was really spewing nonsense he believed, because he kept going.

Amelia I could see. In fact, he laughed, *I thought she was going to challenge me from the start! I'll admit, you were a surprise, Dom.*

Dominic!

Smokey. I turned, catching Evander, who had stopped circling me and licking his wounds. Jumping high, he was about to land over me when I rolled away. Away, and straight into a solid mass beside me.

I snarled, scraping back up to my feet and whirling around to see Smokey's wolf in a heap on the ground, blood spilling from his underbelly, and on the other side of him stood a crazed rogue.

Smokey! I called.

It was clear now that Evander had been about to back me into a trap between him and a rogue wolf. But Smokey had jumped in the way. Nathan snarled, engaging the rogue in a quick and painful death. Watching Nathan really fight was a thing of brutal beauty.

Smokey lifted his head, his old white face staring at me calmly.

I'll be fine, kid. He coughed, blood seeping out of the sides of his mouth. *End this. Avenge Liam. Avenge all of them.*

Smokey coughed again, and I turned back to Evander.

You cheating coward! I roared. *I'll kill you!*

My wolf let out a harsh barking sound, and we rushed at Evander, smacking our claws across his face, dragging fresh lines of blood across his eyes. I jumped off of him before he could retaliate, then struck again. This time, teeth latched onto his throat.

It's over, Evander, I told him, and bit down.

He let out a gurgling howl; I had punctured his throat for sure. But with one last kick from his back leg, he lashed out and slammed all the weight he could put behind the blow into my already torn-up stomach.

My jaw jerked, tearing out the remains of his throat as I slumped backwards.

The rain fell, and my vision blurred as I watched the last traces of life disappear from Evander's body. Blood flowing out of his wounds, mixing with the muddy field he lay on.

I swayed, only just staying on my feet.

Dom! June cried. I could feel her coming closer, but there was no way for me to discern the direction it came from.

Then the true realization hit me as I heard a sound I wasn't sure I'd actually hear in my lifetime. Not used on me, at least.

The call of a new alpha.

A loud, proud note with a bittersweet hint in it. One wolf started it. It could have been Amelia, but I wasn't sure. Another quickly joined the first. Then another, and more wolves until I registered that the fighting around us was finally stopping and the wolves of Moonpeak were free to see Evander's body.

Dom! June had reached me. She had blood around her mouth but otherwise seemed fine. She inspected me as I stared blankly at Evander's body. It was finally over, but he'd left something behind that still needed attention.

I started moving. I leaned over and nudged June's face with my own, then walked to a still gray figure a short distance away.

Now I could see the wolves around me. I saw injuries and blood. I saw the bodies too. The only blessing now was that the mindless rogues outnumbered the Moonpeak wolves among the corpses, but too many familiar faces were there.

For the survivors, recognition and surprise still sat plainly on their faces. This had really happened, and it wasn't Amelia to come back from the past to take care of Evander. It was John's pup.

Even Jerod, Carmine, Dani, and Ryker watched silently, letting our pack have our moment to stop reeling from the fight.

Tanner, June choked out.

I glanced at her. She stood over the body of a smaller wolf. Broken spine, from the look of it.

I'm sorry, June, I said. She shook her head and kept walking. Observing the bodies. Whether she knew it or not, it was exactly what a luna would want to do after a battle.

Dom, you're bleeding pretty badly, Aaron said.

I ignored him and kept walking. Amelia stood next to a familiar old gray wolf, and my heart tightened. Jack and Carson padded over to join her. The rest of Moonpeak was silent as they watched me and June walk through the dead.

Hannah and Linda had made it out with minor injuries, but Bruce didn't make it at all. One of the wolves Nathan had brought was so badly injured in one eye that I wondered if even a wolf could recover from it. Alpha Bernard looked torn to pieces, but he didn't flinch or complain from it. Brutus, one of the wolves from his pack who had come with Bianca, was dead.

My feet stopped in a bloody puddle. The still form of a once-great wolf lay before me. Rain fell hard as it tried to clean the sins of the night.

I lifted my head, meeting Amelia's gaze. In unison, we raised our heads and let out the mournful call of a lost loved one.

Others were quick to join us. In just a brief moment, the whole pack was singing a song for Smokey.

Fucking hell. A very faint sound came across the mind link. The whole mind link, every Moonpeak wolf nearby could hear it.

I stilled, the notes of mourning fell away and silence replaced it.

I ain't dead... yet... boy, Smokey's soft but distinct thoughts came through clearly.

Smokey? I choked out.

Smokey! Carson chimed in.

I rushed to turn him over. Part of his neck was badly broken, but somehow the old bastard was hanging on. The other Blightfang came close, hovering to see him for themselves.

Smokey! I called. *You're alive.*

Hold on. June pushed forward. *Oh my god, get Doc. Doc!*

Coming, Luna.

Doc pushed through, scraped up pretty good but still standing. He and June took over, looking at Smokey and trying to gently nudge his body into the best possible position for healing while Smokey called them every name under the sun.

But he was alive! The old bastard was alive, barely. And I owed him my life.

417

The first rays of daylight began to peek through the mountaintops around us. The moon's demanding journey was fading, and the stronger wolves could start shifting. I shifted first, all the while keeping an eye on Smokey's situation.

"That was one hell of a night, Alpha Dom." The giant of a man who must have been Bernard came over to me, Amelia with him, and Bianca was shifting right behind them.

"You did it," Amelia said, looking behind me at Evander's body in the background.

"Yeah," I said.

"Took your damn time about it though," she snapped, then looked at me with a smirk.

"When are you going to get off my land, Winter Wind bitch?" I asked back.

Alpha Bernard laughed, patting me on the back a little harder than necessary.

June gasped, causing my head to snap in Smokey's direction. But it wasn't Smokey who had distressed her.

"You're a mess!" June cried as she rushed to my side. Only now did I look down at my burning torso in its human form. The skin was pretty well shredded, and I would be bleeding through bandages for a while, I was sure.

I winced as she put her fingers lightly over some of the exposed muscle.

"I've got Smokey, June," Doc said. Now in his human shape, he was having an easier time maneuvering Smokey's injuries.

She turned back to inspect my torso closer.

"I can't let this slide," June said, looking around for more shifted wolves. "Aaron! Can you go get my red bag from the village? It's in my living room. I need my medical supplies."

"Yes, Lun . . ."

We both glanced up at Aaron, his expression of shock startling us.

Then he took off. Blazing across the field and heading straight for the pack house of all places. I could see people coming out now that the moon was down, Anna leading the village children into the sun. They looked shaken by the evening's events as they came to find their parents. I just hoped their parents weren't among the dead.

Right after the children, Naomi half carried a naked woman out the doorway. The woman looked disoriented, alarmed, and her eyes widened as she and the rest of the Moonpeak pack watched Aaron run at full speed to her side before he embraced her.

"Oh shit," June whispered. "Is that . . . ?"

She gently took one of my hands and pressed it to a bad wound on my stomach. "Hold pressure to that, I need to check on Kat."

June ran off at full speed, rushing to the side of the new bite and Aaron. After a moment's discussion, they began to walk back this way.

I started to chuckle until it hurt my stomach. I looked over my remaining wolves. At Smokey, who miraculously held on for his life, even now with Doc at his side. At the wolves who remembered me from ten years ago, the wolves who were new since then. The old, the young, the strong, the weak. The dead.

Whatever came of it, they were mine to take care of. Mine and June's.

"Dom, this is Kat, my best friend." June came back, introducing a terrified-looking human to me and the rest of the naked and bloody wolves.

"She was crazed most of the moon," Naomi said. "Just at

the end she managed to turn, and we walked her through turning back."

"June Bug." The girl looked close to tears. "What is happening?"

"Shh, it's gonna be okay now. You did so good, Kit Kat. Here, sit with me on the grass. And Aaron here is probably going to keep a hold on you. Can you let him do that for now?"

"You mean like hold me steady?" Kat asked.

"Um . . . yes. That." June got them settled and sitting down as she sat next to Kat, checking her pulse and soothing her. Aaron, exhausted and filthy as he was, looked completely refreshed despite the night behind us. I didn't know what June's friend from Seattle was doing all the way out here, but she was definitely shaken after a traumatic night.

A traumatic night for us all. I sighed, looking around the field at the expectant faces full of questions.

"Moonpeak pack." I called around the field as the last of us was shifting from our fur. "I, Dominic, swear to uphold the values of a proper alpha."

Nods of approval and a few cheers made their way around.

"At my side, I present to you Juniper, your luna."

The cheers were a little more enthusiastic this time as the pack started to realize what was happening. Really realize that I wouldn't sit in the pack house like a king on his throne, working alone and above the rest.

"I name the ever-loyal and fiercely strong Aaron as my beta if he will have me." I looked down to where Aaron was holding his newly found mate in his arms. He paused, stunned, then nodded. That earned us a few more cheers.

"Moonpeak pack, it's over. From here on out, we're a proper pack once more."

The wolves dropped the cheering altogether and lifted their heads as one. Some human throats mixing with some wolves, they let out the howl of a unified pack. It would reach the Salt Fur pack. It would reach the humans. It would ring across the mountains, and the rivers, and the trees.

Moonpeak pack was finally free.

Now, and for as long as I had breath in my body and June at my side.

Moonpeak was finally free.

CHAPTER FIFTY

JUNE

"June."

I groaned, rolling over onto something hard and warm. That hard and warm something grunted.

"June, wake up."

Opening my eyes, my first view was Dom's chest. Bandages that looked like they needed changing.

I sat up. "Dom, your stomach! I'm so sorry."

Dom was sitting on our bed, already wearing pants and holding a plate of apple slices and toast.

"I'm fine, the bandages can come off now, it's been hours."

"I'll be the judge of that. If it was up to you there would have been no bandages at all," I said as I unwrapped his torso. "How long was I out?"

"Maybe three hours, but you told me to wake you when Kat was up and when Jerod left. Well, Kat just woke up, and Jerod is waiting on you before he leaves. Or rather, Carmine is making him stay to say goodbye."

I finished pulling away the last of his bandages. His wounds still looked tender, but a human would have been days, if not weeks, before this level of healing. A wolf's body was still a medical marvel to witness.

"Okay, no more bandages," I said.

"Told you so," Dom mused.

"Don't push it or I'll put them all back on," I teased. "Let's go say goodbye to Carmine and Jerod first. I'll want to spend a lot of time catching Kat up."

"Eat something first." Dom handed me the plate of toast and apples.

"Thanks." I took the plate, stuffing an apple slice in my mouth and then setting the plate on the bed long enough to locate a shirt and shorts. The pack probably didn't expect me to look presentable today, but I could at least wear clothes.

"Okay." I picked the plate back up and we started walking. "Let's go."

We left our small house, which probably wasn't going to be our house much longer since Dom was alpha now, and I was his luna. I looked around at the village as we walked down the main street, and Dom led us to the pack house.

It was odd to look at the untouched village, knowing the deep and bloody scars of battle that still littered the field just down the hill. Most of the pack should still be sleeping after a long night, despite the midday sun that shone overhead.

"Did you even sleep this morning?" I asked, popping another apple in my mouth.

"Jerod has been working in Evander's office and basement since the battle ended. Ryker, the dragon, helped burn the rogue bodies. Dani, the witch who came with him, cleansed the earth for us."

"You're avoiding my question," I said, starting on my toast.

"There, I see Carmine," Dom said, pointing to the front gardens of the pack house.

There she was indeed, still naked but lounging on a garden bench and probably as exhausted as the rest of us. She looked up as we got close.

"June." She stretched, yawning. "I wasn't napping. Promise."

I'd miss her terribly, the first wolf friend I'd ever made. She stood and I gave her a big hug. "Thank you for coming last night. We owe you and Jerod, big time."

"Nonsense, Evander was a stain in the wolf community. Any of my pack would do the same," Carmine answered.

"Are you leaving soon?"

"Yes, I can't wait to take mon amour back home. We have a ferry booked that we need to be on tonight," Carmine said.

"I'm going to miss you," I said.

"Oh, June." Carmine reached out to hold my hands in hers. "You haven't seen the last of me. And if only you'd put a damn phone tower out here, we could talk more!"

"Dom, is that something we can do?"

"I have no idea," he said. "But I'll look into it."

"Oh, and I need to make a request to the new alpha and luna of Moonpeak," Carmine said. "I request permission to bring unmated wolves for visits. After all, I found my mate here, maybe we can make some more matches."

"Permission granted," I squealed, giving her another hug. "But maybe wait until after we've cleaned up."

Carmine laughed. "Next summer, then. We have several teens I believe will be shifting this year anyway. I'll have a whole batch of horny wolves for you, how's that?"

"Mon amour!" Carmine waved as Jerod, Dani the witch, and Ryker the dragon came out of the pack house.

"Jerod," Dom said. "All finished?"

"Yup." Jerod walked over to put an arm around Carmine. "I've got lots of new toys to play with, Ferdinand just took the last of Evander's stash for me. I can't say it wasn't exhausting to purge the house of the smoke, but the free ingredients are a definite bonus. Maybe I'm glad I got involved after all."

"You owe me, Jerod," Dani said. "And you still haven't told me where you've been since the fight in Seattle. Which reminds me—"

Dani turned to Dom. "I never got to thank you before you left. I can't say we met on good terms but you were there for the fight. So, thank you. And thank that bitch of a boss for me, I'd rather not see her myself."

Dom snorted. "Trust me, we wanted to fight Apollo as much as you did. And, we're even. You were here last night for whatever Jerod did to nullify Evander. If anything, we owe you an apology."

"Speaking of which," Jerod said, "that antimagic field is permanent. Or at least, it will last about a thousand years, so as far as you're concerned, it's permanent. The only real thing that can be done here now is cleansing."

"Which I did, by the way," Dani said. "The battlefield, the pack house, and most of the village, really. The bad-magic energy hanging around here was insane. No wonder these people were passively letting that dick get away with his weird behavior."

"Thank you," I said. "It's going to make it a little less uncomfortable to have to move into that place."

We looked up at the pack house for a moment. Yeah, I'd probably want to burn every piece of furniture Evander touched and replace it with new. Soon.

"Well, that's about that," Jerod said. "Ryker here probably wants to get his mate back to wherever they set up their love den."

"I *do*," Ryker rumbled, slipping a hand behind Dani and grabbing a handful of her ass. "And you better not call me for bullshit like that again."

"Come now, you're not telling me it was too heavy for a dragon to hold." Jerod snorted. "Befvelzetah couldn't very well hold his eternal burden and drink the magic in the village at the same time, now could he?"

"Hmm." Ryker narrowed his eyes at Jerod. "Still, never again, warlock."

"Yes, yes, I owe you one." Jerod waved off Ryker's concerns with a hand as he turned to Dom. "Anyway, congrats, Alpha. We'll be going now. Good luck with everything, I suppose."

"You're welcome back any time," Dom answered. "Especially if this antimagic thing applies to you too."

Dani laughed and elbowed Jerod in the ribs. "That's what you get, you saucy asshole."

"All the same," Jerod said. "Goodbye, wolves of Moonpeak. I've got a very different bunch of wolves to go impress."

"Oui," Carmine said, leaning in and kissing Jerod's neck.

The warlock blushed, shocking me until I looked closer and saw the fresh teeth marks in his neck.

I grinned as I watched Carmine nudge the mark on her mate's neck.

"See you later, June. Dom." Carmine winked at us, and the odd mix of wolf, warlock, witch, and dragon walked down the hill and away.

"I can't say I'll miss them," Dom said.

"They did help us." I giggled. "Come on, I need to check on Kat."

I walked with Dom into the pack house and to one of the guest rooms we had set up for displaced and visiting wolves. And Doc's clinic was overflowing, so he'd moved his patients here to the first floor, where he could keep a close eye on them.

We passed by a room where I could clearly hear Doc sigh as Smokey cursed him out. It reminded me how close a call Smokey had really had, and it warmed my heart that he was well enough to swear at anyone now.

At the end of the hall, a shifted wolf lay in front of the last door. Guarding it silently and watching as we approached.

Dom kneeled, looking the wolf in his eyes. "June wants to talk to her. I know it's hard, Aaron, but she doesn't know anything about us yet."

Aaron growled lightly, but shifted enough that I could get through the door.

"Thank you, Aaron," I said. "Kat will get there in time, but let me have today with her, okay? She's been through a lot."

Yes, Luna, Aaron said. *Naomi is in there too.*

"That reminds me," Dom said. "My beta needs to get his ass in gear and help me with the village. Come on, let's take your mind off of it for now. She's safe, she's with your luna. That should be enough for now."

Aaron sighed and got to his feet. He didn't shift, but he reluctantly went with Dom, giving me some space to be with Kat.

Once they were around the corner, I knocked on the door.

"Kat? It's June."

"Come in." The voice wasn't Kat's, but Naomi's.

Kat was sitting up in bed, wearing a pair of Naomi's old pajamas. Someone had found her a hat too. I was glad; her head got cold when she wasn't wearing a wig. Naomi sat in a chair nearby.

"June." Kat sniffed. Her eyes were puffy; she'd been crying.

"Kit Kat." I sat on the side of the bed and took her hands in mine. "I'm so sorry you got dragged into this."

"It's my own fault for sticking my nose where it didn't belong," she whimpered. "Naomi filled me in. Sounds like you got mixed up by accident too. I still don't believe the werewolf thing entirely, but . . ."

"Kat." I sighed. "You turned last night."

"It feels like a bad dream," she answered, her voice shaking. "A really, *really* bad dream."

I hugged her tight. "I don't know what to do for you from here."

"I'm staying with you," she said.

I moved to look her in the eyes. "That's a big decision to make in one day."

But Kat wiped her face with her sleeve and shook her head. "It's easy. I don't have a job and we lost the apartment."

My heart stopped. "We what?"

"We were talking about finding a better one, anyway, and I had no idea how long you'd be gone. You were acting like it would be a while, and after I lost my job and the accident in the plaza happened and all, our landlady let me pay out our lease early. I used the money you sent me and the money I got from the new plaza owner. Oh! But our stuff is fine. I shoved it in a storage unit. I figured a hundred bucks a month is a lot easier to handle than a whole apartment with utilities. I just had such a strong feeling that I needed to come and find you."

"I'm just glad you're safe." I said. "Honestly, most of my stuff is replaceable, but I do have some things like my old picture album and the clock Granny left me and stuff like that. But you're more important, and you're safe."

Kat sniffed. "And since my family is all in Arkansas it's not like I don't still have a long way to go to see them either way. Canada, Washington, it's a plane ride or a really long drive regardless. At least now I can stay with you."

"You're lucky, Kat," Naomi said. "Evander is . . . was an evil and manipulative man. Chances are that you were just in the wrong place at the wrong time. Since you were bitten, he was probably waiting to see if you survived a shift, and if you had, you'd be in his house just like I was." She shivered.

"He's gone," I reminded her. "You have nothing left to fear from him. Besides, you have Nathan now."

Naomi's face took on a warm smile. "Yes, I have Nathan. And my sister, and all the others. They came back."

"They did," I said. "I guess this makes us neighboring lunas."

"I guess it does. I'm so glad Dom found you. He deserves all the happiness in the world after what's he's been through."

"We all do." I sighed. "And speaking of mates . . ."

"Whoa, hold that thought," Kat said. "Naomi told me about it, but I'm still not on board with it. Just . . . let's not use the term *mates*, okay?"

I sighed. "Okay, I understand. But we're going to have to do something about Aaron."

"I have a suggestion," Naomi said.

"Yeah?" Kat asked.

"Why don't we refer to Aaron as your blind date," Naomi said. "We can set up something simple, like maybe dinner tonight or lunch tomorrow. You can meet him as a date, something you're more used to, and from there you can choose to call him boyfriend or not. It's up to you."

Kat let out a sigh of relief. "Yeah, I like that. I like that a lot."

"I'll talk to Aaron, then." I grinned. "Thanks for the idea, Naomi."

"Of course, I'm happy it works for you." Naomi smiled, standing up. "Well, speaking of mates, I should go find mine."

"Tell him I said thank you for taking over our patrols while we dealt with the aftermath," I said.

"Oh, it's our pleasure. We're as happy that Evander is gone as you are. I hope to repair the lost bonds between Salt Fur pack and Moonpeak pack. We were close once. We even shared full moon runs and new moon picnics together sometimes."

"I can promise you, we want the same thing," I told her. "Thanks for all your help, Naomi. Would you like me to have the things from your old room boxed up and taken to Salt Fur?"

Naomi looked thoughtful for a moment, her eyes distant. When she looked up at me again she smiled. "Burn it all. Please."

I knew the sentiment. "I will."

That brought a wider smile to her face. "We'll see you later, June. Congratulations, Luna."

I gave her a wave as she left, closing the door behind her.

"We should get you some breakfast." I turned to Kat. "Or lunch, or something."

"I think I want clothes first," Kat said looking down at her pajamas. "Before you burn Naomi's old things, can I grab an outfit?"

I laughed. "I'll get you something for now and we'll get you a new wardrobe as soon as we can."

Kat smiled. "Okay. I'm going to shower then."

"Go for it. I'll run home and get you some things."

I left her to get cleaned up, and left the pack house.

"June," Dom said. He was waiting for me, leaning on the side of the building. "How is she?"

"She'll bounce back," I said. "Kat's a tough girl."

Dom nodded and pushed off the wall, coming over to hold me in his arms.

"Where's Aaron, I thought you had work to do?" I asked.

"I have him running the whole territory," Dom said. "He needs to run off a lot of energy and give Kat space."

I nodded. "Thanks for that. I know she'll come around, but she does need time. I'm just on my way home to get her some clothes, actually."

Dom frowned. "Give her something that covers a lot of skin. For Aaron's sake."

I laughed. "Okay."

"Come on," Dom said offering his arm. "I'll walk with you, my luna."

I smiled and looked out over the village. It was waking up to the aftermath of a terrible night, but little acts of life were already getting back to normal.

Chickens were being fed. Gardens were being weeded. Wolves were on their front steps, talking to neighbors. Visibly shaken, but recovering.

Moonpeak was now in our hands, and I would use my life to protect it.

"Let's go, my alpha," I said warmly.

And side by side, we walked through our village, a new era for Moonpeak ahead of us.

ACKNOWLEDGMENTS

The third book in my very first publishing deal is done! It somehow took a lifetime and no time at all. What a strange feeling to be in the position to look back at the stories as they went from Wattpad to bookstores. This book challenged me in many ways, but in the end, I'm pleased with how it turned out. For that, I have several people to thank.

As always, I want to thank the W by Wattpad Books team. Deanna, Irina, Delaney, Austin, Robyn, Fiona, Rachel, Rebecca, and everyone else who worked with me this year in one way or another. You make publishing fun, and as low stress as I'm capable of being. Which isn't a lot, but thank you for making a dent in that. The agents I've worked with, Amanda and Ali at Spencerhill Associates, thank you for everything. I would be lost without you.

To the friends who have given me a little extra support and hype this year as I struggled to edit down a very large manuscript, thank you. Tyreek and Tia, you two come to the top of my mind for support this year, and I could never replace you. Brooke, Liliana, Katie, Ashley, and honestly so many more of you, thank you for being there. Malinda, thank you for being my friend and for taking my first official author photo.

My husband, Josh, deserves many thanks for this book. Not only has he put up with me and my impostor syndrome from the very beginning, I can also honestly say you wouldn't have a *Dirty Lying Wolves* if it wasn't for him asking if I was going to do a wolf book. Regularly. For months. Really, babe, you can stop now. My mom and sisters also deserve thanks; you guys have always been nothing but supportive of me.

Last, but possibly most important, I need to acknowledge two of my biggest sources of inspiration and determination. You picked me up when I was at some of my lowest points during this process. You've lifted my spirits, given me hope, and fueled me to finish the work that needed to be done to make this book ready for shelves. High Rise Bakery, and Plate & Pour Bakery, you truly have no idea how many chapters were fueled by a coffee and a scone.

Thank you to everyone in the industry, thank you to friends and family, and thank you to all the readers. I can't wait to see what's next, and I hope you're all with me for the next project.

ABOUT THE AUTHOR

Sabrina Blackburry is a fantasy author from central Missouri. She has a love for morally gray characters, fated love with a touch of magic, and passionate women finding their place in the world. When she's not writing, Sabrina enjoys adding plants to the collection on her front porch, sewing for the local renaissance festival, and hiking.

THE ENCHANTED FATES SERIES

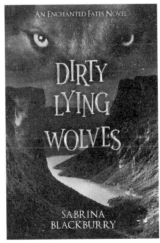